W9-BWH-467

Secret Service

Also by Tom Bradby

Shadow Dancer
The Sleep of the Dead
The Master of Rain
The God of Chaos
The White Russian
Blood Money

Secret Service

Tom Bradby

Atlantic Monthly Press
New York

Copyright © 2019 by Master of Rain Ltd

All rights reserved. No part of this book may be reproduced in any form or by any electronic or mechanical means, including information storage and retrieval systems, without permission in writing from the publisher, except by a reviewer, who may quote brief passages in a review. Scanning, uploading, and electronic distribution of this book or the facilitation of such without the permission of the publisher is prohibited. Please purchase only authorized electronic editions, and do not participate in or encourage electronic piracy of copyrighted materials. Your support of the author's rights is appreciated. Any member of educational institutions wishing to photocopy part or all of the work for classroom use, or anthology, should send inquiries to Grove Atlantic, 154 West 14th Street, New York, NY 10011 or permissions@groveatlantic.com.

This book is a work of fiction and, except in the case of historical fact, any resemblance to actual persons, living or dead, is purely coincidental. Every effort has been made to obtain the necessary permissions with reference to copyright material, both illustrative and quoted. We apologize for any omissions in this respect and will be pleased to make the appropriate acknowledgments in any future edition.

First published in Great Britain in 2019 by Bantam Press
an imprint of Transworld Publishers

Printed in the United States of America

First Grove Atlantic hardcover edition: November 2019

Library of Congress Cataloging-in-Publication data available for this title.

ISBN 978-0-8021-4803-2
eISBN 978-0-8021-4825-4

Atlantic Monthly Press
an imprint of Grove Atlantic
154 West 14th Street
New York, NY 10011

Distributed by Publishers Group West

groveatlantic.com

19 20 21 22   10 9 8 7 6 5 4 3 2 1

To Claudia, Jack, Louisa and Sam

Secret Service

Prologue

KATE HENDERSON GAZED through the windscreen at the steady drizzle and tried to hold back her increasingly familiar sense of dread. 'Stop it, Rav.' Her deputy was rhythmically tapping the steering-wheel, as he always did when he was bored or nervous or both.

'You're in a shit mood today,' he said.

'Thanks. That'll definitely help.'

The radio burst into life at the same time as the street in front of them.

'She's bolted,' a voice announced over the static, as Lena Savic raced past them, a vivid dash of colour in the drab London day.

'Fuck,' Rav muttered. He and Kate each grabbed a door handle and sprang out of the car.

Lena wove her way through the Kingston lunchtime shoppers with the deftness of an international rugby fly half, her long blonde ponytail swinging. Kate followed her along the pavement while Rav ran down the middle of the road, shouting at her to stop.

Lena darted left into a yard at the rear of a dry cleaner's. She scrambled onto the lid of a refuse bin, bounced up to the top of the wall behind it and crashed down onto the neighbouring corrugated-iron roof.

Kate followed her. She almost slipped off the coping that topped the wall, but regained her balance and jumped clear of the roof onto the tarmac. She rolled once, straightened, and followed as Rav blocked the only exit.

Lena realized she was trapped, spun around to face them, like a cornered wildcat, then ducked into the gloom of a bicycle workshop. She charged up an iron staircase but the windows there were barred. She had propelled herself deeper into the trap.

She came back down the stairs with a bike chain in her hand as a tall, close-cropped mechanic in an oil-stained boiler-suit emerged from a side office. 'What the fuck—'

'Stay where you are!' Rav yelled at him.

Up close now, Kate could see the girl's piercing blue eyes and high cheekbones. Her mouth was twisted in a defiant snarl that revealed a set of gleaming white teeth, at least two of which were broken or chipped. A childish, crudely drawn cross was tattooed on one forearm. The expression of the cartoon *femme fatale* that rippled across the other bore more than a passing resemblance to her own.

'Put it down, Lena,' Kate said.

'Who are you?'

'You need to come with us.'

'Who are you? How do you know my name?'

'Put down the chain.'

2

'*Put it down!*' The echoing command came from a uni-formed police constable, who had appeared at her shoulder.

Lena lunged, swinging the chain so fiercely that Kate felt the rush of air on her cheek as she side-stepped to avoid it.

'Put it down, Lena,' Kate said again. 'Or this is going to get much, much worse for you.'

'I've done nothing wrong.'

The constable nodded at his companion and closed in on her.

Kate stepped back and watched Lena struggle, a wiry five foot five, full of rage, spitting and biting as she tried to fight them off.

She was exactly what they needed.

An hour later, Kate leant against the glass of the one-way mirror in the local police station as she watched the two female detectives at work. They emerged after a few moments, closing the door carefully behind them.

'She's all yours, ma'am,' the older of the two said.

Kate nodded. 'Thank you.'

At seventeen, Lena was barely two years older than Kate's own daughter and the contrast was haunting. The terrible circumstances of her birth and upbringing shone through the anger in those blue eyes. She was staring straight ahead through the glass. She knew she was being watched, and dared her tormentors to do their worst.

Kate left her shoulder bag where it lay and slipped into the room. She placed a slim folder on the table between them and sat down. 'Good afternoon. My name is Sarah Johnston.'

Lena stared at her.

'You still claim you don't know how the bracelets got into your bag?'

'How did you know my name?'

'I'll come to that in a moment. How did the bracelets get into your bag?'

'*He* put them there.'

'Who is *he*?'

'I told them!' She gestured at the policewomen's point of departure. 'The store detective. He came over and asked if I would go out for a drink with him. I said no. Then he arrested me, took me to the stock room and said he would only let me go if I gave him a blow-job.' Her English was good, her accent only faint. She was a bright girl, who had evidently learnt fast. 'So who are you? How did you know my name?'

Kate picked up the remote control, gestured at the screen on the wall and pressed play. They both watched the footage, which clearly showed the security officer inspecting her bag and lifting out three gold bracelets. 'And yet there they are.'

'He planted them!'

'So you say.'

'He was harassing me. He must have slipped them into—'

'I know he did,' Kate said. 'I told him to.' She opened the folder. 'You're here illegally, Lena. You do understand that we'll have to send you home?'

Lena shook her head slowly.

Kate pushed a freeze frame from a CCTV camera across the table. 'Recognize this?' It showed Lena, in a short skirt and knee-high leather boots, on a street with a man in a leather jacket. 'Milos Bravic, one of Europe's most notorious sex traffickers. A monster, as I hardly need tell you. I can

4

only imagine the courage and guile required to escape his clutches and recreate yourself as the clean-cut au pair from Clapham.' Kate handed Lena a shot of her walking into Clapham Junction station in blue jeans and a crisp white shirt, her tattoos carefully hidden.

'Who *are* you?'

Kate spread three Belgrade police photographs in front of her, and glanced through the accompanying statements as if she was acquainting herself with them for the first time. 'You insisted that those bruises to your face, neck, upper body and breasts were the result of falling off the bunk bed you shared with your sister.'

Lena closed her eyes. And Kate caught a glimpse of the wounded child within.

'We know your stepfather beat you, Lena. But what else did he do to you?' Kate turned the page. 'Here's the X-ray of your sister's skull from the hospital on Kralja Milutina last weekend. This time, he managed to keep his handiwork away from police scrutiny.'

Lena didn't lift her gaze from the floor.

'Look at it, Lena. Your sister is home alone, except for your mother and your stepfather. And you know what that means.'

Slowly Lena shook her head. 'You are not a policewoman.'

'No, I'm not.' Kate glanced at the photograph. 'My daughter is the same age as Maja. She even looks a little like her.' It was a line Kate might have used anyway, but it also happened to be disconcertingly true. 'I know what I would be feeling if he'd done that to her.'

Lena looked up at her. 'Who are you?'

'I'm with the British Secret Intelligence Service.'

'What do you want?'

5

'You.'

'Why?'

'You sold yourself to the sex traffickers to get here, then managed to escape their clutches. You're clearly a remarkable young woman and I need your help.'

'How could *I* possibly help *you*?'

'We have a job for you. It's simple, straightforward and not unpleasant. If you were prepared to do it, I'd help you in return.'

'How?'

'We would allow you to stay in this country. We could arrange for your sister to come and join you. We'd pay you enough to tide you both over for a while and enable you to get somewhere to live.'

'How much?'

'Enough.'

'And we could both stay here?'

Kate saw something like hope spark in her eyes, despite the air of brittle cynicism that was her first line of defence against the only world she'd ever known. She nodded.

'For ever?'

'If you wanted to.'

'We would have . . . passports?'

'That's a complicated process, but in time . . . We always look after our own.'

'Why me?'

'The job requires a young au pair or nanny who speaks Russian. It needs someone with courage, which you clearly have in abundance.'

'Many people speak Russian.'

'We need someone who is not Russian but comes from a country that Moscow would view as being within its sphere of influence. It's a job that requires tenacity, toughness and intelligence. You would be perfect.'

Lena stared at her. 'What would I have to do?'

'The same kind of work you've been doing in London for the last few weeks.' Kate reached for the folder and extracted a final photograph. 'This is the *Empress*. She'll be cruising the Mediterranean this autumn. The owner's son and his wife need an au pair for their three-year-old son.'

Lena gazed at the massive, gleaming super-yacht. 'And what would I have to do for *you*?'

'Once in a while, we'd want to talk about what you might have seen, who came, who went. That's all.'

'I'd be a spy?'

'Just eyes and ears.'

'Who is the owner?'

'He used to be the head of Russia's Secret Service.'

'So I would be listening to him?'

'Yes. And some of his friends.'

'A suicide mission.'

'No,' Kate said. 'You'd be employed by a reputable Western agency. The worst that could happen is that you'd be summarily dismissed and thrown off at the next port.' She waited.

'They'd kill me—'

'You'd be fired. There would be angry words, but no more. The owner belongs to that small group of oligarchs who are still able to store most of their money in the West and haven't been impacted by sanctions. We have, of course, deliberately chosen to keep it that way. He couldn't afford the scandal that would erupt if anything happened to you somewhere other than his own backyard.' She treated Lena to a warm, motherly smile. 'A few weeks in the sun and your life will be truly your own.'

'The Russians do what they want, wherever they want. There. Here. They don't care. Everyone knows that. Milos and all those other bastards in Belgrade – they all answer to the big bosses back in Moscow. Serbia is just a playground for them. So they do what they like.'

'Not the ones who keep their money where we can find it.'

There was a very long silence. Eventually Lena said, 'I can't do it.'

'I'm very sorry to hear that,' Kate said, 'but not as sorry, I think, as your sister will be.'

A single tear rolled down Lena's cheek. She brushed it away, clearly furious with herself for betraying weakness. 'The Russians kill whoever they want to kill. All over the world. Here in England, at home in Belgrade. Everybody knows that.'

Kate leant forward again and laid a hand on Lena's forearm. 'Maja really does look like my daughter, Lena. I know that's the kind of thing someone in my position would say, but it's true. My girl is sleeping safely in her bed just a few miles from here. I'd do anything to protect her. If you look into my eyes, you'll see that. *Anything.*' Kate gave her a gentle squeeze. 'You've had to become the mother neither of you had. And that's not fair. I'm guessing your plan is to go back and rescue her when you can. So, now you have a choice. Go home and let that monster do what he will with you both, always supposing you can escape the clutches of Milos and his traffickers. Or do what I ask, and save not just yourself but Maja too.'

Kate slid the picture of Lena's sister closer to her. 'Take a look at what he did to her last week, then tell me you want me to leave.'

Lena recoiled, and Kate gripped her wrist. 'You can do this, Lena.'

'No . . . *no*. I can't do this. The Russians kill everyone . . .'

'They won't need to, if you let your stepfather do it first. We can move your sister beyond his reach. Starting today. The moment you say yes to me, we can start looking for ways of getting her over here, ways of helping her.'

Kate allowed the silence to lengthen between them. When Lena looked up again, she adopted an expression of regret. 'If you don't take this offer, you'll leave me no choice. You'll be going back there. To him, to this, and to the mother who did nothing whatsoever to help you. Maja won't stand a chance.' She paused. 'I'll give you a few minutes to think about it.'

She stood up, went to the door and left the room.

Rav was leaning against the far side of the glass. 'Well?'

'She'll need a moment or two. But she's our girl all right.'

Rav turned and stared at the crumpled figure in the interview room. 'You can be a ruthless bitch. You know that, don't you?'

1

KATE PLACED THE mug of heavily sweetened tea carefully on Stuart's side of the bed. 'Morning, Rocky.'

Her husband was splayed across the mattress, snoring loudly. He reeked of alcohol and cigarette smoke, and the black eye he had achieved the night before was darkening nicely. He groaned in acknowledgement and she opened the curtains to let in the dawn.

'Jesus . . .' he said.

'Not exactly. I do a passing impression of Mother Teresa, though – rather too often for my liking. You need to get up.'

'What time is it?'

'Six thirty.'

'Fucking hell.'

'As you will no doubt recall, it's the school's National Costume Day. Gus will kill you if you put him in a kilt. And so will I.'

'What about Fi?'

'She's going as a Swede.'

Stuart pushed himself up onto his elbows. 'Why?'

'Because she's fifteen.'

'What does going as a Swede involve?'

'I don't know because she won't tell me. And I'm not sure I want to know. You definitely won't.'

'Great.' He sipped his tea and looked at her overnight bag by the door. 'Where are you going?'

'I'm worried you really are getting Alzheimer's.'

'No, wait, I do know . . . Of course I do. You told me. I'm sorry. Vienna.'

'Almost. Istanbul.'

Stuart looked at his watch. 'I have a conference call at eight thirty.'

'Then you'll have to delay it.'

He rubbed his stubbled cheek. 'Right, right.'

Kate moved back to the bed and sat beside him. 'Was there anything left of the goalpost?'

He looked confused.

She pointed at his eye. 'When you got home at dead of night, you kindly woke me up to tell me you'd collided with a goalpost.'

'Oh, shit, yes . . . Sorry. No. It was in a terrible state.'

'Do you think it might be time to acknowledge you're too old for this game?'

'It would be fine if all the other bastards weren't so young.'

She touched his hand. 'I have to go. I'll sort Nelson out, then you're on your own.'

'When will you be back?'

Kate got up and went to grab her bag. 'You should know better than to ask.'

'How about a goodbye kiss?'

'No. Because (a) you absolutely stink, and (b) you don't mean just a kiss.'

'You are an incurable romantic.'

Kate made it to the door before she relented. She came back and gave him a kiss that she allowed to linger. 'You are my one true love . . .'

'Stay a moment . . .'

'No!' She pulled herself free of his octopus arms.

Stuart groaned again, in frustration this time, and turned over.

Kate went downstairs. She put her phone back on charge, then wiped the island clean in the pathological way she always did when she was leaving or returning home. She took down Nelson's lead, clipped it to his collar and pulled him to the front door. Once upon a time any trip to the park would have sent their white and tan Beagle into raptures, but he was ageing now, fat, lazy and grumpy. He lingered on the pavement and only advanced when tugged hard. His collar kept slipping over his head. 'Come on, you old codger,' she said. 'I really don't have time for it today.'

She crossed the road and coaxed him through the park and up towards the river. The sunlight filtered through the trees and sparkled on the water. Nelson had perked up a bit – perhaps it was the weather. His belly almost brushed the ground as he went. Kate insisted it was just his fur, but Gus had taken to googling 'animal fat farms'. The dog had been with them almost since Fiona was born and Kate could see he was approaching the end of the line. 'All right, then. Don't say I didn't warn you.'

She started back. Nelson never needed a lead on the return journey because it meant the end of his morning torture and the strong possibility of food. When they got home, he slumped into his palatial basket in the corner of the kitchen. Kate put his breakfast in front of him, but he didn't stir. He gazed at her mournfully from beneath eyelids that drooped with age. She knelt down to stroke his head. 'You're almost done in, aren't you, old chap?'

Kate cleaned the island one last time, then picked up her bag and headed for the door. Anton was this morning's driver, and he was her favourite because he didn't like to talk beyond their exchange of greetings.

'Would you like the radio, ma'am?' he murmured.

'No, thank you.' As if there wasn't enough to be depressed about already. Kate rested her cheek on the window, relishing the cool of the glass. She wished she could share Stuart's easy and uncomplicated relationship with sleep. But then, while he knew about her mother, of course, and her slow and terrible decline, he didn't know that Fiona wanted to dress as a Swede so that she could look like a porn star and thus, in her mind, increase her chances of getting together with the inappropriate boy in the sixth form. And he couldn't know about Operation Sigma, which was about to unfold in Istanbul and had deprived her of any lingering chance of a good night's rest.

She'd got clearance for it on a series of half-truths, but it represented a huge amount of work and expense. She had to make it pay. And she had to make its pay-off look like a lucky break.

The *ping* of Rav's incoming WhatsApp message interrupted her thoughts. *All set. See you when you land.*

True to his word, Rav was waiting for her in Arrivals, with an umbrella. A savage electrical storm was raging over the city.

'You brought the weather,' he said, as she climbed into the car. 'And it's messing with the signal.' He handed her his phone. The pictures on it streamed live but not fluidly from their camera on top of the Hotel Kempinski.

Kate watched a black Mercedes pull up in the centre of the screen. Three young women got out and trotted on high heels towards a motor launch bobbing beside the quay. 'How many does he get through?' she asked.

'They're the third lot since we arrived. He appeared to be having some kind of party last night – old men and a lot of young women. He must be keeping Viagra in business.'

'Is Mikhail there?'

'Not yet. He's landed, but went straight to the embassy. Katya checked into the Kempinski with their kid.'

'What time is Lena's interview?'

'Six. We arranged the meet for between four and five, so you'll be in position in good time.' Rav tapped the driver's shoulder. 'Let's go.'

'You've briefed the teams?'

He smiled. 'Don't worry. It's all good.'

'I do worry, Rav. I always worry. That's my job.'

'Well, if you worried less you'd sleep more, and we'd all be the better for it.'

She touched his arm and he gripped her hand in return. As far as a chief and her deputy could be, they were close friends. Rav was quiet, laconic and intense. The son of two Pakistani doctors, he'd only come out in his mid-twenties and had yet to tell them he was gay and living with his partner, Zac. But, then, no one kept secrets like members of the Secret Service.

'We should go straight there,' he said.

'Where are we set up?'

'Four Seasons. Not far from the Kempinski. We have a team on the roof with a good line of sight to the stern of the yacht.'

Kate looked again at the video stream on Rav's phone. The *Empress* was a sleek multi-storey gin palace with a helicopter pad, a shining beacon of ostentation in the grey afternoon. But even at a hundred and fifty million plus, it had made hardly a dent in Igor Borodin's fortune. Kate's Russia Desk estimated his total net worth at around sixty billion – roughly half the sum accumulated by the Russian president, whom they had assessed to be, by some distance, the richest man in the world.

A former head of the SVR, Russia's Foreign Intelligence Service, Borodin had been a close friend of the president from their KGB days, and they were the principal shareholders – via proxies – in Keftal, which sold the lion's share of the Motherland's oil and natural resources on the world market. Nobody *had* to trade through Keftal, of course, but few wished to contemplate the consequences of trying to go a different route.

Igor's only son, Mikhail, and his new young wife, Katya, had rubbed shoulders with the cream of the British public-school system – at Eton and Downe House respectively – in order to get to know the landscape they intended to dominate or destroy.

Another incoming WhatsApp message prompted her to pull out her own phone.

Stuart: *Had massive argument with Fi over her costume. Is she completely insane?*

She responded: *No. As I said, she's fifteen.*

Stuart often complained he didn't get to spend enough time with his teenage daughter, so now was his chance. Good luck to him.

Their SUV pulled up and they stepped out into a sudden burst of afternoon sunshine. The hot, humid air ramped up the claustrophobic atmosphere of the tightly packed streets. They headed for the entrance to the Grand Bazaar. Kate pulled a scarf from her pocket and wrapped it around her head as they passed a group of women, wearing *niqabs*, walking with a young boy in a clean white T-shirt. As if to emphasize the international flavour of the city at the crossroads of two continents, two old Turkish men sat by a stall selling sweet pastries in front of a Chinese restaurant painted a deep red, with lanterns that swayed in the warm breeze.

Kate's stomach tightened. 'Are the teams out already?'

'No. We told them to spend the day sunbathing and getting drunk on raki.'

'Very funny. You gave them the picture but nothing more?'

'Nothing more, as you said.'

Kate led the way into the covered bazaar. She had a profound affection for Istanbul's easy secularity. Women in headscarves mixed with scantily clad tourists as they moved between tiny stores selling silver teapots and hookah pipes, rugs, Turkish delight, chessboards and handbags. They passed a café where old men sat smoking and watching the world sweep by.

She glanced over her shoulder.

'Relax,' Rav said. 'We're clean.'

That's all very well, but we've missed the signs before, Kate wanted to say. She turned right and swung through a doorway at the end of an alley.

Julie's wide smile and auburn hair lit the money-changer's gloomy interior. She'd become an indispensable part of the team. 'All set.' She draped a scarf over her head and departed.

17

Kate took her seat behind the desk, positioned so that she could see out of the window while remaining almost invisible to the outside world. She picked up a set of worry beads and flicked them over and over her fingers as she thought of the succession of shops, cafés and houses she'd sat in at times like this. Vladivostok, Riga, Kabul, Lahore, Riyadh, Beirut, Cairo – the list was long, but the sensation in the pit of her stomach never changed.

A sitting duck once more.

She'd been cornered only once, in Lahore, and ended up having to fight her way out. An al-Qaeda double had arrived at the rendezvous with two gunmen. All three were dead before they'd managed to fire a single shot. She owed her life that day to the speed of Rav's reactions. For a slight man, he packed one hell of a punch, with a gun in his hand and without.

'So how was the legendary dinner?' she asked, in an attempt to distract herself.

'Grim.'

'Urgh.' She turned to face him. 'What happened?'

'The boy, David, doesn't speak to me. And I wish his sisters wouldn't. It's like they've taken a course in how to lace every sentence with enough poison to wound, but not quite enough to justify a reprimand.'

Rav's partner, Zac, had left his wife and children to be with him. None of them had taken it well.

'It *will* get better.'

'So you keep saying.'

'You have to keep trying.'

'What – until they're fifty?'

'Teenagers are teenagers. If it's any consolation, it's not much easier when they're your own.'

'Well, it couldn't be any fucking worse. They're just bloody rude. And don't start lecturing me again on how tough it is for them. It's not my fault their father's gay.'

'For an emotionally intelligent man, you can sometimes be a right pillock.'

Rav was staring at his phone. 'She's en route.'

Kate glanced at her watch. 'Early.'

'She's clear.'

'Sure?'

'Sure.'

Kate tapped the worry beads against her leg. And, sooner than expected, Lena was in front of her.

'I'd like to change a hundred dollars.'

'Of course.' Kate fished the package out of her handbag. 'Remember what we said?'

Lena didn't answer.

'There's no rush. Just see how freely you can move around the yacht. We'll be keeping an eye on you. You should activate the microphone and plant it where they're most likely to exchange confidential information. Remember to look as if you've dropped something. We don't know where the security cameras are hidden.'

Lena had turned the colour of icing sugar.

Kate pushed the small brown package across the desk, but the girl didn't take it.

'I need some air . . .' Lena raised a hand to her forehead and was a couple of paces outside the door when her knees folded.

Kate leapt to her feet. 'Rav!'

He was already in the alley. Together, they gathered her up and carried her back into the shop, where she shook them off, bent double and vomited.

19

Kate crouched beside her. 'It's okay,' she whispered. 'It's okay.'

Lena was sobbing, in great, lurching gasps.

'Calm down,' Kate said. 'It's all right. Really . . .'

'I can't . . . I can't do it.'

'Just wait a moment—'

'What if they catch me?'

'We've been through that. They won't.'

'But what if they *do*? I can't stop thinking about it.'

Kate took a handkerchief from her bag. She held Lena tight, straightened her and wiped the remnants of vomit from her mouth. 'Just breathe, breathe deeply,' she said, 'and get a grip on yourself.'

Lena did as she was told and her panic gradually subsided.

'I'm here. And you trust me, right?'

Lena nodded uncertainly.

'We've talked about the risk. In the worst case, you could expect an hour or two of shouting. Our relationship with the Turkish security services is good. The Russians simply wouldn't risk anything more than throwing you back onto the quay.'

'But if they—'

Kate took Lena's chin in her hand and fixed her with a steady gaze. 'Believe me, Lena. Please. I have your back.'

Lena tugged anxiously at her ponytail.

'Forget about us,' Kate said. 'Think only of the part you must play. Have you ever been on a yacht like that?'

She shook her head.

Kate smiled. 'I'd love to have a nose around. It looks bloody amazing.'

Lena managed to smile back. 'Why don't *you* do it, then?'

20

'Tempting . . . but, sadly, they know all too well who I am.' Kate touched her arm. 'Come on, enjoy it. It'll be something to tell your grandchildren about.'

'Who says I want grandchildren?'

'That's more like it.'

Lena took a deep breath and picked up the small brown package. She looked up at Kate once more. 'I do trust you,' she said. 'You remind me of my grandmother.'

'I'm not sure that's a compliment.'

'She is very young.'

'With respect, she can't be *that* young.'

'She is a good woman.'

'And she would be proud of you.'

Lena started for the door.

'Next time I see you, we'll work out a plan. There's no pressure. You're there to look around, no more.'

'If I get the job.'

'You *will* get the job.'

Lena turned and the door snapped shut behind her. Kate watched as she passed the window. She didn't look back.

2

JULIE WAS WAITING in Reception at the Four Seasons. 'We might have something interesting.'

She took them up to their suite on the tenth floor, where Danny, their unit technician, juggled a bank of screens. It was a spectacular room in tasteful beige and mahogany with floor-to-ceiling windows that afforded a stunning view of the Bosphorus. Julie was back in place, sitting beside Danny. She pointed to the man on the left of the screen.

'Mikhail,' Kate said. The young Russian was sitting alone on the terrace by the hotel pool, drinking coffee and smoking.

'Now rewind,' Julie said.

Danny maximized the recorded feed from the left-hand side of the screen, rewound about an hour's worth and played the video again. Mikhail walked out onto the terrace in the corner of the shot, and paused to speak to someone at a table by the entrance.

'There,' Julie said.

Danny froze the frame. Kate peered closer.

He highlighted the man's face, then expanded it.

'Sasha Rigin.' Kate straightened. 'Keep going.'

Danny let the playback continue. Mikhail moved on to his own table, unfolded the international edition of the *New York Times* and lit a cigarette. 'He hasn't moved since.' Danny returned to the live feed. Mikhail now appeared to be staring out across the water.

'What the hell would the head of their London Desk be doing in Istanbul?' Rav asked.

'Meeting an asset?' Julie said.

Kate didn't answer. She went to stand by the window and looked down at the choppy waters of the Bosphorus. The wind had got up since they'd arrived. Then she sat on the bed. 'I'd relax,' she said, speaking almost to herself. 'I think it's going to be a long night.'

She turned and focused on the screen. This was the strangest and perhaps most tiring phase of the job. Nothing of any interest took place for very long periods, yet loss of concentration risked missing something significant.

Just after seven, Mikhail, his wife and their young son walked out of the Kempinski, with Lena at their side. 'Looks like she got the job,' Julie said.

Kate allowed herself a smile of satisfaction.

The little boy was already holding Lena's hand as they climbed down the steps into the launch, and kept holding it as they headed out to the *Empress*, clambered aboard and disappeared below deck.

The team ordered room service. Kate had a Caprese salad and water. Rav had pizza. He always had pizza, wherever they were in the world. It was a miracle he was so thin. 'You think it's a coincidence Sasha Rigin is here in the hotel?' he asked.

'No,' Kate said. 'Sasha Rigin doesn't do coincidences.'

'You think we should put a team in there to watch him?'

'No. I don't want to risk it. We just need to be patient.'

At ten, Mikhail's son was spotted sprinting along the top deck with Lena in pursuit. Kate nodded at Rav. It had been his idea to encourage Lena to play hide-and-seek with the child – or any other game that would allow a young nanny to poke around parts of the yacht that might normally have been barred to her.

After that, there was nothing more of any note. At midnight, Kate stood up. 'Okay, let's take shifts. I'm happy to do the first.'

'I'm all right,' Danny said. 'I've had a few weeks' R and R. I'll call you if anything happens.'

'You sure you don't want us to put a tail on Rigin?' Rav asked. 'We might be missing a trick.'

'I'm sure. But let's get a signal in place by dawn.'

Rav frowned. 'Isn't it a bit soon for that? I mean, she's only just climbed aboard. It might spook her.'

'Rigin's presence here really is no accident. I think we're in the right place at the right time, and need to move quickly.'

Rav shrugged. 'You're the boss.'

Kate slipped out to her bedroom next door to the suite. There was no message from Stuart – perhaps he'd navigated around their daughter's desire to dress as a Swedish porn star instead of pressing the nuclear button. But as Kate turned out the light, home was far from her mind. It was always the same when you had someone out there: the sense of responsibility, of vulnerability, was like a shadow over every waking and sleeping moment.

She was awake long before dawn.

The first thing she did was check with Danny that the

signal was out. The team had done its work and ensured a red T-shirt was clearly visible through an open window of the sixth-floor room they occupied at the Kempinski.

Kate breakfasted with Danny, who insisted again that he didn't need sleep. She poured herself a coffee. Soon Julie joined her. She sat down, lit up and offered Kate her Marlboros.

Kate grimaced. 'Not before breakfast.'

Julie held up the cigarette. 'This *is* my breakfast.'

'That's what my dad used to say.'

'Mine too.'

'How's he bearing up?'

'Fine, considering. I sent him back up to Doncaster when I knew I was coming out here.' Julie took a deep drag and funnelled the smoke upwards. 'I told him about your mum.' Julie's mother, like Kate's, had destroyed her family with an ill-judged affair.

'I'm not convinced that would have helped.'

'He doesn't want to open the door to the possibility that she isn't the woman he still tells himself she is.'

Kate sighed. 'I should have warned you about that. It's the only thing I ever really argued with my father about. Have you called your mother?'

'No.'

'I know I should probably shut up about it, but I still think it's better to grasp the nettle.'

'I've thought about it. And I'll never speak to her again as long as I live.'

Kate looked at her young protégée. At times there was an unsettling intensity to her.

Rav joined them. He took a cigarette from Julie's packet without asking. 'I'll do tomorrow night,' he said.

'Did you sleep?' Kate asked.

'Course not. You?'

Kate shook her head.

After a while, they went back to join Danny at the screen. The *Empress* seemed deserted.

At one o'clock, Kate and Rav walked towards the rendez-vous near Taksim Square. They dodged the rackety trams and crowds of shoppers on Istiklal Avenue and chose a café with chairs and tables scattered along the edge of the road. Rav ordered coffee with a hookah and opened a copy of the *Financial Times*. They watched the flow of pedestrians for a few minutes, then Kate got up and crossed the street to the Turkish baths.

She paid her entry fee and was directed down a murky corridor to a small glass-and-wood cubicle. She undressed, wrapped herself in a towel and slipped on a pair of ungainly wooden clogs. She clip-clopped down to the central bath area, where the afternoon sun filtered through slats high in the domed ceiling and cast ridged shadows across the cool stone floor.

Kate allowed herself to be washed in hot water, scrubbed and soaped. After about twenty minutes, a young Turkish woman made her way quietly towards her. Zehra was a friend of the owner, and, more importantly, the eldest daughter of Yusuf, who had been the Service's Istanbul station manager since the 1970s. '*As salaam alaikum,*' she said.

'*Wa alaikum salaam.*' Kate smiled. 'It's so good to see you, my friend.'

'You too.'

'Your father is well?'

'Convinced he'll live for ever.' She smiled. 'Which is rather touching in a man of our profession.'

'He's done all right so far. I rather fell in love with him when we were checking out that Russian translator.' Kate had worked with Yusuf and Zehra on one of her first operations in the Service, an attempt to assess the reliability of a young Russian KGB translator who had offered her services to the British Embassy in Istanbul during the chaotic period after the collapse of Communism. Turncoats were there for the taking, but few in London saw the need to spare the time and expense. Kate had completed the original assessment and passed the girl on to Ian but, as far as she knew, nothing had ever come of it.

'I warned Ian about her,' Zehra said. 'I didn't trust her.'

Kate frowned. 'What do you mean, you "warned Ian"?'

'She smelt of trouble.'

'But I thought he passed on her.'

'I don't think so. But I don't expect she did him much good.'

Kate was still frowning as Zehra turned away. The secrets of the field were best not shared with London, even with an officer you liked and trusted.

'I'm here if you need me,' Zehra said. 'I've seen Rav. We're well covered.' She wandered back down the corridor.

Half an hour later Lena appeared, head up, shoulders back. She was shown to the rear of the marble partition, where Kate was waiting. 'I have time,' Lena said. 'An hour's break every day. They say I can go wherever I want.' Her eyes were bright. 'It is just like you said. Mikhail and Katya are really nice. Alexei is a sweet boy. They are very generous, and say I must not overwork.'

'Did they *encourage* you to leave the yacht?'

'Encourage? They say I can come and go as I want.'

'What about Igor?'

'He doesn't say much. Mikhail and Katya switch between Russian and English because they want Alexei to be familiar with both languages, but Mikhail's father only talks in Russian and is mostly on the phone.'

'Where does he take his calls?'

'He normally leaves us and goes along the deck to an office – he called it the boardroom. He came to eat dinner with us last night, but was only there for a few minutes. Every time he sat down, he took another call and had to go away again.'

'Have you been in the room?'

'No.' A haunted look replaced the excitement in her eyes.

Kate leant forward. 'Lena, I need you to get inside that room.'

'I can't.'

'Listen to me. I think we're on to something here. I saw you chasing Alexei around the decks yesterday. That was clever. You've set up your right to roam. Did he enjoy it?'

'Yes. Very much.'

'Well, now I want you to wait until Igor is off the yacht, or preoccupied with something else. Then suggest another game of hide-and-seek. It doesn't matter where you think Alexei is. All you have to do is go into that room, call his name, crouch down, as if you're looking for him, and fasten the activated microphone beneath the best piece of furniture.'

'I can't do it.'

Kate clasped her wrists. 'You can. You told me that Mikhail and Katya are nice.'

'But not the father. The father is not the same. He frightens me.'

'You'll be doing nothing wrong, Lena. You didn't know that room was out of bounds. You *do not* know that. You'll just be having fun with his grandson . . .'

Lena was smiling now. 'You are a crazy woman. Why does it matter so much?'

'Trust me. It does.'

'Is Maja safe?'

'She will be very soon.'

'If I do it, will that be enough?'

'I really hope so, yes.'

'All right. I cannot promise, but I will try.'

Kate patted Lena's arm, then stood up. 'Enjoy your bath.'

She rejoined Rav at the café to update him. He folded his newspaper and got to his feet. 'You ever worry that it's all going too well?' he said.

'Like I said, I always worry.'

3

JULIE WAS WAITING for them in the hotel's ornate lobby. She held back until the lift doors had shut. 'Guess who just made a special guest appearance?'

'I don't know. God, maybe?'

'Better than that. The Holy fucking Trinity. Markov, Barentsev and Vasily himself.'

'You sure?'

'They're drinking cocktails by the pool.'

They strode out of the lift and into the top-floor suite. Danny greeted them with a megawatt smile and gestured at the biggest of the screens, where three burly Russians, jackets off and ties loosened on the hotel terrace, raised their glasses to the backdrop of the Bosphorus: Markov, head of Directorate S, responsible for agents abroad; Barentsev, head of Operations; and Vasily Durov, the all-powerful chief of Russia's Foreign Intelligence Service, the SVR.

'Fuck . . .' Kate breathed. 'Full house.' She couldn't quite believe her luck.

'Too good to be true?' Rav said.

Kate continued to stare at the screen. He had a point. 'So Igor's been busy. They're all his people.'

Another man came into the frame and shook the hands of those around the table. 'Rigin again . . .'

'So, why would Rigin be here with the big boys?' Julie asked.

'My money says not just for happy hour,' Rav said. He turned to Kate. 'If we get anything, you're going to look like a genius.'

'That's because I *am* a genius, Rav. And we'd better bloody get something or you're all fired.' She sat back. The op had started as a fishing expedition. Now it was something else. Rav had ordered food and a bottle of wine, but she picked at the pizza and avoided the wine.

Half an hour later, the four Russians stood, slung their jackets over their shoulders, sauntered to the edge of the quay and boarded the launch. Igor emerged onto the bridge wing and watched them power towards the *Empress*. The microphone was activated and the tension in the suite ratcheted up several more notches as they saw Lena and her young charge racing around the lower deck and disappearing inside.

Igor greeted his guests with bear hugs, and ushered them below. Kate realized she was chewing her fingernails. Rav grabbed Julie's cigarettes, lit up and went to stand by the window.

The yacht was a blaze of light, but there was no sign of anyone on deck and the microphone fed them only static. Kate

31

could stand it no longer. 'I'm going to the gym. Call me straight away if you get anything.'

She was halfway down the corridor to her room when she heard Rav behind her. 'You going to level with me?' he asked.

'About what?'

'Everything.'

'Such as?'

'C'mon, Kate.'

Kate shook her head, though she knew what was coming.

'You insisted Igor was still more active than we knew so, all right, I bought the operation. Just. Maybe it'd be worth all the time, effort and expense, not to mention Lena risking her scrawny neck. But it looks like you're going to win the lottery here. And that's a bit too much of a coincidence to be credible.'

'You mean *we're* going to win the lottery.'

'We know each other far too well for this, Kate.'

She still didn't answer.

'I backed your hunch. And so did the top floor. But I don't buy that this was just a coincidence, and neither will they. You knew they were going to be here. How?'

She gazed at him steadily.

'Are you going to deny it?'

'Let's just get on with it, shall we?'

'It's one thing keeping it from me, but if anyone on the top floor thinks you have an undeclared source of intelligence, they'll go crazy.'

Kate went back to her room, relieved to have got away without giving Rav a straight answer. She went down to the gym and pounded the running machine for longer than she'd intended. She showered and returned to the suite where the surveillance equipment was set up. Danny shook his head to indicate nothing had changed.

Shortly before midnight, a black Mercedes van pulled up outside the hotel foyer. Half a dozen women spilt out and were shepherded through Reception to the quay beyond the pool. Rav peered at them as they waited for the motor launch. 'Bet they don't come cheap,' he said.

They picked up something on the microphone feed shortly after one in the morning. Danny leant forward and adjusted the volume dial. They heard a girl laugh, then giggle and moan encouragingly. Before long, she was panting as unconvincingly as her male companion was grunting loudly.

'Fuck's sake.' Julie groaned. '*Please* tell me Igor hasn't just invited them there for a sex party.'

'Hookers are part of Igor's hospitality shtick.' Kate lowered the volume. 'But I very much doubt that's Vasily getting his rocks off in the boardroom.'

'Top deck,' Rav said.

Danny maximized the close-up of the yacht's stern. The three most powerful men in Russia's Foreign Intelligence Service had gathered there, with Vasily at the centre – but they weren't drunk enough to have forgotten their own standard operating procedures. They kept their backs to the shore.

'Lower deck,' Rav said.

Danny pulled up the screen and closed in on Igor's son, Mikhail, leaning against the rail next to a blonde hooker.

'Go on,' Kate said.

Danny enlarged the screen and peered closer. Lip-reading was one of his many skills. 'She's asking questions in English. Where does he spend his time? All over the place, he says. Mainly Moscow, these days, but he travels a lot in

Europe. He's . . . expecting to spend a few weeks on his
father's yacht. Paying homage, he jokes . . .

'She doesn't seem to know whether to laugh. Where is his
favourite place? Zermatt. He loves skiing. She loves skiing,
too. She once spent a winter in . . . somewhere . . . didn't
catch it . . . Oh, Cortina. She also loves Venice. But for the
fucking, not the skiing. She asks . . . Oh, okay, what would
he like to do to her? He can do anything. Anything he likes.
He's not answering. He seems shy, she says, but she likes to
make sure her clients have lived out their most extreme fan-
tasies, so she's happy to do anything he wants. She's—'

'We can see what she's doing, Danny,' Kate said.

'She's asking if he'd like some Viagra. She has her own
supply. He says, yes, that would be good.'

'So would being heterosexual, maybe,' Rav said.

'It makes it harder, longer, better, she says. Her English is
a bit stilted. I can't quite make . . . Well, she's trying to arouse
him, whispering something . . .'

'Is his wife still aboard?' Julie asked.

'Yes,' Kate said. 'But Igor makes it very clear that fucking
hookers regularly is a fundamental duty of manhood, and a
prerequisite for membership of the Mafia class. He thinks
his son and daughter-in-law are dangerously Westernized
already, so this is his way of reminding them of the chau-
vinistic imperatives of Russian power politics. Mikhail
won't dare to refuse. Katya won't dare to object.'

The hooker led the apparently unwilling Mikhail inside.
The three men on the upper deck had also vanished.

'You should go to bed,' Rav told Kate. 'This could take days.'

'With those guys on board? Are you kidding? They're
here for a reason.'

They heard the door to the boardroom open and close,

34

then voices. They listened in silence. Even with the level of technical wizardry the Service could deploy, the microphone's performance had been heavily compromised by its size, so the conversation came and went. To begin with, they seemed to be talking about Moscow Centre's internal politics.

'Who is Kyril?' Kate whispered.

'Not sure,' Rav muttered. 'GRU, maybe.' Moscow's military intelligence arm had a substantial foreign operation of its own. The tension between the two organizations was notorious.

Igor was talking now. He offered the men cigars and disappeared to the far end of the room, frustratingly out of earshot for a minute or more.

When he came back, Vasily, whose voice was familiar to them all, said, 'Now is our moment.' He was speaking in Russian, which all of Kate's team spoke fluently. They leant closer to the speaker on the desk.

'What makes you so sure?' Igor asked.

'The Prime Minister has prostate cancer. He will resign this week.'

They could hear Igor lighting the cigars. 'Who stands in our way?'

'The woman in Education, perhaps. But there will be other candidates, of course.'

'Viper can help.'

'Yes. We will have to wait and see. But we won't need to for long. Viper says—'

Somebody must have moved a chair or table, because there was a screech that had them all covering their ears and the voices became much fainter. Danny tried to work his magic with the dials, but to no avail.

'Fuck,' Kate said. She leant further forward. 'Turn it up.'

Danny kept trying. 'I think it's been damaged. This is maximum volume.'

They leant even closer, but hearing anything was next to impossible.

'It's on record,' he said. 'I'll see what I can get with some enhancement.'

Kate moved to the window. Rav and Julie lit up. Rav offered Kate his cigarette and she took a few puffs. 'If the PM was sick,' Julie said, 'wouldn't we know?'

'I've not heard a whisper,' Rav said.

'But let's assume for a moment they know something we don't,' Kate said. 'They were implying they would have a dog in any leadership fight. So who's their guy?'

'How do we know it's a guy?' Julie said.

'And how do we know that "Who stands in our way?" refers to their candidate,' Rav asked, 'and not someone – or something – else entirely?'

Kate took another drag of his cigarette. ' "Who stands in our way?" And "There will be other candidates . . ." They absolutely must have their own horse in the race. And, given their enthusiasm for interfering with the democratic process, it would be more of a surprise if they *weren't* trying to pull some stunt. If they've tried it in other countries, why not in the UK? Some of our politicians probably come cheaper than others elsewhere.'

'And who the hell is Viper?' Julie asked.

'"Viper can help".' Kate shook her head. 'It could be anyone – a politician, someone in Whitehall, a newspaper editor.'

Rav trod his stub into the stone floor of the suite, then picked it up and put it into the ashtray. 'Ian's going to love this. It'll bring out all his inner machismo.'

'The foreign secretary has to be prime suspect,' Julie said.

'He served in Kosovo with the Paras. The Russians were all over that place like a rash.'

'That's a bit of a leap,' Kate said. 'And probably wise not to rush into pointing the finger at our nominal superior.'

'We can hardly ignore him,' Rav said. 'Every piece of speculative crap in the last five years puts him on the list of leadership front runners.'

'I'm not saying we should,' Kate said.

'Has Stuart heard any whispers? It looks like his boss is in the clear,' Rav said. 'Unless, of course, they're already fucking us about.'

'A lot of people in the party want someone from the next generation,' Julie said, 'so Imogen could easily be in the frame. But the field is actually pretty wide.'

'Right,' Kate said. 'Julie, you stay here and keep an eye on Lena. Rav and I will get the first flight back in the morning. Well done, everybody. They may still be talking about this operation in fifty years' time.'

She turned at the door. 'Especially if we crash and burn.'

4

IT WAS ALMOST four in the afternoon by the time Kate reached the space-age bubbles that controlled entry to Vauxhall Cross. Rav had gone home for a change of clothes, so she rode the lift to the fifth floor alone.

The office occupied by C, the head of the Secret Intelligence Service – currently Sir Alan Brabazon, a tall, good-looking man, who'd made his name in his dealings with Russia and the former Soviet Union – was not quite as magnificent as his wood-panelled executive dining room on the top floor, but it still boasted a spectacular view of the Thames and the Houses of Parliament, their stonework gold in the occasional shaft of sunlight.

Sir Alan's desk stood in the middle of the room with two open laptops – one internal, one external – at the ready, but he ushered Kate and her boss, Ian Granger, head of Europe and Russia, to the soft seating area in the far corner. Unless he had bad news for you, he served coffee and biscuits, which Ian could never resist.

Ian was lean and wiry – tales of his Iron Man triumphs were legendary for their tedium – with wavy blond hair he allowed to curl over the nape of his neck, like a 1970s rock star. He was clever, and couldn't resist letting everyone know it. He also had a tendency to state the blindingly obvious as if it were biblical revelation. Kate had just about found a way to cooperate with him until Sir Alan had named her as one of his potential successors the previous summer. Their relationship had since been plunged into the deep freeze.

'I think we have to be realistic,' Ian said. 'Don't you, Alan?' Ian's version of being realistic was to agree that someone else must have made a mistake. He tugged at his cuffs. He had once made a point of telling everyone in the office that he had his suits, shirts and shoes handmade on Savile Row. It had been his way of auditioning for entry to the inner sanctum of the establishment. He'd dropped the references since diversity had become the management's watchword, and begun stressing his state-school credentials instead. He hadn't lost his taste for the clothes, though.

C displayed quality tailoring with a great deal less effort and more pleasing effect than his colleague. He picked up Kate's file, raised his tortoiseshell-framed glasses and cast his eye once more over the transcript. 'Realistic, Ian?' he said. 'In what way, precisely?' His stillness was unnerving, and even Ian was not immune to it.

'Well, we start with a basic credibility problem. Are we really being asked to believe that three of the most powerful men in Russia's intelligence hierarchy – arguably the three most powerful – suddenly turned up on a yacht in the

Bosphorus to discuss these vital and sensitive matters at a time when we just happened to have an intelligence operation in place?'

Sir Alan's gaze was steady. Silence was another of his weapons, and he used it now.

'It's a classic misinformation ploy,' Ian said. 'They're hoping to spark up a witch-hunt among our political elite for whoever is their "dog in the fight", as Kate puts it, and a mole-hunt across Whitehall and beyond for this rather colourfully named agent "Viper". They must be laughing their heads off in Moscow Centre already. And they'll split their sides if they get a whiff of the possibility that we might be taking it seriously.'

Kate's cheeks reddened. She hadn't expected Ian's assault to be quite so obvious.

'Fair comment, perhaps.' C lowered his spectacles and gave Kate his undivided attention. 'What do you think?'

'Perfectly fair,' she said, 'but not entirely reliable.'

'Let's roll with it for a minute,' C went on. 'The clear implication here is that in a potential leadership contest – and I'll come back to the premise in a minute – our foremost adversary will have a candidate.' He was still looking at Kate.

She nodded again.

'Who?' he asked.

'We've looked at it all ways,' she said, 'and, honestly, your guess is as good as mine right now. Some backbench MPs say they want one of the new generation, but in a lightning-strike contest, I think it'd be difficult to imagine someone more or less unknown to the public becoming a serious candidate. Which means it probably has to be a current member of the cabinet, and Vasily would be aware of that. So, to be talking about this seriously, their man – or woman – must already be close to the top of the tree.'

'Well, we can rule out Imogen Conrad at Education, since they helpfully – but perhaps too helpfully – identify her as the principal barrier.' C twirled his glasses and gazed, apparently absently, at the Houses of Parliament. 'So I guess that leaves Simon Wishart at Defence, the chancellor, and our very own foreign secretary.'

'Meg Simpson would be an outside bet, though the NHS strikes might have done for her.'

C rose to his feet and moved to the window, as if seeking inspiration from the home of British democracy. 'I've known the foreign secretary for a very long time, and it's no secret that I'm not his biggest fan. But it's a bit of a stretch to perceive him as a potential agent of a foreign power.'

'Unless they've found a pressure point . . .'

'Hmm. He's never made any great virtue of marital fidelity, so it's equally hard to imagine that some video of him with even a roomful of hookers might cause him any sleepless nights.'

'Given everything, we should stick this recording in the bloody bin where it belongs,' Ian said, almost under his breath.

'What do you mean, "given everything"?' Kate said.

'It's just another Russian conjuring trick. They love these things.'

C turned from the window and walked back. 'What Ian means is that we've been caught out before and, no doubt, will be again. But I'm afraid we need to take each case on its merits. That has to be the golden rule. They want us to let each drop of invective and every tissue of lies poison the well. Then they *would* have achieved their aim.'

41

'How have we been caught out before?'

'Ian ran the Russia House before you, and I did before him. So we've all been on the receiving end of the Kremlin's fantasy factory's output.'

'Should we talk to MI5?' Kate asked.

'Of course not!' Ian almost choked on his coffee.

'It's a bit early for that,' Sir Alan said, more smoothly. 'I may not have long to go in this chair, but I think even I have to be sensitive to the fact that James Ryan is the foreign secretary and thus our direct superior. As luck – if it is luck – would have it, we've been offered an easy means of testing this. According to the transcript, the prime minister is going to resign this week. I've heard not a whisper that he's unwell, let alone that he has cancer. If that proves to be correct, we'll need to take it all seriously. If not, we can come back to it. Agreed?'

Kate nodded. Ian followed suit reluctantly.

'I'll say this for the Russians,' C said, 'they certainly conspire to keep life interesting.'

Kate followed Ian to the lifts. He hit the call button as if it was an explosive device and waited with a disproportionate degree of impatience.

'Have we come across something like this before?' Kate asked. 'It would be helpful to know.'

'No,' he said. 'Not that I can think of. I mean . . . not specifically like this.'

The doors slid open and they got in. 'If there *has* been anything similar, then I guess—'

'As you should know, Kate, it's the first rule of the Desk to assume that everything you get fed by the Russians is manufactured. Start there, and you can't go far wrong.' He hit the wrong floor button, cursed and tried again. The doors closed.

'While we're on the subject of manufacturing, did you take up that translator I checked out in Istanbul? Irina?' Kate asked. 'I've been meaning to ask.'

'No.' He gave a sigh of what might have been exasperation. 'Why?'

'Just wondered. I met our Turkish connection in a bathhouse and remembered the last time I'd been there.'

'Jesus,' Ian said. 'She was a nobody, with zero prospects. And that was a lifetime ago.'

'Of course. It's all flooding back now.'

The doors opened. They got out and turned their separate ways.

'Have a good evening,' Kate said.

Ian didn't bother to reply.

She walked down to her small corner office overlooking Vauxhall station. Rav was scrutinizing an aerial photograph of the foreign secretary's home in Hampshire on his laptop screen. 'He's got a very big house for a man who has only ever really been an army officer and an MP.'

Kate smiled. 'As you never tire of telling me, the ruling classes have deep reservoirs of inherited cash, so that doesn't prove anything.' She signed the stack of expenses forms on her desk and put them in the out-tray for Maddy to process.

Later, when she called home, Stuart answered. 'I'm coming,' she said.

'Exciting. How was your trip?'

'Very good.'

'Did you get what you were looking for?

'More than.' She ended the call and stood. 'See you tomorrow, Ravindra. Sir Alan wants us to leave it for now.'

He carried on tapping away.

'You did hear me, didn't you? C said to park it for now. It sounded like an order.'

'I heard you.'

'Sometimes you bear a striking resemblance to my son.'

'Have a nice evening.'

'Is Zac at home?'

'He's with his parents.' Rav looked up. 'In Scotland.'

'Well, don't stay here all night.'

Kate swapped her heels for trainers and retrieved her coat. 'Funnily enough, Stuart and I are having dinner with Imogen Conrad and her husband tonight.'

Rav swung around. 'Are you going to ask her about the PM's health?'

'I don't see any harm in saying I've heard a rumour, do you?'

He raised his palms. 'Could have come from anywhere.'

Kate thought about this. 'You're right. See you tomorrow.'

'I can hardly wait.'

She always walked home, rain or shine. It wasn't the capital's most scenic route, but provided time for reflection. She thought about what Ian had said. The Russians loved misinformation almost as much as they loved agents of influence and raw intelligence from inside government departments. But she had been extremely careful, right from the start, about how and when details of the Istanbul operation were disseminated.

Ian knew that Igor and Mikhail were the intended targets, and had signed off on the cost, but he hadn't known – or asked to know – how they had planned to get a microphone inside the yacht. The security teams setting up and manning the equipment and sweeping the approach to the money-changer's cubby-hole in the bazaar had been told no more than they needed to know. Danny had had no idea of what they were up to until he'd done his techie stuff that night. Only she, Rav and Julie knew all the details, including Lena's identity. It was inconceivable to her that either of her close colleagues could be compromised. And if the operation was secure, how could the SVR have believed they were planting misinformation via that microphone?

And the final possibility: that the man who'd let her know that the cream of Russia's intelligence hierarchy would be meeting on Igor's yacht had done so only to manipulate and deceive her . . .

No. She'd thought of that. Night and day. And continued to dismiss it.

It was not possible.

He would never lie to her.

It had started raining again so Kate ran the last hundred yards to her front door. The mood in the house matched the weather outside. Gus was at the kitchen table, shackled to his Facebook feed on the iPad they'd bought him for Christmas. He had his headphones on to shield him from the yelling match taking place upstairs. Kate removed them. 'What *is* going on?' she asked.

'What do you *think* is going on?'

'Well, I've just come in from several days' rather complicated and demanding work and while I am, by common consent, a genius, I'm not blessed with second sight. So how about you just tell me?'

'They're having an argument.'

'You don't say. About what?'

'Guess.'

'Your father wouldn't let her go out until she'd finished her homework.'

'That was the last straw. But they've been at it since you left.'

Kate kissed her son's head and wrapped an arm around his chest. 'Hello, Mum, how lovely to have you back.'

He grunted.

'How was your trip? Oh, it was fine, thank you, Gus. It went rather well, actually.'

Now he was smiling at her. 'You were away?'

'Cheeky,' she said.

He gestured upstairs in the direction of the shouting. 'We missed you.'

Kate took off her raincoat and hung it in the hall, then came back, kissed Nelson, and lay down for a moment beside him.

Gus wrinkled his nose. 'I thought you told us not to kiss anyone until we knew where they'd been.'

'You're right,' she said. 'He does bloody stink.'

'He's old,' Gus said. 'You'll smell that bad when you're his age.'

'Nice.'

'Granny does. Which reminds me, the care home called.'

'How long ago?'

'Twenty minutes.' He scratched his head theatrically with his stylus. 'Or maybe yesterday.'

'What did they say?'

'Not much. They asked you to call back. Not urgent.'

Kate picked herself up and went to join the skirmish on the landing.

Stuart just looked at her. '*Now*,' he said.

'*No!*' Fiona's response wasn't discernibly muffled by the door that separated them.

46

'It was *not* a request!'

'Go away! I hate you!'

He held up an imaginary white flag and eased past Kate. 'All yours.'

'Welcome back, my darling,' Kate said, as he disappeared downstairs. 'How was your trip? Oh, actually, it went really well.'

But Stuart was long gone.

She moved to the bathroom door and knocked. 'Hon, it's me.' She waited. 'Fi, it's me. Mum.'

'Actually, I have a pretty good idea who "me" is.'

'Can you open up?'

'Why?'

'For starters, because I haven't seen you for a few days. And because I love you and missed you terribly.'

'That I doubt.'

'All right, but the loving-you bit is true. And because you've clearly had an argument with Dad and, honestly, he looks a bit cross, which probably means you're even crosser, and because I'm tired and would like to progress to a cup of tea without too much more time elapsing.'

Kate waited again. No one had warned her about the titanic reserves of patience one required to deal with teen-agers. The door was eventually unlocked. A few moments later, it opened. Kate took a step forward.

'*Don't* come any closer!'

Fiona sat on the edge of the bath, her eyes puffy. Kate sat down beside her. 'So . . . I'm guessing Dad wouldn't let you go out tonight.'

'He's a total jerk.'

'Well, he can be, but we've all been there. I suspect he was concerned about your homework.'

'I'll do my homework! I always do my homework!'

Kate drew her daughter gently but firmly towards her and hugged her. 'I assume you wanted to go and see him.'

Fiona didn't answer.

'You won't believe me, but he'll like you more for not jumping every time he calls.'

'You know literally nothing.'

'True.' Kate stood. 'But I have to go to the home now and see Granny.'

'Is she all right?' The concern in her daughter's voice was instant and genuine and reminded Kate – not for the first time – that the children reacted to her mother with an affection she'd never managed. There had to be an explanation for their desire to excuse the older woman's many faults, but she couldn't conjure one up.

'I'm pretty sure the dementia is here to stay. Aside from that, I should think so.' She paused. 'A cup of tea can be very soothing. Will you join me?'

'I'll come down in a minute.'

Kate took that as a 'no'. She kissed her daughter once more and returned to the kitchen.

Stuart already had the kettle on. It was as close as he got to telepathy. 'What is *wrong* with her?'

'It's a long story.'

'I'd like to hear it. I've never met anyone more irrational and unreasonable in my entire life. And that includes you.' He smiled, came over and kissed her tenderly. 'I'm sorry, my love. How was your trip?'

'It was – potentially – incredibly successful.'

'Can you say why?'

'Not really. But we'll see.'

Kate and Stuart sat at the table for another half-hour,

grappling with the infinite mysteries of his favourite subject: logistics. They took in the school run, a weekend he was trying to plan in Norfolk, Christmas and what to do with her mother (hope she's dead), and an invitation he wanted to accept to a five-a-side football tournament in Bristol.

Kate countered by asking whether he'd booked the villa in Greece for half-term, as agreed. He hadn't.

After that, she left again, taking Gus's silence with her.

As she closed the door, Stuart fired two parting shots. 'Don't be late,' he said, since she was a notoriously poor timekeeper at home, which was odd for a woman whose workplace measured it in life and death, and 'Have fun,' which was obviously heavily ironic. Fun was one thing she was absolutely guaranteed not to have down the road with her sick mother.

The phone call turned out to have been about an unpaid bill, which she might have guessed. The home was a genteel establishment for elderly residents who liked to consider themselves a cut above the rest. It suited her mother down to the ground.

When she could finally delay the dreaded moment no longer, Kate went up to the eleventh floor. Lucy sat by the window in her room, staring out over the treetops in the park. A carer was clearing away the evening meal.

As she pulled up a seat, her mother turned to her. 'Hello, love,' she said. It was so long since she had recognized her daughter at all – let alone at first sight – that Kate had to suppress a tear.

'Hi, Mum.'

'How lovely to see you.'

Kate tried to smile. 'I'm sorry, I've been away for work.'

'You're always *so* busy.'

'I know. I'm sorry.'

'The children came. It was charming to see them. Gus is going to be a very big boy. He's like a gangly giant already.'

'He's growing fast. It's hard work keeping him in clothes.'

'I don't know why Fiona has to dress like that. What's wrong with her?'

'She's a teenager, Mum. You may remember having one yourself.'

Lucy smiled. 'Well, yes, I do. You used to wear those awful lurid trousers and went out with a boy who had a pierced ear.'

'Pete Carter, the trainee anarchist.'

'Stuart was with them.'

The first hint of the minefield. 'Well, yes. He would have brought them. He's their father.'

'Hardly said a word. Cat got his tongue?'

'He's been very busy too. And we don't have a cat.'

'You want to watch him. I've told you that before. He's a nice enough man, but I don't trust—'

'Let's not go there, Mum, all right?' Kate was not in a mood to take lessons in trustworthiness from her mother, and she had long since decided that Lucy's basic issue with Stuart was that he was too much like Kate's father. Which, in her own eyes, was his shining virtue.

Lucy shifted uncomfortably in her seat. 'Oooh. Would you mind getting me my pills? They're next door.'

Kate went through to her mother's bedroom, and took a couple of very deep breaths. The pills were on the lurid pink and gold bedside table her mother had always treasured, but something else had stopped Kate in her tracks: the photograph of her father smiling on a Cornish beach, which had once taken pride of place beneath the lamp, had been replaced by one of a man with a pencil moustache and striped swimming trunks.

Kate sat for a moment on the bed, in an attempt to contain her fury. Then she picked up the pills and went back to her mother.

'What's wrong?' Lucy asked. 'You look like you've seen a ghost.'

'Perhaps I have.'

5

'OH, DON'T BE so silly.' Lucy took two large white tablets out of their blister pack and gulped them down with a glass of water. Kate hoped they might choke her.

'You've replaced the picture of Dad with one of David Underpants.'

As her mother met her gaze, Kate realized she knew precisely what she was doing. Nothing about this moment was lost in the mists of memory. There was no shame, no regret. It occurred to Kate that the bedside mission might have had nothing to do with the urgent need for medication.

'Don't be a prig, Kate. It doesn't suit you.'

'Where's the photo of Dad?'

'Oh, I don't know. Somewhere.'

Kate stared at her mother. Even now, after all the water that had flowed under the bridge, the old bitch's capacity to wound took her breath away.

'Honestly, where's the harm in it?' Lucy threw up her arms

extravagantly. 'They're both dead, for God's sake. And I will be soon!'

Not soon enough, Kate thought. 'I don't know how to answer that,' she said eventually. 'Apart from noting that you were married to one of them – my *father* – for fifty years, and the other destroyed our family life.'

'That's your opinion.'

'It's absolutely everyone's opinion.'

'Oh, well,' Lucy said. 'Why does it matter *now*?'

Kate took a deep breath. 'I can't believe you have the gall to ask that. To you, clearly, *incredibly*, it doesn't. But it might have occurred to you that it could possibly matter to me. Just a *bit*.'

The corner of Lucy's mouth began to twist in the way it always did when she was thwarted. 'You were nowhere near as much the apple of your father's eye as you like to think, you know. And he was never the man you imagined. So you might want to get him down off that pedestal and see him as—'

'I don't need any instruction on how to view my father, thank you. Neither do I want your demonic version of how he felt about me. And as for David bloody Underpants, I—'

'I don't know why you insist on calling him that.'

'Because he was a ridiculous figure, a testament to your towering misjudgement. And why you think I would ever give a shit what you of all people think of Stuart, I can't imagine.'

Lucy sighed. 'You were *such* a disappointment to your father. To both of us. We so wanted to have a boy. Then everything would have been different.'

On other occasions, duty – she possessed her father's stoicism, and drew inspiration from his relentless good humour – had forced Kate to sit there and soak up the bile, but not today. 'I'm going now,' she said. 'Call me if you're dying.' She reached the door. 'And I might come back to say goodbye.'

Kate burst out of the home. The wind and rain tugged at her hair as she charged through Battersea Park towards the river. She wanted to scream her rage at the night sky. It had been Stuart's idea to move her mother there, in the fond belief that having work, home and filial duty within walking distance of one another would reduce the burden on her, but having Lucy so close had achieved precisely the opposite. It was a dark cloud in the morning and a thunderhead at night. Not to visit meant guilt. Visiting meant hurt. How did people end up like that?

David Johnson and his wife Emma had been their oldest and best family friends. Their daughter Helen had been more or less a sister to Kate, and young Neil the brother she had never had. They'd gone on holiday together every summer, to the same bungalow by the same Cornish beach. Even now, Kate could see David in his unprepossessingly snug swimming trunks as they played tennis in the garden or cricket on the beach.

And then one day the friendship and the laughter had come to a sudden end. There were no more Sunday lunches and neither of Kate's parents talked about the impending summer holidays. Worse, when Kate had plucked up the courage to call, Helen had taken the phone from her brother and said simply that they couldn't be friends any more.

It took several weeks for her father to get round to a partial explanation of what had happened, sufficient to allow logic and her imagination to fill in the rest. Her mother had been having an affair with David Johnson, perhaps for many years. His wife had now decreed that the two families were never to speak again. And they never did.

A year or two later, Kate had urged her father to leave her mother, and the worst of it all was that she had thought less of him when he wouldn't, or perhaps couldn't. His dependency – weakness, even, she sometimes had to admit – had fuelled her mother's cruelty.

Kate reached the river wall and looked down into the dark, swirling water. She had always suspected her mother of continuing to see her lover over the years, and her extravagant reaction to David's untimely death long before her husband's had more or less confirmed her suspicions. Kate blamed the rain for dampening her cheeks. What kind of wife and mother fucks her husband's best friend? And what part of that woman had lodged itself genetically in her daughter?

If Kate could have run away from the reality of her upbringing at that moment, she would have done so, but she had long since known there was no escape. The shame followed her like a shadow. She walked home and put her arms around Stuart – who was leaning against the cooker, staring at his phone intently.

'Is it Christmas?' He looked at her. 'What happened?'

'Lucidity, that's what. She recognized me straight away. I can't remember the last time that happened.'

'And? What did she say?'

'Not much. But quite enough. She's thrown out the picture of Dad by her bedside and replaced him with David Underpants.'

'So you had an exchange of pleasantries.'

'Indeed.'

'Oh, shit.' Stuart hugged her. 'That's the last time you do

55

that. From now on I'll go, once a week, and if she tries any-thing on with me, she's going to get it with both barrels. I'll chop her up and bury her under the back patio. And the picture of that weirdo in his very tight trunks can join her.'

Kate put her hand to his chest. 'It's a nice idea, and you're positively heroic. But she's *my* mother.'

'That is a matter of opinion.' He glanced at his watch. 'I was going to point out that you are very slightly late, but under the circumstances I'll let it go. However, in the nicest possible way, you do need to get into the shower.'

Kate followed Stuart upstairs, her hand resting between his still quite finely honed shoulder blades. She loved her husband for many of the same reasons she'd adored her father. He was funny, generous and kind. He had an insatiable curiosity about the world, and a lively mind. 'My dreamboat,' she said.

'They still handing out the wacky-baccy at the home?'

Kate had a bath, not a shower, and took her time. She could tell that Stuart was torn between hurrying her because they were going to be late, and relaxing her to the point where she might feel like rolling around before they left. She dried herself slowly and shook out her hair.

'We really need to get going,' he said. 'But do you want to fool around for a bit first?'

'Do you mind if we save it for the weekend? It's been a punishing few days.'

He came over and kissed her. 'Of course not. But it'd better be good.'

She began to dress. 'What happened with Fi?'

Stuart sat on the bed. 'She wanted to go out. I said that was fine, but I wanted to see her essay on the Tudors before she went. She said she *would* do it, but in her own fucking time and . . . Well, you can imagine the rest.'

'You did the right thing. Frankly, anything to keep her away from Jedhead.'

'I don't think that's your most brilliant domestic strategy.'

'You haven't met him.'

'She's fifteen, not five.'

'You just wait.'

'Still, I don't think we can start trying to control who she sees. That never ends well.'

Kate inserted a pair of earrings and they went downstairs. Stuart was filling Nelson's water bowl when the doorbell sounded. Kate answered it.

'Good evening, Mrs Henderson.'

'Hello, Jed.'

Of course he was called Jed. He was six feet tall with enough hair gel to keep a toiletries company in business for a year.

'How are you?'

'I'm very well, thank you, Mrs Henderson.'

His polite and sincere smile seemed at odds with the tattoo wrapped around his neck, and the numerous piercings. Ashamed of herself, Kate tried to smile back. 'Can I help you?'

'Is Fi around?'

'I'm here!'

Fiona came down the stairs at speed, barely dressed and waving a sheet of paper. 'There,' she said, shoving it at Stuart as he came to join Kate at the door. 'The Tudors. An illuminated manuscript.'

'That must explain the ink splotches. But where exactly do you think you're going?'

'Out!'

'Wait!'

Kate turned back to the tattooed youth. 'Jed, I'm very sorry, but would you mind holding on a moment?'

She closed the door and faced her daughter again.

'You said I could go out if I finished my essay,' Fiona told Stuart. 'And, look, I *have* finished it.'

'I did not say you *could* go out if you finished it. I merely said you couldn't because you hadn't.'

'What's that? Russian?'

'You're not going out with him,' Kate said.

Fiona swung back towards her mother. 'I'm not going out? Or I'm not going out *with him*?'

'The distinction is academic. Because you are not going out, full stop.'

'Why not?'

'At this point, honestly? Because I say you're not.'

'And that's, like, an argument?'

'Kate . . .' Stuart said.

'She's not leaving this house, Stuart, and that's—'

'I can't spend the rest of my life wrapped in cotton wool,' Fiona said.

'Let her go for an hour,' Stuart said. 'And no more.'

Kate hated it when Stuart did this, but continued to face her daughter. 'I'm not trying to wrap you in cotton wool.'

'Yes, you are. You always do. You come home and treat us like porcelain dolls. Well, he's not the Russians and he's not the Chinese and he's not ISIS. He's a really nice seventeen-year-old boy.'

'He's nearly eighteen, and you are only just fifteen.'

'And you are two years younger than Dad. That's how it's supposed to be!'

Stuart took hold of Kate's arm. 'Let her go for an hour.'

Kate shrugged him off and stepped back. She went to get her coat, trying without success to hide her rage. She heard Stuart open the door, give the boy strict instructions on when to return his daughter and scold Fiona for the incredibly sloppy presentation of her essay. 'You'll have to do it again when you get back.'

All Kate heard after that was 'Thanks, Dad,' and the front door banging.

Stuart was waiting for her in the hall.

'I hate it when you undermine me.'

'You were being unreasonable and you know it. You can't protect her from poor judgement, and you'll make her choices worse if you try. Besides, he seemed like quite a polite lad to me.'

'I shan't let it go because you did undermine me.'

'I steered us both to a more reasonable course of action that will reduce the chances of her running away to Gretna Green with him. Or the nearest tattoo parlour . . .'

6

STUART PILOTED HER swiftly out of the house and took her hand in the Uber. She wanted to push him away but knew she couldn't justify her irritation. Fiona was right: she *was* too protective.

They bowled into the restaurant with profuse apologies to Imogen and Harry.

'I don't know why you bother saying sorry,' Harry said. 'You're always late.'

'It's Jed's fault.'

'Of course it is . . . Who the hell is Jed?'

'You may well ask. It's a story for the third bottle.'

Harry wasn't much to look at – his nose was flat and wide and he'd long since lost his once-flowing locks – but Imogen was very pretty, with dark hair cut in a neat bob, long lashes and startling green eyes. Kate had met her about seven years ago, when Imogen had first been appointed as a junior minister in the Foreign & Commonwealth Office and Stuart had been her private secretary. She had moved on to Health and eventually into the cabinet as the secretary of state for Culture, Media and Sport. She'd graduated to Education a year ago in the last reshuffle, and had asked Stuart to join her.

Since their children were young and the badlands still some distance away, Harry and Imogen were always hungry for tales from Planet Teenager. Stuart got a great deal of mileage out of Fiona's love-struck angst and the appearance of the tattooed Jed on their doorstep.

Kate didn't say much. Her attention drifted back to Lena on the super-yacht. She wondered what she was doing. Only the progression of the conversation to politics and the security of the prime minister's position brought her back. Imogen was in full flow, hiding her ambition none too convincingly behind protestations of loyalty as much now, in private, as she did in public. With a small majority and a lot of self-generated errors, the prime minister's fate was a matter of almost constant debate.

'How long do you think he's really going to stay on?' Kate asked.

'Out by Christmas, we said, then Easter. But he's still there. I think the basic truth is that our beloved foreign secretary will never force the issue because he's not as confident as he pretends to be that he would win.'

'I thought the PM looked bone tired the other day,' Stuart said. 'Maybe his wife will force him to quit.'

'When do they ever do that?' Harry asked. He was on his third gin and tonic already, and had taken to tugging his corduroy jacket as tightly as possible over his belly, a nervous gesture that gave away a preoccupation with his swelling girth. Imogen had already shot him a few warning glances, though she herself had had a couple of glasses of red wine.

'You haven't heard any rumours about his health?' Kate asked.

Imogen frowned. 'Why do you ask?'

'Something I picked up. Crossed wires, probably.'

'Well, you would know.'

'Maybe, maybe not.'

'What's supposed to be wrong with him?'

'There were just rumours he might not be in the best of health. I wondered if you'd heard them.'

'No, but—'

Their waitress passed the table and Imogen stuck out her hand so far it almost blocked her progress. 'Could we have that bottle of red wine sometime in the next decade? I've asked a couple of times already.'

The waitress stammered an apology. Harry stared uncomfortably into his glass as she departed.

Imogen locked her sights on Kate again. 'I mean specifically. What did you hear?'

'That he hadn't been well.'

'In what way?'

Kate shrugged. 'No more than that.'

'I mean flu or fatigue – or something more serious?'

'I honestly don't know any more.'

'C'mon, Kate. You know everything.'

'Leave it, love,' Harry said. 'It's probably one of those things Kate can't talk about, and we shouldn't press her.' He winked at Kate. 'However much we might want to.'

The waitress came back with the second bottle of red wine. She seemed nervous – Imogen did that to people – and a slightly clumsy twist of the bottle after filling her glass left a couple of spots on the frilly cuff of Imogen's shirt.

'For God's *sake*!' she exploded.

'I'm so sorry,' the waitress spluttered, her gaze transfixed on the two red dots on the cream material as if they were blood. 'I'll get a cloth . . . some salt maybe . . .'

'*No!*' Imogen barked. 'This is a McQueen, for fuck's sake.'

The waitress brought a salt shaker from the neighbouring table and Imogen snatched it away from her, then insisted on seeing the manager and explaining loudly that it was a *designer* shirt. He looked as confused by the significance of this as Stuart might have been, but promised to pay for it to be expertly cleaned or replaced. He said he wouldn't charge them for the evening's wine.

Harry made one attempt to intervene, but was swiftly silenced and reduced to staring into his drink. Stuart offered his boss discreet support, tut-tutting once or twice, then adding, 'Hopeless,' and 'Ridiculous,' for good measure. Kate couldn't think of any other situation in which Stuart would have behaved like that: he hated rudeness. But when Imogen shone her light on people, she could do no wrong.

After the drama had played out, Stuart and Imogen were drawn back to work chat, which left Kate wondering whether Imogen had behaved so oddly because she really didn't know about the PM's illness, or because she did. Perhaps it was just her driving ambition, which was aroused at the slightest scent of a rival's blood in the water. But Kate had a strong sense that Imogen would be a very good liar.

And good liars made good spies.

Kate closed her eyes. It was the curse of the case officer to be able to see every possibility in the most nuanced detail.

Kate and Harry listened to their spouses half-heartedly, chipping in about holiday plans and kitchen extensions until, after the main course, Stuart excused himself. Kate noticed he took his phone – the digital detox agreed the month before was going well then – and returned ashen-faced.

'Fuck me, Kate, sounds like you were spot on. The PM is about to make an emergency statement. Robert Peston tweeted that he thinks he's going to resign.' Stuart handed Kate his phone and she passed it around the group. There was a stupefied silence.

'At almost ten o'clock at night?' Imogen said.

'Somebody must have been about to break the story,' Stuart said.

'I think he's got cancer,' Kate murmured. She looked at Imogen. 'That was the rumour.'

'You *do* know everything,' Imogen gushed, but Kate thought her expression was more guarded than impressed.

They paid quickly and hurried to Harry and Imogen's, only two streets away. On the television screen, Robert Peston was standing in front of a podium outside Number Ten Downing Street. The prime minister had been hoping to go on for some time, he said, but a sharp deterioration in his condition had forced a snap decision.

No sooner had he said that than the prime minister emerged from the iconic front door. His tall and beautiful wife stood beside him. They held hands for a moment before he began. 'I'm sorry to bring you here at this late hour,' he said, 'but news I received earlier today has forced my hand.

'I was diagnosed with prostate cancer three weeks ago. I had hoped that it could be effectively treated, and that I would be able to carry on with my work more or less uninterrupted, happy to be cared for by the brilliant staff of the best healthcare system in the world. However, though hope is by no means lost, the news I received today was less encouraging.

'I thought about taking a break from the business of government for a short period but . . .' he looked across to the media scrum that had been quickly assembled before him '. . . after talking it over with my staff and my family this evening, it was evident to me that this is not practicable. The country can never have a part-time prime minister, for whatever reason, and I would be letting you all down if I were to attempt it.

'I'm sorry again to have brought you here so late, but I was warned rumours might start to circulate and I wanted you to hear this from me. It has been a great privilege to serve my country, by which, of course, I mean all of you. I hope I will be able to do so again in some capacity, but for now, from this office at least, it is goodbye.'

He took his wife's hand once more. Tears were running down her cheeks. He waved to the cameras and led her back inside.

'Shit,' Stuart said.

'Oscar-winning,' Harry said.

Stuart turned to Imogen. 'Are you going to stand? You have to! James will be on the phone already.'

Imogen looked shell-shocked, which was more or less how Kate felt. She glanced at an incoming message from Rav. *Bingo*, it said, with an excitement she couldn't match. She disappeared to the loo, closed the door and sat, elbows on her knees, while she messaged back: *Now what do we do?*

His response arrived via WhatsApp. *Focus on who runs. Investigate (the foreign secretary first, but the rest too, INCLUDING Imogen). Return to source operation and see what more we can get. And let's not forget 'Viper'. Why might he/she be in a position to help? PS Your call, but think we'll have to bring in 5. I know Pete Gibbs. Smart.*

Kate put the phone into her pocket. Pete Gibbs headed up a highly secret unit at the heart of MI5, tasked with investigating all attempts to infiltrate British public life. Rav was probably right, but Kate intrinsically disliked widening the circle of knowledge. No matter how tight the procedures and how careful the intentions, it would become harder to shield the original source of the intelligence. She had promised Lena she wouldn't put her at risk, and she had every intention of sticking to that pledge, even if she hadn't yet stepped in to shield the girl's sister.

In the taxi home, Stuart was pretty high on the night's events. 'She'll win.'

'She'll run him close, but she won't win.'

'She's young, she's telegenic, she's smart. Take a look at the polls. The fall-off in support for the government amid the under-thirties has been calamitous, and she's the only one who stands a chance of winning them another election.'

'She's all of those things, but they won't endear her to the party rank and file.'

'Well, I think you're wrong, wrong, wrong.'

'We'll see.'

By the time they got home Gus was asleep, but Fiona was still poring over her computer. 'I heard the news,' she said, when Kate looked in. 'Poor guy.'

'Somehow we never expect someone in such a position of power to be struck down by something so ordinary.'

'It sounded like he's about to die.'

'It did rather, didn't it?'

'His wife was crying a river. What's he like?'

'Decent enough. When push comes to shove, the sort of man you want to have in a job like that.' Kate moved over to kiss her daughter.

'I was back on time,' Fiona said defensively.

'I'm sure.'

'He's not the boy you think he is.'

Kate sat on the bed. 'He's just much older than you, love.'

'You mean he has loads of ink and piercings.'

'I don't want to have another argument. I just urge you to be careful and go very slowly.'

'You mean about sex?'

'Sex with him would be rape, so that is not a good idea.'

'Of course it wouldn't be rape!'

'Statutory rape. You're a long way from sixteen. He would go to jail, which is not something either of you would be happy about.'

'No one would know.'

Kate took Fiona's hand. 'I'm not trying to imprison you. I'm just trying to look out for your best interests. I'm not going to discuss sex because you're too young for that. If you're still going out with him in a year's time, perhaps it's something we can talk about. If he waits that long, maybe he *is* the boy you think he is.'

Fiona pulled her hand away. 'You have no idea how out of touch you are.'

'I have to be in work early, so I may not see you in the morning. Have a good day.'

Kate went to take off her make-up, then brushed her teeth and climbed into bed. Stuart would normally be snoring by now, but he was wide awake. 'You can't beat a bit of political intrigue,' he said.

'Hmm.'

'And it would be quite exciting if our friend became the most powerful woman in the country.'

'You're forgetting the Queen.'

'I'm serious.'

'It would be complicated, that's for sure.'

'Do you think she'd ask me to go with her?'

'I imagine so.' Kate leant over and kissed his cheek. 'Just make sure you don't spill anything on her *designer* shirt.' She rolled over. 'Now go to sleep.'

He did, but she didn't.

At least, not for long.

At two in the morning, she was woken by a vivid dream in which she discovered Lena's mutilated body in a wood, signs of torture clearly visible on her face and neck, arms and breasts.

Kate sat up with a familiar feeling of panic in her chest. She got up, her body covered with sweat. She went to the window, drew back the curtain and looked down into the street. It was deserted. She breathed in deeply and exhaled slowly, as the psychotherapist had taught her, and after a while the panic began to subside. She went downstairs, made herself a cup of tea and sat on a stool alongside the kitchen island to drink it.

With a start she realized that Stuart was behind her. She swung around.

'What is it?' His voice was creased with worry.

'Oh, same old.'

'Work or home?'

'We have someone out there, a young girl I recruited, not much older than Fiona. Our daughter is risking her virtue, but that girl is risking her neck – and the lack of balance was getting to me.'

'I often think you have everything under control, but . . .'

Kate sighed. 'Maybe it's what happened in Lahore with

Rav – or my mother, I don't know. But the dread in the pit of my stomach is always the same.'

'Have you seen your counsellor recently?'

'Not for a few months. I thought it was getting better.'

'You're the most conscientious and careful woman I know so I'm totally sure you're doing everything you can for the girl you have out there.'

'I hope so, but she's there because of me. That's hard to get out of your head in the middle of the night.'

Stuart sighed. 'We've talked about this. I know it's an important job and you're very good at it, but we agreed it's not worth damaging your health. You have to be able to leave it locked inside that fortress. You can't bring it home, and leave part of yourself behind. That's not a good deal.' He kissed the top of her head. 'If I can help, call me.' He walked to the stairs.

'You do help, my love. It's not really the work but the sense of vulnerability that I can't help bringing home,' she said. 'No brothers, no sisters, no father, no mother to speak of. Work is intellectual stimulation, God is a fantasy. In the balance sheet of my life at dead of night, it's you, Gus and Fiona in the plus column. That's it. Nothing else. Whatever may trigger it, it's the fear of losing you all that brings on the dread.'

'But we're not going anywhere.'

'How do we know what Fate will decree? My love for all of you is paralysing at times. If I didn't know about the threats out there, I wouldn't be so gripped by the need to man the barricades. But I do.'

'I understand. Of course I do. But in the morning, I'll still emerge from the duvet looking like a demented wild boar, as you have been known to suggest, Fiona will still be a hormonal teenager – though hopefully over her Swedish-porn-star phase – and Gus will still struggle to utter five words before breakfast. Normal transmission will continue. And we'll live for the day, not for all time. Because that is what we all have to do.'

'But in the middle of the night, I fear the threat rather than revel in the joy.'

'You can't protect us from life. And you'll squeeze the humanity out of us if you try.'

'I don't want to protect you from *life*—'

'You are not your mother, Kate. You're not going to do what she did, and our family will not go the way of your own. Keep your anxiety locked away with her and with your work. Back here, you simply need to have faith in us.'

She smiled at him. 'I know. I'll be up in a minute.'

'You're a nutter,' he said, and disappeared back to bed.

7

THE FOLLOWING MORNING, the meeting with C was early enough to take place in his dining room on the top floor of MI6 Headquarters in Vauxhall. Kate rode the lift up and gave her overcoat to Beddows, the butler, who ushered her wordlessly into a cosy room with a dramatic view of Big Ben. If it was designed to convince guests that this was where real power rested at the heart of London's innermost establishment, it could not have done a more successful job. Even the carpet seemed thicker than anywhere else in the building.

Sir Alan and Ian were already eating bacon and scrambled eggs. Rav was pushing some fruit and yoghurt around his plate. He never ate breakfast and rarely lunch. He was the archetypal night owl.

Beddows poured Kate some coffee. Sir Alan was already in full flow, and Rav was the beneficiary. 'I see no reason to waste time drawing up a huge list of potential runners and riders for the leadership. We can assume that if one of them is a Russian agent, he or she will stand. So as each candidate declares they list themselves as a potential suspect. We can safely predict the foreign secretary will put himself forward, so you should begin your investigations there today. The same, too, I think, with Imogen Conrad. Since they effectively represent each wing of the party, they may end up as the only candidates.'

'I still think we should wait and see if we can get some corroboration,' Ian said. 'If there's any kind of leak, it'll be hugely—'

'We can't wait. And there won't be a leak.'

'We *know* the Russians. What if this *is* just another—'

'We're damned if we do and damned if we don't. I'm well aware of that. But for now the greater danger is inaction.' Sir Alan was glaring at him.

Kate caught Rav's eye.

'We're not talking about a thin stream of intelligence from a single agent,' Sir Alan went on. 'We're discussing a conversation involving the most senior officials in the SVR that we can all listen to and form a judgement on. We'd look ridiculous if it emerged we'd just sat on it.'

'Rav suggested we bring in Pete Gibbs from Five,' Kate said.

Ian responded like a scalded cat: 'Out of the question.'

'I understand your reluctance,' Kate said, aware that Rav was still deploying his best poker face, 'but are we not under an obligation to inform them?'

'Yes,' C said. 'And indeed we will, in due course. But for now I want to keep the knowledge we have within this building. It's our intelligence. We own it and we need to take care of it.'

'Imogen Conrad stays on my list,' Kate said, still trying to distance herself from the glimpse of egocentric volatility she had been treated to the previous evening.

'Agreed. We should remain open to all possibilities. If Istanbul is an attempt to wrong-foot us, then it's conceivable that she *is* their woman and the foreign secretary their enemy. More prosaically, we may need to provide evidence ourselves some day that we conducted our investigations in an even-handed manner from the receipt of that first intelligence.'

'Any no-go areas?'

'Run the slide rule over everything. Finances, relation-ships, sex lives. Conduct yourselves exactly as if you were assessing the vulnerability of a foreign agent to an approach. We can simply pass it off as routine positive vetting, brought forward as a result of this contest.'

'But don't get bloody caught doing it, all the same,' Ian said.

'That might be difficult.'

'I'm sure you'll manage, Kate,' Ian said. 'We all know how resourceful you can be.'

'There is one other thing,' C said, glossing over Ian's waspishness. He tapped the file. 'Viper can help, they said. So who is Viper?'

No one answered.

'If he or she exists, we must confront the possibility that they have a desk inside this building.'

Kate glanced at Ian, who was staring out of the window.

'And, if somewhere else, then in what way can he or she "help"?'

'Could be anyone,' Ian said. 'In Number Ten, Whitehall, a journalist . . .'

'Let's start with the most senior civil servants around the

secretary of state for Education and the foreign secretary,' Sir Alan instructed. 'Talk to GCHQ. Start with the basics: lifestyle, phone records, travel history. See if you can spot anyone or anything that sticks out. And I want you to go back to the source *here*.' He was pointing at the file.

'In what sense?' Kate asked.

'The only way they could be pissing us around is if they saw us coming. And if you were as tight with your procedures as I would expect you to be, that should have been more or less impossible. So let's not give up on the source of it. Your agent is still in place. Let's plant other devices. Let's see what else she can tell us.' He tapped the file. 'Looking through the transcripts again this morning, I think we should resume our focus on the son, Mikhail. If he's gay, he'll be finding an . . . outlet somewhere, even if it's not in Russia.'

Kate glanced at her phone. 'A message from Julie. The yacht disappeared overnight.'

'Then let's track it – and be there when it reappears.' He flipped the file shut and nodded to them, their audience over.

'Bang goes our quiet autumn,' Ian said, as they waited for the lift.

Kate raised an eyebrow. 'I hadn't figured you as a season-of-mists-and-mellow-fruitfulness fan.'

'You're going to need more help. Who would you like me to bring in?'

'Ops teams later, of course, but we should start off by trying to do it ourselves.'

'Excellent.' He adopted his habitual expression of messianic zeal. 'You're not alone on this, Kate.'

She glanced at Rav and tried not to laugh. Ian had never

taken to her deputy, whom he had made a habit of ignoring. They rode the lift down in silence. When they reached their floor, Ian turned away without another word.

'What's he hiding?' Rav asked, when Ian was out of earshot.

'You might have to ask his tailor.' She grinned. 'He's at his most disconcerting when he starts trying to be helpful.'

'No, I mean specifically. He said, "We know the Russians, but what if this *is just another* . . ." Then Sir Alan cut him off. So, just another what?'

'He said something similar the other day. I didn't read too much into it. We know how Moscow works. They may well be misleading us.'

'No, no. That isn't what I'm saying. He and Sir Alan were looking at each other and they were talking about something specific they were aware of but we weren't.'

'If that's the case, I'm still not.'

They reached their office and the telltale signs of Rav's vigil: a McDonald's bag in the bin, half a dozen styrofoam coffee cups.

'Did you go home at all?' Kate asked.

'No.'

'What did you find?'

'All kinds of interesting things. If you get me a coffee, I'll give you a presentation.'

'You don't need another coffee, but it's a deal. Just give me a second to log on.' Kate stepped into her own small glass-walled office. As she sat at her desk, there was a knock on the partition door.

'Do you have a moment?'

Kate turned at the sound of Sir Alan's mellifluous tones. 'Yes, of course.'

He closed the door behind him. 'It seems like only yesterday

I sat here, enjoying the same uplifting view of Vauxhall station.'

'You must miss it terribly.'

'Promotion does have its drawbacks.' C leant back against the filing cabinet. 'I didn't want to say anything in front of Ian but I'm not naive enough to believe that the intelligence gathered from Istanbul was solely down to luck.'

Kate didn't answer.

'Kate, I know every agent, every source we have in your neck of the woods. And since you started this job – my old job – I have noticed the occasional gem of information, whose origin I cannot completely fathom, creeping into the reports crossing my desk. Somebody tipped you off that one or more of those men were going to be on that yacht, didn't they?'

Kate stared pointedly out of the window.

'Clandestine sources are beguiling, but dangerous. They allow us to be manipulated and misled, with potentially serious consequences.'

'Is that what Ian was alluding to?'

'Yes.'

'It would be helpful to know how we were misled.'

'In an operation that began very much like this.'

'That doesn't tell me anything remotely useful.'

'It's a matter that is now closed on the orders of our political masters. But it's the oldest story in our profession. You think you're buying gold, only to find you've paid a lot of money for highly coloured glass. But back to the present. I'd like to know if the impetus for this operation came from a source you haven't declared.'

She looked at him, sifting her options. 'Yes, it did.'

'Who was he – or, indeed, she?'

'I gave him my word I wouldn't say.'

'That wasn't what I'd call a request, Kate.'

'Well, I'm sorry. I can't tell you. I won't break my word – for you, or anyone else.'

'How very noble of you.' C switched off the light in his eyes. 'So where does that leave us? Perhaps we should be looking for someone you met during your time at Cambridge. Most probably on your year in Russia. Since then, he or she will have risen to a position of some importance in the Russian intelligence community – or perhaps their foreign service – and your contact is . . . episodic. Getting warmer?'

He waited out her silence. What a cool customer he was.

'You're a clever and ambitious woman, Kate. If I looked in your vetting file, I guess I'd find the name I'm looking for somewhere down the list of declared contacts from your Russian sojourn. I don't think you'd have been foolish enough to omit all mention of a contact of this . . . significance.'

'You probably could, but I still can't say.'

'I'd respectfully suggest that you're adopting an unnecessarily inflexible position.'

'Perhaps. But I think you'd do the same. It's one of the many reasons why I've always admired you. It comes down to a basic principle: you either trust my judgement or you don't.'

'Alas, in the real world, it's not as simple as that.'

'I'm not trying to challenge your authority. You're a very large part of the reason I'm still slaving away down here day after day. As I said, I gave my word.'

'Is it possible you were set up?'

'No.'

'How can you be so sure?'

'Instinct.'

'A sometimes mercurial guide, if I may say so.'

She turned to face him. 'You're right. He's someone I got to know when I was studying in St Petersburg, long before any of this.'

'A lover?'

She hesitated a moment too long. 'No.'

'You should tell me, if so.'

'No,' she said emphatically. 'Someone who might have been in other circumstances. I'd met Stuart by then.' She paused. 'I'd heard nothing from him for years until he turned up in London.'

'Possibly not by accident.'

'I've thought about that, of course, but I met him at an American Embassy reception about three years ago and we chatted for a few minutes. I heard nothing more until this time last year when I had an anonymous letter in the post. It said we should watch Igor closely as he moved around Europe. We already were, as you well know. And then I got another letter a month ago.'

'Saying what?'

'Just tipping me off about a meeting of senior intelligence officers on Igor's yacht on the Bosphorus. We already had an operation in mind. We'd been planning to try to find a way to get close to Mikhail, so I just brought it forward.'

C remained impassive, except for a faint ripple of the jaw muscles. 'Very well. There are things *you* don't know. Vasily is not as powerful as he once was inside Moscow Centre. There are those who believe that his attempts to interfere with the democratic politics of the West are a distraction, which might prove costly. They're trying to persuade the Russian president he should concentrate only on the country's direct sphere of influence, and leave the West to unravel by itself. So perhaps you've been used. And perhaps you haven't.' Finally, he smiled. 'We all like to think our relationships are special. But let's not forget Moscow plays a very long game. From now on, I want to know everything, Kate. No secrets.'

'Of course.'

'I'm glad we understand one another.' He opened the door. 'Good luck.'

He shared his smile with Rav, who slipped in as soon as C had rounded the corner.

Kate forestalled Rav's question. 'He wanted to remind me of the almost inestimable size of the can of fucking worms we've just opened. Now I really will get your coffee. Wait here.'

Kate went down to the kitchen and closed the door. She could feel the heat in her cheeks. She punched the machine. Rav joined her before it had spewed out the second latte.

'You're so incredibly impatient,' she said.

'You'll already know point one of the briefing I was about to give you.'

'I don't. But I feel sure you're about to enlighten me.'

'I've been putting our foreign secretary under the microscope.'

'All night?'

'All night. And there is a great deal I have to tell you. But page one, paragraph one, *point one*: guess who was at school with him.'

'Sir Alan. It's not a secret.'

Rav was not remotely deflated. 'I bet you don't know this: they were in the *same house, in the same year.*'

Kate frowned. 'You're right. I didn't know that.'

'It's your highly over-privileged world. How many boys is that?'

'It's not my world, Rav.'

'You went to private school.'

'I went to a small Quaker school where you were expelled if you failed to get straight As and where the playing fields had been sold off to build a block of flats. It wasn't Eton.'

'Eton doesn't accept girls.'

'Don't be pedantic.'

'Okay, but how many do you reckon?'

'In a year in a house? I don't know . . . twelve, thirteen, fourteen?'

'He gives the impression he doesn't think much of the man he calls our "nominal" superior, doesn't he?'

'Well, yes, though he's reasonably discreet about it. And I don't see why it matters that much.'

'But it's *interesting*, right? You know how the establishment likes to stick together? It excludes you just as much as it does me, and you went to Cambridge.'

She thought about it for a moment. 'Yes. It is interesting.'

8

BACK IN KATE'S office, Rav pulled up a chair and deposited his pile of notes on her coffee table. He flipped around the three files in front of him so that the one marked 'Conrad' was on top. 'I'm going to start with your friend Imogen, if you don't mind, because although there's less to report, in some ways it's more interesting.'

She waited.

'Her finances look commensurate with her role and her husband's job with Oxfam: one house, which you know about, in London, and no sign of any other wealth. She gets a hell of a lot of abuse online, I mean really disgusting stuff – rape threats, the works.'

'She's a woman in public life and has made the mistake of being pretty.'

'Well, the internet is not a flawless intelligence resource, but I can't see any rumours of extra-marital affairs or anything else that might be used against her. However, her record on Russia is a bit odd.'

'What sort of odd?'

'When she became a minister, she was very voluble, particularly about the murder of Alexander Litvinenko, which had happened a few years before she joined the Foreign & Commonwealth Office. She took a very tough line, demanding stiffer sanctions and actually getting them imposed on a wider section of the president's inner circle. In 2012, she was invited by the Foreign Affairs Select Committee to accompany MPs on a fact-finding mission to Moscow, St Petersburg and, of all places, Ekaterinburg, Ipatiev House—'

'Where Tsar Nicholas and his family were assassinated. And?'

'And she's barely spoken publicly about Russia since.'

'2012 . . . She must have got promoted to Culture, Media and Sport around then.'

'Later that year.'

'So her silence on that subject is hardly surprising.'

'Maybe.' He was flicking through to the end of the file. 'But on most of her other favourite subjects – human rights in China, Tibet, Saudi – she has continued to be quite frequently and widely quoted. At a conference fringe event last year. At a discussion on shaping the modern world at the Chalke Valley History Festival a few months ago. On Russia, however, even with the Salisbury nerve-agent attack and everything that followed, nothing.'

'Have you got a list of who accompanied her on that Russian trip?'

He fished it out and handed it over. 'Interesting or not?'

'The trouble is, once you start looking for things that

might seem extraordinary, then graduate to the curious absence of the ordinary, that way madness lies.'

Rav flipped open the second file. 'Okay, our illustrious foreign secretary, James Ryan, of whom the reverse appears to be true. Leaving aside the moments when he's had to be critical – such as the attack on Salisbury, for example – he's said incredibly little about Russia, which is intriguing, given that he's been foreign secretary for half a decade. He's filled acres and acres of newsprint on the US, Europe, Saudi, Yemen, Israel, Syria, ISIS, the Middle East in general, China, North Korea, Japan – but Russia only rarely, and he's been only mildly critical, even of its role in Syria.

'Before Salisbury, he was on record as saying, "At least the Russian president knows what he wants." And in general, he's the least hawkish of the cabinet, perhaps surprising, given his time in the military. He has never been in favour of pursuing and confiscating the assets of the London-based oligarchs. And the Foreign & Commonwealth Office has been kind enough to remove sanctions and travel restrictions on eight more members of the president's immediate circle – to "improve relations" with the Motherland.'

'Cosy? Or merely pragmatic?' Kate mused.

'I've looked into the possibility of some kind of *kompromat* on the foreign secretary and I'm with C on this. His reputation as a shagger is so Olympian that even if they had footage of him in bed with any number of women – or men, or even goats, for that matter – they'd have no real hold over him.'

'You never know what really goes on behind the scenes in a marriage, though. Perhaps Sophie chooses not to believe the rumours, but would find the evidence utterly devastating.'

'She seems to have learnt to live with the fact that he has at least one love-child.'

'Is *said* to have a love-child.'

'Have you seen the pictures?'

'No.'

Rav pushed across a printout: a young boy holding a woman's hand in a playground. To say he was the image of James Ryan was understating the likeness between them.

'Hmm. I see what you mean. All the same, wives, husbands – partners – can always blind themselves to what appears obvious to everyone else.'

'Not sure I agree, but let's park it for now. His financial status is puzzling. He left school at eighteen and joined the military. Only made it to major before quitting, and after a very short spell in business, he became an MP. Yet he has a house in Chelsea, that pile in Hampshire I showed you, a cottage in Cornwall and sends all three of his children to public schools, whose fees for each child are now almost forty grand a year.'

'The privileged among us mostly pay for their children's education through inheritance. It's what keeps the class system afloat.'

'Not in this case.'

'Go on.'

'His dad was also an army officer. He died two years ago, leaving everything he had to his wife. She lives in a cottage near Basingstoke and holidays in James's Cornish shepherd's hut. Sophie's father was RAF and her mother was a nurse and they're both dead. The mother left an estate valued at just over half a million three years ago.'

'That's not nothing.'

'Enough to pay the school bills, possibly, but not the rest of it. She also has a sister.'

Kate glanced over the relevant paperwork. 'What next?'

'Follow the money. I'll look into what he did after leaving the army. We should also try to speak to people who knew him at school and in the military, particularly, I would say, during his time in Kosovo. Can I at least ask Five for his vetting file?'

'No.'

'That will make everything harder.'

'You heard what Sir Alan said.'

'Fair enough.' Rav reached for the last file. 'Viper. Potential suspects.'

The names were listed under just two headings: *Imogen Conrad* and *James Ryan*. Stuart made an early appearance.

'Sorry,' Rav said.

'For what?'

'If there's ever a review, we're both going to look stupid if we leave him out.'

'Of course,' Kate said. 'Perhaps I'll discover he has a secret gambling habit. It might explain how all our money seems to vanish into thin air.'

'I don't think I'd want someone in my team investigating Zac.'

'Then you should have more faith.' Kate handed back the dossiers and eyed the McDonald's wrapper. 'Not good,' she said. 'But the coffee is probably worse. If you insist on being here all night, you're going to have to cut down or you'll be dead before you're forty.'

He gave her an unwitting glimpse of unutterable sadness. 'I'll be dead long before I'm forty.'

'That's an extreme and frankly stupid thing to say.'

'Trust me. I will be.'

'Don't talk like that, Rav.' Kate looked into his eyes and saw the vulnerability he worked so hard to hide. Rav had always felt unloved and unworthy in his parents' estimation, which left him prone to often crippling depression. It was a reminder that she was not alone in her unresolved demons.

Rav slipped out and closed the door behind him.

Kate tapped her keyboard and opened the Records entry portal. Zehra's response to her question about the translator she'd assessed in Istanbul still nagged at her. If the recruitment *had* gone ahead, why had Ian lied about it? She typed in her own name and staff code and entered *Irina Demidova* in the search bar. A few seconds later, she was rewarded with *No items found.*

Maddy knocked and entered. 'Morning. I hear Istanbul went well.'

'Yes, it did. We're going to be very, very busy.'

'That'll make a nice change.'

Maddy was in her early forties, tidy, steady, married and childless. She was one of those women who could be annoyingly pedantic – pedestrian, even – over detail, but would always have your back. She was also a world-class gossip, which had its uses in that building. 'You might want to come and watch,' Maddy said. 'He's out of the blocks already.'

Kate joined Rav in front of the TV screen on the far wall. As an apparently impromptu press conference was being set up outside the Foreign & Commonwealth Office in King Charles Street, Kate passed Maddy the list of MPs on the Moscow trip. 'Can you get me in to see one of these champions of the people this morning? Angela White might be favourite – she's been around a while and is quite vociferously anti the Russian president.'

Kate checked that she was not about to sit on anything, then perched on the edge of Julie's desk. It was bare, save for the picture of her brother, Jason, who'd been killed on the top deck of a bus during the 7/7 London bombings. She'd always said she was there to play a meaningful part in the war on terror but, bright as she was, plenty of department heads gave her a wide berth. She'd been to places not many others had experienced, even in a building like this, which set her apart.

A suave, dark-haired man emerged onto the street and approached the microphones. Rav picked up the remote and pumped up the volume. James Ryan paused for a moment, glancing about him. 'Thank you very much for turning out at such short notice. I'm sure you were all as shocked as I was last night to hear what the prime minister had to say. His service to our country has been exemplary and we hope and pray he will be successfully through his treatment and back to front-line politics in no more than a heartbeat. We know he's in the hands of the best health-care professionals anywhere in the world today.'

'Why do they all say that?' Rav asked. 'It isn't true, and they don't mean it.'

'The prime minister's legacy is a great one,' Ryan continued. 'He's led this country with an energy and optimism that are the envy of other world leaders. A golden future awaits us as a proud, independent, free-trading nation, developing new and exciting relationships with countries across the globe.'

He surveyed his audience.

'Was he the original model for Action Man?' Kate whispered.

'If it's him against Imogen Conrad,' Rav said, 'it'll be the best-looking political contest in British history.'

'He's too smooth for me,' Maddy said. 'I wouldn't trust him to put out my rubbish.'

TOM BRADBY

'None of us would choose to be here today . . .' the foreign secretary went on.

'You fucking would,' Rav whispered.

'. . . but I have never denied that, if the moment were to arise, I would aspire to lead our great party and our wonderful country. Such sad circumstances serve to remind us that in adversity there is always opportunity – and today the question before you is, who can give this country the bold and optimistic leadership it needs?

'I count myself truly fortunate to have had so many calls of support from colleagues, urging me to run. And so this morning I announce with considerable pride that I will be putting my name forward. I'm sure an open, exciting and vigorous contest awaits us. May the best man – or woman – win! Thank you!'

As the assembled reporters shouted questions, the foreign secretary turned smartly and re-entered his domain.

Maddy put down her phone. 'Angela White can see you now, if you have time. They'll come down and get you from Reception at Portcullis House.' She followed Kate into her office. 'Any expenses from Istanbul?'

'Somewhere. I'll put them on your desk.' Kate picked up her coat, then hesitated. 'Maddy, you know I don't like to ask about your stint with Ian . . .'

'I've never understood why you insist on being so scrupulous. He wouldn't.'

'I don't want to put you in an awkward position.'

'You mean like I was the whole bloody time I worked for him?'

Kate smiled. 'All right. Do you recall him recruiting a woman called Irina Demidova? I assessed her in Istanbul. Originally a relatively lowly secretary in the KGB, but she may have progressed beyond that. Ian told me yesterday that he never moved forward with her, but I'm not so sure.'

'I don't, but that doesn't mean much. If he told me it was Wednesday, I'd still check a calendar.'

'But if she *had* gone on the payroll, it would have been down to you to process it through Finance?'

'Probably, unless she was one of the little secrets he liked to keep.'

'If she *had* gone on the payroll, Finance would still have a record, right? I mean, if the management committee wants to take someone off the books, they can remove them from the central system, but there's no procedure for taking it out of the accounts?'

Maddy closed the door quietly behind her. 'That's a pretty big question. What's going on?'

'I have to keep everything tight for now and I'm not sure this is relevant anyway.'

Maddy shrugged. 'I really don't know. You'd have to talk to Rose.'

'I thought you might say that.'

Kate walked down the back stairs to the Operations Room on the floor below. Maddy's visceral dislike of Ian was partly explained by his attempt to get her sacked for incompetence, as a result, she said, of her having refused his advances. Only the fact that she had once worked for Sir Alan had saved her.

Danny's colleague Hamid was staring at a set of screens in the far corner of the Ops Room. 'Morning,' Kate said. 'You look knackered.'

He manipulated the mouse on the pad in front of him and pulled up a satellite feed displaying the progress of Igor's yacht. 'Headed for Greece, at a guess, but not in any particular hurry.' He moved to the screen on the right. 'There was something we missed, though.' He fast-forwarded through the stream of video from the top of the Kempinski. 'Danny went through the pictures from the very small hours . . . And here we are. Four thirty in the morning . . .'

A group of men were getting onto the launch, speeding in to the shore, offloading on the quay, then walking towards the hotel. At the head of the group, which included Vasily and his colleagues from the Russian Intelligence Service, was Igor.

'They got into two separate Mercedes, drove to the airport and took off in a private jet bound for Moscow.'

'No sign of Mikhail, his wife and son or the au pair disembarking?'

He shook his head. 'As far as we can tell, they're still on board.'

'Will you tell me as soon as they get within reach of a dock?'

'Sure. Danny's packing up in Istanbul and heading home. Is that all right?'

'Yes, but I'll want him to turn straight round and head out to wherever they make landfall.'

'I'll give him the good news.'

Kate took the lift to the ground floor. Rose's office was only just far enough above the exterior walkway to afford its incumbents a view of the river. 'They put us here,' her aunt had once told her, 'because they'd be only too delighted if someone planted a bomb on the wall and the whole Finance team got blown to smithereens.'

Rose's secretary had poorly dyed blonde hair and a lurid green cardigan with bright brass buttons pulled tightly across her chest. Jane was originally from Poland in the days when it had laboured under Communist rule and looked like she'd never left. Her manner was pure Iron Curtain too, and it was a mystery why Rose was so loyal to her. 'She's in a meeting,' Jane announced, as Kate approached, allowing herself a rare moment of delight.

'No problem. Will you tell her I dropped by?' Kate glanced at the frames on Rose's desk, which included photographs of her husband and beloved dog Stanley, Kate and her father, arm in arm on the Ridgeway, just above Rose's home.

Rose Trewen was Kate's father's sister, and the principal reason Kate had joined the Service. She was also as close to a mother as Kate had ever enjoyed, though the depth of their emotional connection was not something either tended to advertise at work.

'Can I help you with something?' Jane asked.

'Don't worry. It can wait.' Kate turned away, then thought better of it. 'Actually, could you do a system search? We're doing some internal vetting.'

'I am sure Rose would want us to help.' Jane's accent was still strong enough to make that sound like a threat.

'Could you check whether we've ever made any payments to an Irina Demidova?'

Jane turned to her monitor, tapped away for a few moments, then went very still. 'You will have to speak to Rose about that,' she said.

'Oh . . . of course. I'll come back later.'

Kate emerged from Security into a close afternoon. Banks of dark cloud brooded over Vauxhall station, threatening to explode at any minute. She thought about the expression on Jane's face when her screen had sent her a message she clearly hadn't expected.

It seemed obvious that Ian *had* recruited Irina Demidova. So why was he so evasive at the mention of her name?

91

9

KATE CLEARED SECURITY into Parliament at Portcullis House with unexpected speed. The fig trees on the other side of the barrier seemed to reach up to the great glass roof, but she had little time to admire them.

The woman who came to meet her was tall and slightly forbidding. She tucked a strand of long, grey-streaked hair behind her ear as if rebuking it for an act of momentary dis-obedience. 'Angela White,' she said. 'I was passing through from the House, so I thought I'd take you up myself.' She swiped Kate through the glass security portal and gestured at the light and airy piazza beyond. 'I'm guessing you've been here often enough.'

'Not really.'

'You were admiring the fig trees. Quite right too. They cost our loyal taxpayer four hundred thousand pounds. Oh, the glory of the Blair years. Those were the days!' She broke into an unexpected smile and gestured at the coffee shop. 'Would you like to come up to the office or stay down here?'

'Probably best to have a little peace and quiet.'

'I assumed as much. Let's go up.'

Angela led Kate up to a small but well-appointed suite on the third floor, which overlooked Big Ben and a slice of the river. She smiled again. 'You have no idea of the native cunning required to get an office like this.'

'With a view like that, I might have been tempted to indulge in a little light skulduggery myself.'

'Tea?'

'Coffee, if it's on offer.'

Angela motioned to her smaller, more intimate chamber with an even more spectacular perspective of Big Ben. Kate sat on the sofa by the window, as invited. 'The chimes must be deafening.'

'Oddly, you get used to them, to the point when you look out for the strike of the hour as a signal to go and do something, and somehow always miss it.'

'It's a hell of a place.'

'It is, but I try not to let it go to my head. My seat isn't exactly a marginal, but it wouldn't take much of a turn in the tide . . .'

'You've been here a while, though.'

'Seventeen years. It only feels like five lifetimes so far.'

Angela's assistant brought in a tray of tea, coffee and biscuits. They were silent for a moment as they helped themselves and settled back in their seats.

'Have you ever wanted to be a minister?' Kate asked.

'No. An MP is what I am, and what I shall remain. That's partly to do with the children – we have three, all grown up now – but also because I think one has to choose early on in here between ambition and principle, and I found it too hard to win my seat to readily let go of the things that really matter, which perhaps sounds a bit priggish. I try not to stand on my principles too often, which is harder than it might appear . . .' She sipped her tea. 'Sorry. I imagine you didn't come all the way here to discuss my less than impressive career.'

'I can't help feeling that choosing integrity over office is pretty impressive.'

'Kind of you to say so.'

Kate put down her cup. 'I know you must be busy, so I'll get to the point. My office was probably rather vague—'

' "Opaque" is a word that springs to mind.'

'I can't stress strongly enough the sensitivity of what I'm about to discuss. Which is a roundabout way of saying that after listening to what you've just told me, I'm going to speak more openly than perhaps I would otherwise.'

'That sounds . . . dangerous.'

'I've kept up to speed on much of what you've said at the Foreign Affairs Committee hearings, and you seem to have a very dark view of modern Russia.'

'Are you suggesting I'm wrong? After the nerve-agent attack in Salisbury, I thought it was generally accepted—'

'My God, you're not wrong. It's a gangster regime and the Russian president is the nemesis of everything we hold dear. In his view, a great modern Russia requires a corrupt, weak and supine West. He is the most serious and well-organized enemy of Western civilization.'

'Go on.'

'Oh, I could be here for hours. He's everywhere. He's trying to provoke war with Georgia via the breakaway republics in an attempt to deter NATO from admitting it to membership. He's funding and equipping right-wing para-military groups in Latvia, Estonia, Lithuania and even Slovakia. Look closely on the satellite pictures into some of the camps these groups are building in the middle of the countryside and you'll see armoured cars and stashes of semi-automatic weapons. What would they need those for? A long while back you alerted the committee to the Russian president's attempts to undermine the operation of Western democracy and since then, of course, it has exploded into the public consciousness in America and everywhere else. But it isn't just the false social-media accounts and the hacked emails, the leaking and assistance given to candidates of dubious views who once might not have had a cat's chance of high office.'

Angela was listening intently now.

'They're doing much more than that. We know that they're trying to bribe, bully or blackmail leading figures within these walls. What could be more satisfying than having Western leaders as your agents of influence? Which brings me to the current leadership election. We're trying, very carefully, to check out the main candidates, so I'd be grateful if you didn't read anything significant into the choice of individual I'm here to discuss.'

Angela's gaze was now hawk-like. 'Isn't that MI5's job?'

'Yes. But in this particular case, because of the nature of the original intelligence, we need to pursue things ourselves, at least initially. If we find evidence that it's correct, Five will be fully briefed.'

'Okay.' Angela visibly relaxed. 'I'll try to keep my trap shut.'

'About seven years ago, you went on a trip to Russia with Imogen Conrad. At that point, she was a junior minister in the Foreign & Commonwealth Office.'

'I did, yes.'

'Was there anything about her conduct on the trip that struck you as odd or worthy of note? Anyone she saw, anything she said?'

'That's a rather open-ended question, if I may say so.'

'True. But I think you know what I'm driving at.'

'All right. I'll tell you what I really think of Imogen Conrad, in the privacy of this room. She's what you might call a man's woman, at her brightest and most vivacious when there's a man around she wants to impress. She *is* attractive – what men would call sexy – and she knows it. I think she likes to feel she has the men around her exactly where she wants them. She is, consequently, not someone who finds women – particularly jobsworth backbench MPs – of much interest. So, mostly, I find myself somewhat impervious to her no doubt considerable charm.'

'How did that particularly manifest itself in Russia?'

'To be brutally honest, she didn't seem especially interested in the place or its issues, which struck me as curious for a young minister early on in her brief. And less than sensible, given that her colleagues on the trip – mostly women, unusually, in this instance – might one day play a role in her future, as now seems about to be the case.'

'So she didn't speak to you?'

'She didn't speak to anyone very much. She had various flunkeys with her, all men, at least one of whom she appeared very friendly with indeed.'

'Which one?'

'Oh, I can't remember. Some Scottish fellow.'

Kate suddenly found herself concentrating very hard on the floor. 'Did he have a name?'

'I suppose he must have done.'

'Someone from her private office?'

'Probably. He seemed to be with her all the time.'

'What did he look like?'

'I really can't . . .' Angela leant forward. 'Are you all right?'

'Yes. Fine. Sorry, just a little warm.' Kate composed herself. 'Do you think she was having an affair with this man?'

'I really don't know. I didn't consider it my business. But . . .' She tilted her head to one side. She was still looking intently at Kate. 'On the last night we were taken to the ballet at the Mariinsky and they slipped away the moment the official part of the evening was over. I saw them coming in together later that night. They looked . . . Well, I don't quite know how to put it. I think you understand what I'm getting at.'

'And if something had happened between them, the Russians might well have been aware of it?'

'We were all warned to be careful. I'd be amazed if she and her team weren't given a similar briefing.'

Kate could feel the colour in her cheeks now. She stood, too quickly. The remnants of her coffee spilt across the low table and onto the floor. 'Oh, God! I'm *so* sorry.'

Angela whisked some tissues out of a box on her desk and began to mop up. 'Don't worry about it.' Kate stood awkwardly by the door as she deposited the soaked tissues in the bin. 'There, no harm done.'

'Thank you for your help. And your time.'

'Was there . . . anything else?'

'Yes. No.'

'Well, it was a pleasure to meet you.'

'Likewise.' Kate realized she was still glued to the threshold. 'There is one other thing. A long shot . . . I don't suppose you kept a list of who was on that trip by any chance?'

'I very much doubt it, but I'll let you know if we can dig it out.'

Angela insisted on taking her back downstairs. Stuart's incoming message made Kate struggle to engage in further small-talk. She and Angela shook hands slightly awkwardly at Security, and she tipped out into the spitting rain on the Embankment, then returned to her phone screen.

She's standing! High excitement here! Official statement later this afternoon.

Kate crossed Westminster Bridge, head bowed against the gusting wind. She wanted to avoid the office, so slipped into Waterloo station to hide in the upstairs Pret a Manger. She ordered a coffee and sat looking down over the departure boards.

She closed her eyes.

No, no, *no* . . .

She knew nothing. There was no evidence of anything.

Imogen must have had more than one Scottish adviser. And, if Angela had unwittingly been talking about Stuart, there was no evidence of an affair. They got on well. She knew that. They were friends. Stuart hated the ballet, so a couple of mates hurrying away from a cultural evening with a dowdy group of MPs would have been no big deal.

She opened her eyes again and scanned the cluster of passengers waiting for their train to appear. 'You can pick a destination,' her father had once told her, 'but you can never predict the journey.' He'd been talking about his marriage, an oblique answer to an oblique question, since they never spoke directly of her mother's infidelity and the pain it had inflicted on him.

The years had not dulled the shame of her mother's affair, the burning sense of injustice on her father's behalf, and

Kate's humiliation at being the daughter of a woman who could behave in such a way.

She thought about what Stuart had told her only the night before. 'You can't protect us from life. And you'll squeeze the humanity out of us if you try.' What had he meant by that?

She had spent so long worrying about not becoming her mother that she had never really considered the possibility that Stuart might turn into his father. Alec Henderson had run out on three marriages in quick succession. Stuart had somehow retained a cordial relationship with him throughout, and never been more than mildly censorious of his father's inability to keep his trousers zipped.

Kate selected a sandwich and a compact beetroot-coloured drink brimming with good health. Half an hour later, she had wrestled herself back into some kind of equilibrium.

'How did you get on?' Rav asked, when she walked back into the office.

'Something and nothing, as my granny used to say. Maddy, can you find me a list of everyone on that FO Russia trip, not just the MPs?'

'I'll call the Foreign Office now.'

Rav followed her. 'I've started with his schooldays. Found a guy who sounds dull, provincial and tediously reliable. Rupert Grant. Same house, same year.'

'Good.'

'Believe it or not, he still lives close by. So much for devotion to the Empire. It's about two hours on the train. You want to go now?'

Kate looked at the clock on the wall. 'No. I have to be home in reasonable time tonight. Let's do it first thing tomorrow.'

'Okay. I'll focus on his time in the army and in business before he became an MP.'

'We should take a careful look at trips to Russia as well. More lists for Maddy. She'll love that.'

Kate nudged the door shut with her foot as Rav went back to his desk. The pain behind her eyes was blinding now. She reached into her drawer, knocked back four ibuprofen and stared blankly at her computer screen, then pulled herself together and logged on.

If Imogen Conrad was her subject, she needed to treat her like any other. She googled her name and began to read about her friend as if she was a stranger. She hadn't got much further than an article in her constituency news-paper when Maddy put her head around the door. 'She's standing.'

Kate joined the others in front of the screen as Imogen and her team approached the bank of microphones. 'Do you ever wish we could wind back time,' Kate asked, 'and scrub what we think we know from our minds?'

'Not really,' Rav said. 'It's going to put us all through the wringer – but that's nothing new, and if we end up nailing some bent politician, then few things would give me greater satisfaction.'

'Good afternoon.' Imogen was now at the microphones. She looked uncharacteristically nervous. 'Thank you very much for turning out at such short notice. As you know, there is a vacancy at the head of my great party. But before I talk about the hole in our lives that needs to be filled, can I first pay tribute to the prime minister for all he has done for us and, more importantly, for our country? There have been many tributes already. And rightly so. There will, no doubt, be many more. Some will be less genuine than others, but I

100

dare to believe that anyone who knows anything at all about life here at Westminster will be aware that my admiration for him is genuine and heartfelt. I am very, very sorry to see him go.'

She paused for a moment, surveying the massed ranks of commentators assembled in front of her. 'However, we must now look to the future. We must look closely at how we as a party can best continue to serve the interests of this great and diverse nation. The question I ask myself is no different from the one you must be asking: who is best placed to take forward the prime minister's vision of a country at ease with itself and with the modern world, a nation determined to make the best of the opportunities that now present themselves?

'I have been overwhelmed – slightly stunned, in fact – by the number of hugely encouraging calls I have already received today from colleagues, some of whom you see with me now, and from my very supportive constituents. I have been persuaded, therefore, that I should indeed put my hat into the ring. I am here to announce my candidacy for the leadership.'

Imogen allowed herself a modest smile at the flurry of dutiful applause from the MPs – largely men, Kate noted – behind her. She was hitting her stride.

'I will set out my vision for our country in more detail in due course, but I want to flag one issue today, which I believe stands out over and above all others. It has been the privilege of my life to serve as the secretary of state for Education. As we now make our way in the wider world, it is imperative that we have a workforce educated to the highest possible standards. Without it, we will simply not be able to compete and thrive. A previous prime minister once listed his priorities as "Education, education, education." Whatever one may think of his legacy, I would like you to know that I am *deadly* serious. I have already tried to improve standards in the state sector and force private schools to do more to help local state schools, but I intend to go much, much further. And that cannot be achieved without a significant – perhaps a *very* significant – reallocation of resources.'

She smiled again. 'The fine detail is for another day. For now, I thank my colleagues for their support, my constituents for their trust, and I thank you all for coming.'

Imogen turned to accept another burst of applause from the phalanx of party faithful, and walked away from the microphone.

'Class act,' Rav said. 'She's going to give him a run for his money, and he's a fool if he doesn't know it.'

Maddy was at her shoulder. 'The list you asked for.'

Kate took the sheet of paper, walked back into her office and closed the door. As a minister, Imogen's name headed the page, and was followed by those of the officials who had travelled with her: *Stuart Henderson, private office; Alastair Macintosh, special adviser; Callum Rennie, Foreign & Commonwealth Office press office.*

Her suspicions and uncertainties closed in on her, like a winter's night, and it took her a considerable amount of time and willpower to beat them back. Of course her husband was noticeably Scottish, but she was pretty sure Alastair, the special adviser, spoke with a broad Glaswegian lilt. And for all she knew, Callum Rennie might be a kilt-wearing, skean-dhu-waving Highland reeler too.

Kate returned to her screen and continued her trawl. For someone who was now a serious prospect as future leader of her country, Imogen had made very few waves. She was interrupted by another of Stuart's increasingly overexcited messages: *She's going to promise to double – DOUBLE – the education budget. That will create a few waves!!! Just working out where the money is going to come from. Xxx*

Kate switched her phone to silent and tried to concentrate on Imogen's life, work and finances. After a relatively futile hour or two, punctuated by increasingly graphic images of a variety of unwelcome stains spreading across Imogen's McQueen, she gave up, changed her shoes, and headed for the lifts.

Maddy managed to catch her before she headed out into the night. 'I forgot to say – Rose came looking for you. She said she had to leave early today, but will be in tomorrow. Do you want me to fix a time?'

'Oh. No, don't worry. I don't think . . . It's not important now. I'll bend her ear next time we bump into each other.'

Maddy's normally imperturbable brow creased. 'Are you all right, Kate?'

'I'm fine. Yes, fine. Why?'

'You don't look quite yourself.'

'No, really. I'm just a bit tired. I need to get home.'

10

WHEN SHE GOT back Stuart was still out. 'He's at Imogen's,' Fiona said. 'Busy planning to take over the world.'

Kate took off her coat, trainers and socks. She padded across the cold floor in bare feet. 'Where's Gus?'

'How on earth would I know?'

'Sisterly concern, perhaps.'

'I have no idea what that even is.' Fiona headed for the stairs.

'Did you feed Nelson?'

'Er, no. Sorry . . .' And then she was gone.

Nelson eyed Kate dolefully.

'Believe me, I know just how you feel, old chap.' She loved her children more than life itself, but the gap between the affection they professed for the family's pet and the care they were prepared to offer him never failed to irritate her. She crouched down and eyeballed him again. His tail wagged with dim enthusiasm. 'So, are *you* pleased to see me, at least?'

He rolled onto his back. 'You're really just hungry for love, aren't you?' She scratched his belly for a while. 'Join the club.'

She stayed by his basket longer than she'd intended, then got up, filled his bowl and put it in front of him. He didn't move for a while, but as she walked away to make herself a cup of tea, he forced himself upright and picked at his dinner.

Ten minutes later the door slammed open and shut and Gus blew in.

'What's wrong?' Like all teenagers, he had broadcast his mood at twenty paces.

He clenched his teeth and then his fists. 'Why do you *always* ask what's *wrong*?'

Kate stared at the ceiling and said a silent prayer. She followed him upstairs. Before she could ask anything else, he said, 'I got dropped.'

'From what?'

She instantly regretted asking. Of course she knew from what.

'The A team!'

'No! Did Mr Wilson give you a reason?'

'He didn't say a thing. Just put the list up on the board. Without my name on it. At the beginning of term, he said he might make me captain. And now I've been bloody dropped!'

'Perhaps—'

'Perhaps nothing. He said I was his guy, the one the rest of the team looked up to. And now he's chucked me on the scrapheap!'

Kate moved into his room and leant against his chest of drawers. It was a source of irritation to her – and near apoplexy to Stuart – that the teachers in the school they were bankrupting themselves to pay for frequently didn't seem to feel the need to communicate in any meaningful way with the children in their care. At least, not where the things they actually minded about it were concerned.

'I don't want to discuss it,' Gus said.

'Who did they pick instead?'

'Adams.'

'Bizarre.'

'What would you know?'

'Dad says he thinks you're one of the best players in the school, not just the team. He was saying the other day he thought you might make it into one of the club academies.'

'Dad thinks I'm going to play for Scotland. He doesn't know *anything*.'

Kate could see the hurt in her son's eyes, but couldn't think of anything to say that might help. She kissed him and withdrew quietly, wishing Stuart was there. His predictable anger at the decision might at least help convince their son he was the victim of a genuine injustice rather than simply not good enough.

She knocked on Fiona's door and slipped into the room. Her daughter sat cross-legged on her bed, bent over her laptop.

'How was your day?' Kate asked.

'Fine.'

'What did you get up to?'

'Not much.'

'How were lessons?'

'Fine.'

Kate knelt and started to pick up her daughter's discarded clothes, fold them, and pile them neatly on the chair.

Fiona didn't look up. 'Please leave those where they are.'

'I'm just trying to—'

'No, Mum. You're just trying. End of.'

Kate stopped, mid-fold. 'That's not massively polite.'

'It's my room.'

'And it's my house.' Kate carried on folding, wondering how, try as hard as she might, she always sounded like her own blindingly unreasonable mother at such times.

'*Our* house, actually,' Fiona said. 'After all, Dad pays half the mortgage, doesn't he?'

'I'm really not going to have this argument again.' Kate finished her self-appointed task and rose to her feet. 'Is it my imagination or are you in a rather more bullish mood today?'

'I have no idea what's in your imagination, Mum.'

'Has something happened?'

'No.'

'What's going on with Jed?'

Fiona shrugged. Her eyes were still fixed on the screen, but she wasn't concentrating on whatever it contained now. A worrying sign.

'What does a shrug mean?'

'If I tell you, you'll only freak out. So I'm not going to tell you.'

'Please promise me that you haven't—'

'We're *going out*.'

Kate sat down on the bed.

Fiona raised her palm. 'I don't want to talk about it.'

'Well, I do.'

'There's absolutely nothing to say.'

'I'm going to need you to promise me that you won't, under any circumstances, take things further than—'

'Than what? A coy glance? The occasional swoon? It really isn't your problem.'

107

'You're fifteen. If you were to . . . make a mistake—'

'I'd get an abortion. It's no big deal.'

Kate bit her lip. Her daughter knew how to push every one of her buttons and did so with a precision she found enraging. 'As I've said to you before, I know you better than anyone else does. And I know that beneath that teenage exterior lies a sensitive, loving and caring young woman. You'd find having an abortion a seismic experience. You'd carry it with you for the rest of your life.'

'Not everyone is you, Mum.'

'And not everyone is you, either. Maybe to some of your friends it's no big deal. But I promise you, my darling, it *would* be for you.'

Fiona was still avoiding her gaze, but Kate knew her daughter well enough to be sure that she had got through to her. 'Just go slow, that's all I ask. And I wouldn't tell Dad you and Jed are definitely going out.'

Fiona finally looked her in the eye. 'He's a lot more reasonable than you are.'

'What's that supposed to mean?'

'He's not intent on protecting my purity until I'm an old maid.'

Kate stared at the raging bag of hormones and insecurities beside her. 'Let's leave it there before we both say something we might regret.'

She closed the door behind her and went downstairs. Sometimes being the only adult in the room, in the whole house, was too exhausting for words. She made a cup of tea and started to plan supper. This is not a chore, she told herself. This is therapy.

She scanned the shelf for inspiration. Her cookbook selection was a series of foreign missions, but without the endless waiting and life-threatening confrontations. She messaged Stuart to find out when he might be back and got a swift reply: *Eating at Imogen's. Big crew here. Come over when you're done.*

Dinner was like a party at an undertaker's. She got half a dozen words out of Gus and only a few more from Fiona. She had to tell both of them several times to put away their phones, and in the end simply left them to it. 'Perhaps you would be so kind as to do the washing-up,' she said. 'I'm going to spend some quality time with your father.'

She didn't get a response to that either.

It was a balmy night and Kate decided to walk. The route took her past her mother's place and she looked up at her window to see if the light was on. It wasn't. She tried to push away the dark cloud that seemed to wrap itself around her. The worst of it was that she understood why her mother was the woman she was. Abandoned as a baby in Galway, she had spent the first four years of her life in a convent before being adopted by an austere Catholic family in Limerick. It was hardly surprising that she had little understanding of how to give or receive affection.

Kate ended up so lost in thought that she wandered past Imogen's house, despite the very obvious presence of two photographers and three journalists outside it, and had to double back. They didn't pay her much attention as she rang the bell and was ushered in without question or introduction by a young woman she'd never met.

Kate offered her hand. 'I'm Stuart's wife.'

Her greeting was left hanging in the hallway with the discarded coats as the girl's hurriedly retreating back screamed, *I'm busy with very important stuff,* which reminded Kate of how much she detested the breed of apparatchik that managed to attach itself to politicians on the rise.

The sitting room was full of people, perhaps twenty in all. Most were on their smartphones. Kate recognized quite a few ministers and MPs. Stuart sat on the sofa, next to Imogen, poring over a vital strategic document. The intensity of his concentration suggested that he might have forgotten that the two of them weren't in the process of discovering a cure for cancer.

Kate waited, suddenly awkward and unsure. Eventually Imogen's young special adviser materialized and greeted her. He was called Ben, or possibly Steve. They had come and gone with bewildering speed over the years. 'Stuart!' he shouted, pointing at Kate.

Stuart raised a hand, hauled himself to his feet, came over and treated her to a perfunctory kiss. His eyes were wide with excitement. 'We have sixty guaranteed names, with twenty more actively leaning in our direction.'

'Active leaning. That's my favourite kind.'

'We don't think James Ryan has any more – and we have a hunch the new intake of younger MPs is coming our way.'

'Has anyone else declared?'

'No – and the smart money says they aren't going to. Support for Imogen and James is sufficiently strong and evenly split for any other contender to seem like an also-ran from the start. They're all trying to bolster their future careers by hitching their wagons to one or the other – and an awful lot of them are still playing hard to get, to maximize their price.'

'But Imogen won't win when it goes to party members, will she?'

'Conventional wisdom says no, but I'm not so sure. Her message on education is striking a chord and I think people are tired of talking about our place in the world and the great free-trade opportunities that seem mostly a mirage.

110

They want someone to focus on everyday issues. Plus she has bags more charisma.'

Either his tone or the look of pure joy on his face meant Kate couldn't stop herself asking, 'Do you think you should be here?'

The air momentarily left his balloon. 'What do you mean?'

'You're a civil servant.'

'I'm helping out as a friend.'

'All the same . . . there are a lot of politicians here.'

'There are indeed. And they're all on the team.' He leant closer. 'Honestly, you can be a bit of a killjoy sometimes.' He gave her a peck on the forehead. 'Go home, if you want to keep your distance. I'll be back in a bit.'

He returned to his seat beside Imogen, who looked up, caught sight of Kate, waved and pulled a face – *Oh, God, what have I got myself into?* – then returned to the sheet of paper in front of her. Stuart did not glance up again.

Kate waited a few moments more, ill at ease, then walked home. She felt a bit stupid in a way she couldn't quite articulate, or perhaps didn't want to.

Gus was appealingly meek when she kissed him goodnight, and he hugged her tight when she said that she was sure his father was right: he was very good and would win through in the end. He even listened when she delivered a short speech about adversity making one stronger. She quoted Jonny Wilkinson as an example of someone who'd had setbacks but gone on to conquer the world. It was no more than guesswork, but she rather liked the sound of it – and so, apparently, did he.

Even Fiona was in a more malleable mood. 'I'm sorry I shouted at you,' she said, 'but it is *my* life.'

Kate got in a bit of a speech there, too, about the value of people who love you and have your back. Much to her surprise, Fiona said, 'You never had that, did you?'

She pulled the duvet up to her daughter's neck and kissed her forehead, as she had done so often when Fiona was a little girl. 'Granny has many strengths,' she said, as outrageous a lie as she'd told all day, 'but thank you for thinking of me.'

She retreated to the bathroom to remove her make-up and brush her teeth, then read for a while, although she was still finding it strangely difficult to concentrate. She turned out the bedside light, but couldn't sleep. She tossed and turned. She picked up her book again, but without much success.

It was one in the morning before Stuart crept in, as quiet as a herd of elephants. 'Good God, are you still awake?'

'Just . . . reading.'

'Why didn't you go to sleep?'

'I don't know. I suppose I was waiting for you.'

'Why?'

'God knows.' She attempted a grin. 'Sometimes it's nice to chat. How's it going?'

'Much as I said earlier.'

'You really think she's going to win?'

'I do, which will be fucking amazing. There's every chance I'll be right there at the heart of it.'

'That would be . . . great.'

'You didn't sound like you thought so earlier.' Stuart was naked except for his boxers and socks. He almost fell over as he tried to take off the socks. He was more pissed than she'd thought.

'Put it down to the spy in me. I always feel uncomfortable in a roomful of politicians.'

Stuart made his way uncertainly into the bathroom and noisily brushed his teeth. Sometimes she thought a separate bathroom was the key to lasting happiness.

He tumbled onto the bed, fiddled with the light switch and stifled a belch.

'Aren't you going to kiss me goodnight?'

He did, then immediately turned his back on her.

'Have you spoken to your father recently?' Kate asked.

'No. Why?'

'Just wondered. Is he still with Suzy?'

'Of course.' Stuart faced her again. 'Why do you ask?'

'You said they were arguing a lot, that's all. And he has a habit of moving on.'

'He's been with Suzy for twenty years. Your point being?'

'I don't have a point. We haven't seen them for a bit.'

'You always have a point.' Stuart sat up. 'So come on, what is it?'

Kate felt cornered, which she hadn't anticipated. 'I'm sorry. I don't know what I'm saying, really. I sometimes feel stupid. Out there in the real world, people spend their lives shitting on their nearest and dearest . . .'

'What on earth are you talking about?'

'You say I'm not my mother. But why am I so obsessed with what she did? I mean, my father forgave her – and is anyone faithful for a lifetime anyway? Why do I—'

'Stop it, Kate. And to answer your questions: (a) yes, they are. And (b) it wasn't only your father your mother hurt, but you. Yes, people do behave badly to their nearest and dearest and, yes, I know, it's your job to be up to your neck in it – and sometimes well beyond. I understand why you stand guard over our family with such ferocity. I know you want something in this world of shit to be true and honest.

113

But we're all well aware of that, believe it or not, and we're good for it. So do us all a favour and leave your work where it belongs. Home is another country. We care for each other here. It's a place to relax. Now get some sodding rest. You'll be a lot less likely to start at the wrong shadows.' He turned over once more and was asleep in seconds.

Which was more than could be said for his wife. Kate lay there, staring up at the ceiling, long into the night. When she finally drifted off, it was not for long. She woke up bathed in sweat, despite the chill in the room. The image that had loomed at her from her dreams was Lena drowning in an unusually murky and turbulent stretch of the otherwise clear blue waters of the Mediterranean Sea. She went to the window and peered out as the first harbingers of dawn crept through the deserted streets.

11

KATE DECIDED NOT to catch the train to the West Country. She had no desire to share their findings, or even their gossip, with a carriage full of eavesdroppers on the return journey. She got up, took Nelson out and left a note telling Stuart she'd taken the car.

In her eagerness to leave the kitchen, she knocked his iPad off the work surface. She cursed silently as she knelt and plucked it off the stone floor. And more loudly when she saw the crack in the top right-hand corner of the screen. Her husband was very particular about his possessions, especially those of an electronic persuasion. She toyed with the idea of leaving an apologetic Post-it note, but decided it would be better to confess later, face to face.

She parked in front of Rav's house and tapped out a WhatsApp message. *Am outside. No hurry.*

He was with her in less than five minutes.

'Wow. That was quick.'

'Not sleeping much.'

'Me neither.'

Kate pulled away and started winding through the west London traffic.

'Music?' Rav asked.

'Why don't you dazzle me with your conversation?'

'It's too early for dazzling. How was your evening?'

'I spent a lot of time channelling that book you gave me on how to deal with extremely awkward teenagers. And that was just when I was with Stuart.'

'Did it work?'

'It stopped me committing murder, so in that sense, yes, it did. He was at Imogen's, planning their takeover of the world.'

'Is that wise of him?'

'I'm not sure it is. But I got an earful when I suggested he might want to think about it. How about you?'

'Zac's still with his parents, so I was just meandering about.'

'When's he back?'

'He didn't say.'

'How are his parents?'

'You mean physically, mentally, spiritually – or with me?'

'I guess mostly the latter.'

'I haven't seen them since we went up there for Easter. I've spoken on the phone to his father a few times. I find him a lot easier than the mother. But, well, it is what it is. It's one thing your son leaving his wife and three children, but it's a bit of a twist in the tail when it turns out he's gay as well. I think they want to come to terms with it, but I'm not sure they ever will.' Rav turned to her. 'Did you get anything on Imogen yesterday?'

For a moment, Kate toyed with the idea of keeping the information to herself. But she withheld nothing professionally from Rav, and not much personally either. 'The MP I saw was very measured, sensible and credible. She obviously doesn't like Imogen much. She said they didn't see a lot of her on the Russia trip because she appeared to be quite wrapped up with one of her male advisers.'

'Which one?'

'She wasn't sure. I think it was a young guy who was her special adviser at the time, but I'm going to have to check that out.'

'Have you talked to Stuart about it?'

'No. He was on the trip, so if it comes to it, I will. But it'll be hard to do it without giving some hint of what I'm after, so I'm going to hold off for now.' She glanced at him. 'How about you? By the look of you, I'd say you'd been up half the night. And it's becoming a habit.'

'Lots of interesting circumstantial stuff. You won't be surprised to hear that our man in King Charles Street was the liaison officer with the Russians in Kosovo. He had a young Montenegrin interpreter whose *Like* button he'd have wanted to press, judging by her social-media profile, even if she had the good sense to resist him. I'm trying to locate someone who served with him there. And I'm still circling the money and the security business he set up after he left the army.'

They chatted a little more, then drifted into silence. Rav slept. He'd always been good at napping. She was hungry and needed coffee, so pulled off the dual carriageway to stop at a Little Chef. In the event, she dragged him in for breakfast, possibly because it summoned appealing memories of the trips she had made with her father and sometimes her aunt Rose to see their parents in Fowey. Her mother rarely accompanied them. She'd had little affection for her parents-in-law, and they'd made no attempt to hide the fact that the feeling was mutual.

It was almost lunchtime before they reached Sherborne. They lost their way a few times around the abbey and ended up having to park by the station, then retraced their route past an attractive public garden, still bursting with colour in the autumn sunshine, to the bottom of the high street. Rupert Grant's estate agency was three shops in from the corner.

Grant stooped slightly, perhaps from a lifetime of apology for being so tall – six feet three or more. He was greying at the temples, and had the laconic, charming smile of a man now at ease with himself. He greeted them as if this was the most exciting thing to have happened to him for a while, and took them upstairs to his office.

Coffee poured, biscuits distributed and niceties exchanged, Rav cleared his throat for the business at hand. 'Mr Grant, I hope you'll excuse me for saying this, given that we've so rudely imposed ourselves on you, but it is imperative that you do not disclose our conversation to anyone. Is that all right?'

'A matter of national security?'

'I'm sorry if that sounds overly dramatic, but in essence, yes.'

'I find it difficult to imagine what I could possibly reveal in this charming rural backwater that might shake the estab-lishment to its core, unless it stems from my time in Hong Kong, but go ahead. You certainly have my word that what is said in this room will stay in it.'

'What did you do in Hong Kong?' Kate asked.

'I was based there for fifteen years. Commercial property.

This is the family business. We only came back when my father died.'

'Our questions relate to two of your former school friends,' Rav said.

'So are you MI5 or MI6?'

'The Secret Intelligence Service, MI6.'

'Sir Alan is your *direct* superior?'

'He is,' Kate said.

'And my old sparring partner, the Right Honourable James Ryan, also has a degree of influence over your destiny . . .'

She nodded. 'Two reasons why this whole situation is potentially extremely awkward. But we should stress that the focus of our enquiries is not our boss.'

'Well, that's certainly livened up my day. Carry on, do.'

'I'm afraid we can't tell you precisely what we're investigating,' Rav said, 'but rest assured that it's entirely routine in the context of modern intelligence operations, and no accusation or suspicion is implied or intended.'

'We're just trying to build up a picture of the kind of man the foreign secretary is,' Kate added. 'From those who have known him best.'

'I haven't seen him for more than three decades.'

'But you spent five years in very close proximity when you were at school. I imagine you got a pretty good handle on him.'

Rupert Grant thought about this. He sipped his coffee and appeared to lose himself for a moment in another world. 'I'm not so sure, to be honest. It was a very long time ago. A different life. And I wouldn't say it brought out the best in any of us.'

Rav was about to jump in but Kate raised her hand. They waited. If she had learnt one thing from Sir Alan, it was the value of silence.

'I can tell you what I remember, but I'm really not sure how it could be of the remotest use.'

'We'd be grateful.'

He picked up a shortbread biscuit, tapped it on his plate, then put it down again. 'First, it was a pretty rough environment. We were hunkered down just along the road there, almost overlooking the games pitches. A rather forbidding pebble-dashed building, no longer a boarding-house. It would have benefited from modernization, as the particulars might have put it.

'The housemaster was a good man, but remote, and the place was run almost entirely by the boys, which, if you have any knowledge of the public-school system, is another way of saying it was more *Lord of the Flies* than *Goodbye, Mr Chips*. In retrospect, it seems to me rather like prison. Except that there wasn't much homosexuality, as is commonly supposed. In fact, the atmosphere was pretty homophobic. The few chaps who were probably gay had a very rough time indeed.

'Sherborne was a rugby-playing school, so much of its life was conducted as if it were an extension of the games field.'

Rupert sipped his coffee again, perhaps because he couldn't quite bring himself to look them in the eye. 'There were several baptisms of fire. When we arrived, there was a boy in the year above whose favourite trick was to lurk in the changing room, on top of the lockers, and urinate on our heads as we threw on our kit.'

'Charming,' Rav said.

'Not our future foreign secretary, I should probably add. But, as I said, it was a bit of a zoo at times, and I don't think it brought out the best in any of us. Frankly, I found the whole thing terrifying. In fact, I barely spoke for that first year. But over time, I found my voice, and my place, and I ended up really enjoying it – loving it, even – because the camaraderie was akin to what I imagine you might experience in war or any extreme environment where men are pushed together.'

'So how did the two of them cope?' Kate asked. 'Rumour has it they didn't much like each other.'

Rupert frowned. 'Who told you that?'

'It's just the impression we've got.'

'Then someone is trying to throw you off the scent. They were best friends. We began life in dormitories and we spent our rugby-free waking hours outside of lessons in what was known as the day room – essentially lots of desks lined up in a row. In the second year, we graduated to a study, which in due course we were allowed to sleep in as well. As far as I recall, Alan and James shared one until we were given single rooms in our final year.'

'I guess that would end up sealing a friendship,' Rav said. 'Or make you the best of enemies.'

Rupert looked from one to the other as if they were hard of hearing. 'They weren't just friends, they were inseparable. Most of the rest of us switched roommates periodically. They stuck together, through thick and thin.'

'Are you suggesting that there was something more than—'

'Good God, no. They were both heterosexual, James rampantly so. I think they just got along. They had the same sense of humour, the same slight detachment from the life of the school. I think their response to the madness of the first year was to join forces and, after that, saw no reason to open up much to anyone else.'

'Slight detachment, you say . . . Could you elaborate?'

Rupert shook his head. 'It's quite difficult to explain. It was such an odd environment. James and Alan were the unofficial leaders of our year all the way through. They *were* the establishment, if you like. Well, Alan was. He was head of house and so on. James was a maverick, uncontrollable in some ways. Always smoking, endlessly up at the girls' school, mostly in the middle of the night. It was a miracle he wasn't expelled – though that might have been because Alan usually covered his back.'

'So they were the gamekeepers *and* the poachers,' Rav said. 'How did that work?'

'They knew how to play the system. And when caught between a rock and a hard place, they were able to come out with the most bare-faced lies, never turning a hair. We were all rather envious. I'm not in the least surprised that James went on to become a politician and Alan rose to the top of an organization like MI6. It was what they were destined for. You could say, I suppose, that it was what our school life – or their experience of it – trained them for.'

'You paint quite a picture,' Kate said, 'both vividly illuminating and more than a little confusing. What did you *personally* think of them? Did you like them? Did you trust them?'

Rupert didn't answer immediately. The striking of the abbey clock seemed to prompt him to do so. 'No,' he said. 'I didn't like them. People are often rude about public-school boys and girls, which I understand. We have a terrible habit of hanging together as a tribe, which can be intimidating, even if we don't intend it to be. And it's no accident. It is an extraordinary experience, not good always, but certainly unique.

'Back then, we spent five years in a tumble-dryer lined

with sandpaper. Some people were destroyed by it. Some were just numbed. Some simply lost their rough edges. The Jameses and Alans of this world worked out how to insulate themselves from the harsher elements of the environment, sometimes at the cost of their companions.

'One consequence was that beneath our often unattractively pompous exterior, we developed quite a high level of social skill, and not just of the cocktail-party variety. Most of us are now rather good at navigating our way around conflict and pouring oil on troubled waters. All of which is a very long-winded way of saying that we learnt how to get along.

'So, if you asked James what he'd thought of me then, supposing for a moment that he could remember, he would probably say, "He was a good man." And, yes, we had a laugh and rubbed along fine. On the day we left, we parted with a warm handshake and a genuine smile. But I haven't seen him since, and there's probably a reason for that. I thought him just . . . well . . . immoral, on a very basic level, really intensely unprincipled.

'He had a good brain and was brilliant in an argument. We'd stay up late at night in the dormitory, even as very young boys, arguing about everything under the sun – it was a surprisingly stimulating environment – but he would change his position on a whim, then argue as if it were his most deeply held conviction, even if it was the polar opposite of what he'd defended to the hilt the previous night. We used to say to ourselves, "It's just James," but there was something quite disturbing about it.'

'Did that manifest itself in how he treated people?' Kate asked.

'Not in how he treated us. I certainly wouldn't have relied

on him, but he wasn't mean or unpleasant. He was quite good to the juniors and even stepped in to defend one or two when they were being given a hard time. I'd go so far as to say that the house was better run when he and Alan were in charge than it was before and possibly after.'

'If not "us",' Kate said, 'then who?'

'I found his treatment of women pretty distasteful. He was a good-looking guy. A lot of the girls carried a torch for him . . . Perhaps I needed to get out more.'

'Or perhaps you had a point.'

'What about Sir Alan?' Rav asked.

Rupert repeated his shortbread ritual. He could not be accused, Kate thought, of glibness. 'Alan was different. I'm not sure I liked him much more, though. He was a stickler for the rules, particularly when it came to the lower forms. He was unyielding, strict even, though never with James. He was capable of great charm, but I found that the closer you got to him, the less warmth he exuded. He was quite Machiavellian – which is uncomfortable in a teenager. Again, he wasn't someone I would have chosen to go to war with.'

'Why not?' Rav leant forward. 'I mean precisely.'

'James would have given a rousing speech on the eve of battle. But you wouldn't trust him not to desert, or to sell your rations to a black-marketeer, or even defect to the enemy, if he thought it would be more profitable. Alan wouldn't have hesitated to send you out on a mission he knew to be suicidal, if that was what the orders said. And he'd do it with a glint in his eye.'

12

THEY GOT A bite to eat in a delicatessen on the road that led past the abbey and began the return journey in silence. The sun was bright on the honey sandstone of the terraced houses along the way, so the journey felt like a slow departure from a bucolic idyll. 'He was very thoughtful, insightful and articulate,' Rav said, as they passed the turning to Warminster, 'but I can't help wishing we hadn't come.'

'Don't be so feeble.'

'Well, let's recap. He told us that the foreign secretary is an unprincipled bastard, who could easily have sold himself or his granny to a foreign power, and that our own superior was his best friend, despite vigorous attempts to claim otherwise.'

'Wasn't it you who suggested we should just treat this like any other case?'

'That was when I wasn't thinking about it properly.'

'Well, man up.'

Rav stared out of the window as they approached Stonehenge. 'Thanks. I appreciate the pep talk.'

'We have no evidence of anything yet. It was a moderately compelling but ultimately insubstantial portrait of the pair as young men. I'm not sure anyone I was at school with would have said anything much more positive about me.'

'You were the class swot. There's nothing wrong with that.'

'At school, there's everything wrong with it.'

'I thought you said that was the point of your school.'

'It didn't make it popular.'

'Well, anyway, did you miss the bit where I reminded you that our hitherto trusted leader was best mates with one of our potential traitors, yet goes to great lengths to indicate the polar opposite? Don't you find yourself wondering why he does that?'

'All right, Rav. I get it. Now calm down.'

He didn't, though. And neither did she.

The Ops Room updated them on the *Empress* as soon as they got back to the office. Kate, Danny and Rav studied the satellite footage of Igor's super-yacht arriving at the port of Gavrio on the Greek island of Andros, and watched Mikhail and his wife wander along to an ice-cream shop on the quayside with Lena and their son in tow.

'Why Gavrio?' Rav said. 'Not really Mikhail's kind of town, is it? Looks like a port that time forgot . . .'

'It's a stop-off point for the Piraeus–Mykonos ferry,' Danny said. 'Maybe he's planning a day trip.'

Julie had just landed at Heathrow from Istanbul, so Kate immediately rerouted her to Athens, and booked herself and Rav on the first flight out the following morning. She messaged Stuart to say she'd be late home, and left Rav to handle the operational paperwork while she ordered up another mic from the technical team, then took a closer look at Gavrio.

When she was finally ready to go home and pack, Sir Alan popped his head around her door. 'Athens-bound?'

'Yes.' She glanced not too pointedly at the wall clock. It was past nine. 'First thing.'

'Good call. Have you briefed Ian?'

'I was going to email him in the morning.'

'Don't worry. I'll talk to him.'

She was momentarily surprised by his sudden interest in a routine operation and wondered how he'd found out about it so quickly. Perhaps he had come via the Ops Room.

He advanced towards her desk and placed a photograph in front of her. Kate found herself staring at a grainy surveillance shot of a man climbing into a car on what looked like a London street. She felt her cheeks redden again, not just because of the sudden clash between principle and ambition.

'I believe his name is Sergei Malinsky,' C said. 'But you won't need me to tell you that.'

'I don't mean to be impertinent, but I haven't changed my mind. I made my position clear.'

'Are you saying you don't trust me, Kate?'

'I have trouble trusting anyone.'

'Join the club. A handicap, perhaps. Or possibly an advantage.'

'Time alone will tell.'

'You won't be taking my place, nor should you be, if you don't learn to put the interests of your country and, indeed, of this organization before your own. I don't know what this guy is to you – friend, lover, performing seal – and I don't care. Your files make it pretty clear – to me, at least – that he's your undeclared source. So why would you fail to ID him when you'd already listed him as a previous contact in your vetting?'

She met his penetrating gaze but did not answer.

'The most benign interpretation is that he wanted to be off the books and, in deference to whatever relationship you had – or have – with him, you felt duty-bound to respect that. Correct?'

Kate watched the minute hand on the clock pass the quarter.

'I'm trying to help you here, Kate. It might be a good idea if you contributed to that admirable objective.'

'I will, if you can tell me why you're pushing this to breaking point.'

'Because you and I need to be able to talk honestly. And not simply about this.'

He waited, but she still wasn't going to budge.

'Let me tell you what's at stake, both professionally and personally,' he said. 'Your intelligence suggests that our superior, the foreign secretary, or one of his rivals for the premiership, is an enemy asset, assisted by another agent somewhere in Whitehall, perhaps inside this building. That leaves two possibilities: either we're being subjected to a calculated campaign of misinformation, or it's true. Either way, the threat to our organization and, indeed, our democracy, is of the severest possible kind. Do you agree?'

'Yes, I do.'

'Then let me tell you what is at stake personally. I don't shout about it much, but I have known the foreign secretary for a very long time. The fact that we were at school together is a matter of public record, though for obvious reasons I tend not to highlight our close proximity – or that we were friends, good friends.

'In recent years, our relationship has soured. Like most politicians, he favours the kind of expediency that I find . . . discomfiting. And if he discovers that we're investigating him as a possible traitor, he'll flay us alive. All of us. Do you understand that?'

'Yes, sir. I do.'

'Less of the "sir", if you don't mind. I simply cannot hope to plot a course through this area of turbulence unless I have all relevant information. And Sergei Malinsky is a piece I lack.'

Kate looked at the photograph again.

'Perhaps I need to remind you that it's often wise to go back to basics if you're to have any chance of assessing motive and reliability. It's perfectly possible that they found out about the prime minister through some other channel, and saw a chance to embarrass us. I think your man Sergei was where it began. So I need to know what he's up to. Who does he really work for? Where do his loyalties really lie?'

Sir Alan ran a manicured index finger down the length of his cheek. 'I'm not trying to catch you out, Kate. You do know that, don't you? The question here is whether or not we're a team.'

'Whoever he may or may not be, I don't know who he works for. All I can say is that his information has proved one hundred per cent accurate so far.'

'All right. I'll back off. But I will say this. Whoever your . . . contact may be, you need to find a way to activate him, and reassess his motives for giving you this information. And I want to know about that meeting. I *need* to know about that meeting. Is that understood?'

'Yes.'

The index finger moved from his chin to the picture of Sergei. 'A piece of friendly advice. Admitting something of this nature only when forced to, even though it was inevitable that I – or someone else – would find out in the end, is not . . . sensible. It speaks of some kind of flaw you might want to think about.' He paused. 'Good luck in Greece.'

On his way out, Sir Alan seemed hardly to notice Rav, still hunched over his desk. Kate closed the door behind him, went to the window and looked down at the people scurrying in and out of Vauxhall station in the rain. She could still feel the colour in her cheeks.

Kate had first met Sergei on a wintry afternoon in January 1992. The Soviet Union had been falling apart and she'd taken a break from her lonely studies in central St Petersburg to catch the train to Tsarskoe Selo fifty minutes outside the old Russian capital to spend the afternoon looking around the Alexander Palace, the unprepossessing yellow stucco building that had been home to the last Tsar of Russia and his family.

Sergei had been a volunteer at the palace and offered to show her around the dowdy, poorly kept rooms that the Romanovs had occupied. He'd claimed he wanted to practise his English. She'd insisted he endure her still shaky Russian. They turned out to share an obsession with the life and times of Tsar Nicholas II, Emperor of All Russia, one of the most infuriating and tragic figures in world history: a good, kind, devoted husband and father, who was as stubborn and foolish a leader as had ever lived. His wilful inflexibility had perhaps lost his country the chance to take its place gradually in the democratic landscape, and had pitched it instead into a nightmarish experiment from which it had still to emerge.

Sergei was the son of an elderly couple who lived on Vasilevsky Island, close by the old stock exchange. His father was the caretaker at the Ice Palace, home of the SKA St Petersburg ice-hockey team, and Sergei had ended their tour of the last tsar's rooms with an offer to join him at a game that evening.

Later she had spent many hours wondering if it was only loneliness that had prevented her refusing. That evening, they hardly watched the game. They talked about politics with enormous passion. Sergei's maternal grandfather had been an important figure in the Leningrad Communist Party and had fallen victim to one of the very last of Stalin's purges, so his family had had even more reason than most to be happy at the demise of the old regime. Sergei's enthusiasm and excitement at the prospect of a new and democratic society emerging from the rubble of the old Soviet Union was utterly infectious, but he was unnerved by the chaos and feared that old Russia herself – the great steppes that he maintained had barely changed in a century, a place to which he held a romantic, almost mystical attachment – would end up a poor and backward nation rather than the first-world country he believed it should be.

Afterwards he'd taken her to a basement bar just off the Nevsky Prospekt that had become a favourite haunt of student radicals. He introduced her to some of his friends, but somehow it was always his bright eyes in the centre of her vision. They drank beer and vodka shots, and she could hardly stand when she tipped out onto the snowy streets in the crisp hours of the early morning.

He walked her home to her seedy digs on the top floor of

a run-down building at Podolskaya. He hooked his arm through her own, but made no attempt to kiss her. Kate was conscious of a faint twinge of regret at his reticence in the few seconds between when her head hit the pillow and she passed out, fully clothed.

In the sober light of dawn, she remembered she hadn't even told him that she had a boyfriend – and not just any man: Stuart.

After that, he called every evening. She didn't answer for almost a week, but was caught out when she thought it was her father. He said he would be round in ten minutes. She went out for a long walk by the Neva. When she got back, he was still waiting, sitting on the step of her tenement in his thin leather jacket.

'You're a fucking idiot,' she said.

'I know you have a boyfriend,' he said, 'but I am happy just to be your friend.'

She'd wanted so badly to renew his acquaintance that she'd let that line go and invited him up for a cup of coffee. After that, they were inseparable.

Sergei's parents had welcomed Kate, their son's English 'friend', into their lives, and for a while she had felt almost part of the family. By the time the summer came, she was spending weekends at their primitive wooden dacha on the Gulf of Finland – which Sergei's mother's family had some-how managed to hold on to after the execution of her father – and everyone assumed they were lovers.

And that was very, very nearly true. When she thought of him even now, she could still feel a twinge of the ache that had gnawed away at her that summer. She'd certainly lusted after him: with his dark stubble, blue eyes and steady gaze, he was nothing if not handsome. But it was worse than that. He had a droll, laconic sense of humour and made her laugh, more than anyone before or since. More even than Stuart. Slowly, inexorably, she had come to accept that she loved him.

Lucy, predictably enough, had told her to go ahead and roll in the hay with Sergei. 'The Russians must have more hay than they know what to do with,' she'd said. 'And you only live once.'

But she wasn't her mother. And since she was already committed to Stuart, that summer had been about proving it. It was the last time she'd ever asked her mother's advice, and on the plane home, she had pushed Sergei forcefully from her mind – right up until the moment she'd bumped into him at the reception at the US ambassador's London residence.

He hadn't changed much. His languid lopsided smile was as ready as it had ever been. A wife and mother now, she'd felt no more than a pleasant hint of the old glow, and they had reminisced happily for half an hour about their time in St Petersburg and the turns life had taken since. He had joined the foreign service, he said, and been posted to Hanoi, then Washington, between long periods chained to a desk in Moscow. He'd never married. 'Your fault,' he'd told her, with an easy laugh. 'You broke my heart.'

Kate had considered the encounter no more than a pleasant interlude until the letters had started arriving. There had been four in total, written in his unmistakable flowing hand and accompanied by a clear instruction to burn upon reading. The first two had been full of relatively inconsequential information, but the third had directed her towards a chain of secret companies controlled via a Swiss lawyer by two of the Russian president's closest friends. And then the tip-off that Igor's super-yacht was a meeting place for the power brokers of Russia's intelligence elite in early autumn each year – a place to meet up, plot and gossip, away from the eyes and ears of Moscow Centre.

She might well have set up the operation anyway, or something like it – Igor and Mikhail had long been targets – but she had to admit it was doubtful she would have pushed it through so hard and so fast without Sergei's impetus.

All of which left her with Sir Alan's questions: why had he done this? What *were* his motives?

The truth was she trusted him, as absurd as that would sound were she to articulate it anywhere beyond the confines of her own head. Lovers they might not have been in the physical sense, but she *knew* every fibre of him. He'd done it *for her*.

And it had worked. Without the knowledge of the prime minister's condition, she would undoubtedly have put it under Ian's heading of misinformation, but how else could the Russians have known such an intimate secret were it not for a source – or sources – close to the heart of the British establishment?

Kate stayed in her office until close to midnight, and left with a strict instruction to Rav that he should stay no longer, which she knew he would ignore.

In the lobby, she caught sight of a familiar figure. 'Rose . . .'

Her aunt turned. 'Kate, my dear . . .'

'You're here late.'

'C wanted something. And what he wants, he gets.'

'He's just been on my case, too.'

'Yes . . . I don't know what's going on. Something's got to him.' She clasped Kate's hand. 'How are things on the top floor?'

'Ian bats his little-boy-lost eyes at our political masters and everyone else has to watch their backs. Alan will prevail, but it's like watching a tired old lion trying to keep the pack's most ravenous cub at bay. Ian makes no attempt to hide how much he wants it, these days.'

'But he won't get it. He's cut too many corners, and that will come back to haunt him.' Rose's smile lit her penetrating blue eyes and handsome features. 'But, most important of all, how are *you*?'

'Oh, fine.' It occurred to Kate as she said it that she had no idea whether that was true. 'I think.'

'Jane mentioned you were looking for me.'

'Oh, yes. It wasn't urgent. Something that didn't quite chime from way back. If I gave you a name, I wondered if you'd be able check if someone was ever on the books.'

'I think the most honest answer is that it depends.' Rose looked towards the entrance. Kate had the sense that her aunt knew exactly what she was talking about, even if she was pretending that she didn't.

'I'll pop down at some point.'

'Of course. Any time.'

As they made their way towards the security portals, Kate tried to convince herself that her aunt was not being deliberately evasive.

'Stuart called me this afternoon,' Rose said quietly.

'Oh, yes? What about?'

'Your mother.'

'One of our favourite subjects at the moment.'

'He's right, you know.' Rose touched Kate's shoulder. 'You're not your mother and you never will be. You need to see her for what she is: a difficult and damaged woman, who deserves our pity, not our anger.'

135

'I'm her daughter. I can change what I think, perhaps, but what I feel is a different matter. I suspect pity is out of reach.'

'Well, I'm here for you if you need me.' Rose took Kate in her arms and, for a moment, in the warmth of her embrace, Kate found herself close to tears. 'Come down to us for a weekend,' Rose said. 'I haven't seen the children for far too long.'

'The way they're behaving, you won't want to.'

'They're great kids and charm itself with us. So you must be doing something right.' Rose kissed her niece and strode out into the night.

Stuart was sitting on the edge of their bed, hunched over his iPad. She was at his shoulder before he noticed her, and he almost jumped out of his skin. 'Christ,' he gasped. 'Don't *do* that!'

'Don't do what?'

'That spy shit. Save it for the day job.'

Kate was taken aback. He looked startled. Guilty, even.

He clicked off the iPad and put it on his chair. 'Sorry,' he said. 'You gave me a shock.'

'Why did I give you a shock?'

'I didn't hear you come in.'

'You look like someone caught in the act of emailing his mistress.'

'Oh, for God's sake.' He got up and went into the bathroom. 'I should be so lucky. Where have you been?'

'I have to go away in the morning.'

He came out again, toothbrush in hand, foaming at the mouth. 'Why?'

'Sir Alan thought I deserved an all-expenses-paid holiday.'

'Very funny.'

'Work.'

'What kind of work?'

'An op.'

'Where?'

'Greece.'

'Thanks for telling me.'

'I just did.'

Stuart went back into the bathroom and completed his nightly regime more noisily than he needed to. It didn't take a genius to spot that he was spoiling for a fight when he returned. Kate knew she had overplayed her hand.

'When did you find out you were going to Athens?'

'I didn't say I was going to Athens.'

'Well, through Athens, I assume. Don't split hairs.'

Suddenly overwhelmed by tiredness, she dropped her bag on the chair and sank on to the bed. 'I'm sorry,' she said. 'I should have called. We have something quite big going on, and new intelligence came through earlier this evening.'

'You can't go.'

'I don't have a choice.'

'You can't. Whether or not you approve of what I'm up to, the next few days are critical for Imogen's campaign. I can drop the kids at school in the morning and probably pick them up, but I can't be tied to the house in the evenings.'

'Fi will keep an eye on Gus for a few hours.'

'Who's going to feed them?'

Kate gave a sigh of exasperation. 'You knew it was going to be like this, Stuart. We talked it all through. You agreed to—'

'I agreed to do my level best to support you.'

'Look, maybe I could delay my departure to the second flight tomorrow, so I can take them to school . . .'

Stuart circled around her. It was not a good sign. 'Is this to do with national security or your own personal ambition?'

'I'm going to pretend you didn't say that.'

'All right, then. It's standard Service advice that one's closest relative can be briefed on some detail of one's activity in order to share its burden. Or words to that effect. That's the deal, isn't it? So what the fuck are you doing in Greece that can't be done the week after next?'

'Investigating a serious and credible attempt to undermine British democracy during this leadership election.'

'What the hell is that supposed to mean?'

'We bugged a boat and overheard some major Russian intelligence officials cooking up something horrifying.'

'About what?'

'A significant attempt to undermine and corrupt our democracy.'

'Come off it, Kate. We're doing a pretty good job of undermining our so-called democracy all by ourselves. Which is why I'm doing what I'm doing, by the way. A few spotty wankers in Vladivostok posting crap on Twitter is hardly a global conspiracy.'

'You're right. But the possibility that one of the candidates for the leadership is a Russian spy isn't so easily dismissed.'

'Which one?'

'We don't know. Yet. That's what we're trying to work out.'

For the first time she could remember, Stuart seemed not to know how to respond. He got into bed and turned over.

'When did you buy a new iPad?' Kate asked.

'What are you talking about?'

'I'm really sorry – I knocked yours on to the kitchen floor

this morning and cracked the glass. But you've got a new one.'

There was a momentary silence. 'The office swapped it.'

'I didn't know it was an office one. I wouldn't have worried so much.'

'I asked them to fix it. They loaned me another in the meantime.'

'Christ, some government departments are freer with their cash than others.'

'Go to sleep, Kate.' He switched off the light.

She had little choice but to swallow her resentment and get undressed in the dark. She went to the bathroom and took a long, hard look at herself in the mirror. Then she switched off the light and sat on the toilet to try to calm down.

Stuart could be a grumpy git on occasion, but he had a point. She should have called him earlier. His willingness to hold the fort at short notice, at random moments, was more remarkable than perhaps it should have been.

She went back into their room, got into bed and tried to sleep, without success. The iPad loomed. Had his department really supplied a new one at the drop of a hat? That wasn't her experience of government procurement. And why had he been so startled when she'd appeared at his shoulder?

She tossed and turned and tried to think about other things, but the doubt kept nagging. She retrieved Stuart's new iPad from beneath his sweater, left him snoring, and took it down to the kitchen. She said hello to Nelson and made herself a cup of herbal tea.

Pretty much anyone could have cracked Stuart's passcode, since he only ever remembered his own birthday. He'd never have made any kind of spy.

Once in, she glanced through his emails and texts. Weirdly, months of archived texts appeared, and not just those sent through iMessage, but nothing of any interest. She accessed his WhatsApp exchanges with Imogen and scrolled down and down. Nothing to set the alarm bells ringing there either. Just endless discussions about MPs and ministers who might or might not be joining the cause, policy ideas, media enquiries, the procedural tedium that one would expect of a professional relationship between a politician and a trusted aide.

Kate went back upstairs, replaced the iPad and slipped into bed. This time, finally, she slept.

13

THE JOURNEY TO Andros was longer than she'd bargained for. They flew into Athens International, hired a car and drove to Rafina, a sleepy port just south of the capital. They shared beer, pitta and Greek salad in a taverna on the quay and sunned themselves at the water's edge as they waited for the ferry. When it arrived, the port burst into life with the organized chaos that is the hallmark of so much of Greek life. They waited their turn at the back of a long queue. 'Do you think the fact we have a ticket for this ferry will make any difference?' Rav asked.

'No.'

They got on, just when it looked as if they might not, and Kate was preparing to argue the toss with the men waving cars and lorries forward. They locked the car and went to catch the sun on the upper deck. As the ferry cast off and steamed away, Kate watched the mainland dwindle into the distance, lost for a while in pleasant memories of a childhood holiday when her father, Aunt Rose and her husband had taken Kate away without her mother. She couldn't remember which island they'd visited, the memory little more than an imprint of sound, scent and colour, with a rare feeling of happiness and contentment.

Rav came over and insisted on briefing Kate on his trawl through the company accounts of James Ryan's security business. It had managed to rack up losses of almost a quarter of a million pounds in three years on a very modest turnover, before it was wound up. He'd then acted as a consultant for a while before entering politics. It begged a number of questions, not least who had bankrolled the venture.

It was more than two hours before the ferry cruised in towards its destination. Andros was a big island, more rough and rugged than its prettier cousins with sparse rocky hills, but the whitewashed cottages in the port of Gavrio were as attractive as any. The ferry steamed into a sweeping turn, past the fishing boats bobbing against the harbour wall, then backed onto the jetty. Kate marvelled at the efficiency of the seamen this time as they lowered the ramp and had the cars rolling off within seconds. They went downstairs to discover they were holding up a line so got in swiftly and disembarked.

Julie was waiting for them on the main road ashore. 'You're burnt,' she said. 'It's still hotter than you think.' She slid into the rear of the hire car and directed Rav, who was driving, to the end of Gavrio's main street.

It was a tiny town, full of small shops and stalls, and cafés with white sofas where tourists watched the chaos along the main street as if it was the most interesting thing that had happened all afternoon, which perhaps it was. Julie directed them and they wove through the speeding mopeds, then drove over the hill to their hotel on the beach at the far side of the town.

'It's not exactly the Bel-Air.' Julie wasn't kidding: the reception area was like a set from the seventies classic *Saturday Night Fever*, with a ceiling that hoped to be mistaken for a distant galaxy.

They all had rooms along the poolside, and sat out for drinks and dinner on the terrace. Danny had already set up, and the surveillance team was billeted in a bed-and-breakfast halfway down the main street, ready to start work the next morning.

'What have they been doing on the yacht?' Kate asked.

'It seems very quiet. They've been ashore once – you probably saw the pictures – but went straight back on-board once they'd bought ice-creams. We've seen Lena and the little boy on the deck a couple of times today, but there's been no sign of Mikhail and his wife.'

'Any idea why they're here?'

'None, really, apart from the obvious. It's not the most popular destination for foreign tourists, which may be why Athenians love the place. A load of them have holiday homes here. It's pretty, in its own way, so if you were planning a tour of the Cyclades, it would be no hardship to stop here for a day or two.'

'How far is it to Mykonos?'

'A couple of hours, I guess. I'd have to check.'

'Perhaps Mikhail intends to head there by himself. Is it still the gay capital of the Med?'

Rav remained staring into the still waters of the pool.

'Ground Control to Major Rav. That question was beamed in your direction.'

'Oh, Christ, I don't know. It's not really my scene. I think things have moved on a bit, but I imagine it's the kind of place you might get some action if that was what you were looking for.'

'Can you ask the surveillance team to be ready to infiltrate and wire a room at short notice?'

Julie nodded. 'Are we looking for the same kind of play?'

A young couple had wandered in, holding hands, and settled at the far end of the terrace. Kate pulled her chair forward and turned her back to them. Rav and Julie leant in. 'We'll give Lena another bug, but the boardroom isn't likely to yield much while Igor's in Moscow. So Mikhail's our target. We know he loves England. I think there has to be some doubt as to the depth of his loyalty to modern Russia, and he certainly isn't going to want his father to find out how he likes to entertain himself on his nights off.'

'You think it's possible Igor doesn't know?' Rav asked.

'Who goes digging around for uncomfortable truths about their own loved ones?'

'Psychopaths, like Igor.'

'So here's our challenge. Even if we pick something up on the mic, Ian and the others will dismiss it as deliberately planted. If the foreign secretary wins this contest and makes it into Number Ten, our investigation is going to get even more difficult, or perhaps impossible. We need something more tangible, and we need it quickly. If we can corner him, Mikhail may be able to ID the agent of influence, and Viper. That would give us enough to open a formal investigation.'

Julie didn't look convinced.

'What is it?' Kate asked.

'Just worried about tomorrow, that's all.'

'Why?'

'We're proceeding on the assumption that the Russians

are in blissful ignorance. What happens if Viper has already alerted them to our investigation, and they're on the lookout? The moment we meet up with Lena, they'll know how we came by our intelligence.'

'How could they know?' Rav asked.

But they were all well enough aware of the answer to that. If Viper was inside the Service, rather than somewhere else in Whitehall, it was possible they knew the truth already.

Kate swirled the ice in her gin and tonic. 'We'll be as careful as we possibly can be. Lena's safety is our first priority, of course. But some days we just have to roll the dice.'

'We could wait,' Julie said. 'Sit back and watch.'

'That's not necessarily going to make any difference.'

When Rav disappeared to bed, Julie didn't follow suit. Kate sensed she wanted to talk. 'Are you all right?'

Julie finished her vodka and lime. 'Not really.'

'Anything I can do to help?'

'It's Jason's birthday.' She covered her eyes. 'I'm *so* sorry. I had to tell somebody. And that somebody, inevitably, was going to be you.'

'How old would he have been?'

'Twenty-six. I've been thinking today what I've thought on this day every year since – if we hadn't argued that morning, if I hadn't shouted at him and he hadn't skipped school . . .'

'Then everything would have been different. Of course. But you were just a young girl, and you had to be a mother to your little brother. You didn't have a choice. And I know that's one of the reasons you can't forgive your own mother, and I know I should stop trying to persuade you to give it a go. But *every* tragic accident is dogged by a haunting amalgam of what-ifs and if-onlys . . .' She gazed at the dregs in her own glass, aware that her voice was becoming slightly slurred, and that she wasn't completely sure how many times they'd re-ordered. 'Anyway, in a hundred years, we'll all be dead. So in the great sweep of human history, whether you live long or short doesn't matter that much.'

Julie took a moment apparently to reflect upon this nugget of timeless wisdom. 'I'm not sure that helps, to be honest.'

'I have a doctor friend who told me the other day that the number of genes we have is actually statistically small. So another way of looking at it is that we get reconstituted – remade, if you like – fairly frequently anyway. Next time, perhaps he'll live long enough to be a boring old fart. Then you'll be sorry.'

'Are you telling me you believe in reincarnation?'

'In a way I am, yes. I don't believe in God – there are too many, all with competing theories about life, the universe and everything – but I try to take some comfort in the idea that there probably is an answer we haven't yet found. And in the meantime reincarnation makes about as much sense as anything else. Have you spoken to your dad?'

'Yes. He wasn't in great shape. He never is today. He thinks if their marriage hadn't fallen apart, Jason and I wouldn't have argued in the first place.'

'And what about your mum?'

Julie shrugged.

'Despite what I just said, dare I suggest, not for the first time, that this might be the moment to—'

'I've tried.' Julie snapped the cocktail stick she had been toying with. 'She destroyed us. And she doesn't regret it.'

Julie was close to her father, who, like Kate's, still carried a torch for his adulterous wife and had never remarried. Julie had blocked her mother out of her life until the previous January when, partly at Kate's encouragement, she had agreed to a meeting in a pub, providing the joiner her mother had run off with years before was not present. Her mother had appeared to be as good as her word – until the joiner had turned up for an apparently spontaneous 'hello' as they ordered coffee.

An incredibly acrimonious argument had followed, and Julie had walked out, vowing never to speak to her mother again. Kate thought she was unlikely to relent. But from her own experience she knew that rejecting a parent entirely in such circumstances was perhaps an act of self-harm.

When the waiter next approached, Julie shook her head at his offer of another drink, but Kate sensed she still wanted company. 'Are there ever times,' Julie said, 'when what we do keeps you awake at night?'

'I'd like to say it gets better over the years, but I can't. What's getting to you?'

'Lena, mostly. That any mistake we make is likely to be fatal for her. And what we learnt in Istanbul. I feel its weight more than perhaps I should.'

'Well, you're not alone. We're right at the cutting edge. But isn't that why we got into the business in the first place?'

'I suppose so.' She smiled ruefully. 'Sometimes, when I have to cancel yet another date, I wonder.'

'You have time on your side, not to mention brains and beauty. It's a rather fabulous combination.'

Julie conjured up another smile, but this one was tinged with sadness. 'I love working for you. I don't know that I'd want to stay if you moved on.'

'Why not?'

'Ian gives me the creeps, and some of the other senior men aren't much better. And . . . well, you know how it is. I can manage the pressures and the anxieties that fuck me up in the middle of the night because I believe in you. And I trust you. So there we have it.'

Kate took her hand. 'There are plenty of people like us. And though I won't say that Ian or even Sir Alan exudes much warmth, you'd be surprised at what they're capable of when the chips are down. We're all on the same team, whatever might obscure that in the day-to-day.'

Not long after, Kate said goodnight and went to her room. She lay down, hoping that the combination of too much gin and the slowly rotating ceiling fan might help her drift off. Instead, they made her feel dizzy. She grabbed a bottle of mineral water and sat by the sliding glass door that led out to the pool, looking up at the sky.

There was something different about Julie, these days. She couldn't quite put her finger on it. A softness, an uncertainty, a vulnerability? Hints of all those things, though none quite fitted. Maybe the vodka had encouraged her to display the cracks in the emotional armour she'd worn since her brother's death. Kate couldn't make up her mind if that was a good thing. Or perhaps she still couldn't confront the possibility that the qualities of an attractive human being were likely to prove fatal to a spy.

She tried to think through tomorrow's operation, but her mind was dragged back to Stuart and the iPad.

She began to wonder if she had imagined knocking it off the counter. When you lack sleep, your brain can do that to you. She circled the issue for a while, without achieving clarity and building a mountain of self-doubt. Why was she suddenly suspicious of Stuart? She hadn't doubted him before – not in all the years they'd been together. In fact she'd probably given him more substantial grounds for suspicion than he had ever provided for her. If the wish really was father to the deed, she was on the thinnest of ice – because she had wanted to sleep with Sergei in that dacha.

Sergei Malinsky.

'I believe his name is Sergei Malinsky,' C had whispered in her ear. 'But you won't need me to tell you that.'

Ever since Sir Alan had come to her office, she'd been thinking about how to handle his laser-like insight into her source. He must have gone through every one of her positive vetting files and worked through every individual she had ever listed, cross-referencing, then eliminating each until he had found Sergei. It was tempting to bury her head in the sand and hope it went away, but that was not realistic. And Sir Alan had every right to question the motives of her original source. Given what was at stake, she probably needed to rekindle her connection with Sergei.

The first step, at least, would be easy. This year's soirée was in less than a week's time, and the unanswered invitation from the US ambassador was in her bag. What followed would be increasingly fraught with risk – and not just that of being caught in the vortex of East–West power politics.

Kate closed the glass door and crawled back into bed. She concentrated on slowing her breathing. She needed sleep.

14

IT CAME EVENTUALLY but, as ever now, not enough. She got up at dawn and strode along the rugged coastline until she reached the succession of beaches that stretched away to the south. She commandeered a sun-lounger and stared out to sea for a while, then walked back to the hotel for breakfast – fruit, Greek yoghurt and honey. She was installed in Danny's room with a cup of coffee before eight.

One of the cameras the surveillance team had installed was focused on the yacht, the others on the street by the quay, which was still empty, save for a scattering of early-morning shoppers. Kate sat and watched nothing much happening. It was going to be a long day.

'You know what?' she said, to no one in particular. 'I think I need to take a look around.'

Julie agreed to come with her on the recce – there was no sign of Rav yet – and they retraced the route they'd driven the previous day, back down the hill to the harbour. Gavrio was a world away from the teeming labyrinthine alleys of Istanbul, so they began at the part closest to the sea, settling at a table outside an ice-cream shop at the far end of the quay.

A host of small boats busied themselves in the lee of Igor's super-yacht, which looked as if it had been teleported from another galaxy. Kate scanned their immediate surroundings, then went to the back of the building and checked out the toilets.

Julie glanced up when she emerged into the sunlight.

Kate gestured at the ice-cream shop. 'It's certainly far enough from the yacht and there's a good view of the approaches. But let's go for a wander.'

Kate led the way towards the far end of the harbour wall, to a street of cafés and bars with seating areas that offered glimpses of the boats without being in clear view of the people aboard them. They doubled back behind the main street, where shops selling food, clothes and beach kit were interspersed with the odd travel agent and car-hire firm. The cobbled alleys were still largely deserted.

Kate was sweating by the time she got back to Danny's room at the hotel. 'Where's Rav?'

Danny didn't move from his screens. 'Haven't seen him.'

'Go and wake him, would you?' she said to Julie. She poured herself another coffee. Her third.

Julie reappeared without Rav and raised both palms, but they were diverted by Danny: 'We're in business.'

They joined him in time to see Mikhail usher Lena, his wife and son onto the motor-launch. The door squeaked open again and Kate shot it a sideways glance.

'Sorry,' Rav said sheepishly. 'Needed to clear my head.'

They watched Mikhail's group clamber onto the quay and lost sight of them periodically as they drifted from shop to shop, then picked them up again as they settled in a café at the far end of the strip.

'How do you want to play this?' Julie asked.

'Let's sit tight.'

The family ordered coffee, pastries and ice-creams with apparent relish, but Lena only picked at hers. They didn't need Danny's close-up to see that she was very, very nervous.

Kate felt her phone throb in her pocket. *Meg Simpson from Health is standing. Complicates it a bit for us.*

Another message followed a few moments later: *We'll have to have a run-off with MPs now, before going to party members. Should still win through, but it'll be close. First debate on Sky News tomorrow night. Heavy preps tonight. When u home?*

'On the move,' Rav said.

Kate shoved the phone back into her pocket as Mikhail threw a wad of euros onto the table and put his arm around Katya's shoulders. They leant into each other affectionately as they sauntered away.

'You sure you're right about his orientation?' Rav asked.

'Totally.'

'You think they have an . . . arrangement?' Julie asked.

'He wouldn't be the first gay man in history to be living a lie.'

The group appeared to be in no hurry to get back into the launch. Mikhail and Katya boarded first, then Lena handed down their son, but stayed where she was. The three waved to her as they pulled away.

'Let's take the car,' Kate said. To Danny, she added, 'Tell Ralph I want a clean sweep of the town.' She unfolded her sunglasses, slipped in her earpiece, taped the microphone to her neck, draped a scarf over her head against the sun and hooked a shopping basket over her shoulder.

They drove down the hill and swung the car around just in front of the ice-cream shop. Kate waited, listening to the sound of static in her ear.

The seconds crawled by. She watched a child with her parents throwing a tantrum over ice-cream.

And then the relief of hearing the stentorian Scottish brogue of Ralph, the head of their surveillance team on Andros: 'All clear.'

Kate climbed out of the car and strolled along the sea front. She began to fill her bag from the mouth-watering display at a grocery stall by an intersection on the way to the quay, from which she could see in four directions without appearing to be paying undue attention to anything other than the largest tomatoes she'd ever set eyes on.

She spotted Lena emerging from the pharmacy sixty metres away. She paid the stall's proprietor and strolled in her direction, slowing momentarily as their paths crossed. 'The ice-cream parlour,' she murmured. 'Paradeisos. Just back from the quay.' She went into the pharmacy, bought a packet of Nurofen and glanced across the harbour. There was no sign of anyone on the deck of the *Empress*. Mikhail and Katya must have gone below.

Lena was seated inside the entrance of Paradeisos, tucking into a bowlful of something smothered with cherry sauce. Kate ordered a frappuccino and sat at the neighbouring table. She sipped her coffee while Lena looked steadily out at the sea. When she had finished, she went to the toilet. About thirty seconds later, Lena tapped on the door. Kate eased her in and turned the lock.

'There's nothing much,' Lena said. 'They're really nice

people. They never talk about Russia or politics or his work, only about Alexei and holidays and food and where they will go skiing this winter and they also ask a lot about me and my family and—'

'Take a breath,' Kate said. 'It's all right. We have time.'

'Two minutes, you said before. Never more than two minutes.'

'Do you know where they're going next?'

'No.'

'Do you know where Igor's gone?'

'Moscow, they said.'

'How long for?'

'They didn't say.'

'Where does Mikhail go when he receives a call about work?'

'I don't know . . .' She thought about it. 'I guess in that boardroom place. Yes, he goes there sometimes.'

Kate took another tiny microphone from her pocket. 'What you did last time was brilliant. But these bugs are quite fragile, and can be easily disturbed.'

Lena stared at the device.

'Just do exactly what you did last time. Before Igor gets back.' She slipped it into Lena's pocket.

Lena stayed where she was, her back against the door, barring Kate's exit. 'I still get scared sometimes. So scared I can't breathe.'

Kate reached for her hand. 'You're doing really, really well. The most difficult bit is over. Once Mikhail leaves the yacht, we'll take you out. But for now, I just want you to keep an eye on him and Katya . . .' Kate tried to release her, but Lena clung to her.

'You should go now, Lena.'

154

'Have I truly done well?'

'Better than you can possibly imagine.'

'I am frightened.' She gripped Kate's hand more tightly. Her gaze was imploring.

'You're a star. We won't ever forget what you've done for us.'

'Is Maja safe?'

'Yes. We have her under surveillance. We can't intervene until we lift you out. In case Igor's people are watching.'

'Something good can come of this, can't it?'

'It can, Lena. It really can.' Kate gently prised her hand free and kissed the girl's forehead. 'Go now. Be safe.'

By the time she had retrieved her groceries and emerged onto the quay, Lena was already stepping into the launch. She watched the water churn beneath the outboard as it powered back to the *Empress*.

Kate walked up the hill to join the others. 'Anything?'

'Not a ripple,' Danny said. 'Ralph and the guys are still out there.'

'So the town is definitely clean?'

Danny shrugged. 'As far as we can tell.'

Kate sat on the sofa in Danny's room and exhaled slowly.

'Did she have anything?' Rav asked.

'Only that Mikhail and Katya have been very nice to her. I've given her the new mic.'

Danny stayed where he was while they went for lunch on the terrace. Kate called Stuart several times, but he didn't pick up. He messaged at teatime: *Sorry frantic day will call later. Hope all going well. Everything under control here. Xxx*

In the early evening, Kate left the room to try Stuart again, but the line went to voicemail. Julie grabbed her before she could press redial. 'She's on the launch.'

155

'Shit.' Kate hurriedly followed her.

Back in Danny's room, they all took their usual positions. Lena stood alone in the bow of the launch as it closed on the quay. Once alongside, she stepped off and ducked under the awning of the nearest café.

Kate took a series of slow breaths. This didn't feel right.

'Where is she going?'

The other three were watching her closely now, waiting for a decision. If Kate put Ralph and the surveillance team on her tail and the Russians were watching, it risked exposing her.

And yet . . .

It had been clean all day. Why would they be testing her now?

'Any sign of her?' Kate asked. You could feel the tension crackling in the room now. They could all see the screens. Lena had disappeared.

'Do it,' Kate said. 'But tell them to keep their distance. Maximum discretion.'

Danny spoke into the microphone on the desk, then fiddled with his laptop and maximized the feed from a camera listed as Bravo Four. The screen was suddenly filled with the image of a lone figure disappearing rapidly down an alleyway in the gathering darkness. It was just about possible to make out that it was Lena.

'Where the fuck is she going?' Kate asked. 'Come on, Lena, don't do this to me.'

'Look.' Danny pointed at the neighbouring monitor. Igor's yacht was now making a tight arc as it headed towards the harbour mouth.

'Something's wrong here,' Kate said. 'Where the fuck are you going, Lena?'

They turned back to the Bravo Four feed, but the guy carrying it had stopped dead. 'She went into that door on the right,' Danny said. 'The one at the end.'

Kate's heart was thumping. 'Get someone around the back!'

On the largest of the screens, the *Empress* was now steaming towards the spot where the sun had almost sunk into the sea.

Danny brought up another feed: Bravo One. 'Back door,' he confirmed.

'Sure?'

He was studying a map of the town. 'Yup. Has to be.'

There was no sign of life in either shot. No lights, no people passing.

'For fuck's sake,' Kate said. 'Go in.' She started towards the door. 'Go in hard, both sides.'

As Danny gave the instruction to the team on the ground, Kate sprinted towards the hotel entrance, Rav and Julie half a pace behind her. At the bottom of the slope, they swung into the cobbled alley leading off the quayside. Rav had fired up Google Maps on his phone: he was trying to look at the screen and run at the same time.

It took them less than a minute to locate the house. It wasn't difficult: the front door was hanging off its hinges. The surveillance team were already combing through the place. 'Where is she?' Kate asked Ralph, a slight five feet ten of Scottish skin and bone whose appearance belied his strength and agility.

'No sign of anyone.'

Kate doubled back. 'Spread out,' she told Rav and Julie, then called over her shoulder, 'All of you.'

She hurried up to a nearby square, where a handful of

tourists were eating in the lee of a church. She turned left at the top of the hill and began to work her way back down towards the water sweeping everything in the arc of her vision, one way and then the other. She could not afford to lose Lena. She was not going to lose her.

She was in deep shadow now. A solitary street lamp flickered uncertainly ahead of her. She spotted Rav beside a battered white Fiat that looked as if it had been recently abandoned, its rear doors and boot thrown open.

The shutters of a nearby apartment block banged in the wind. Kate moved towards it. She held up a hand when they were a couple of metres short of the entrance. She and Rav stopped in their tracks.

Kate pushed open the door with infinite care and stepped inside. A hint of movement and the glint of gunmetal at the periphery of her vision prompted the response that had been second nature since her training at Fort Monckton all those years ago. Her swiftly raised hand sent the silenced round up the stairwell. She grasped the barrel and reversed it against her assailant's wrist until she was able to rip the pistol – a Sig Sauer P226, complete with suppressor – from his grasp. She fired twice into his groin and was about to give his knees the same treatment as he went down when a fist cannoned into the back of her hand and launched the weapon into the shadows.

The second man had a blade, and she slammed herself into the wall only just in time to avoid his thrust.

She and Rav backed away, then darted up the stairs. It was virtually impossible to disarm a trained killer with a knife, and neither of them was about to try.

Rav wrenched a fire extinguisher out of its wall bracket as they arrived on the landing, and sent a chunk of plaster tumbling down the way they had come. They turned and stood their ground. It was pitch black, except for a sliver of moonlight, so they had to rely upon the sixth sense that had saved them from a bullet in the head moments before.

Kate strained her ears for the slightest sound above the distant howl of the wind.

They waited.

It was two against one, but the odds were still with him. Kate and Rav needed him to commit, to make the first move.

The air molecules in the stairwell were momentarily re-arranged as the knifeman lunged forward. Rav blocked him with the fire extinguisher and Kate swung behind him, wrapping her right arm around his neck.

He knew exactly what she was doing and tried to reverse the blade and thrust it towards her, but she'd planted her elbow between his shoulder blades and was beginning to close down his carotid artery.

Rav feinted at his chest and brought the canister down on his wrist, but the man had been swiping at thin air by then, confused as to whom he should have been targeting. His weapon skittered across the floor, and five seconds later, he dropped like water.

They stood over him, breathing hard. Rav felt for the pulse in the man's neck, but they both knew it was a formality. She heard him run his hands through every pocket, sensed rather than saw the shake of his head, then followed him down to the ground floor to retrieve the pistol.

As he stepped back towards the shaft of moonlight that was forcing its way between the leading edge of the door and its frame, she saw that something was troubling him. He stopped and seemed to sniff the air for a potential attacker. Kate froze as the shaft suddenly widened and a third man burst into the hallway, weapon raised, muzzle in the aim, with her as its prime target. But Rav had already raised the Sig, and double-tapped the intruder, centre mass, before the man's eyes had adjusted to the darkness.

They stepped back into the shadows and listened. 'You mustn't keep saving my worthless neck,' she muttered eventually. 'It's getting embarrassing.'

'No, it's not,' he whispered. 'It's the only way I know right now of persuading myself I'm not completely useless.'

Kate selected the torch app on her phone and they circled the building. If Lena had ever been there, Kate had to acknowledge that she wasn't now. She sat down on the stairs. 'Now what?'

Rav shook his head.

'Kidnap, murder?'

'I don't know.'

'We'll have to talk to Athens.'

Rav pointed at the corpses. 'They'll go mental.'

Kate stood. 'Let's go.'

When they got back to the hotel, she called the MI6 station chief in Athens. He sounded miffed not to have been told of the operation and said the Greeks would be furious when they discovered it was being conducted on their soil without their knowledge. But Kate was the ranking officer and she cut him dead. 'We need to find her,' she said. 'So please just do it.'

They found Julie again on the quay. 'You've cut your face,' she said.

'They were waiting for us.'

Julie glanced at the blood on Rav's right hand. 'Yours?'

He shrugged. 'Possibly. Possibly not.'

'Where are they now?'

'In a stairwell. Do you have anything?'

She shook her head, trying, Kate thought, to keep last night's demons away. 'She's vanished. Like a ghost.'

'She can't have vanished!' Kate insisted.

'Ralph and the team have been over every inch of the town and of the house. They must have bundled her into a car by the back door before we could get the camera there.'

'Talk to GCHQ and the CIA. See if there was any satellite cover.'

Kate and Rav retreated to Danny's ops room and reviewed the footage from the main cameras in forensic detail, then the feeds from each member of the surveillance team. They all told the same story. Lena appeared on the deck of the *Empress*. She did not look distressed or concerned. She climbed down onto the launch and came ashore. She walked towards the awning of a café, then disappeared. No more than sixty seconds later, they picked up her receding figure in the darkened alley, heading towards that doorway.

And then nothing.

They reran the alley sequence again and again.

Lena's hair. Lena's clothes. Lena's shoulder bag. Lena's walk.

But they only ever saw her from the back. It would take painstaking motion-capture analysis to be sure it was her.

Kate glanced at her watch. It was almost eleven o'clock. About four hours since Lena had climbed aboard that launch. Her phone rang. It was the Athens station chief. 'The Greeks are raging. It's going to take me a few hours to calm them down enough to help.'

'We don't have a few hours.'

'I'm doing my best, Kate.' He was called Nick and they'd met once, at an unarmed-combat refresher course at Fort Monckton five years before.

She hung up. The phone rang again. This time it was Ian. She didn't answer.

'I'm going to take a shower,' Kate said. She turned to Julie. 'Would you mind dealing with the police? You can't miss the building. It's full of dead Russians. And there's a white Fiat Punto outside with its doors open.'

'Always supposing they *were* Russians,' Rav said. 'They didn't say anything, even when we got up close and personal. And they were sterile.'

'Couldn't you *smell* them?' Kate said. 'They were Russian all right.'

Kate didn't get into the shower immediately, though she badly needed to wash off the blood and the unmistakable odour of failure. Maybe if she just sat on the bed for a while she could persuade herself that Lena had found another great place for ice-cream, then nipped back for a fun evening with those nice people on board the *Empress*.

She glanced at her phone. There was a missed call from Stuart, but she couldn't face getting back to him now. Besides, her hands were shaking so badly she'd probably press the wrong button. It was a long time since she'd killed a man, but it didn't get any easier.

She looked around the room, searching for distraction. Then she got up. Something wasn't right. The rug had been moved. Its edge was no longer quite parallel with the floor tiles. And the tiles were cleaner than they had been that afternoon.

Housekeeping didn't operate in the evening.

She went into the bathroom, but nothing there seemed to have been disturbed. She studiously avoided catching sight of herself in the mirror above the sink. Instead, she went back to the bedroom and pulled open the wardrobe door. There, against the wall, staring at her sightlessly, was Lena's body, naked and covered with blood.

15

AT ELEVEN O'CLOCK the next morning, Kate stood in a gloomy basement room with peeling green paint and four rickety air-conditioning units. The Greek capital's Forensic Science Centre in Antigonis Street was some distance from state-of-the-art.

If Lena looked at peace, she knew it had much to do with the sympathetic attentions of Dr Minakis and her assistant. The senior pathologist was a woman of around Kate's age, with a warmth and passion for life that Kate had learnt, perhaps counter-intuitively, to associate with those in her profession. She looked at Kate over her reading glasses. 'Nothing complicated. They drugged her.'

She pointed at the needle mark in Lena's upper right arm. 'We don't yet know what they used, but will do as soon as we have run the tests. I will let you know, of course.'

Dr Minakis lifted Lena's right wrist. 'They bound her. I don't know why. I don't think she was in a position to struggle. We have found dog hair beneath her nails, perhaps from the boot of a car. There might be something for you there.'

'We've found the car,' Kate said. In the middle of the night, the CIA had come back with the requisite satellite coverage. It showed Lena being bundled out of the back of the building they had seen her entering and into a grey Renault Espace. They had killed her in the car, then driven straight to the hotel, where two men could be seen depositing the body in Kate's room. They drove on to a beach a few miles further down the coast where a dinghy was waiting to take them to a fast boat that returned them to Athens. They boarded a private jet at the airport. It had filed a flight plan to Georgia, but had rerouted once it was close to Russian airspace.

It had all been planned with the kind of ruthless efficiency of which the Russians so often showed themselves capable.

'The rest you can see. They cut her throat. We can all be thankful that she died swiftly.'

'Thankful' wasn't the word that echoed in Kate's head. The sight of Lena's lovely young face, the clear blue eyes and unblemished complexion, was almost harder to take than the livid gash beneath her beautifully sculpted chin. She was haunted by the contrast between her own privileged daughter and this girl who had come from nothing and been forced into taking a risk she hadn't sought to try to save her sister and make something of her own life.

Forced by Kate.

It had been her call. Her idea. Her operation from the beginning. Irrespective of the findings of an inquest, she was in no doubt about who deserved the blame. She had witnessed death often enough. She had ordered it, and seen the whites of its eyes. But she knew she would never be able to wash the taste of this one out of her mouth.

She became aware that Dr Minakis had stopped talking, and was looking at her sympathetically. 'I'm sorry for your loss.'

Kate nodded, and had some difficulty swallowing. Not for the first time, she took momentary refuge in procedure. 'I'd like to know what drug they used, Doctor.' Kate gave her a card with a Foreign & Commonwealth Office cover but an email account that was routed through to her via a number of digital blind alleys.

She saw herself out. Rav and Julie were waiting on the street. 'How did you get on?' she asked.

'They're still mightily pissed off that we didn't let them know we were here,' Rav said, 'but they'll get over it. They're even more worried about the Russians than we are.'

'Have they found anything else on Andros?'

Julie had been liaising with the local police and the coast guard. 'You want me to get an Uber? We could make the afternoon flight to London.'

Kate squinted against the late-morning sun. 'Please. I'm tempted to find somewhere I can bury my head in the sand, but I need to go home and face the music.'

'Two minutes,' Julie said.

Too tired to talk, Rav and Julie shared a cigarette. Kate stepped back into the shade and leant against a wall.

'Don't stare at me like that,' Julie said.

'Like what?' Kate said.

'Like you're wondering why I look so shit.'

'There are quite a few things I can't get my head around right now, but that's not one of them.'

166

'Good. Because I haven't been crying. It's just the smoke.' She held up her Marlboro and managed a weak smile. 'Gets in my eyes.'

Kate insisted Rav and Julie go straight home from Heathrow, and wished she could do the same. Ian was waiting for her in his office, blinds drawn and the lights down low. He looked like thunder. 'Have a seat,' he muttered. 'Coffee? Tea?'

'Coffee might help. I haven't had a lot of sleep.'

'Suzy's gone home, so I'll get it myself.'

He vanished before she could offer to go.

Kate glanced at his books. Nearly all non-fiction, politics or history. Margaret Thatcher's memoirs. Andrew Roberts on Napoleon. Le Carré's novels occupied one entire shelf. Who did Ian think he was? George Smiley?

A framed photograph of him dressed from head to toe in Lycra and holding a bike above his head at the top of a mountain pass took pride of place on the far wall. The not-completely-spontaneous shots of the family in the Alps, on Mustique and at the Monaco Grand Prix alongside it sent a message that was rather easier to decode. His desk was covered with snaps of his wife and three teenage boys. As he never tired of reminding anyone who came within reach, he and Ella had met at Oxford. She ran her own internet retail business, now reputedly worth a fortune. Ella dutifully attended all office functions, but she looked a little wearier each time. After a throwaway comment a few years back – 'Show me *one* middle-aged couple who has sex any more' – Kate had begun to appreciate why she might turn a blind eye to her husband's many office affairs. He was spectacularly unsubtle about it, so she couldn't possibly have missed the signs.

Ian returned with her coffee. 'Two sugars,' he said. 'Thought you might need it.'

'Thank you.'

He sat on the sofa opposite her, tugging his trousers up a little above the knee – another of his annoying habits – then crossed his legs, as if this was a languid philosophy tutorial rather than the dissection of an operation that had led to the death of a girl in her charge.

She expected a barrage of questions about every twist and turn of the Andros mission, and every decision she had taken along the way, but Ian was a lot more clinical. 'We started work as soon as you called last night. Thank you for the rapidity of the heads-up, by the way. I appreciate it. I brought in a team and we began by looking at traffic through Athens airport.'

He flipped open the file on the coffee-table in front of him and pushed across a selection of CCTV images from the immigration hall and photographs of five men from their own files. 'Recognize them?'

She tapped three. 'They were the guys who ambushed us in the stairwell.'

'One of their specialist wet teams,' Ian said. 'I'm afraid the Serbian girl never had a chance. And the fact that you got the better of them does you great credit.'

Kate left the pictures where they lay.

'Check out the time stamp on the CCTV grabs,' Ian said. 11.27.

'They hired a speedboat in Rafina for cash and were on your island less than an hour later.'

Kate continued to stare at the pictures. 'So they knew.'

'Someone must have alerted them that you were on your way to Andros.'

'But we didn't take the decision to go until . . . well, early evening the previous day. I'd have to go over the timeline, but—'

'Exactly.' He let that hang in the air for a moment. 'So they do have a source. And I'd hazard a guess that he or she is inside this building.'

'So Viper is real.'

'I'd say so, wouldn't you?'

Kate needed to buy time to think. She stood up, went to the window and looked out through the blinds. 'How much do you think they knew?'

'Let's take a different route. What *could* they have known? Or, more precisely, what *could* someone have told them? The surveillance team first. More of them, so more possibilities. But, so far as I'm aware, they knew nothing beforehand, except that Andros was your target. Why would they think that would be of any interest to Moscow? And why would Moscow have wanted to send a wet team – which is, after all, not without risks of its own – for some unknown operation in a European backwater?'

'Do you think they knew about Lena?'

'My guess – and it's only a guess – is no. At least, not initially. I suspect they knew that you and your team had somehow gleaned intelligence on their assets and wanted to make quite sure that your source was shut down. To put it another way, they knew the int came via you, so it was *you* they were tracking.'

'You think they'll suspect Mikhail?'

'Depends on how unreliable they reckon he is. But even if they did, they wouldn't move against him. He's Igor's son. I'm afraid that someone saw you with Lena near that quayside and drew their own conclusions.'

169

In despair, Kate came back and sat down.

'We all make mistakes, Kate.'

'Not like that we don't.'

'Yes, we do.'

'She was just a kid.'

Ian waited until she had composed herself. 'So who knew that you were about to get on a plane to Athens?'

'My team, obviously.'

'Anyone else in your office, apart from you, Rav, Julie and Maddy?'

'No. And even Maddy didn't know. She went home early.'

'All right. You emailed me, so I was aware. Who else?'

'Danny. And C.'

'Did you tell anyone beyond the three of us?'

'No.'

'Your husband?'

'Well, yes. I guess I did say I was going to Greece, but not to Andros.'

'That might have been enough. He knows the form, of course. But could he have let any of that slip to anyone else, however inadvertently?'

She hesitated a moment too long as she turned over the possibility he had mentioned it to Imogen. 'No. He was brought up to speed again in the latest vetting round. He knows that *anything* I tell him or talk to him about is sacrosanct, and can't be discussed elsewhere, under any circumstances.'

Ian's eyes seemed to glint in the low light, as if he sensed her doubts. 'Did anyone in your team behave in *any* way you thought worthy of note? Did they appear uncomfortable? Did they disappear for a period, or do anything you remember thinking was odd at the time?'

Kate recalled Rav's disappearance on the morning of Lena's death. He'd be the last person on earth to betray her. So why was she even giving it a second thought? 'No,' she said.

'How much did you tell Sir Alan?'

Kate stopped in her tracks. 'What do you mean?'

'When I arrived here in the morning, he clearly knew about the operation. But I hadn't briefed him. Had you?'

Kate cast her mind back to the late-night stint before she'd left for Athens. 'No. I didn't formally brief him.'

'But did you talk to him about it?'

'Yes. He came to my office.'

'And?'

Kate shifted uncomfortably.

'Did he ask you where you were going?'

'No! He didn't need to. He seemed to know. He said, "Bound for Athens in the morning?" Something like that.'

'How did he know it was Athens?'

'He said we should move as soon as the *Empress* docked. You heard him. So I guess Danny must have told him. Why do you ask?'

Ian pursed his lips. 'Don't be naive. If you don't know where this is headed, then you should. In all likelihood, the foreign secretary is going to win the leadership contest and become prime minister. So I don't need to explain, to you, at least, that we're holding a tiger by the tail. And sooner or later, as is the way of such things, it'll turn and bite us on the bum. Then the hard-faced hatchet men across the river will launch the mother and father of all investigations.'

'I don't understand.'

'Oh yes you do. We all have to protect ourselves. And we can only do that by ensuring that our loyalty is – above all – to our country.'

Kate narrowed her eyes.

'Sir Alan is a school friend of the foreign secretary,' Ian continued. 'He will admit to it when he has to, but generally chooses not to shout about it. You know as well as I do that, when push comes to shove, children of the establishment always stick together. So all I'm saying is that we may have to answer for our conduct one day, and we need to be aware of that.'

'Are you saying C could be Viper?'

'I'm saying that *no one* here is above suspicion. Not me, not you, not Rav, Julie or Danny. And not Sir Alan – particularly given his close connection to James Ryan.' Ian sat back. 'To begin with, to be fair to all of us, anyone in Whitehall or beyond could be Viper. But this operation changes everything. Now we know he or she is in this bloody building. So from now on I'd like any information you uncover to come direct to me, please.'

Ian stood up.

Her audience was clearly over, so she rose with him. He put a hand on her shoulder. 'You must be . . . exhausted.'

'That's one word for it.'

'C wants to see you in the morning. Go straight up as soon as you're in.'

He ushered her out and she returned to her office in a daze. She sat at her computer and stared out into the darkness.

Her phone sounded. She glanced at the readout and pressed the green button. 'Hi, love.'

'Are you back?'

'Just got to the office. Sorry, I was about to ring.'

'Could you get over here? I'm at Millbank, waiting for this debate.'

Kate frowned in confusion, her mind blank. 'What debate?'

172

'The first of the TV leadership debates. It's on Sky News tonight. It's meant to focus primarily on foreign affairs, so James Ryan has the upper hand and we need all the help we can get.'

Kate glanced at her watch. 'I was about to go home and see the kids.'

'They're fine. We'd appreciate a bit of assistance. Imogen's nervous. She's less confident on foreign-policy stuff.'

'All right. I'll come over.'

Given what she'd previously said about feeling uncomfortable around Imogen's campaign, Kate had to suppress her irritation at being asked to help directly. But since Stuart had provided cover for Athens with no warning, she wasn't in a strong position to object. She went out into the blustery autumn night and decided to walk along the river and over Lambeth Bridge. The lights of the Houses of Parliament shimmered on the choppy waters of the Thames.

The TV crews outside the offices of Number Four Millbank showed little interest in her. She swept through them unhindered and up to the Sky News office. She gave a fake name to the security people and was just wrestling with the absence of any ID to match it – she had left it in her desk – when Stuart appeared and talked her in.

He kissed her perfunctorily and led her down the corridor. 'I know I'm not supposed to be here,' he said, 'but she needs me.'

Imogen did indeed look nervous, drained of her usual poise and self-assurance. She was heavily made-up and muttering quietly as she scanned her notes. Neither she nor the two male aides alongside her acknowledged Kate's presence.

Stuart interrupted: 'Imogen.'

She finally looked up, smiled at Kate and came to kiss her.

173

'Sorry, we have a minute to sum up our vision for the country. Which is, honestly, impossible.'

'I'm sure you'll be great.'

'It's such an unnatural thing, speaking for a minute. Oh, well, what will be will be.'

She was about to go back to her papers when Stuart stepped in. 'Kate's here to help on the stuff we talked about.'

'Oh, yes,' she said absent-mindedly. 'I was going to take a tough line on Russia – strict economic measures, sanctions and so on, and a broad alliance against them, but I do think we have to be careful to avoid a march to war.'

'Given the way the Russians have been deliberately trying to undermine Western democracies,' Stuart said, 'not to mention their enthusiasm for cold-blooded murder on our streets, attempted or otherwise, I think they should be the focus of our attacks. I mean, who knows what they may be up to in this election? Look what they did in the US!'

Kate glared at him.

He carried on regardless: 'Our guys have been doing some analysis. A lot of social-media accounts heavily support the foreign secretary – more than you'd think he might merit – and an equal number say the vilest things about you, Imogen. I think we should tell it as it is. The new Cold War.'

One of the aides finally tore himself away from his phone. 'We think they're bots, like we saw in the EU referendum – fake automated accounts, set up and later deleted. Quite a few have already gone.'

Stuart was looking at Kate for some kind of reaction. 'What do you think?'

'About what?'

'Is that possible? Isn't that the kind of thing the Russians are always doing?'

Kate shrugged. 'I don't know. It's not really my area.'

Stuart's face reddened. He stared at the floor. But if the tension was there for all to see, neither Imogen nor her assistants noticed it. She was too preoccupied with her notes, and they with their phones.

'I'll leave you to it.' She didn't meet Stuart's eye. 'I'll watch in the lobby.'

She fetched herself a glass of water and sat in a corner with a clear view of the TV screen on the wall. The foreign secretary swept in, late but unfazed, even though his cohort of aides could barely conceal their panic, and she shrank back to avoid being seen. She'd never been asked to brief him, but it was increasingly on the cards, and she wasn't keen to have him feel – or, worse, know – that he'd seen her before.

He chatted cheerily to the Sky News producers and allowed himself to be led to the make-up room. He exuded charm, she thought, whatever his critics might say.

The debate began about ten minutes later.

James and Imogen both had a natural ease in front of the camera. If it had been a dating show, they would probably have hit it off immediately and rushed away for a wild weekend in Brighton, leaving Meg Simpson, pale, technocratic and dull by comparison, to stand beneath their window and complain about the noise. But about ten minutes in, James got to her.

'I think we've probably had enough of the public-school charm,' Imogen said. 'After all, it's provided us with little but uncertainty wrapped up as destiny.

'It's not that I don't care about our relationship with the European Union – in the past and the future – and our place in the world. But right now I'd prefer to be talking about the scale of our social-care challenge or the still significant size of the deficit, not to mention our national debt. I'd like to talk about our students struggling with ever-increasing fees. They can't get a well-paid job or buy a house. I'd like to talk—'

'You do believe in capitalism, don't you, Imogen?' James shot her and the invited audience his trademark megawatt smile.

'I do. Enough to want to save it.'

'And if we don't get out there and build our trade across the world, as our forefathers did, then we won't have the money to do all the things you've so thoughtfully listed. And while I admire your ambition to double – to *double* – the education budget, you have not yet begun to let us know how you plan to fund—'

'*That* is how we compete in this brave new world you and your fellow posh boys have created,' Imogen said.

She was rewarded with a ripple of applause. Imogen was coming across as younger and fresher than her fellow contestants, with ideas that hadn't been talked to death over the past few years, but Kate still found it hard to tell precisely how well she was doing.

She was certainly right about politicians failing to confront the things that really mattered. The ageing population, a health service that couldn't continue in the way it had without an enormous injection of cash, unaffordable public-sector pensions, the fact that no one had a plan to build anywhere near enough houses, or that all public-sector finance projections relied on high levels of immigration, which the government was determined to reduce.

On and on. It seemed never to change.

And that was before you got to the really intractable issues – a deeply hostile Russia, and a China that grew in power each day without taking a single tiny step towards genuine reform. Who would want to talk about that when you could fill the airwaves with irrelevant shit about our place in the world from morning to night, dreaming up deals with every country and planet this side of Mars in the fond belief that it equated in some way to trade?

It was pathetic. They were pathetic. So pathetic she couldn't take any more. Her head hurt, and filling it with more politics wasn't the cure. She decided to walk home, in the hope that it might make her feel a bit better. She set off through the night, head down, mind drifting. And by the time she got to their front door, she had more or less forgotten her irritation with her husband.

16

WHEN SHE GOT into the house, Fiona and Gus were already asleep, so Kate went straight to bed. But an hour later she was still trying to bury herself in a book when Stuart arrived back.

'Where did you get to?' he asked.

'I was tired. I didn't think you'd notice my absence.'

'What's that supposed to mean?'

'It's supposed to mean exactly what it said.'

'You want to explain to me why you've been so weird these past few days?'

'I have no idea what you're talking about.'

Stuart put his hands on his hips. 'So now we're going to do the bit where we pretend we haven't been married for ever?'

'We might not be for very much longer if you keep salivating over Imogen twenty-four seven.'

Stuart stared at her. She could tell he was genuinely shocked, and cursed inwardly. She hadn't meant to say it.

'What the fuck are you talking about? She's one of our best friends!'

'One of *your* best friends, if we're being brutally honest.' Kate immediately regretted saying that, too.

'Is that why you were so weird when I asked for your help and advice on Russia?'

'You were inviting me to comment on something I'd told you in literally the deepest confidence – the most sensitive national secret that only five people know.'

'I was absolutely not! Everyone knows you're the local Russia expert. I was inviting you to chip in on whether you thought we might be the victims of a well-known modern intelligence warfare strategy. The use of bots and fake accounts has hardly been the deepest, most sensitive, only-five-people-know national secret during God knows how many recent elections, has it?'

His blood was up, but it wasn't just bluster. She knew she had wounded him, genuinely and unnecessarily. 'I'm sorry,' she said. 'I had an operation that went very badly wrong in Greece.' Suddenly she couldn't stop herself. 'I recruited a blameless young girl to work for us. Actually, "recruited" is too nice a way of putting it. I blackmailed her into it. And then, in the middle of an operation, she disappeared. Rav and I went looking for her and got ambushed in a stairwell and had to kill our three attackers. Back at the hotel, I had to wash the blood off and change my shirt. I found the girl in my cupboard, with her throat cut. So . . . I'm probably not in the best frame of mind.'

Stuart was dumbstruck. She watched the emotions sweep through him, anger giving way to incomprehension and then, eventually, pity. 'Oh, shit, Kate,' he said. 'I am *really* sorry.'

'No. It's my fault. I shouldn't have taken it out on you.'

He came to sit next to her and rested a hand on her leg. 'I don't know what to say. That is . . . *horrible.* Are you . . . all right?'

'Physically, yes. I'm fine. It's a long time since I had to fight my way out of a stairwell, but Rav is young, fit and very good. We're both okay.'

She looked at him. 'So, yes, you're on the money. The Russians are ruthless murdering bastards. But I can't say that in public, and especially not now.'

'What will the consequences be?'

'Of her death? For me, not good. For the Service as a whole, it depends.'

'On what?'

'Everyone is looking over their shoulder now. The Russians knew we were coming, so someone must have told them.'

'Who?'

'That is a very good question.'

Stuart had turned his back to her. 'Yours is a brutal business. I sometimes forget that. Or maybe I try not to remember it. Politics is sweetness and light by comparison.'

'War *is* brutal. And that's what it is.'

He looked at her again. 'Do you ever worry about the damage it's doing to you?'

'All the bloody time.'

Stuart began to undress, perhaps to make what he said next appear less loaded. 'Do you think it's possible to be the warrior you need to be and the wife and mother you want to be?'

So there it was. The question Kate could not and would not ask herself, articulated clearly between them at last.

She knew what his answer was, but she couldn't get her head around it now, so she let the silence play out.

He appeared to be deep in thought. Then he said, 'The Russians definitely killed this young girl?'

'I'd better stop talking about it. We've already got down to which of us knew exactly what, when.'

Stuart went to do whatever Stuart did in front of the bathroom mirror. After a while, he came back, removed the electric toothbrush from his mouth and stopped it for a moment. 'You should see the abuse and trolling Imogen gets online. It's off the scale. James hardly has anything like it. Don't you think that's strange, given what a complete dickhead he is? I reckon they're trying to swing the election in his favour. I can't help feeling it's all connected.'

'They?'

'Your Russian pals.'

Kate closed her book and switched off the light. 'I need to sleep.'

'Will you keep me posted? It feels important.'

'Right now, we're looking at a total shutdown, even when it comes to sharing certain information with each other internally.'

Stuart went back to the bathroom to finish off, then quickly slid between the sheets next to her and spooned her, which he hadn't done for as long as she could remember. She wrapped his arms around her waist and folded them over her stomach. It felt very good to be held.

'I do love you,' he said.

She felt his breath against her neck.

'And I have some good news.'

'I can hardly wait.'

'I went to see your mother. I agreed we'd take her down to see your aunt Rose this weekend.'

Kate was too exhausted to protest. 'A whole day with my mother. My cup runneth over.'

'On the plus side, she'll be on her best behaviour – she always is when the kids are around – and we might get the chance to murder her and dispose of her body on the way back.'

'As long as you do the time, I'm up for it.'

'Okay. Let's work up a plan in the morning.'

He turned over and, seconds later, was snoring quietly.

'To answer your question,' she whispered, 'do I think it is possible to be a warrior and the wife and mother I want to be? No, I don't.'

17

SIR ALAN'S MESSAGE had said: *Early meeting at the RAC Club. How about breakfast there at 8.30?*

Kate knew that the early meeting was in fact his morning swim and, sure enough, chlorine was the aroma she detected as she kissed him in the lobby.

'Sorry to drag you over here,' he said. 'But sometimes escaping from Mission Control can be productive.' He led her to the upper atrium, with its beautiful domed ceiling, where a red vintage Ferrari had been parked on the carpet. 'I'd recount its history for you in some detail, if I had the slightest interest in motor vehicles.'

'Well, thank God you didn't drag me to an automobile club.'

His eyes sparkled. 'Indeed.'

'I thought you were a member of the Travellers?'

'I am. But it's impossible to go there without feeling ... noticed.'

The waiter leapt to attention as they moved through into the dining room. 'Good morning, Sir Alan!' He took them, without further discussion, to a table that was carefully hidden from view and where there was no prospect of being overheard. It was exactly the kind of place you would expect a spymaster to be taking his breakfast. Sir Alan had learnt his trade in the KGB's heyday, and old habits died hard.

'How are Stuart and the kids?' he asked.

'Stuart is well. The children are teenagers.'

'Ah, yes, been there, got the scars to show for it. And so has my wallet. You'll be pleased to know they emerge as surprisingly sophisticated and likeable human beings.'

'I'll hold you to that.'

The waiter took Sir Alan's order of scrambled eggs and smoked salmon. Kate wasn't hungry, but asked for the same, and coffee.

Sir Alan leant towards her. 'I just wanted to offer you my support,' he said quietly. 'I know how it can feel when an operation goes wrong, especially one in which a young girl lies dead. But we're fighting a war, as you know, and however much we attempt to guard against it, the innocent are often casualties. There is no merit or sense in blaming yourself, and I hope you're not going down that road.'

'I'd love to take a different one entirely, but I can't.'

'Why not?'

'Because I *am* to blame.'

'Is that what Ian said?'

'No. He was quite decent about it, actually.'

'I'm sure he was. He'll be positioning himself and, no doubt, in his situation I'd be doing the same. He's already looking forward to the day when this explodes into the public domain and costs me my head.'

'I'd like it if that didn't happen.'

'So would I. In the meantime, allow me to share my vision of the future. The first bout of the leadership contest on Monday will see Imogen and James go through to the run-off vote with the party members. Ballots will go out very soon afterwards. It's even possible that one or other of them will stand down, paving the way for an immediate coronation. Although it shouldn't make any difference, we all have to consider the political reality. Once one or other is prime minister, we're going to find it difficult to continue to investigate him or her without the most solid evidence imaginable – which, let's face it, is a rare luxury in our trade. Or, to put it another way, if we don't nail this in the next few days, we may have to park it for ever, with potentially incalculable costs for our country. The clock is ticking now and we need a result fast.'

The waiter returned with a large silver jug of coffee, but knew better than to invade Sir Alan's personal space without invitation. He got the nod, poured for them both and left the jug.

Sir Alan took a sheaf of papers from an inner pocket, unfolded them and placed them on the table. 'I had GCHQ take a look at what's going on across the web. The vast majority of the most suspicious activity is swinging behind James, although they seem to be refuelling Imogen as well, to try to throw us off the scent.'

'What if that's just another part of the misinformation ploy?'

'It could be. But I think we're better off assuming they have a dog in the fight and want him to win. If they really have compromised him, their reward will be considerable.'

'If they compromised him, how did they do it? And how do we prove it?'

'I've known James Ryan long enough and well enough to be in no doubt that there is nothing in his sexual closet that would trouble him. He can't keep his flies done up and might have illegitimate offspring in every port, for all I know, but I don't think that would embarrass him unduly or surprise his wife. I'm not quite clear about the basis of their marriage, but conventional fidelity doesn't come into it.

'He's always been greedy, though. His father was a gambler and womanizer, who was periodically penniless after he left the army. James was constantly worried that he was going to be pulled out of school. I've always wondered how he manages to fund his lifestyle, and send his children to the most expensive establishments in the land without apparently breaking sweat. So, my advice is to follow the money.'

'Rav is on to it.'

'I know. I've spoken to him already this morning. Beyond that, I want you to concentrate on two things. First, Mikhail. Danny says the *Empress* is moored off the coast a little way from Andros, but as soon as it pulls in anywhere else, let's put a team on the ground. This time I don't want anyone but me to know.'

'You want to cut Ian out of the loop?'

'I'll tell him what he needs to know. In addition, I want you to keep me informed about Sergei.' His gaze was steady again, those grey-blue eyes boring into her own. 'This is the last time I'm going to ask. I understand personal loyalty, but this goes beyond that.'

'You make it sound like a test.'

'Everything is a test. Of your suitability for high office because, as you well know, this is about the integrity and security of our country. And nothing – at least nothing we do – is more important than that.'

The waiter brought their food. Kate looked at her plate. 'I'll try to make contact with . . . my source, but there's no way of hurrying it. The US Embassy reception is next week, as you know. If he doesn't turn up there, I don't know any other way of making contact without colossal risk for him.'

'You should know that Ian is also aware of Sergei's existence.'

Kate failed to hide her surprise. 'How?'

'He might be a selfish shit, but he's no fool. He asked the same questions as I did, and arrived at the same conclusion.'

'He came to talk to you about it?'

'Yes. I told him you had been lovers—'

'I didn't sleep with him. Ever.'

'That comforts me not at all. Love is infinitely more dangerous. Anyway, suffice it to say that he didn't buy it, and I'm not sure I do either.'

'Buy what?'

'That Sergei was helping you out of long-held affection. Ian suggested there were only two realistic possibilities – that Sergei was manipulating you for his own ends, or those of his masters in Moscow, whoever they may be.'

'You said there were two possibilities.'

Sir Alan gazed at her from beneath hooded eyelids. 'Or that he had recruited you a long time ago.'

'You think I'm Viper?'

He finished his scrambled egg before he answered. 'I believe the former explanation is more likely. But I prefer to keep an open mind. Either way, it would help if we could place Sergei within the system. At the moment, we're coming up blank. We have no idea what he does and are therefore struggling with motive.'

'But Ian favours the latter?'

'Yes. Though it may occur to you, as it has to me, that this might be a convenient way of diverting suspicion from himself.'

Sir Alan tilted his head in the direction of his empty plate, and her still full one. Kate gave him an apologetic smile. 'It's a terrible waste, I know. But I'll just stick with the coffee.'

Sir Alan had an appointment in Downing Street, so Kate walked on alone. As she skirted the Horse Guards end of St James's Park, she saw the prime minister's wife emerge from the rear gate and set off for a jog. She looked pale and drawn, and who could blame her?

Kate accelerated past the Foreign & Commonwealth Office as it started to rain, and jumped into a cab in Parliament Square.

When she finally got to work – it would have been quicker to crawl on all fours along Millbank – Rav was at his desk. He didn't hear her approaching.

'Morning.'

He responded as if she'd set fire to his trousers. 'Shit! You gave me a shock.'

'What's wrong?'

'Nothing.' He shook his head vigorously, but somehow without conviction. 'C's asked me to refine the search for Viper. These are the names.' He handed her a handwritten note. Kate featured. So did Ian, Rav, Julie, Danny and C. 'So I'm in the unusual position of having to investigate every one of my superiors. Thank God I never liked you.'

'The job is the job, Rav. You'd be the first to say it – just put one foot in front of the other, and we'll see where it lands.'

'I've asked Maddy to start pulling the phone records as

soon as she's in.' He sucked his enviably white teeth. 'Mine will come to you.'

'If someone inside this building is betraying us to a foreign power, I'd like to think they were smart enough to avoid giving themselves away that easily.'

'I'm pulling everything else as well.'

'Good.' But Kate could tell that wasn't what was troubling him. 'Spit it out.'

'I've got a lead on the foreign secretary's African business activities. The man is now a teacher and lives in Oxford. We should get going.'

'We will. As soon as you tell me what's on your mind.'

Rav gazed at her. 'The initial feedback on our original Viper search group.' He opened his drawer and took out a dossier. 'I've been going through it for most of the night. I can't find anything at all unusual on anyone around the foreign secretary. We've got every email they've ever written that mentions Russia, and if they *are* working for Moscow, they've been doing a great job of hiding their true feelings for a very long time. The same is true of those around Imogen Conrad.' He cleared his throat uneasily. 'Except . . .'

'Except what?'

'I've been agonizing about this, actually. I imagined what I'd feel if this was about Zac. I wouldn't want to know. But I think you would.' He handed her a wad of papers. 'Stuart calls Imogen a lot.'

Kate's heart was pounding, but she was determined not to show it. 'So he should. He's her right-hand man.'

'The night before last, when we were in Greece, he called her at three in the morning. I tracked her phone. Half an hour later it was in your house, which I guess means she was too.'

Kate turned the pages of the call log. Rav had circled those he thought unusual or worthy of note. She found the one at three in the morning. There were several more for the hours beyond midnight. 'I'll take a look,' she said.

'I'm sorry, I—'

'It's fine, Rav. You did the right thing.'

Kate picked up the file and retreated to her office. She closed the door and wished she could bar it. She sat down and stared at the log again. After a while, her vision blurred. She could feel sweat on her palms, her forehead and at the back of her neck. She had an overwhelming urge to pick up the phone, call Stuart and yell at him.

Rav knocked and entered before she could stop him. She didn't dare turn round. 'I'm sorry,' he said again.

'For what?'

He hesitated. 'There's almost certainly an innocent explanation. I sometimes call *you* at three in the morning.'

'I understand. I'll deal with it.'

Rav didn't move. Kate turned to face him. 'I said I'd deal with it, Rav. Okay? It's absolutely not your problem. Leave it to me.'

'But that's kind of the thing. I *do* have to deal with it.'

'What do you mean?'

'Well, you *know* what I mean. Given what's at stake, it obviously isn't appropriate that you deal with it so I must. I'm going to cross everyone else off the suspect list for Viper, but I need to transfer Stuart onto the new one.'

'Rav—'

'The pattern of phone calls is . . . odd. Not suspicious or anything, but odd. At the very least, he had access to your movements in Greece, so—'

'Rav, this is my husband we're talking about.'

'I know. I get that. It's awkward, but—'

'It's a bit more than fucking awkward.'

He put up his hands. 'All right. But in all . . . well, ninety-nine per cent probability, there's nothing to it. Like I say, we regularly call each other at three in the morning. It's a matter of internal record, though, that these logs have been delivered to me. The only line of interest in them is glaringly obvious. If I hand it over to you and the case is ever subject to review for any reason, we'll both end up being hung out to dry.' Rav waited. 'I'm just covering your back, Kate. I hope you know that.'

Kate watched the grey clouds gather above Vauxhall station. 'Fine,' she said. 'You're right.' She thrust the papers back at him and turned on her computer.

'I can go to Oxford on my own,' he said.

'I'm coming to Oxford. Just indulge me for sixty seconds.'

He retreated to the door.

'And I'll need to see whatever you get on Viper, when you get it. If you don't mind.'

Kate drove to Oxford in one of the office Astras, mostly in silence. She tried to conjure up a vaguely convincing reason as to why her husband might call Imogen at three in the morning if they were not lovers. She couldn't. And that ate away at the logical, rational part of her brain until it was hard to concentrate. Eventually, Rav said, 'For the avoidance of doubt, I assume you'll check Zac's phone records as well as mine. It's your duty to do so. And *I* would. If I were you.'

Kate wasn't in a mood to answer.

'So, just to be clear, I *don't* want to know what you find. I mean, do what you have to do for work, but if there's anything else – anything at all – I don't want to know about it.'

'You're making a bit of a mountain of this, Rav.'

'No, I'm not. You seem to forget I've known you for a very long time, and I can see exactly what it's doing to you, even though, given what I know of Stuart, I should think there is almost certainly an innocent explanation. And I'm not as robust as you . . . so, I'm just telling you that I don't want to know.' He waited. 'Do you understand that?'

'I get it. There won't be anything, so let's just forget about it.'

To change the subject, Rav filled her in on their visit. The man they were going to see had worked with the foreign secretary for the brief period after he left the army. 'The *Guardian* ran a story a few years back saying Blandwick Security did some work for Mugabe and his family,' Rav said. 'James threw his lawyers at it, but the only man the *Guardian* quoted was Blandwick's in-country manager, David Snell. I don't know whether he left Zimbabwe by choice or not, but he's now a teacher at the Dragon School.'

'Quite a change of career.'

'The *Guardian* seems to have given up on the story after that. They've never written anything else.' Rav had bits of paper all over his lap. 'Blandwick was wound up after three years. Its income stream tells an intriguing story. The losses were pretty chunky. Ryan was a consultant for a few years afterwards, working mostly in Africa.'

'None of which sounds out of the ordinary for an ex-soldier.'

'Perhaps not. But just before he became an MP, he bought that house in Hampshire for £1.75 million. Two years later, he applied to build a swimming pool with an elaborate pool-house complex. And the year after that, he bought the mews house in Chelsea for £2.2 million.'

'Maybe he won the lottery.'

'The African lottery, perhaps.'

'It's hard to see what that has to do with Russia, though.'

'I agree.'

18

THE DRAGON SCHOOL was in a leafy part of north Oxford and David Snell lived in an apartment at the rear of the school.

He had the tanned, leathery skin that appeared to be the preserve of southern Africans of a certain era. 'You're late,' he said. 'I've been waiting for you.' He ushered them into a small, gloomy sitting room, where the furniture was down-at-heel, the paint grey and peeling in places. The mantelpiece was crowded with bronze trinkets and wooden carvings, but the walls were completely bare except for an old water-colour of the African bush. There were no photographs. If David Snell had a family, there was no evidence of any affection for it.

'I suppose you'll need tea.'

'No, thank you,' Rav said. 'We're fine.'

'What is it you want of me?'

'We need to ask a few questions.'

He indicated that they should sit down.

'I'm sorry to be blunt,' Rav said, rehearsing his usual spiel, 'but I'm afraid we must ask you to treat the following conversation in the strictest—'

'I know who you are, for God's sake. And I know the drill. I wasn't born yesterday. I also have a geography class to teach, so please get to the point.'

'We'd like to ask you about your work at Blandwick Security,' Kate said.

'It was a long time ago. What do you want to know?'

'How long did you work for James Ryan?'

'About two years.'

'How did you meet him?'

'He came out to Zim to look for a country manager for a new security business he said he was setting up. He had a friend who'd been in the Recces in South Africa. That's the equivalent of the SAS there—'

'Thank you. We're aware of what it was.'

'He recommended me. I met James. I worked with him for a few years. That's it.'

'What did you do?'

'Not much. He was looking for business, guarding big international firms and their premises. But, first, there weren't many doing any work in Zim, and second, insofar as there was any business, he didn't win it.'

'Did you work for Mugabe?' Rav asked.

'Everybody in Zimbabwe worked for Mugabe in those days. He had a hand in pretty much every concern in the country. We did some work briefly for a South African foodprocessing company, which had a subsidiary owned by one of Mugabe's relatives, but the *Guardian* story was basically bullshit.'

'Did you see much of Mr Ryan?' Kate asked.

'No. He travelled a lot, throughout Africa. Even when he was in Zim, I rarely saw him.'

'So he paid your salary,' Rav said, 'and you sat around waiting for him to call with business, which rarely materialized.'

'I rarely sit around. His was just one contract I had. We agreed it was flexible.'

'But he paid you a retainer?'

'Correct.'

'Annual?'

'Yes.'

'And he rarely asked you to do a huge amount in return?'

'Also correct.'

Kate leant forward. 'If you don't mind me saying so, Mr Snell, something about this doesn't entirely add up.'

He glared at her, but she didn't flinch.

'Which is a polite way of saying that I don't think you're telling us the *whole* story.' She was glad he didn't have a weapon within reach. 'Look, we aren't trying to catch you out. This is just a series of routine enquiries being conducted as part of a vetting—'

'That's what you said last time.'

Kate frowned. 'What do you mean, last time?'

'You said all this when you came here before. I spilt my guts out to you and nothing came of it.'

'Mr Snell, unless I'm going prematurely senile, I can say with some confidence that I have never set eyes on you before in my life.'

'Your people.'

'Which people?'

'I don't know. I can't remember his name. Some guy asking about James bloody Ryan.'

'From the Security Service or the Secret Intelligence Service – MI5 or MI6?'

'Six.'

'Are you sure?'

'Of course I'm sure. I was in the same business back in the Rhodesian war. I served in the Central Intelligence Organization, then the Selous Scouts.'

'Can you remember their names?'

'There was just one guy. Ian something.'

'Granger?'

'Maybe.'

'What did he look like?'

'Slimy. Unreliable.'

'I mean physically.'

'Five ten, dark-haired, receding hairline, slim. Looked like the kind of guy intent on trying to recover his youth – trim and fit.'

'What did he want?'

'Exactly the same as you. Same questions. Tell me about James Ryan's business, and so on.'

'And what did you say?'

'I told him that James Ryan was an unreliable cunt and that whatever he was doing in Harare had nothing whatsoever to do with the business he hired me for.'

'Which means?'

'He was there every five minutes. It's my country, for Christ's sake, and there's no one I don't know.'

'What was he doing there?'

'Crawling so far up the Mugabe family's backsides you could have seen his head whenever they opened their mouths.'

'To what purpose?'

He looked away.

'To what purpose?' Kate repeated.

'I don't know.'

'It looks to me like you might have a pretty good idea.'

'He left his briefcase in the office one day on one of his rare visits to us. I shouldn't have looked through it, but I did.'

'Go on.'

'I realized that whatever he was doing with his time, it had precious little to do with us. And I left.'

'What was in the briefcase?'

'Nothing very much. Except business cards and letterheads with his name on from a company called Hamilton Capital Management, which I had never even heard of.'

'What did it do?' Rav asked.

'I have absolutely no idea.'

'If you had to guess?' Kate said.

'Someone had to be keeping the Mugabes afloat. The country was bankrupt and there was practically nothing left to steal. So that was an opportunity, right, for anyone who wanted to buy assets or influence. The assets went long before, so who would be interested in buying influence? The Chinese . . . Shit, I don't know. Take your pick.'

'That's a bit of a leap, if I may say so. The Mugabes still controlled the rights to the country's natural resources.'

'He wasn't a mineral engineer, let me tell you. The rumour was he was a bag-carrier. That's all I can say.'

'What do you mean, exactly?'

'Moving money and assets around for the Mugabe family and outside investors who wanted to buy influence.'

'You heard that from old friends in the CIO?' Rav asked.

'Old friends and new. Like I said, Zim is a small country.'

'And you told all this to Ian Granger?'

'If that was his name, yeah, sure I did.'

'Do you have any idea where the money came from?'

'No.'

'You mentioned the Chinese.'

'It was a guess. They were trying to buy influence and assets all over Africa at the time and still are, as far as I know. They thought it was going to provide the natural resources they'll need in the future.'

'What about the Russians?'

'The same, but for them it's more like getting back to the days of the Cold War. It's the Soviet mentality – they want every country in the world in their sphere of influence.'

'Did you ever see James Ryan with any Russians?'

'I hardly saw him, like I said.'

'But specifically . . .'

'No, I never saw him with any Russians.'

'But he was bringing large sums in and out of the country and Moscow might have been the source of the cash?'

'Might have been.'

'If you had to guess?'

'I've told you as much as I know. The cash came from somewhere, but where exactly I couldn't say.'

Kate and Rav left David Snell to his unfortunate pupils and began their journey back to London.

'What the hell was all that about?' Kate asked, as soon as they were in the car.

'Maybe Ian had an investigation and it just ran into the sand,' Rav said.

'I'll check it out when I get back.'

They were silent for a while. 'I'm sorry about earlier,' Rav said eventually.

'About what?'

'Maybe I should have dropped it. Like you said, Stuart is your husband.'

'Of course you shouldn't, for all the reasons you gave.' Kate turned to him. 'I'm not talking about this again. Stuart might turn out to be a lot of things, but I've been married to him since you were a child, and I can assure you infidelity is not his vice.'

'I envy you your certainty.'

'Are you trying to make this worse?'

'No. It's not about you. It's about me. I've met Stuart. I can see why you feel that way about him. But how can we ever really *know*? I love Zac. I think he's a genuinely solid guy. But I don't know that I trust him a hundred—'

'Let's drop it, Rav.'

'You once told me you didn't trust anyone.'

'It's just a phrase I use to shut people up. I shouldn't.'

'You said it was one of your problems, but maybe it's everyone's.'

'It's just the business we're in.'

'You said it had nothing to do with the business we're in.'

'You really shouldn't have such a good memory.'

'I sometimes wish I didn't.'

'I'm fond of you, Rav, and I think you know that, quite apart from the fact that you've saved my life on more than one occasion—'

'And vice versa.'

'—but I'm still going to kill you if you don't shut up for a while.'

Rav did as instructed. And Kate tried to think about what the schoolmaster had told them. The problem was that suspicion was not only corrosive but explosive. It could dynamite the certainties that underlay not just a marriage but a life. What possible reason could Stuart have had to call Imogen at three in the morning? And why would she immediately come to their house?

Back at Vauxhall, Kate tried to force herself to focus on something else. She logged in and searched the records for any reference to Snell. The database came up with one result but no corresponding file.

Kate called the Records Office. 'Hi, Duncan. Kate Henderson from Russia Desk. I'm trying to locate the records for a David Snell. I have a feeling he was interviewed in connection with a prior investigation. His name comes up when I do a search, but I can't find the file.'

'Let me take a look. What did you say his name was?'

'Snell. David Snell. From Zimbabwe. Ex-Rhodesian Central Intelligence.'

'Hold on a second.' Duncan put down the phone. He was gone for a few minutes. 'There was a file,' he said, when he came back, 'but it has a red flag. It's been closed.'

'By whom?'

'I'm sorry, Kate, that's above my pay grade.'

Kate was about to hang up when she tried one last throw of the dice. 'Is there a Finance reference?'

'Yes.'

'Could you give it to me?' As he spoke, she jotted the number on a piece of paper and went straight down the back stairs to Rose's office.

'I'm sorry, Kate,' Jane said, 'but she went early today. Said she was having guests for the weekend.'

'That's us, so I can't complain.'

'Oh!' Clearly Jane didn't know what to make of that.

'She'll be exhausted by Monday,' Kate said, 'so cut her some slack. My mother's coming too.'

'I'll need her to authorize any discussion on the matter you raised the other day,' Jane said defensively.

'I understand that.' She didn't, though, now she came to think of it. 'I'll talk to her. But this is about something else.'

'Oh,' Jane said again. She looked relieved, which in itself told a story.

'I just wanted to see if we have any codes for a guy called David Snell. Ex-Rhodesian CIO.'

Jane tapped her keyboard reluctantly. The ability to use the Department of Finance to reverse into the filing system was something few understood. Every trainee had to spend at least a week in every department. Most took a mental break during their time in Finance, but Kate had spotted weaknesses in the system that not even the senior management entirely understood, and which hadn't been eradicated during numerous upgrades.

'There are quite a few references to a David Snell.'

'Could you give them to me?'

The printer buzzed, then Jane handed her a sheet of paper, which she took down the corridor to the Records Office. Duncan Black had a shock of curly red hair and skin as white as alabaster. He was lost in his iPhone. He snapped to attention when he saw her badge. 'Sorry!'

'Duncan, I've just been given these codes from Finance, and I need to have the corresponding files, please.'

He didn't look convinced. He'd probably never had a request like that before. Kate gave him the warmest of smiles to discourage him from questioning her. He retreated to his screen and she heard the printer going seconds later.

Duncan came back with her cover sheet and a thick wad of paper. 'We've got all these.' He pointed to the eight or nine at the top of the list. 'But this one is the most recent.'

'So . . . where is it?'

'Not there.'

'How can it not be there? It's got a direct corresponding Finance reference.'

'Like I said, it's been closed.'

'By whom?'

'I'm not supposed to say. Someone on the management committee.'

'Right.' Kate frowned, as if trying to work out what to do. 'But Rose Trewen, the head of Finance, wants it. And she's on the management—'

His cheeks began to match his hair. 'She closed it.'

Kate stared at him. It took her a few beats too many to recover. 'Ah. Okay. Thank you for your help.'

She went back to her office, which was deserted now. Maddy's desk light was still on, but the corner that Rav and Julie normally occupied was in darkness.

Kate sat at her desk and interrogated Duncan's offering. David Snell had been an occasional informer for the Service in the final days of the Rhodesian war, but there was nothing else to be gleaned.

Maddy returned and handed Kate a small stack of paperwork, kicked off her shoes and tucked her feet beneath her on the soft chair next to her desk. She was the only person who ever did this. Comfort corner, she called it.

'I can tell you have bad news for me,' Kate said.

'Complicated news.'

'Go on, then.' Kate leant back. 'I'm not sure today can get much worse.'

'Rav said I needed to start asking GCHQ for material on the new list for Viper. I've only got the phone records so far.'

'Go on.'

'It might be nothing but it did kind of leap out at me.' Maddy handed them over. 'Julie and Ian.' She pointed at the circled numbers. 'The top sheets are hers, with his number circled. The bottom sheets are the reverse.'

Kate turned the pages. Far too many for there to be any doubt. 'Jesus . . . She always claims she can't stand the sight of him.'

'The heart has its reasons.'

'I'm not sure the heart plays any role in this. And it's not a crime. They're two consenting adults. He's married, but that's his business, not ours. It shows there's no accounting for taste, but little else. Unless I'm missing something.'

Maddy pulled the face she used when she wanted Kate to question her own judgement. Mostly, her commitment to covering Kate's back was endearing, but occasionally – like now – it was annoying.

'It honestly doesn't matter,' Kate said.

'Except that Ian is *always* trying to undermine you.'

'Don't worry. Really. Whenever he gets on his Savile Row-clad high horse, I remind myself of Stuart cornering him at the Christmas do.'

Kate had been forced to ban her husband from office parties after he'd told Ian, when playing Diversity Snakes and Ladders, that being a woman trumped state-school GCSEs every time 'so she's always going to slaughter you'.

'But now we have a mole-hunt,' Maddy said, 'during the course of which he'll be doing everything in his power to point the finger elsewhere.'

Kate took the papers and locked them into her drawer. 'I

really appreciate this. Thank you. But that's where these belong for now. And where *is* Julie? I need to talk to her about Lena's sister.'

'C is on the case. She flies to Serbia tomorrow, first thing.'

'Why is C on the—'

'He said it was his moral responsibility.'

'In what way?'

Maddy shrugged. 'An agent lost on his watch.'

Kate tried to hide her irritation at being outside the loop. And the idea of Julie and Ian as lovers was bizarre. Maddy was hovering. 'Come on, Maddy, spit it out.'

She handed over yet more paper. 'Rav's phone records.' She grimaced. 'And Zac's.'

'Okay,' Kate said. 'I'll take a look.'

'It's just . . .'

'I'll take a look, Maddy.'

'Right,' Maddy said. 'Have a good weekend. I'll see you on Monday.' She'd long since mastered the art of lowering the curtain without leaving her audience in any doubt as to her true feelings.

Once she'd gone, Kate glanced over Rav's records. Nothing of note. But as Maddy's expression had made clear, Zac's were less comforting. Zac's Scottish trip had been Rav's excuse for spending so many nights at his desk. But his partner's phone very clearly placed him at his former wife's Fulham address.

Kate shuffled them to and fro on her desk. She went and fixed herself a coffee, then came back and drank it. When she'd run out of excuses not to, she picked up her phone and dialled Rav.

'You've got the records,' he said.

'Yes.'

'So why are you calling?' There was real anger in his voice. 'I told you not to.'

'He hasn't been cheating on you.'

Rav was silent. He didn't invite her to go on, but neither did he ask her to hold back.

'He hasn't been in Scotland. He's been with his kids at the house in Fulham.'

There was a long, long silence.

'Rav?'

'I *told* you not to fucking tell me, Kate. I *begged* you. Don't you understand *anything*?' He severed the connection.

19

KATE TOOK AN extra turn around Battersea Park in the fading light. Part of her wanted to burst through the door and ask Stuart about his three a.m. phone calls. Another part wanted to give him the benefit of the doubt, and do nothing more to disturb the already troubled surface of their pond. He'd only ask her why she didn't trust him, and she couldn't blame him for that because she'd have asked exactly the same question if the shoe was on the other foot.

When she got home, Stuart already had the car more or less packed. But the washing-up had not been done, or the bins put out, and the house was still a tip. Kate sublimated her anger and frustration by tearing through it at speed. She pulled the overstuffed bin-liner free and Stuart tried to leap to her aid as she carried it across the kitchen. 'I'll do that.'

'Just make sure the kids are ready to go,' she hissed, as she stormed past him, only to have it burst over the paving stones. Kate stared at the scattered contents for a moment, then caught sight of their neighbour watching through her sitting-room window. She didn't know whether to laugh or cry.

She scraped up the mess, almost on autopilot, until she found something stuffed into a tin of Nelson's dog food. A condom wrapper. She stared at it for a while, her rage reignited, then went back inside, unrolled a sheet of kitchen paper, wrapped it up and shoved it into her pocket.

When she had finished, Stuart had the good sense to avoid any further conversation. Kate gave him a wide berth and climbed the stairs. She went into the bathroom, locked the door, slumped into the Lloyd Loom chair and put her head into her hands. Her heart was thumping and her hands were shaking more than they had after their encounter with the SVR wet team.

Eventually she managed to lift her head and gaze out of the window. After the endless wind and rain, it was a beautiful autumn evening, but the clear sky mocked her instead of restoring her spirits. By sheer effort of will, she managed to quieten the tumult in her mind and body, then left the refuge of the bathroom and busied herself with her packing.

Stuart pushed open the bedroom door. 'Are you all right?'

'Why wouldn't I be?' She felt as if her facial features had been carved in stone, and his expression told her she wasn't wrong.

'You don't look . . . well.'

'I'm fine,' she muttered. 'Considering.'

'I don't think you should have gone to work today.'

She looked at him as if he was speaking a foreign language.

'You can't just shrug off what happened in Greece, Kate. I can see the impact it's had on you. No one is superhuman.'

'I'm fine.'

'No one would be fine after what you've been through.'

'Well, I am.'

He hovered uncertainly. 'There's something I need to tell you,' he said.

She couldn't remember ever seeing him so nervous.

'I have a terrible feeling you're not going to like it.'

She sat down on the bed, with her back to him. 'I suspect I already know.'

'Try not to go crazy. I can explain.'

'It had better be good.'

He came to her side of the bed, but she couldn't bring herself to look up at him.

'Jed is coming with us. For the weekend.'

'*What?*'

'I did say don't go crazy.'

'What do you mean, Jed's coming with us?'

'Please bear with me, Kate. I know it's not ideal, but it's actually not crazy either. The Swedish porn star and I had an argument. Actually, it was worse than that. But in the end she said the situation was really very simple – she wanted to see Jed this weekend, and would only come to Rose's house if he could join us. I offered her every argument you would have done – believe me – but you know how goddamn stubborn she can be. In the end, I thought, I'm tired, you're tired, what the fuck does it matter? It's a fight we don't need to have. I called Rose. She was fine with it. Separate bedrooms and no corridor-creeping, obviously.' He put a hand on her shoulder.

Kate shrugged it off. 'Okay.'

'Honestly? Jeez, you *have* had a bad week. I didn't think you'd agree in a month of Sundays.'

'You know she's doing this to provoke us?'

'Of course she is. But if we roll with it, she'll get tired of fighting.'

'I doubt it.'

Ten minutes later Jed arrived. He'd removed some of the metalwork from his piercings and selected a strange ethnic coat for his weekend wear. 'Th-thank you very m-much for inviting me, Mr and Mrs Henderson,' he stammered, anxiety pouring off him in waves.

'It's our pleasure, Jed,' Stuart replied, gripping his outstretched hand while Kate was still struggling to concentrate.

Jed climbed through to the third row of seats in the back of the car, and Fiona followed. Kate's mother was less obliging when they picked her up, but obeyed, uncharacteristically meekly, when Stuart instructed her to sit next to Gus. She stared stonily ahead as they crawled along the Embankment. Gus and Fiona were on their phones and Jed stared out of the window.

'What was today like?' Stuart asked Kate.

'Difficult.'

'There's an awful lot of traffic,' Lucy said.

'Yes, there is, Mum.'

'Can't you do anything about it?'

'Her people usually clear the roads in advance,' Stuart said, 'but they're having the day off.'

'It's a disgrace. Where *is* everyone going?'

'Out of London for the weekend,' Kate said. 'Just like us.'

'Why on earth are they doing that?'

'God knows, Mum.'

Stuart started to laugh.

'So many cars. There is a *lot* of traffic.'

'I was thinking poison,' Stuart murmured. 'But I may just resort to a blunt instrument.'

'It's not funny.'

'Who is that boy?'

'Which boy, Mum?'

'The one in the back, with that awful jacket.'

Gus snorted. Like father, like son, Kate thought.

'That's Jed. He's a friend of Fiona's. We just introduced you. And it's a very nice jacket.'

'He looks simply *awful*.'

Kate swung around. 'I'm so sorry, Jed. My mother isn't very well.'

'It's fine, Mrs Henderson. Fiona told me. I understand.' He gave her a sheepish grin. 'And I worry about the jacket, some days.'

'I don't know *what* you're talking about,' Lucy said. 'There's *nothing* wrong with me.'

'I know, Mum. You're an example to us all.'

'Always have been,' Stuart said. 'Or so I've been told.'

'People in glass houses . . .' Lucy muttered. 'If you ask *me* . . .'

'Thank you for the words of wisdom, Mum, but we're not asking you.'

'Who *is* that boy?'

Kate glanced over her mother's shoulder and rolled her eyes at Jed, who suddenly, and rather delightfully, followed Gus's example.

Over the course of the next hour, the state of the traffic and the offensive nature of his jacket shared top billing in Lucy's increasingly monotonous string of complaints. Gus took cover beneath his headphones, and Fiona handed Jed one of her earpieces to share. Kate tuned in to Kenny Rogers on Magic FM. When her mother suddenly went silent, she hardly dared breathe, but looked back as the traffic on the

211

M40 cleared and saw that all four of their passengers had fallen asleep.

'Have you told the girl's parents?' Stuart murmured.

'Mother and stepfather. I don't think they're going to miss her. That's where the trouble started.'

'Hmm. Doesn't it always?' He risked a grin as he glanced in the rear-view mirror.

'Julie's going to Belgrade, to try to rescue her younger sister.'

'Is that wise?'

'It's the least we can do. By which I mean the least *I* can do.'

'Not everybody wants to be rescued,' Stuart said, keeping his eyes peeled for the slip road that would herald the final phase of their journey. 'Did you ever think of that?'

Kate's aunt lived with her ex-investment-banker husband in considerable style just beneath the Ridgeway in the Oxford-shire countryside. A pair of wrought-iron gates glided open as they turned off the road and closed again as they made their way along the gravel drive to where Rose and Simon were waiting at the grand entrance of their Georgian mansion.

'Bloody hell,' Stuart said. 'Is it my imagination, or does this place get bigger every time we turn our backs on it?'

After the greetings, Simon showed Kate and Stuart to the folly at the far end of the formal garden, which was done up in the luxury one might expect of the finest country-house hotel, complete with roll-top bath and a fireplace in the bedroom. 'We'll keep an eye on Lucy and the young,' he said, 'but Rose thought you two could probably use some privacy.'

At dinner, Jed was the centre of attention for the first two courses. Much to their distress, Rose and Simon had never had children of their own, and asked him the sort of questions that made Kate embarrassed by her own lack of the right kind of curiosity. He answered with scrupulous politeness and gentle wit. His parents were doctors, his father a GP and his mother a psychiatrist. 'When we got up her nose as kids, she used to hit us with textbooks.'

Stuart winked at Kate, but she was still in no mood to wink back.

Lucy stared at 'that boy' throughout the meal, as if she were about to launch another wave of invective but she held back, perhaps because she'd suddenly remembered her habitual need to cast herself in the role of Fairy Godmother in front of the grandchildren.

Simon and Stuart pitched into an animated discussion about the state of the nation over port and Stilton, then retired to the billiards table. The children went to watch TV, and Rose escorted Lucy to bed. Kate was painfully aware that she had said hardly a word during the evening, and knew her aunt had sensed something was wrong.

When she came down, Rose tore Kate away from the washing-up and made herbal tea for them both. 'What the hell?' She smiled. 'You only live once!'

They settled next door by the fire, a lovely room with low beams, antique panelling and modern Scandinavian fixtures.

'You look tired,' Rose said.

'Looks can be deceptive.' Kate sighed. 'I'm completely and utterly knackered.'

'Work, the children, or both?'

'Both, probably. But I guess my mother deserves a fair amount of the credit.'

'Jed is a nice boy.'

Kate nodded and sipped her tea.

213

'You don't have to tell me anything if you don't want to,' Rose said.

'It's more a question of where I should start.' Kate gazed into the fire. For a moment, she thought of telling Rose about the condom wrapper in her pocket and the suspicion that was tearing her apart, but she couldn't bring herself to articulate it. 'Don't *you* feel tired sometimes?'

'I'm not in the front line in the way you are.'

'I suppose it depends how you define the front line. I could put it down to losing someone this week, a young girl who deserved an awful lot better, and knowing beyond a shadow of a doubt that it was my fault. I could also claim it's because we're all overworked and underpaid. I might even blame it on the fact that, like every middle-aged woman, I find trying to be a mother and a wife at the same time as a warrior for truth is not as easy as we all feel the need to make it look. But I'd be able to live with that if I didn't feel we're being overwhelmed by an incoming tide that we're completely powerless to hold back.'

'I suspect that every generation has to grapple with its own version of that.'

'But in the old days, it seemed like a fair match, didn't it? We faced off against the KGB. The two intelligence services, each at the heart of their respective establishments, locked in combat, with a succession of victories and defeats. As long as we could spot their feints and sleights of hand, we could go home reasonably secure in the knowledge that our world – the safe, civilized, *free* West – would continue along its relatively well-maintained tram tracks. It isn't like that any more. They go behind us and around us and beyond us to the people and the country at large, whipping up hostility and division and dissent, their tentacles reaching down a thousand different alleyways. I don't know which front we should be most energetically defending now. And the only thing I can say for sure is that it's a battle we're losing. It's not just that they come over here and murder people right under our noses, but they get a distressingly large number of people to believe it's all a conspiracy by the *British* government. It's bloody surreal at times.'

'But that makes what we do more important than ever, doesn't it? Which at least gives our work a sense of urgency and purpose.'

'That's what I keep telling myself.' Kate looked up. 'While we're on the subject of urgency and purpose, can I ask you something about work?'

'Of course,' Rose said, but her smile was suddenly devoid of its usual warmth.

'Who decides to put a red flag on a file?'

'The management committee.' The flames danced in her eyes. 'As you well know.'

'Sorry. And, yes, I do know.' She paused. 'I was looking into something last week. I mentioned it to Jane.'

'Oh?'

Kate frowned. Rose's expression remained opaque. But it was impossible that she didn't know. 'I was asking about someone I had to assess for recruitment a long time ago.'

'And you tried Registry?'

'Yes, I did. And the file on her was closed. I tried to use Finance to reverse-engineer an enquiry, as you once taught me. I was pursuing something else today, and that led to a dead end too, with another big red flag.'

'It happens.'

'Rarely, though. At least, I thought that was the theory. And the odd thing is, I know of no connection between those two files. So why would they both be closed? It's a bit of a coincidence, isn't it?'

Rose shrugged.

'It *had* to be by order of the management committee? There's no other way?'

'Yes. And no.'

'But you're on the management committee.'

'Not present at every meeting.'

'One of the red flags was signed by you.'

Kate had rarely witnessed the flint at Rose's core, but did so now. A reminder, perhaps, if one were needed, that you didn't get to the top of the Service without it.

Rose leant forward to throw another log onto the fire.

'You're not going to help me, are you?' Kate said.

'Of course I'm going to help. But I won't put either of us in a position we might both regret.' She turned. 'I look upon you as a daughter, you know that. And I feel a tiny bit responsible for luring you into the Service. But for those endless conversations on the way to Cornwall, you might have been safely installed at Goldman Sachs by now, earning a king's ransom.'

'Not really my style.'

'Your father always held me responsible, and he was right. So, I will *always* do my best to help you. But there's a handful of things that are more important than family, and this is one of them.'

'Is that a piece of advice?'

'Possibly.'

'To do what?'

'Tread carefully.'

'What's the connection between the two closed files?'

'That's not treading carefully.'

There was a long silence as Rose appeared to weigh up how much she should say. 'Ian,' she said eventually. 'He's the connection. But he dragged in Alan. And Alan is unlikely to forgive him for that.'

Despite the fatigue and the alcohol, Kate's brain was turning faster now. 'So that's what they meant when they talked about "another" attempt at disinformation. Ian brought in Irina, but kept her to himself. And she sold us a pup.'

'Correct.'

'What breed of pup?'

'We paid Irina a lot of money over quite a number of years. She was Ian's prized asset and he dined out on her. She seemed to be a never-ending source of quality material. And some of it was undeniably true. You know how clever the Russians are. They hooked us with lots of sprats so that we'd swallow the mackerel whole.'

'The mackerel?'

'Sorry. We're getting a bit zoological here, aren't we? The mackerel was cast-iron intelligence that the German treasury minister was a paedophile who had been caught and turned by the Russians. We had everything – internet history, emails, phone records, videos of him with a series of under-age boys . . . Hideous, of course. We went over and over it. It was totally convincing. Everything checked out.'

'Except it was all fake.'

'Every single bit of it.'

'And we'd already handed it over.'

'Worse than that. The foreign secretary had used it as leverage. So it blew up in his face in the most embarrassing way imaginable. It was a miracle no one on the German side leaked it to their press.'

The fire crackled, and sent up a small shower of sparks. 'If

217

that was Ian's operation – if he owned it from first to last – why didn't it ruin him?'

'The second closed file gives you your answer. But I can see you no longer need it.'

'He'd been digging around in the foreign secretary's African business interests. And there was plenty there.'

'They say knowledge is power,' Rose said. 'But sometimes it's a burden, too.'

'Why is your name on the file closure?'

'I think Alan's a good man. I always have. He's been loyal to me, and I have to him. He was taken in by this when he shouldn't have been. Shutting down the Africa investigation was the price of keeping him in his job, and I thought it was worth paying. But everyone knew he was a school friend of the foreign secretary, so his name on the closure would have made him a hostage to fortune.'

'What about Ian?'

'We had no choice but to leave him where he was. He knew too much.'

'Did the Africa file trace the source of the foreign secretary's cash?'

'Not to my knowledge. Mugabe or his cronies, I assume.'

'The other day you told me Sir Alan seemed preoccupied with something. Do you know what?'

'No. He's been more than usually secretive.'

'There's something he might not want to share with you, under the circumstances,' Kate said. 'A week ago we received intelligence that suggested one of the leading candidates to replace the prime minister is working for the Russians.'

'In what capacity?'

'We don't know the what, why or how.'

'What about the who?'

'It's very likely to be the foreign secretary.'

Rose nodded, as if it made complete sense.

'The same source suggested there's a mole, probably inside Vauxhall Cross, which would explain why we lost the girl. The op appears to have been compromised from the word go.'

'So you're on a mole-hunt.'

'Yes.'

'How close do you think you are?'

'It's a small pool. Half a dozen people knew enough to put the Russians where they were at the time they were there: me, my two assistants, Danny from Ops, Ian and Sir Alan.'

'This story doesn't have a happy ending, Kate.'

20

'IS THERE ANY way I can help?'

'No. You've given me too much already.'

Rose got up and kissed her. 'As I said, you're the daughter I never had. But now you need to go to bed.' She took the empty mug from Kate's hand. 'You need to rest and recharge. Simon and I will look after the children and your mother in the morning. Why don't you and Stuart take that fabulous walk along the Ridgeway, have lunch at the White Horse? I'll send Simon to pick you up afterwards.'

'Rose . . .'

She stopped at the door. 'Yes, my love?'

'Do you ever think you can have too much knowledge?'

'In our business?' She pursed her lips. 'Not if you want to win. And you've always been very competitive. In what we laughingly call real life? Perhaps.'

Kate hadn't meant in their business, of course, but she didn't correct her aunt.

She almost collided with Jed as he emerged from the ground-floor loo. 'I'm so sorry, Mrs Henderson.'

'Night, Jed.' She headed for the door into the formal garden.

'Er, Mrs Henderson . . .'

She stopped and turned.

'I know you don't think much of me, although you were very nice about my jacket, but the thing is, I *really* like your daughter. I get that you're worried about the age issue, but I . . . I care for her. A lot.'

'I can see that, Jed. And I'm sorry if I appear unwelcoming. I have a lot on my plate right now so please don't take it personally.' She felt herself smile at him in a way she hadn't managed with anyone recently. 'Goodnight.'

The tension seeped from her shoulders as she walked through the garden. The perfectly sculpted box hedge brushed her leg and she ran a hand through an ornamental rosemary bush, snapped off a sprig, rubbed it between her fingers and raised them to her nose. The night was still but for the sound of the breeze in the treetops and the distant hum of traffic. An owl hooted as Kate gazed up at the constellations above her. She glanced about her. All was still.

She meant to wait up for Stuart, but her eyelids grew so heavy once she'd burrowed beneath the duvet that she couldn't stave off sleep a moment longer. She woke to find Stuart leaning over her with a bone china cup of tea. 'Role reversal,' he said. 'I've been given strict instructions from Rose.'

He drew back the curtains and let in the bright morning sunlight. Kate sat up and sipped her Earl Grey. The four-poster bed afforded a magnificent view of the rolling hills beyond the garden's ancient stone walls, and of the blue sky above them.

'Apparently, we're embarking upon a major expedition to the White Horse, and leaving the children to your mother's tender mercies.'

'Rose said she and Simon would look after them all.'

Stuart threw himself onto the bed. 'Well, I couldn't think of a better idea if my life depended on it. Let's get going. It's a beautiful day.'

'What time did you turn in?'

'Late.' He hauled himself up again and went to the bathroom. 'Simon's Lagavulin is invariably a mistake, so I'm going to have to blast up that hill to eradicate the traces.' He turned on the shower. 'You must have slept well. You were snoring when I came in.'

'I was *not!*'

His grin appeared around the door. 'You most certainly were.'

She showered while he dressed, and then they had a huge family breakfast. Afterwards the two of them set off, feeling only moderately guilty. The children had been more than happy to be left behind. Gus and Fiona viewed a long country walk as the least amusing of all adult tricks, and Jed was not about to contradict them.

The merest hint of cloud brushed across the sun as they climbed towards the horizon, but the sky was clear again as they drew closer to the ridge, and the green fields below them were luxuriant in the sunlight. 'On a day like this,' Stuart said, 'there's not a shadow of a doubt that Jerusalem was builded here . . .'

'Hmm,' Kate said. 'Pity about "those dark satanic mills".' Her nose was running, so she reached into the pocket of her jeans and almost took out the condom packet wrapped in its sheet of kitchen roll.

It burnt a hole in her pocket and her mind for the rest of the climb.

Stuart's phone *ping*ed and he fished it out of his Barbour.

'You need to switch it off,' she said.

'Controversial.' He smiled at her. 'But all right.'

'So?'

'So what?' he asked.

'What was the text about?'

'Ah – now who's breaking her own rule?'

'What's happening?'

'Imogen is on a media round tomorrow morning. She's going to announce that she plans to review Trident and redirect all savings entirely to the Education budget.'

'Bloody hell. Does she mean to ditch Trident?'

'Not immediately, but that might be the outcome. She wants a nuclear deterrent, just doesn't think it has to be Trident in this day and age. On Monday she'll share a stage with three retired admirals, two generals and an air chief marshal who will all say they think she's right.'

'The press and the party will go crazy.'

'Some of the press, perhaps. The party? I'm not so sure. The idea is for a new kind of leader with new priorities and ideas for a new generation. If she looks and sounds like the future, she may well swing it.'

Kate walked on in silence. It was a bold play. She wondered what the Russians would make of it.

'You've been a bit odd this week,' Stuart said, from behind her.

'Have I?'

'You know you have.'

'I'm sorry.'

'About Imogen, I mean.' He took her arm and swung her around. 'What *is* eating you?'

'Nothing.'

'Come on, Kate. Tell me. I can't stand tiptoeing around in no man's land.'

'I just wonder if you're having an affair.'

'For God's sake . . .'

'What on earth were you doing, calling her at three in the morning?'

He gaped at her, dumbfounded. 'You're spying on *me*?'

'The Russians have someone inside our organization, for fuck's sake. Or close to one of the candidates. We had to pull your phone records along with everyone else's.'

'What do you mean?'

'A spy, a sleeper, a mole.'

'How do you know?'

'The same way we know about our foreign secretary possibly being one of theirs.'

'And you thought it was me?'

'Of course I didn't. But my team couldn't exclude you or me from the search. They'd get carpeted and sacked if it ever came to light. They pulled everyone's logs. Yours show just how much you call her. Which is fine. But I've found it difficult to explain why you might have needed to speak to her in the middle of the night.'

'That's difficult to explain, is it?'

She shook herself free. 'Of course it bloody is.'

'Even though you regularly call your team at all hours?'

'That's different.'

'Why? Because your job is more important than mine?'

'It's *different*. I was away in Greece. You were on your own with the children. You called her at three in the morning, and half an hour later, her phone was located inside our home.'

'So I must have been fucking her?'

'Were you?'

'I am not going to dignify that with an answer.'

'Don't lie to me, Stuart.'

'Jesus, Kate . . .'

She retrieved the kitchen towel, shook out the condom wrapper and handed it him. 'So explain this, why don't you.'

Stuart took the gold wrapper as if it were about to burst into flames. He stared at it for a moment. 'You're right. I did put this in the dog-food can and shove it in the bin.' He looked at her, his gaze cold as ice. 'And that is because I found it under the sitting-room sofa. Why was it there? Not because I can't wait to hump my boss the moment your back is turned but because that was where your new best friend Jed left it.

'I confronted Fiona. She admitted she'd lost her virginity to him while I was upstairs in our bedroom watching television. She begged me not to tell you. Begged me. I didn't promise not to – after the last lecture you gave me – but reckoned I'd wait for a better moment, given everything you have on your mind. And, yes, I echoed every point you apparently made to her the other day, including the legal definition of statutory rape.

'So let's move on to the phone records – not that I should have to answer your stupid questions. Someone in our department got himself arrested in Scotland for allegedly downloading child pornography. We were shitting ourselves about the news leaking first thing in the morning. You were away. She texted me. I called back. Of course, if I was shagging her, I wouldn't have *had* to call back, would I? I'd have been right there on the kitchen table with her. But that clearly never occurred to our local neighbourhood super-spy. She came over, we talked it through, she went away again. *End of.'*

Stuart was shaking with rage. Kate reached for his arm and only succeeded in tugging at his sleeve as he stepped further away.

'All right,' she said. 'I'm sorry . . . really sorry. I've been under a lot of pressure.'

'Fuck your pressure, Kate. Fuck your job. And fuck you.'

He stormed on up the hill and she let him go. He was a big, strong, athletic man and he could move at quite a pace when he wanted to. For half an hour or so, he charged ahead and she struggled to keep within fifty metres of him. When he eventually slowed, she closed in on him and this time wrapped her arm around his. 'I'm truly sorry,' she said.

He turned to her.

'Truly.' She saw his features soften, and dared to hope that the worst of his fury had blown through. 'I'm not going to try to excuse myself,' she said. 'Except to say that my love for you has always been a kind of madness.'

'It's incredibly hurtful, Kate.'

'Of course it is. But it's not really about you. After what my mother did, I find it difficult to trust anyone. You know that.'

'Honestly – screw your mother. Jesus, seriously, let's do her in and bury her here, under the Ridgeway, and then we can move on. I'm well up for it. I don't want to live with someone who doesn't trust me to be as good as my word. It's totally debilitating, and just a bit fucking depressing . . .'

'I know, I know.' She drew him closer and kissed him.

He gripped both her arms, took half a pace back and looked into her eyes. 'I need you to be in no doubt that I would *never* betray you.' His voice cracked. 'I never have. Never even wanted to.' He smiled at her sadly. The skin around those big blue eyes crinkled in a way she had always found almost impossible to resist. 'Even though you're emotionally autistic, frequently remote and preoccupied, you're still the one.'

'A ringing endorsement. Lucky me!'

'We love who we love. Sometimes, as you say, it's beyond reason.' He kissed her this time, the palm of his hand gently cupping the back of her head. 'On the plus side,' he said, 'you're still unbelievably sexy and have a great sense of humour.'

They held hands along the ridge, and her footsteps were lighter than they had been in a while. Until her thoughts returned to the condom wrapper.

'I suppose I should talk to Fiona,' Kate said.

'I suppose you shouldn't. I've already said everything that needs to be said, and issued every warning that needs to be issued. Besides, we've had enough tension in the house, so just leave it.'

'I'm her mother.'

'True. And I'm her father. And parenthood, as I recall, is a shared responsibility. Even though we both know "literally nothing".' He let go of her hand, but only long enough to mime a pair of quotation marks in the brisk autumn air.

Later they walked arm in arm to the folly, peeled off their hiking gear and sat in front of the fire, which one of their hosts had lit. Still later they lay together in the roll-top bath and then Kate sat naked in the deep armchair by the fire, the relief still washing through her like a drug. Stuart caressed her with the languid ease that only long experience can muster. He massaged her feet, then ran his fingertips over her knees and the inside of her thighs, and brushed his lips across her stomach.

She rested her hands on the back of his head as his tongue darted ever lower, and arched her back, losing herself in the sheer, exhilarating pleasure of the moment in a way she would not have imagined possible only a few hours ago.

They lay in each other's arms, by the fire, occasionally glancing up at the hands of the mantelpiece clock, willing it not to march them too briskly to reality. Eventually Kate raised herself on an elbow and kissed him. 'Let's get dressed and head over for supper before people begin to wonder what we're up to.'

She had a quick shower and was humming as she got dressed. As they strolled through the garden to the main house, she stopped for a moment by the rosemary bush. She picked another sprig and raised it to his nose. 'Rosemary,' she whispered. 'For remembrance . . .'

When they arrived in the kitchen Rose was frying slivers of foie gras, as Simon eased the cork out of a bottle of chilled Muscadet. 'Ah, the young lovers,' he said easily. 'Time for something restorative, I fancy.' He poured the wine and handed Kate a glass.

'And why not indeed?' She could hear the children joshing with their grandmother in the sitting room over the burble of the radio. Even Lucy seemed caught up in the magic of the occasion.

Rose turned as Simon held out her glass, but her expression was a mixture of curiosity and alarm. 'Oh, bloody hell,' she said.

'What?'

'Imogen.' She motioned Stuart in the direction of the radio.

Puzzled, he reached across and turned up the volume.

'The Westminster Confidential website has published a tape of the minister for Education having sex with one of her aides, which appears to have been filmed in a hotel during a government-sponsored visit to the Russian capital.'

21

KATE PUT DOWN her glass, swung around and rushed out into the garden. Stuart trailed her as she sprinted across the grass and into the folly. He was beside her as she opened her laptop on their bed, firing the same question at her, again and again: *'What the hell are you doing?'*

It took her seconds to find the site and the tape. She hit play and they were suddenly watching graphic images of flesh against flesh. They froze, unable to tear their eyes from the screen.

The quality of the footage was incredible, the action as explicit as any porn film. Imogen straddled a man, whose face was out of frame, her head tipped back as she panted and writhed, her small breasts bobbing. She giggled as, eventually, she raised a shapely knee and eased herself off her lover.

The camera tracked up his glistening torso and Kate finally saw his face.

It wasn't Stuart.

It was Andy or Connor or Gregor – or somebody else entirely.

'Would you like to turn it off now and tell me what the bloody hell is going on?' Stuart's tone was icy again.

Kate closed the screen. She breathed in deeply and gave herself a moment. 'The Russians must have leaked it.'

'What do you mean?' He looked horrified.

'They want Imogen out of the race. Who is he?'

'Andy Mac.'

'Did you know they were an item?'

'Suspected. Not knew. They were pretty discreet. But, honestly, I only care how you and I behave. I don't want to be the world's moral policeman.'

'Was Andy on that now legendary Russian trip?'

'As far as I remember, yes.'

'And they were fucking each other back then?'

'No idea.' Stuart was shaking his head. 'You thought it was me,' he said.

'No.'

'That was why you dashed across here, like a scalded cat. Even after everything we've said and done today, you still thought it was me.'

'I know what the Russians are trying to do. I think about it almost every waking moment, and most sleeping ones, too. The last few hours have been the most wonderful escape from that reality – but this just took me back with a bang.'

'For a spy, you're a shit liar. And for the record, the children and I are going to need a bit more than a few hours away from that reality.' Stuart grasped her arm and gripped it tight. 'That's it, Kate. That's the last time you doubt me. Understood?'

She nodded.

The door banged shut behind him.

Kate sat on the bed, shaking. Her phone pinged. A message from Rav: *Have you seen it?*

She WhatsApped back: *Hard to miss.*

It would be quite a turn-on if I was straight.

Then: *In fact, it's still a turn-on – she has a hell of a body and so has her stud.*

Inappropriate, Kate replied.

She lay back and stared at the gathered silk canopy of the four-poster, relief still flooding through her. Stuart annoyed she could handle, Stuart angry, even. But Stuart a liar would have killed her.

The phone sounded. 'I can't speak, Rav,' she said.

'My sources tell me she hasn't been shagging him for a while, so they've sat on this for years.'

'Have we got a trace?'

'GCHQ don't hold out much hope. It'll have arrived on a USB stick, in the post.'

'I'm here with my family, Rav. I have to go.'

'It puts her out of contention, wouldn't you agree?'

'Yes.'

'There's something else. More on Ryan's little business venture. Guess where it was incorporated?'

'British Virgin Islands?' Kate sighed. 'Belize?'

'Belize. Via a Panamanian law firm. But here's the interesting bit: GCHQ have pinned François Binot as the intermediary.'

'Christ.'

'Yup.'

Binot was a legendary Swiss lawyer who'd once worked for the International Criminal Court in The Hague, helping to compile cases against Ratko Mladić and the other butchers of

Bosnia. But in the early 2000s he appeared to have switched course to represent, or at least assist, some of those he'd previously been investigating. He had quickly acquired a reputation for taking on tasks and individuals others would not contemplate and before long had found his way into the orbit of the Russian president. It was Binot who had set up the offshore companies that stored the wealth of the Russian president's closest associates. He was the president's bagman. 'How the hell would James Ryan have come across him?'

'Kosovo. Ryan served there, and the last work Binot did in The Hague was on those accused of war crimes in Kosovo. I can't prove a connection, but I'd bet you any money they met there.'

'I have to go,' Kate said. 'Let's talk in the morning.'

'I want to get on a plane to Zürich first thing, to try to get in front of Binot. Will you authorize?'

'No, Rav, I won't. I want a proper risk assessment and I'd also like a discussion about what getting in front of him is likely to achieve. Apart from alerting everyone involved as to how much we know.'

'I'll go anyway.'

'No! Stay right where you are. We'll talk about it in the morning.' She waited, but he didn't hang up. 'I'm sorry about yesterday,' she said.

He didn't reply.

'If it had been infidelity, I wouldn't have told you, but I thought you needed to know.'

'But don't you see, Kate? It *is* infidelity. Worse, even. It makes a mockery of everything we've been through together.'

'Have you spoken to him?'

'No. And I'm not going to.'

'Rav, I really think—'

'It's none of your fucking business, Kate. It wasn't your job to tell me, and I asked you not to. I don't want a lecture, and I don't want to talk about it again.'

Rav cut the call and she put her face into her hands. So much for a break from reality.

Perhaps inevitably dinner became a low-key affair. They paid the price for Lucy's earlier good humour, and Rose put her to bed early. Simon kept the conversation ticking over, mostly talking to the three kids about their lives, plans and hopes.

Fiona was particularly forthcoming, announcing that she now wanted to be a doctor, despite having little previous aptitude for or interest in science. Since the source of this newly discovered passion was obvious enough, neither Stuart nor Kate sought to puncture her balloon. Only Jed felt obliged to share the profession's drawbacks, based on his experience of his parents' lives.

Kate wondered whether her daughter's sudden volubility had something to do with the tension in the air between her and Stuart. She could tell that Rose knew something was wrong too, but she didn't want to talk about it tonight, so turned in straight after they'd finished eating. She heard Stuart come to bed hours later, reeking of whisky, and found herself thinking how strange it was that you could sense your husband's wakefulness in the dark, yet not be certain of his fidelity. She felt ashamed for doubting him.

The journey back to London began in silence, but Kate knew she could rely on her mother to make matters worse. It was just a question of when.

'Rose says you don't look after me properly,' she said.

Kate continued to stare out of the window.

'She says you don't come to see me enough.'

'She actually said she was worried that Kate was working too hard,' Stuart said, 'which is not quite the same thing.'

'Your father would be ashamed of you.'

Kate let that go, too. Her mother was like a spiteful child, who would go on prodding until she got a reaction.

'He always said you were selfish.'

Stuart kept his attention fixed on the road ahead. 'That quarry a few miles back would be a good place to hide a body.'

Kate glanced over her shoulder. Gus was sitting next to Lucy again, with his headphones in. Fiona and Jed were in the row behind, their heads together as they watched something on his phone. 'I said I wanted you to do the time,' she told him, 'but, actually, I wouldn't mind doing it myself.'

Stuart smiled and reached for her hand. They locked fingers.

'I'm so sorry,' Kate said.

'You're an idiot,' Stuart replied, 'but, thankfully, you're my idiot.'

Kate found Magic again, to discourage her mother from offering further contributions.

'Who do you think leaked the footage?' Stuart asked.

'No prizes for guessing that one.'

'How?'

'In a manner we won't be able to trace. The simplest way, probably. Put it into an envelope and sent it to the website, which is unscrupulous enough to have run it without any checks.'

'You think it could be fake?'

'No. They've used fake videos to devastating effect in the past, but you can always tell it's real when the quality is so good. The Russians like to shoot their porn in high definition.' She paused. 'How is she?'

'Devastated, needless to say. Harry has taken the kids and gone to his mother's. Would you mind popping round to see her tonight?'

'Will that help?'

'I don't think she should be alone. And I suspect she'd rather have a woman to talk to. Also, I've persuaded her not to pull out, and I think a word or two from you would help. If that wouldn't be above and beyond the call of duty.'

'I'm afraid it's now her duty to go on running. And to win, though I doubt she has any idea what she's really up against.'

'That's what I said you'd think. But she needs to hear it from the horse's mouth.'

Kate looked at him. 'I'm sorry, darling, I really am.'

'I know you are. But it's water under the bridge. Just don't bloody do it again. You are not your mother and I am not my father. And that's all there is to say.'

In the early evening Kate went round to Imogen's. There was a sizeable media pack outside the front door, so at first she kept her distance and messaged her. Together they devised an alternative route through the side entrance of a neighbour's garden and over the dividing wall.

'In other circumstances,' Imogen said, 'I'd find this funny.'

Moments later, Kate was inside the house and Imogen made her a cup of tea. They sat at the kitchen table. 'I know I shouldn't say this,' Imogen said, 'since, in a very literal sense, I made my bed and now have to lie in it. But I feel almost as if I've been raped.'

'That's a pretty understandable response.'

'It's bloody out there for ever now, and I have no desire to show my face in public again. I mean, what happens if my parents see it?'

'No one you care about is ever going to set eyes on it.'

'The internet is today's version of the Wild West. All the newspaper websites are running the video with the bits helpfully pixellated, while giving every reader a shortcut to the unredacted version. I mean, some porn videos are less explicit.'

'On the plus side, thank God you have such a great body.'

Imogen looked at her, clearly aghast. And, for one terrible second, Kate thought she had misjudged the moment. But then Imogen burst out laughing. And started to cry.

Kate touched her shoulder. 'I'm sorry, that was a terrible joke.'

'No, it was a good one. And if I lose sight of the funny side of this nightmare, I'll go upstairs and blow my brains out.'

Kate was tempted to give her a hug, but it wasn't her style, so she waited patiently for Imogen to gather herself.

Imogen wiped the tears defiantly from her cheek. 'Christ, what a mess,' she said.

'I hardly dare ask about Harry.'

'He walked out with the children, saying he'd see me in court. Under the circumstances, I didn't feel there was much I could do to stop him.'

'I imagine he'll be feeling pretty humiliated, apart from anything else. But we have to believe that doesn't necessarily have to be permanent, don't we?' Kate sipped her tea awkwardly, marvelling at her own hypocrisy. 'Do you mind me asking you when and where it was filmed?'

'I don't know.'

'How long did you . . . ?'

'On and off for a while.' She snorted with laughter. 'No pun intended. We did a lot of foreign trips together.'

'Were you with him at the time of your Moscow trip?'

Imogen frowned. 'Fuck knows. No, I don't think so. I'm not sure it had started by then. But . . .' she looked intensely sheepish '. . . unfortunately, I have to admit it could have been recorded in quite a number of places. I just don't remember that particular hotel.'

'Hmm. They didn't focus much on the décor, did they? There's no doubt it's you?'

'Afraid not. It's me, all right. I'd recognize those tits anywhere. I've hated them my entire life.'

'I have no doubt whatsoever that plenty of us are currently green with envy.'

Imogen smiled again. 'So, who was holding the camera?'

'Your previous hosts.'

'How can you be so sure?'

'They had the means, the method and the motive. They were on home turf. And they do it all the time.'

'What motive?'

Kate stared at the table. Tread carefully, she told herself. 'I think they'd rather James won this particular race.'

'For the leadership?'

'Yes.'

'Why?'

'They think he'd be more likely to align himself with their interests. And they've already demonstrated countless times that when they make that judgement they're not afraid to try to affect the outcome.'

'But neither of us has talked much about Russia in recent years, have we?'

'You have in the past.'

'Years ago.'

'They have long memories.'

'And that's it? They did all this because of something I said years ago?'

'I think so, yes. And that's one of the many reasons you shouldn't step down from the leadership contest.'

'I can't carry on with it, Kate.' She leant back, spread her hands. 'I just can't. I'm going to have the battle of my life trying to keep my family together. Harry isn't the world's most forgiving man, and he was only half supportive of my ambition in the first place. If I go on, I'll lose any slim chance I have of winning him back.'

'You *have* to stay in the race, Imogen.'

'Why?'

'Because it's important for the country. I'd even go as far as to say it's your duty.'

'What *aren't* you telling me?' Imogen gave her the full benefit of her unblinking almond-shaped emerald-green eyes. 'Come on, Kate, I'm at my lowest ebb here. You owe me the truth.'

'I can't.'

'Or won't?'

'Either. It doesn't matter which.'

'So you want me to throw away my husband and children but you won't tell me why?'

Kate took a couple of deep breaths. 'We think your opponent might be a Russian spy.'

'Fucking hell.' Imogen just stared at her. 'What does that mean?'

'I'm not totally convinced he has an ideological bone in his finely hewn body, so it would mean he's been coerced or bribed into working for them.'

'Are you *sure*?'

239

'No, not yet. But I'm confident enough to break every rule here and tell you why you can't come out with a white flag. And I'll do my absolute best to help you.'

Imogen put her head in her hands. 'Jesus,' she said. 'What is the world coming to?'

'In a way, you should take it as a compliment. The Russians try to acquire compromising material on everyone of influence. The fact that they had something on you confirms their perception of your significance even back then. And choosing not to try to coerce you indicates that they don't believe you would bend. So they kept it up their sleeve to discredit you, if need be.'

'Diabolical,' Imogen said.

'Dirty and immoral. They always have been. Unfortunately, they're also *very* effective.'

'I'll have to think about it. I'm still . . . I just don't know if I can.'

'I'm not going to sugar-coat it. You don't have a choice.'

Imogen looked at her. 'You're a tough woman, Kate.'

'Not always a compliment.'

'From a man to a woman, it wouldn't be. But from a woman, it is. Especially a woman like me.'

'Why *especially* a woman like you?'

'Politics is a dirty word for some people, I know. Even you, perhaps, when you're in the privacy of your own home. It's also a lonely business. And the higher you climb, the lonelier it gets. I'm not completely sure I want it that badly.'

'You once told me that, though it was a terrible cliché, you really did come into politics to make a difference to people's lives.'

'I'd never say that in public – everyone would die laughing.'

'Perhaps. But isn't it also true that the higher you climb, the more difference you can make?'

'Most people don't believe politicians are capable of altruism.'

'Maybe they don't, but I'm not most people. Any more than you are. I work in a world where the threat to us is rawest. And it's very, very real. If people like you and I don't stand up and face it, there's no telling where this story might end.'

'I'll do it if you agree to work for me.'

'That's a discussion for another time.'

'Do we have a deal?'

'I assume you'll take Stuart with you to Downing Street, and . . . look . . . I'd like to count myself as your friend. I will help. I promise you that much.'

Raised voices in the street made Imogen glance towards the front door. 'I'll think about it. I'm ambitious and I do want to make a difference – though there are probably more egotistical and less attractive motives in there as well. But I don't yet know if I want it enough to risk losing my family. Would you?'

'That,' Kate said, 'is a very good question.'

She waited. She'd done as much as she could. There was just one more question she needed to ask. 'Imogen, I'm not sure how best to ask this but . . . is there anything else?'

'Do you mean any*one* else?'

'Both, I'm afraid. Anything financial? Any other . . . affairs?'

'Affairs. Such an odd word, isn't it?' Imogen shook her head. 'No. Even for me, one really bad sin is enough.'

'So there's nothing else that could bite you on the bum?'

'Nothing I can think of.'

'No other . . .'

Imogen's brow furrowed. 'I'm not a scarlet woman, Kate. I made a mistake. Harry and I haven't had the most active of love lives these past few years, and I sought solace elsewhere. I'm ashamed of it. And now I'm paying the price.'

Kate raised her palms. 'I'm not prying. I just need to know what might be coming down the track.'

But, of course, that wasn't the whole truth. Kate walked home with a spring in her step, feeling foolish and relieved in almost equal measure.

22

WHEN KATE ARRIVED at the office shortly after dawn, Julie was already there.

'How was Belgrade?' Kate asked.

'Complicated and inconclusive. I'll explain when we have more time. Have you seen this?'

'Seen what?'

Julie pointed at her screen. 'It's just dropped on the *Guardian*'s website.' The gist of the story was instantly clear from the headline. *MI6 Investigates Foreign Secretary over Links to Russian Intelligence.*

'Fuck,' Kate said.

'C's asked you to go up.'

'Where's Rav?'

'He's in Switzerland.'

'Doing what?' Kate asked, though she knew well enough. He had gone to see the Swiss lawyer, Binot, the insubordinate bastard.

Julie looked confused. 'He said he'd told you about it.'

'Tell him to get on a plane back, and I mean yesterday. That's an order. And if he ignores it, I'll ensure he's fired before the day's out.'

Kate strode into her office, slammed the door and called Imogen's mobile. She answered almost immediately.

'Have you seen the *Guardian* website?'

'Yes. Christ, I—'

'Please tell me you're not responsible.'

'Of course I'm bloody not!'

'Imogen, it's going to save a lot of time and trouble if you're straight with me. I simply cannot afford to—'

'I haven't told a soul. I swear it. I mean, I wouldn't, of course. But I've also barely spoken to anyone since you left. My only incoming call was from my mother, and I can assure you this wasn't at the top of her list of priorities.'

'Okay. Listen. I shouldn't have told you. I'm now going to have to lie about it to my superiors, which makes me feel deeply uncomfortable. And if anyone knew I *had* told you, I'd be out.'

'I may have my idiotic moments, Kate, but I'm not a complete fool. I won't tell anyone. You have my word on it.'

'Are you going to stay in the contest?'

'The first ballot is tonight, so I have only the next hour or two to make up my mind. But I think I have to, don't I? Meg is a good woman, so she might beat him anyway—'

'She doesn't have a chance. You have to stay in. Look, I've got to go. Good luck.'

Kate placed her forehead against the cool metal interior as she rode the lift up to C's floor. She found him standing by the window in his office, but from the set of his shoulders, the view over the Thames was not uppermost in his mind. Ian was already seated, ready for her arrival.

244

'Close the door, please,' C said, keeping his back to them. 'And sit down.'

She pulled up an armchair next to Ian. Sir Alan still didn't turn, maintaining his distance from the pair of them. 'Kate, I'm going to ask you the question I've just put to Ian.'

He swivelled on his heel and his eyes bored into hers, like lasers. 'Did you tell *anyone* outside this building that we were investigating the foreign secretary's links with Russia?'

'No,' she said.

'Not your husband?'

'He knew about my trips to Istanbul and Athens, but he couldn't possibly have connected any of that with the foreign secretary.'

'Is it not the case that your husband works with Imogen Conrad, and that she is a family friend?'

'It is.'

'And that Mrs Conrad is the principal beneficiary of this leak, in both its nature and its timing?'

'I think she may pull out anyway, so I'm not sure that's right.'

'Have you seen her since the sex tape was released?'

'Yes. I went round there last night. She was in a very poor state.'

'And you didn't mention, even in passing, that we're investigating her principal opponent, as incredibly useful as that intelligence would have been?'

'No,' Kate said more tersely. 'I did not.'

'Very well,' he said at length. 'Ian has given me a similar assurance. And I'm right in thinking that the details of what you recorded in Istanbul are restricted to the occupants of this room, plus Rav, Julie, Maddy and Danny?'

She waited for him to continue.

'That is not a rhetorical question.'

245

'That's correct,' she said. 'But Maddy wouldn't have known enough to leak.'

'And the surveillance teams?'

'They'd have been aware of some details about the yacht and possibly about Lena, but no one outside the core group knew of the contents of that recording.'

'What about the people you've spoken to in the course of your investigation?' Ian asked. 'We're going to need a list.'

'Of course,' Kate said. 'But I've conducted or been present at all the interviews to date and, while it was clear in each case that we were asking about the foreign secretary, we gave no hint of the central allegation – and no one could realistically have drawn that inference from any of our questions. We were, of course, punctilious.' Kate thought about Rav in Switzerland. She had no idea whom he'd spoken to there as he closed in on François Binot and his relationship with the foreign secretary, or what he might have said. Another lie she could snare herself with.

'That will have to do, for the time being,' Sir Alan said. 'The foreign secretary wants to see all of us, right now. I then have to see the PM and our colleagues across the river to explain why, if this story is correct, we haven't called them to look into the matter, as we're obliged to do.'

C retrieved his raincoat and homburg from his hat-stand and led them down into the street as commuters continued to pour out of Vauxhall station. Kate was acutely aware of several surprised glances from junior employees among the throng before they turned east against the wind and headed towards Lambeth Bridge.

C liked to walk around London. He made a point of it. And he walked fast. Kate had almost to run to keep up.

'We're going to need to buy some time,' he said, to no one in particular. 'Don't you think?'

'Yes,' Ian said.

'Any ideas?'

'You know what I think. We're being played. Why don't we just say so?'

C didn't respond. Apparently deep in thought, he didn't speak again until they were in the foreign secretary's palatial office overlooking Horse Guards. Very nearly the size of a tennis court, with leather-bound books and red sofas, it boasted the airy grandeur of the empire builders who had once sat behind its enormous desk. The foreign secretary rose from his seat and strode towards them.

'Old friend,' he said, offering Sir Alan his hand. 'Ian, yes, we've met.'

'And this is Kate Henderson from our Russia Desk,' C said.

James Ryan shook her hand. 'The woman at the heart of the action! Very pleased to meet you.' He appeared entirely unfazed by the morning's controversy. 'Have a seat.' He ushered them towards the red leather sofas in the centre of the room and ordered coffee. 'Well, this is a rum business, and no mistake. And all from my old mate.'

'I'm sorry, James,' Sir Alan said. 'We're not going to pretend the *Guardian* story is anything but an embarrassment.'

'My comms people tell me social media is ablaze. I'm being torn limb from limb even as we speak.'

'I think it will be a momentary disembowelment.'

'Well, I should hope so. It's damned uncomfortable. What *is* going on?' He smiled at Kate. 'I suppose you'd expect me to ask that if I really were a Russian spy.'

Kate tried to smile back. In general – and long before the

events of the last week – she did not find him remotely amusing.

'The original intelligence stems from an operation Kate ran in Istanbul,' Sir Alan said. 'We managed to bug a meeting between three of the most senior officers in the SVR. They discussed the prime minister's prostate cancer, before it had been made public. They went on to imply that one of the leading candidates to succeed him was what we would call an agent of influence.'

'And they claimed it was me?'

'It wasn't clear whom they were talking about. We've since been trying to assess the underlying value of the intelligence, and someone has chosen to use this against you.'

'I'm not sure I'm catching your drift.'

'We think, sir,' Ian said, leaning forward, as if taking command of the meeting, 'that we're caught up in a classic Moscow campaign of misinformation – a sophisticated sting – of the kind we know all too well.'

James Ryan glanced at Sir Alan. 'In which case, we don't seem to be learning very much from past mistakes.'

'Early days,' C said. 'And we haven't reached any conclusions yet.'

'Go on,' the foreign secretary said.

'You might ask,' Ian went on, 'how we came to be overhearing this particular conversation – between three of Moscow's most senior intelligence officials – aboard that yacht at the exact moment the revelation was made. In fact, you might ask what they were doing on the yacht in the first place. Does it not strike you as a bit of a coincidence?'

'Now you come to mention it, yes, it does.'

'We were tipped off about that meeting.'

Ian glanced at Kate, and she felt her face redden.

Whatever she had expected from this morning, it was not to find herself humiliated in front of her ministerial superior.

'I see it as a classic attempt to cause us havoc. They obviously found out about the prime minister's condition and decided to use it to plant a series of devices at the heart of our political system.'

'A *series* of devices?'

'There was also the suggestion of a mole in Whitehall, who would be able to assist their candidate,' Sir Alan said.

'What kind of mole?'

'The whole purpose of the operation,' Ian said, neatly dodging the question, 'is to have us chasing our tails, and to create chaos at the heart of our government. So far, their plan appears to be working rather well.'

'Indeed – to the point at which I'm being ripped apart on the morning of the first leadership ballot. Not an ideal situation, if you happen to be in my shoes.'

When he next looked at Sir Alan, the air of geniality had clearly evaporated. 'And what I would like to know is what the fuck you intend to do about it.'

'If you're referring to today's story, nothing.'

The pair glared at each other. If they were seeking to hide any evidence of their friendship, they were making a good fist of it.

'What do you mean, *nothing*?'

'I would suggest that the Foreign & Commonwealth Office put out a general statement to the effect that this is, as Ian said, yet another Russian attempt to interfere in the Western democratic process. And you can add your own denials, of course.'

'That's big of you.' He leant back. 'And what about your lot?'

'We don't comment on ongoing investigations or operations. The fact is that we have intelligence and are looking into it. If we get drawn, we would have to start lying, which we never do. Better to leave us out of it.'

'But your man can brief the press that it's a load of cobblers, as Ian here suggests, designed to alter the course of the leadership election.'

'I have instructed our press liaison to say nothing.'

Ryan's expression lowered the temperature in the room by a further ten degrees. 'That's a brave stance, Alan, under the circumstances, if I may say so.' He shook his head in amazement. 'Especially given that someone in your neck of the woods obviously leaked it.'

'We don't believe that was the case.'

'How could it have been anyone else? You just told me no one else knows about it.'

Kate was watching James Ryan's face. He was trying hard to control his fury, and not succeeding.

'We think the Russians leaked the information,' Ian said smoothly. 'They gave us the intelligence, knowing we'd have to look into it. Then, after a suitable period had elapsed, they leaked that fact, knowing we'd get ourselves into further trouble if we tried to deny it. They're clever. That's no secret. And increasingly successful at exploiting the weaknesses of an open democratic system in the internet age.'

'They're bloody outrageous.'

'It's what modern espionage looks like, I'm afraid.'

'Did you know about the prime minister's illness?' Kate asked.

He peered at her, as if he was trying to recall who she was. 'Did I know what about it?'

'Were you aware he had prostate cancer?'

'No. Er, I don't think I was. No, I was not. Why?'

'We knew nothing of it. We wondered if others in the government or Whitehall might have had some inkling.'

250

'As far as I'm aware, only his wife and doctors knew until the day he resigned. But you'd probably have to check that. Maybe some of the staff in Downing Street? I don't know. No, I . . . No, it was a bolt from the blue for me.'

Kate thought that, for a very senior politician apparently at the height of his powers, he was making very heavy going of a pretty simple question.

Shortly afterwards they filed out. Sir Alan waited until they were halfway across the courtyard before he turned to Ian. 'You'd do us all a favour if you could be a little more adept at hiding your ambition.'

'I was trying to be helpful.'

'Then perhaps you should learn the value of keeping your mouth shut on occasion.'

Sir Alan peeled away in the direction of Downing Street. 'I'm going to tell the PM the bare minimum,' he said. 'I don't want to add to his woes, but we may need his support before this is over.'

Ian and Kate proceeded in silence towards the King Charles Street exit.

'They're pretty good at hiding their friendship, don't you think?' Ian said.

'I don't think the foreign secretary was faking his anger, if that's what you mean.'

Ian wasn't in a mood to walk back to Vauxhall, so he hailed a taxi on Whitehall. They climbed into it by the Cenotaph. As she settled into the back, Kate said, 'Has the foreign secretary ever crossed your radar before this?'

'What do you mean?'

'Have you ever had cause to give him a closer look before now?'

'No,' Ian said. He was concentrating perhaps unduly hard on Big Ben and the House of Commons through the rain-spattered window. 'Never heard a whisper of anything amiss until now, which is what makes me more than a tad suspicious of the whole business.' He smiled. 'Sorry, not what you wanted to hear in there, I know. But at least it got us out of a jam.'

'This is not a game of Moscow disinformation, Ian, and you know it.'

'That's what we always think.'

'I don't care what mistakes were made before. I know what this is. It's true, real. We have not one but two spies.'

'So you're infallible? Sometimes, Kate, your arrogance is a little wearing.'

Kate had been back at her desk for a matter of minutes, and had hardly begun quizzing Julie about giving Lena's sister Maja safe passage, when her office phone rang.

'Kate. James Ryan here.'

'Yes, Foreign Secretary.'

'James will do just fine. I need to speak to you in private. There's a coffee shop in the Tate, the one on the other side of the river from you. I'm sure you know it. Could you meet me there in ten minutes?'

'Of course.'

She hung up, then turned back to Julie. 'Where were we?' His call had interrupted her mid-sentence.

'She's still in hospital and the doc is right on side. They'll hang on to her until we can sort out her visa.'

'And the stepfather?'

'Keeping his distance.'

'Long may it last,' Kate said. 'And if it doesn't, I'll kill him myself.'

23

HER MAJESTY'S FOREIGN secretary had stationed himself in the far corner of the Tate's basement café. Kate spotted his two close-protection officers immediately, though they were discreetly enough positioned not to be broadcasting their presence.

'Thanks for coming,' James Ryan said. 'Let me get you a coffee.'

'Actually, I'm okay.'

'Come on, I'm going to have one.'

'Then an espresso would be great.'

He went to make the order himself. Kate nodded at the protection officers, who had taken a table on the opposite side of the room where they could watch the flow of people coming towards them. She settled into the chair with her back to them as Ryan returned.

'Thanks for coming at such short notice.'

'Did I have a choice?'

'Look, I'll cut straight to it. Nothing is certain in this day and age – and it might be a whole lot closer than most people expect – but I'll probably win this leadership election. Imogen is smart, charismatic, and I wouldn't climb over her to get to Meg, but she won't go down well with the rank and file. If I do make it, I'm going to have to form my own Praetorian Guard in Number Ten at the double, because we all know how events lay siege to a leader. So I'll need to have someone I can trust as head of SIS.'

Kate glanced over her shoulder, an involuntary tic when she had her back to any door, despite the presence of the protection officers.

'I'm not a perfect candidate,' he went on. 'I have a colourful past. There have been too many women, and I cut a few corners in the accumulation of my fortune, the details of which I know are lurking somewhere in your archives. You could have a go at sinking me if you wanted. But I don't think it would even dent me if the sexual indiscretions became public.'

'I'm not quite sure where all this is leading.'

'The point is, I wouldn't paint myself as a saint. And neither would anyone who knows me. But I'm no Kim Philby, and this is the second time Sir Alan and Ian Granger have landed me in it. And twice is at least once too often.'

'I know there was a slip-up a few years ago.'

'A *slip-up*? A calamitous weapons-grade fuck-up, more like, which made Her Majesty's Government in general and me in particular look like absolute arses. We were beyond lucky that the Germans had their own reasons for keeping it secret.'

'I know it was an unfortunate set of circumstances.'

He massaged his steel-blue jaw. '*How* do you know? The

files were supposed to be locked and all details of the affair scrubbed from the record.'

'It's hard to erase things in the House of Secrets if you know where to look.'

'And you know where to look?'

'I do. Yes.'

'That's why I need you,' he said. 'The world affects to hate politicians, and sometimes with justification. But I'm not afraid to admit I want the top job badly. There's so much I feel I could do. I don't mind being denied it for something that's my fault, but this Russian-spy nonsense is prize bullshit.'

He leant forward. He was a handsome man and, against her most fundamental instincts, she could see how the full force of his personality might weaken a woman's defences. 'He may have been a close friend of mine, but I no longer trust Alan, or Ian. Neither their loyalty nor their competence. And this is one screw-up too many – unless, of course, they set out to destroy me, and I wouldn't put that past them. Like I said, if and when I make it into Number Ten, I'll need to surround myself with extremely competent and loyal people I can trust. And it's high time a woman was in charge. Stella and Eliza did a great job at Five, but now it's Six's turn to enter the twenty-first century.'

He was clearly expecting her to answer. 'I'm happy to serve whoever is—'

'That's too mealy-mouthed for me. I'm offering you an opportunity. Give me your loyalty and I'll make you the first female C in British history.'

Kate looked at him properly, perhaps for the first time. There was a directness to his manner – a desperation, even – that was almost appealing. 'What is it you want?'

'I'd like to be kept informed on what the fuck is going on

inside your building. I'd like to know where this investigation is going. And I'd like to know it before everyone else does.'

Kate stared into the dark liquid in her cup. Whatever else, she thought, you couldn't accuse James Ryan of subterfuge. Or subtlety.

'Politics is the art of the deal, Kate. And I'm offering you one.'

'And espionage is a game of snakes and ladders. But, right now, all I can see is snakes.'

'Do you think it's remotely conceivable that I'm a Russian spy?'

'I've lost track of what is conceivable and what isn't.'

'If that's how you see it, I'll leave now. But think about what I've said. Give me your loyalty and you'll get an empire in return. I want a strong, robust Britain, capable of standing up to the likes of Russia and China. I'm led to believe you want the same. So we can be a very good team.' He offered her his hand. It seemed an odd gesture, but she took it all the same. And then he was gone.

She felt like Faustus on the walk back across Vauxhall Bridge. If politics *was* the art of the deal, then this was the opportunity of a lifetime. But if she took it, she'd never be able to look herself in the mirror again.

When she got back to the office she went straight to Julie's desk. 'Have you got hold of Rav?'

Julie shook her head.

'Keep trying, would you?'

Minutes later, Julie was at her door again. 'Your friend is about to say something.'

Imogen was facing a bank of cameras, on the front steps

of her house. She raised a hand to still the barrage of shouted questions. 'Most people will be aware of the events that have engulfed my family these past twenty-four hours,' she said. 'Some may have seen the video, though even the pixellated version should come with some kind of eighteen rating.'

'Nice touch,' Maddy said. She had come to stand between Kate and Julie.

'This poses a number of extremely important questions, of course,' Imogen went on, 'starting with the ones I have to answer. How could I have been so stupid? How could I have treated my husband and children – the people I love most in this world – in such a selfish and careless fashion?

'Some will no doubt believe that these considerations should disqualify me from holding any kind of public office. And the way I feel today, I don't entirely blame them.'

She breathed in deeply. 'But there are other questions, arguably of more importance to the country at large. Who recorded this material? Where did they do it, and why? Who leaked the footage? And for what purpose was it released at this precise moment? I don't have the answers yet but, given what many of us have read in the *Guardian* this morning, we may have our suspicions.'

'Christ,' Kate said.

'She's bloody going for it,' Julie said. 'And, frankly, good on her.'

Kate looked at her askance.

'You're not telling me a sex tape would put the foreign secretary out of the race?' Julie said. 'It would have MPs and party members flocking to him even faster.'

'Fair point,' Maddy said.

'Many of you might, with great justification, take the view that I should now be pulling out of the race to be leader of my party,' Imogen went on. 'I can certainly see many difficult days ahead, as I seek to persuade my family to forgive me for my *un*forgivable behaviour. I don't pretend that it's going to be easy or quick. But these are evidently *not* normal times, and I have been repeatedly told by colleagues during the course of the night that I have a *duty* now to stay in the ring. Given the public's understandable cynicism about politicians and their motives, I can see why you may be inclined to take this with a pinch of salt, but we know all too well now of the Russians' repeated attempts to interfere in our democratic process.

'I have decided therefore that I have no choice but to continue to fight what I believe to be a good fight. I will leave it to my fellow Members of Parliament to judge tonight whether I have done the right thing.'

As she turned and walked away, Kate's screen lit up. *Thank you*, it read. *You persuaded her.*

She messaged back: *What news from the front line?* She was in her office before her phone *ping*ed again. *Support still amazingly solid. Meg uninspiring and no one knows what to make of claims re James. She's still in the game.*

'A couple of sex addicts, and one a foreign spy,' Kate muttered to herself. 'What can possibly go wrong?'

She was scanning the flurry of emails from colleagues sympathizing with her predicament – or what they had inferred from the day's events – when Rav rang. Kate checked the door was closed before she answered. 'What the hell are you doing?'

'I have something,' he said.

'A very short rope. And you're going to hang yourself with it unless you give me a good explanation.'

'You remember my Cambridge mate at the *Guardian*? Did some stuff on the Panama Papers?'

'Vaguely.'

'He had a way in to the Swiss lawyer, so I offered him a trade.'

'What kind of trade?'

'He'd got to one of Binot's former secretaries in Zürich. Turns out Binot was a complete lech. This girl remembered Ryan and the offshore company they set up for him. She also recalls some very large amounts of money being transferred to him personally as well as to the company account. And you will probably guess the source. We might have him.'

'Does she have any paperwork?'

'She says she has evidence of millions of pounds being moved via Zürich from one of the Russian government's cipher accounts into Ryan's personal account in Belize.'

'Fuck.'

'My thoughts entirely.'

'How do we know this isn't the Russians playing us?'

'Because I've met her. And so has my friend from the *Guardian*. She's either on the level or she's the best actress I've ever seen.'

'It seems a tiny bit convenient that we've just happened upon—'

'You say that every time I get a break into anything.'

She bridled, perhaps because there was an element of truth in it. 'And what did you trade for this information, Rav, with your friend from the *Guardian*?'

'Nothing of any consequence.'

'Have you seen their story today?'

'Yes. I mean, no. Of course I didn't bloody give him that! I'm not totally out of my mind. He's looking into one of the Russian president's friends, and the cash being ripped out of the Crimea. I gave him a small contribution. Look, I have to go. I'm meeting her again this afternoon.'

'Be careful, Rav. If she is the real deal, then—'

'Of course I'm going to be careful.'

He ended the call. Kate listened to the rain lashing against her window. Perhaps it was her imagination, but she felt as if the world was closing in on her. She went down the corridor, shut the loo door behind her and splashed water on her face. She looked at herself in the mirror. Her eyes were full of fatigue. 'You're out of your depth, my girl,' she whispered to herself.

She dabbed her face dry with a paper towel and returned to the office as James Ryan was graciously accepting the attention of the cameras and fielding questions from journalists in the rain-swept courtyard of the Foreign & Commonwealth Office. 'It's all just hokum,' he said. 'Arrant, utter nonsense – the Russians up to their usual tricks. But I say to the Russian president, it isn't clever, and it isn't sophisticated, and it isn't fooling anybody any more. We've seen it too many times before and we'd have to be absolute lunatics to fall for it.'

'Do you deny that MI6 is investigating such claims?' one reporter asked.

'I deny they're taking them seriously. I spoke to the head of SIS this morning. They look at mounds of Orwellian misinformation every day and it's their considered view that the idea that I'm linked to the Russians was leaked by the Russians themselves to discredit me, and interfere with our leadership election, as is their wont. You can draw your own conclusions from that. I'm confident that neither the party nor the country is stupid enough to fall for it.'

'So you won't stand down?'

'Of course I won't! In fact, I consider it a vaguely

preposterous question, as will everyone watching.' He smiled at them and waved airily. 'I apologize for making you stand outside in this appalling weather. I blame Siberia for that too. Let the contest go on, and may the best man or woman win. I sympathize with young Imogen, by the way. There but for the grace of God ... And that's a joke, of course!'

He turned and hurried back inside. Kate, Julie and Maddy watched him go. 'Wow,' Julie said. 'He's got some chutzpah.'

Kate sat down at her desk. Her first new email was from Dr Minakis, the Athens pathologist. Attached to it was the final autopsy report. Kate looked through it, trying not to dwell on the photographs, or the fact that they had found the microphone shoved deep into Lena's larynx.

The police report followed. There was nothing in it of any note, of course. The Andros squad had found an abandoned car, but it had been torched, so all forensic traces had been erased.

A sixth sense made Kate turn to find Sir Alan at her door.

'A minute of your time?'

'Of course.'

'We need proof, by the end of the week. Otherwise we have to shut down the investigation into both politicians and Viper, then make clear that we looked into the matter and concluded it was only the Russians pissing around again. The PM's direct order. He may be ill, possibly dying, but he still has all his faculties and, for the moment, his word remains final. He's no fan of James Ryan, it's true, but he seems reluctant to accept that any politician of his seniority is capable of such perfidy.'

'Did you tell him—'

'Naivety may be a beguiling quality in a human being, but not in a prime minister.'

'It's better than having a spy in Number Ten.'

'That's what I tried to tell him, or words to that effect. I even asked if it was possible he might reconsider his decision and delay standing down until after his treatment is completed, but he wouldn't hear of it. I think his wife wouldn't let him. So . . . we are where we are.'

'Why Viper? I mean, Ryan and Conrad I can understand. If the foreign secretary wins, then the country needs to have faith in him, and if we can't prove it's misplaced, we should drop it. But I'm not sure why Viper should be in the same category. Isn't a potential mole inside our walls still a matter for *us*?'

'Not any more. I had to come clean about everything, and the PM's views were extremely clear.'

'How did he look?'

'As unwell as you'd expect.' Sir Alan opened the door. 'I've just come from the Ops Room. The *Empress* has docked at Mykonos. So you could do worse than start there.'

Kate followed him to the lifts.

Danny was, as ever, juggling screens, as if he was in charge of Apollo Mission Control. 'You were right about where he was heading.'

'Who's on board?'

'Just Mikhail. Katya and the kid left for the airport about an hour ago.'

'Okay, Danny, pack your bags. Take all your toys. We're going to need a second surveillance team to join the one on the ground.'

Kate spent the rest of the afternoon with Julie, mapping out the logistics of the operation, then left early and went home to cook Fiona and Gus supper. They were both unusually talkative. Gus was in the A team once more, so his life was back on track, and she wasn't inclined to probe Fiona's happiness long enough to discover the cause. Every time she came anywhere near broaching the subject of sex, contraception and Jed, Stuart's warning rang in her ears. She didn't want another argument. With any of them.

After a shower, she took an age to choose her dress for the US ambassador's party – finally selecting the same strapless stretch-woollen Roland Mouret she'd worn last year. She adored its cinched waist and origami-style sculpted panel, and wearing a red dress to meet a Russian source at an American Embassy soirée gave her something to smile about.

She laid it on the bed and sat at her dressing-table, tying back her hair, keeping half an eye on her phone for an update from Rav. Then she applied her make-up, with infinite care. It had been an age since she'd made so much effort with her appearance.

She almost missed the *ping*.

Bingo. Got him. The documents are devastating.

Proof?

Close. Serious explaining to do. And then some.

She asked where he was and when he was due back, and got no response, then looked up to see Stuart at the door. She wondered how long he'd been standing there.

He eyed her warpaint, and the Roland Mouret. 'Going out?'

'Yes.'

'The US Embassy thing?'

She nodded.

'Will he be there?'

On her return from Russia as a student, Kate had admitted to Stuart that she'd 'developed feelings' for someone else while she'd been away, though she'd sworn on everything dear to her that her relationship had remained platonic (and she'd had to, since Stuart's rage had been terrifying). It had taken him a long time to forgive her, and even to this day, he wasn't above throwing it at her in the heat of an argument.

She'd made the mistake of telling him she'd bumped into Sergei at last year's do, and he'd spotted the crisp, embossed invitation on the kitchen worktop.

'Who?'

'Don't treat me like an idiot, Kate.'

'Never that, Stuart. Never that.'

She shrugged on the dress and turned her back to him so that he could pull up her zip. She could feel his breath on her bare shoulders and neck.

'Shouldn't I be worried when you're sneaking off to see an old lover, and looking good enough to eat?'

'You bought me this.'

'Did I? Must have been channelling Chris de Burgh.'

'And I never did . . . with Sergei. You know that.'

'But you wanted to.' He looked haunted now. 'Isn't that almost as bad?'

'No. It's not.' She turned and kissed him. 'You can't seriously be upset about something that didn't happen more than twenty-five years ago. That would be absurd.'

'Would it?'

'Yes.'

'It's funny,' Stuart said. 'I was thinking about it the other day. I have such a clear picture of that Gulf of Finland dacha – the huge open fire, the ice-hockey pictures on the wall, the low ceilings upstairs, the endless beach and the sun on the still water at first light.'

'It is a wonderful place.' She slipped on her much-loved black patent Gianvito Rossi 105 pumps – she'd had to avert her eyes from the screen of the credit-card reader when she'd tapped in her PIN – and picked up her handbag. 'But slightly odd that it has such a hold on you.'

'Why?'

'Because, as far as I know, you've never been there.'

'That's precisely my point.' The muscles bunched along his jaw. 'It occupies such a vivid place in my imagination because it continues to do so in yours. You've stopped talking about it, but I know you haven't stopped dreaming about the bloody place.'

She sighed. 'I think we've had enough jealousy for one year, don't you? If I was going to sleep with Sergei, I'd have done it long ago.'

'Who said anything about sleeping with him? You're still seeing him, aren't you? And I know you loved him.'

She put down the bag and clasped his cheeks between her hands. 'It's you I've always loved, as I've told you many, many times. This is about something different. This is work.'

'What kind of work requires you to cosy up to an old lover?'

Kate tried not to let her irritation show. 'The kind I do.'

'And what if I said I really don't want you to see him, even if it catapults us to the brink of the Third World War?'

'I'd say that would be fine, after tonight.'

'And why is tonight so important?'

'For all the reasons I shouldn't already have told you.' She held his look. 'This isn't some secret assignation. I'm going to see him very briefly in the middle of a party of about five hundred people.'

'What are you going to see him about?'

'I'm under direct orders from Sir Alan. I *really* can't discuss it. And I *really* have to go.' She blew him a kiss and pulled the door shut behind her.

The ambassador's residence was a comfortable red-brick building, set in its own grounds just north of Regent's Park. The previous incumbent had been a great fan of vinyl and guests had been encouraged to put a favourite LP from his voluminous collection on the turntable in the spacious entrance hall. But it had been all-change since then, and guests were ushered through the hallway now to a marquee in the garden.

Despite the rain, it was still warm enough for the flaps to be furled and some of the guests to have drifted out beyond its confines to smoke or take in the damp evening air. Kate circulated. Several of her US-leaning colleagues were present. Adrian Sandalwood, a direct contemporary and now the main liaison with the CIA, introduced her to a striking, enviably ageless blonde, who turned out to be his opposite number in London. 'You've met Cindy, of course.'

'I don't believe I have.'

'Kate runs our Russia Desk, so she has her hands quite full at the moment.'

'Jeez,' Cindy said. 'Welcome to our world.' She shook her great mane of hair. 'Our politicos are so weak and venal it's a job to find one they couldn't corrupt.' She touched Kate's sleeve with a hand that seemed a little older than her face. 'The first ballot must be around now, right?'

Kate glanced at her watch. 'Yes.'

'His Excellency has left the TV on in the main reception room, so I guess we'll hear as soon as it's out.'

'The result isn't in much doubt,' Kate said.

'You don't think the *Guardian* story will make any difference?'

'Not as much as it would once have done. In our world of fake news, the truth is a matter of opinion. In the meantime, in every other respect, particularly on the charisma front, James Ryan and Imogen Conrad are streets ahead of anyone else. I don't think Meg Simpson has much of a following. I suspect a lot of MPs will waver, but not many will change their vote. Then we'll have to see what happens as they go out to the party members.'

'What about the sex tape? She fucks like a trooper, but that ain't what most folks want in a leader – at least, not when she's a woman.'

'Maybe. But times have changed here, too. No one is shocked by porn any more, not even when it turns out to involve our hitherto superficially blameless political elite.'

'It was an unbelievable piece of work,' Cindy said. 'More of a turn-on than any porn movie I've ever seen. But that might decide it – she has a body most women would kill for, so they definitely won't vote for her.'

Adrian had barely taken his eyes off Cindy during the entire conversation, but they swivelled now in the direction of the terrace, where the ambassador had made an appearance. 'Result imminent,' he announced, in a booming voice.

Cindy and Adrian set off for the reception room, along with almost everyone else, but Kate hung back. She looked up at the trees, listened to the distant hum of the traffic. It was hard to believe they were still in the heart of the city.

'I hoped you might be here,' Sergei said.

She snapped around.

Sergei's smile was as beguilingly crooked as ever. He

wore a sleek charcoal suit, white shirt and woven silk tie. His wavy dark hair – tinged with grey now – was swept back from his forehead and his eyes still sparkled with wry amusement.

'And here I am,' she said. 'So the magic still seems to work.'

'The lady in red. You look as lovely as ever.' He nodded towards the last of the guests jostling for a glimpse of the TV screen. 'Don't you want to know who is through to the next round?' He had to stoop slightly to speak to her, even though she was wearing stiletto heels.

'I have a pretty good idea already.'

'Ah, you mean it's rigged – like one of our elections?'

She arched an eyebrow. 'Rumour has it that this *is* one of your elections. But isn't that rather a dangerous thing to say for a man in your position?'

'Everything between us has always been dangerous.' His deep brown eyes shone with mischief, then burnt with the intensity that had always made her heart beat faster. 'In the end it is always about trust, no?'

'Of course.'

'And what else can you base that on but instinct?' He smiled again. 'Have you placed a bet?'

'No.'

'You should. Your judgement has always been excellent.'

'I've learnt that trying to predict the future is unwise these days. Especially when it comes to politics.'

'True enough.'

'Perhaps *you* should,' she said.

'Me? Who am I supposed to want to win?'

'Something tells me you know the answer to that.'

A big man with a white beard came out onto the terrace. 'Ryan and Conrad,' he shouted across to a colleague.

'So there we have it,' Sergei said. 'Santa Claus has spoken. I'm just puzzled that he isn't also wearing red.'

'It's not Christmas yet.' She bit her lower lip. 'I need help, Sergei. I wasn't going to ask, but I have to. Why did you send me that letter?'

He removed a carefully folded white linen handkerchief from his jacket pocket and wiped a smear of lipstick from her teeth. 'Because time may have moved on, but I haven't.'

She wondered what an onlooker might make of this scene. 'That leaves me none the wiser. Did you play me? Us?'

'Of course not. Did you listen carefully enough to what I just said? It is cold in Moscow. And I am not talking about the weather.'

'There are those at Vauxhall Cross who take the view that you're GRU, and that they've used you to set this in play. You and your colleagues don't think all this messing about in Western politics is in Mother Russia's interests, and you want Vasily and his cronies gone. Is that right?'

'If I was GRU, I wouldn't have known about the meeting they were due to have on Igor's yacht, or what they were there to discuss.'

'My bosses think it's too much of a coincidence—'

'And what about you? Do you think I would use you like that?'

She shook her head. 'I've asked myself that question over and over again, but I cannot believe you would. However, I'm relying on an instinct formed nearly half a lifetime ago. And yet . . .'

He waited. 'And yet . . . what?'

'Why was I prepared to accept it?'

'Why would you not?'

'I don't know who you work for, how senior you are and

who you're really loyal to. There's no one else in the world I'd accept such incredibly sensitive information from, then act upon it without question.'

'I am not anyone else in the world,' he said. 'Has anything changed? Between us, I mean.'

'I don't know.' Kate stared at the grass, her mind swimming with the danger. 'Yes. No. Maybe. Everything has changed. I don't know you any more.'

'Of course you do. I told you, time has moved on, but I really haven't. It hardly qualifies as grand tragedy. And, of course, it is not your fault. I was trying to help you, that's all.'

'You've come close to ruining me. You must know what you set in motion. It's make or break now. I need more – or they'll close this down. And maybe me too.' She hated herself for her beseeching look and tone. 'I need proof, Sergei. Proof.'

'I was trying to help you, Kate. One day you will understand.'

Adrian and Cindy's imminent return robbed her of the opportunity to press the point.

'Ryan and Conrad,' Adrian said, as he reached them. 'So now it gets interesting.'

Kate introduced Sergei and they engaged in uneasy small-talk for a moment, until he excused himself. 'You should come to the dacha again,' he whispered to her, before he slipped away. 'Everything is just as you remember it. And my parents still talk of you often.'

After a decent interval, she went looking for him, aware that her heart was beating much faster than it should.

He appeared to have been swallowed into the night. She wiped the sweat from her palms and closed her eyes to calm the electric current racing through her stomach. How ridiculous. She was a middle-aged happily married mother of two and he'd made her feel like a girl again in no more than a few crisp sentences.

A band had started playing on the terrace, but Kate's appetite for the event had evaporated. She made her way back towards the entrance hall. As she left, Sir Alan materialized at her shoulder.

'Good party?'

'Yes, sir. How about you?'

'It rarely disappoints. And how I wish one could say that more often.' His car was waiting on the front drive. 'Get in,' he said. 'I'll drop you home.'

They were scarcely through the gate when he said, 'I'm hoping you're about to tell me we have a breakthrough.'

'Not really, sir. No.'

'I saw you chatting. Did you not get the opportunity to discuss his motives?'

'I know what his motive was.'

'Love?'

'Something very like it.'

'That might be . . . complicated.'

'Not if I don't intend to make it so. And I don't.' Kate turned to him. 'I'm not sure he knows much more than he told me.'

'Of course he does. There is no conceivable way he would have tipped you off about that meeting without knowing its agenda. And that leaves only two possibilities: the reason you suggest, or to play you – and therefore us – as Ian likes to believe.'

'He's not playing me.'

C shook his head. 'Odd. You told me a few days ago that you didn't trust anyone. So how is it that you trust him?'

It was a question Kate couldn't – or perhaps wouldn't – answer. And Sir Alan's demeanour was considerably less amicable as a result. She stared out of the window at the passing traffic.

'Do you trust your husband?'

Kate turned back to him. 'That's an unacceptable question, if I may say so.'

'No, Kate, you may not. You know the rules.' His tone was even steelier than she had prepared herself for. 'Ian came to me to talk about Viper. He had Stuart's phone records. One or two of the calls take some explaining.'

Kate thought about that. 'I've seen them and I imagine Julie gave them to him,' she said. 'But the number of Ian's calls to *her* would take rather more explaining than my husband working late on a damage-limitation exercise when an official in his employer's department had just been arrested by the police as a suspected paedophile.'

'It's not a revelation to me that Ian's every action has an ulterior motive – and sometimes many of them.' Sir Alan glanced at the kaleidoscope of lights on the windscreen, conjured up by a fresh squall of rain on the glass. 'You don't need me to tell you that we're damned if we go on and damned if we turn back. If we can't stand this thing up, then I'm finished. And so are you.'

'We're trying to do the right thing. What other choice is there?'

'You think that's Ian's philosophy?'

'No.'

'Ian has been waiting for such a moment for a very long time. You saw how he behaved at the meeting in King Charles Street this morning. And it was unquestionably him who leaked that information to the *Guardian*.'

'How can you be so sure?'

'Because I know him. The person it damages in the long run is me. And that is why Ian did it.'

'Surely your long-standing friendship with the foreign secretary will protect you.'

'James is great fun. He's irreverent, amusing – and the most ruthless man I've ever met. In a landscape where rebellion, inconsistency and unreliability are without meaningful consequence, he's a wonderful companion. And I have no doubt our friendship, or his version of it, will endure. He'll still want to invite me shooting or to share a glass from the back of his Range Rover on Twickenham match days. But if I stand in his way, he'll cut me down. And, right now, I'm what stands between him and the job he's always wanted. So . . .' he smiled bleakly '. . . either we find proof that the original intelligence was correct, or it's goodnight, Vienna.'

'We must have this kind of conversation more often,' Kate said. 'It's lifting my spirits no end.'

'There's always the private sector.'

'I'll dust off my CV in the morning.'

Sir Alan didn't speak again until they were coasting down the street to her home. 'I have the measure of Ian,' he said. 'And, in a way, I find that easier to deal with. It's the questions that keep gathering around you that trouble me more.'

'Which ones in particular?'

'I don't think you need me to tell you that.'

His driver had pulled open her door before she could respond. She opted for a polite farewell as she stepped out onto the pavement.

'Goodnight, Kate.'

*

To her surprise – and no little delight – Fiona, Gus and Jed were all hunched over Fiona's computer in her bedroom, watching something together.

'Hi,' Kate said. 'Everything all right?'

Fiona hit the stop button. 'We didn't burn the house down.'

'Well, I'll take that as a positive. Dad not back?'

'Not yet.'

'Okay. I've got some work to do, so I'll see you in the morning.' Kate kissed them both. She almost hugged Jed, then thought better of it. 'I have to go somewhere tomorrow, but I'll be back in a few days.'

She had reached the door when Fiona said, 'Is everything okay between you and Dad?'

She swung back into the room. 'Of course. Why?'

'Nothing. It's just . . .'

'Just?'

'You're hardly ever here together. And arguing a lot when you are.' Both Fiona and Gus were looking at her now. Jed was doing his best to pretend he wasn't there.

Kate sat on the edge of the bed. 'I should have said something. There's absolutely nothing wrong between Dad and me, though I can understand why you might think there could be. We're just going through one of those infuriating periods when we're both overloaded at work by a whole heap of things that can't wait to be dealt with. I'm really sorry if we're distracted and tired and sometimes ratty with each other, and probably with you too. But if there's a problem, it's out there,' – she waved a hand at the window – 'rather than in here.'

'What do you mean?' Fiona asked.

'I can't really explain now. I wish I could, but I can't.'

'Is it to do with the Russians trying to undermine the leadership election?' Gus asked.

This was so far ahead of the perspective she expected of her rugby-mad son that Kate simply stared at him. 'How do you know about that?'

'Our history teacher was talking about it. She said it's the same as they've always done, only worse, because now they're trying to get our leading politicians to work for them. Secret service, she called it. She wrote it up on the board. She said it's how Russia and China will destroy the West.'

'Well . . .'

'Is that true?' Fiona asked.

'That's what I'm trying to find out,' Kate said. 'I mean, in a nutshell. And it's bloody difficult, because they're extremely good at sowing discord, and half the time – most of the time, actually – they're spewing out lies and misinformation, and for us, working out what's true and what isn't gets more complicated with each passing year.'

'Are they threatening you?' Fiona asked.

'No, love. No.'

Fiona was frowning at her.

'What is it?' Kate asked.

'It's probably nothing.' Fiona glanced at each of the boys.

'What is it? Tell me.'

'She doesn't want to worry you, Mrs Henderson. It's just that . . . earlier this evening, there was a knock on the door. And Fi knows very well that you've said never open it when we're here without you at night. So we came upstairs and looked out of the window. There were two men, but we couldn't see their faces. They knocked again. Hard. And then they waited and knocked again.'

'It was really loud,' Gus said.

275

'Jed went downstairs,' Fiona said, with pride.

'Did you open the door?' Kate asked.

'No. I didn't think that was a good idea. And I didn't say anything because I didn't want them to know for sure that we were here.'

'He got a knife from the kitchen, Mum, and waited inside the door.'

Jed looked embarrassed. 'I put on the security chain. They must have heard me, because they knocked even louder.'

'It was terrifying,' Fiona said. 'Jed was amazing.'

'I wasn't,' Gus said. 'I was shitting myself.'

'Don't worry,' Kate said. 'I won't say a word to the A team. And good for you, Jed.' She turned back to her daughter. 'What did they look like?'

'They were wearing black leather jackets and black beanie hats. I couldn't see their faces. I don't know if they spotted us at the window. They never looked up.'

'Why didn't you call me?'

'I . . . We . . .' She glanced at her brother. 'We didn't want to bother you.'

'We would have called you,' Gus said, 'but they suddenly legged it. There were four of them,' he added. Fiona and Jed stared at him, confused. 'There were only two at the door. But I saw two more on the other side of the street. And they all walked off together.'

'Also in black beanie hats and leather jackets?'

'Yes. It was like they were in a gang or something.'

Kate got up. 'I'll be back in a minute.'

'Were they part of a gang?' Gus asked.

'In a manner of speaking. They were delivering a message, meant for me.'

24

KATE MESSAGED STUART to come home as soon as possible. She called the night desk at the office and asked the duty officer to send a detail to the house immediately. She promised to get the necessary clearance in the morning.

Two women and a rather sallow young man arrived about an hour later. Kate showed them around the house and introduced them to Gus, Fiona and Jed. They checked the back garden and all the external locks and asked a lot of questions about the black-leather-jacket brigade.

Once she had finished briefing them, Kate went back upstairs.

'Who are they?' Gus asked.

'One of our security teams.' She saw the look on their faces. 'It's just a precaution.'

'Are we going to be . . . all right?'

'Yes. Absolutely. I'm just playing it safe.'

Gus and Fiona decided they wanted to share a room for the

first time since they were toddlers. Before Kate could offer to drop Jed home, Fiona asked if he could stay as well. 'We'd feel safer,' she said.

Kate didn't have a good reason to object, so Fiona and Gus topped and tailed in Fiona's bed and Jed was assigned the sofa in the corner, which was slightly too short for him. He went to brush his teeth while Kate kissed Fiona and Gus goodnight, and she bumped into him again on the landing.

'Is there anything else I can do, Mrs Henderson?' he asked.

'We'll be fine now, Jed. Thank you.' He was on the way back to the bedroom when she stopped him. 'Jed . . . It's always . . . useful to be reminded one can get things wrong. I misjudged you. I'm sorry.'

He rewarded her with the kind of smile that would probably have melted her heart if she'd been Fiona's age. 'I might have misjudged you, too, Mrs Henderson.' He hesitated. 'And, by the way, that red dress really suits you.'

'Steady, Jed,' she said, hoping he wouldn't spot the pink in her cheeks. 'One step at a time.'

She called Rav's mobile again when she was safely back in her own room. No answer. She tried his home number. No answer there either. By the time Stuart came back half an hour later, she'd tried both numbers more than a dozen times, without success.

She heard him bantering to the team in the kitchen, then his uneven footsteps on the stairs. 'Are you okay?' he asked. He was quite pissed. He always got drunk when he was angry or upset with her.

'Yes. Fine.'

'What's going on?'

'Probably nothing.' Kate was by the window. The Roland

278

Mouret was back on its hanger, and she was in jeans and a dark pullover. 'There were some men outside the house earlier, before I got back. Hammering on the door. Fiona and Gus got a bit scared. Jed's here with them. He was a bit of a hero, actually – went down and put the chain on the door.'

Stuart was getting more sober by the second. 'Who the fuck were they?'

'I don't know.'

'You must have *some* idea.'

'I don't. I'm just playing it safe for now.' Kate picked up her raincoat. 'I need to go out for half an hour. Do you mind holding the fort?'

'Of course not. Whatever you need.'

'I said Jed could stay. Gus is sharing Fiona's bed. Jed's on the sofa.'

'Well, wonders will never cease.'

As she walked past him, he took her arm and pulled her towards him. She forgot sometimes how strong he was. He looked as directly into her eyes as his still slightly blurred vision would allow. 'Are you really okay?'

'Fine. Just being cautious.'

'I'm sorry I wasn't here. Anything you want me to do, just ask.'

She kissed him tenderly. 'It's not your problem, it's mine.'

'It's ours.'

'I won't be long.' Kate pulled on a pair of black trainers and busied herself with the laces. 'I'm sorry – how was tonight?'

'We're through. But God knows what happens next. The party appears to have given itself the rather surprising choice of an adulterer or a Russian spy. It's not politics as we know it, but what is, these days?'

'You can say that again. How is she?'

'Her mood changes about every ten seconds, and she has no idea what to think about anything. It's quite hard keeping her on the level, and I have no idea how she's going to cope with the next few weeks. But at least she's still in it.'

Rav's building was shrouded in darkness. She parked a little way down the road and called both his numbers again. There was still no answer. She tried Julie, who picked up straight away. 'Sorry to bother you so late,' Kate said, 'but do you have any idea where our talented but elusive colleague might be?'

'At home, I guess. I think he flew back in from Zürich at teatime.'

'Where are you?'

'Still at work.'

Kate wondered if Ian was with her. She felt more betrayed by their dalliance than she had a right to. Two lonely adults seeking solace in an unlikely relationship – what was new? 'Could you check the flight manifests, see if he actually got on a plane?'

'Of course.'

Julie rang off and Kate waited.

There was no sign of life inside Rav's top-floor flat. She scanned each vehicle, up and down the street. Nothing out of the ordinary.

Julie called back. 'He was on the BA flight that arrived at Heathrow at five p.m. I'm just checking the CCTV. I'll tell you when I've picked him up.'

Kate realized she'd been half hoping Rav might have decided to go AWOL for a night or two and sample the fleshpots of Zürich. If Zürich had fleshpots. He was addicted to his phone. It was unheard of for him to ignore her calls unless he was deliberately avoiding her. And the alternatives didn't bear thinking about. She pressed the WhatsApp button. *If you're avoiding me because I was shitty with you, then stop it. I need to know you're okay. Call now.*

She switched on the radio, surfed the dial for a few moments and then turned it off. She messaged again. *Stop fucking around. Make contact.*

'Come on, Rav,' she muttered. 'This is *not* funny. Where are you?'

She glanced up and down the street again and got out of her car. There was no answer when she punched Rav's buzzer. She retreated and looked up. No sudden play of lights on curtained windows. Nothing. She got back into the car and pulled up Zac's number. She hesitated for a moment, then thumbed the call button. He answered immediately.

'Zac, it's Kate Henderson.'

There was a momentary silence. 'You've got a nerve,' he said.

'Have you heard from Rav?'

'You mean since the raging argument we had after what you told him?'

'Tonight, I mean.'

'No. He's in Switzerland.'

'He's not. He flew into London earlier this evening. Should be home by now, but I'm outside the flat and there's no sign. And he's not responding to my calls and messages, which is highly unlike him.'

'Perhaps he's as pissed off with you as I am.'

'I wouldn't blame him for that. But he's the most professional officer I know. He'd respond on a work issue, no matter what.'

'Maybe he's had enough of you and your "work".'

'Zac, I'm worried enough about him to call you, despite the abuse I knew I'd get. So, is there any chance you could come round here and let me in?'

There was another silence. 'I'll be there in five minutes,' he said.

In fact it was more like three, his state of mind made blindingly obvious by the speed at which he drove down the terraced street and the screech of brakes as he brought his SUV to a halt. He was a tall, rangy man with a big nose and a generous beard, which seemed intent on invading his flowery designer shirt as he stalked towards the entrance. 'You've got me worried,' he said.

He opened the shared front door and they charged upstairs. He put the key in the apartment lock and turned it until Kate put a hand on his arm and a finger to her lips. She went in first. It was dark, with no discernible movement in the air. She was powerfully reminded of the moment Rav had saved her life in the Andros hallway, and did not turn on the light.

She glided noiselessly down the corridor, turning right into a bedroom. The duvet had been pulled back on one side, as if someone had recently been sleeping there.

On the opposite side of the corridor, state-of-the-art kitchen equipment gleamed in the ochre glow of a street lamp. An electronic clock flashed at her, as if it was waiting to be reset. The room was a testament to what Rav called his OCD, everything so neatly stored it made her wonder if it had ever been used.

Kate took a knife from the magnetic rack by the cooker. She glanced at a photograph of Rav with his arm around Zac on a beach somewhere, stuck to the stainless-steel fridge, and then at Zac himself, framed by the doorway, his face so pale and gaunt that his eyes appeared to have sunk into their sockets.

She moved back into the corridor. Waited. Stepped into the living room.

It was even darker in here, with the curtains drawn. As her eyes adjusted, she saw the silhouette of a naked figure hanging from the ceiling. She switched on the light.

Rav had a belt wrapped around his neck, taut as a razor strop, attached to a wrought-iron ring set into an oak beam that spanned the width of the ceiling. His eyes bulged accusingly at her and an orange had been stuffed into his mouth.

'*No!*' she cried. She grabbed a chair, dragged it across, climbed onto it and tried to lift him down. 'Zac – *Zac!*'

She wrenched the orange from Rav's mouth, wrapped one arm around his waist and struggled to unbuckle the belt. She caught sight of Zac, frozen to the spot, by the entrance to the room. 'Help me!'

But he still didn't move.

Kate slashed and slashed at the leather with the knife until Rav came free. She lowered him to the floor, in the recovery position, bent over him and touched a fingertip to the carotid artery in his neck. She knelt and put her cheek to his mouth, hoping to feel a hint of breath on her skin.

'Rav . . . Oh, Rav . . .'

She rolled him onto his back, placed both palms on his chest and rhythmically compressed his ribcage, counting to herself as she went. When she reached thirty, she pinched his nose between her thumb and forefinger, opened his lips and lowered her mouth to his, desperate to fill his lungs with life-giving air. Once. Twice.

'Rav . . .'

She shook her head.

'No, no, no . . . Ravindra, my dear friend, *please* . . .' She cupped his cheek and rocked back and forth, cradling his head to her breast. 'Don't *do* this to me. Not after everything we've been through. Not like this, not now . . .'

The silence was deafening. She looked up at Zac, still rooted to the spot, as pale as driven snow. He was staring at Rav's body, mouth moving, but failing to form any recognizable words.

Kate pushed past him into the bedroom, pulled the duvet off the bed and used it to cover Rav, as if helping him recover some dignity in this moment of agony would make the slightest difference to either of them.

She stood beside him and looked around the room. Save for the chair she'd moved, the room seemed undisturbed. She switched off the light, went to the window and fractionally eased back the curtain. The street appeared deserted, except for a woman taking her dog for a late-night constitutional on the opposite pavement.

She took out her phone, dialled the SIS night desk and asked them to alert Ian and C. Then she called the police. Then Stuart. She warned him it was likely to be a long night, and that she would also have to go away tomorrow. His voice vibrated with concern and he wanted to know what had happened, but she told him not to worry.

Zac was now seated in the corner, his head bowed. He looked up, still struggling. 'What happens now?'

'The police come, then a load of people from the office. There will be a lot of questions for both of us. And then we get to feel guilty for the rest of our lives.'

'It was me who killed him, not you.'

'Actually, Zac, it wasn't either of us. You don't know Rav very well if you think he would hang himself from a beam with a fucking orange in his mouth because you went back to your wife for a week. Apart from anything else, he'd have wanted something a lot more original.'

'You didn't hear him crying on the phone.'

'Perhaps, but I did know him. And we've seen each other through thick and thin. There's no way on earth he would have wanted it to end like this.'

'So?'

'He made the mistake of calling in what he found in Switzerland. And that call killed him.'

'I don't understand.'

'You don't need to. And perhaps you never will. All you need to know right now is that he was murdered.'

'Who by?'

'I can't tell you. But he wasn't the first and, sadly, he probably won't be the last.'

Kate worked her way carefully through the apartment, and found absolutely nothing of interest. Rav's laptop was missing. So were his phone and the leather satchel he always carried with him. She looked for hiding places, but unless he had thought of something or somewhere very unusual, there wasn't one. She tried to enlist Zac's help, but he had sunk into a state of shock so deep he was barely capable of breathing, let alone speaking.

The police arrived first. They insisted on detaining her and transporting her to Scotland Yard. She waited in a spartan interview room until Ian and Sir Alan arrived. They didn't look as if they'd formed a rescue party. Grim-faced, they took the seats opposite her. 'We've had to talk to Five,' Ian said. 'They've opened an investigation. They'll be in touch in due course.'

'It doesn't take a genius to work out who killed him.'

'They're not looking into who killed him.'

'So, what are—'

'Viper,' Sir Alan said. 'We couldn't put them off any longer.'

'If there's anything you wish to tell us,' Ian said, 'it would help to do so now.'

'Help who?'

'Don't get cute, Kate. It would help all of us.'

'If I had anything new to tell you, believe me, I would.'

Ian took a laptop and a file from his bag. He arranged them fussily on the table. 'We haven't been going behind your back, Kate, if that's what you're thinking.'

'Why would I think that?'

'I've never felt your story added up. Not for one minute. In many ways I wish I could have swallowed it whole. But it just doesn't make sense. And we all have an obligation to act upon any reasonably founded suspicion.'

'That's Orwellian double-think, Ian, if ever I heard it. Why don't you just spit it out?'

Ian stared at her. 'It's not credible that you don't know who Sergei Malinsky really is.'

'I do know who he is.'

'Then spell it out for us.'

'He's a friend from my time as a student in St Petersburg. I lost touch with him, but he must have joined the Russian Foreign Service, possibly the SVR. I agree it's odd we have no record of him, but he wouldn't be the first. You know as well as I do that they keep people hidden in the diplomatic service for so long that we can't be sure of their exact operational role. I met him again at the American ambassador's party, as I've said, and he gave me the tip-off that led to the recording on Igor's gin palace.'

'So this guy, with an unspecified role somewhere within the Russian state apparatus, gift-wrapped this golden intelligence egg out of pure friendship?'

'I don't know why he gave it to me. All I know is that it turned out to be true.'

'You might concede he could have been manipulating you?'

'Yes, I might. But we have been over this. In the end it doesn't matter what his motives were because the information we gleaned from the operation has so far proved to be accurate. Unless the PM is faking it, and cooked this whole thing up with Vasily and the boys for their own amusement. We wouldn't have acted upon any of it otherwise.'

'It's a beguiling theory,' Ian said, 'but just not credible.' He opened his laptop, maximized a file on the screen and hit play. They all watched. 'The Winter Olympics in Sochi,' Ian said, by way of commentary. 'The opening ceremony. Here we have the Russian president, watching his mistress. But who should be sitting alongside him?' He hit the stop bar.

Kate peered more closely. 'Alexander Gregorin. So what?'

'His old friend from their days as liaison officers with the Stasi in East Berlin, now head of the GRU.'

Kate glanced at Sir Alan, who was examining her with such stillness and purpose that she felt like a laboratory specimen. 'How is that surprising? Gregorin is exactly who you'd expect the Russian president to have at his side.'

'You're right, of course,' Ian said. 'But watch this.' He hit play again. The Russian president murmured something in

Gregorin's ear, and, as he leant over to do so, the shot widened to reveal a third man. They were all laughing now.

'My goodness,' Ian said, making no attempt now to conceal his enjoyment of her discomfort. 'Sergei Malinsky, as I live and breathe. Silly me. While we were toiling in the vineyards, trying and failing to work out who he really is, he's risen like a spectre and now sitteth at the right hand of Alexander Gregorin. Except he's one hell of a hidden asset, because we've never seen him in Gregorin's company before – or with anyone else in the GRU, for that matter.'

Kate stared at the frozen image of her friend laughing at the Russian president's joke. 'So the GRU hide people deep inside the diplomatic service as well. How does this change anything?'

Ian planted his elbows on the table. His cheeks were flushed and a lock of his curly blond hair tumbled across his forehead in its enthusiasm to join the celebration. 'Are you really going to tell us you had no idea who he is?'

'That's exactly what I'm going to try to tell you, yes.'

'Or you could admit you're working for him.'

'And what is your evidence for that?'

'This whole operation suits Alexander Gregorin and the GRU down to the ground. Or indeed the underground. They embarrass the SVR and us at the same time.'

'I thought you said I was being manipulated?'

'I did think that – before I knew who he fucking was! Why would you keep that a secret from us unless you were working for him?'

'You think *I'm* working for the GRU?'

'I'm saying that's one of the vanishingly small number of conclusions one can draw from the facts now in our possession.'

Sir Alan stood. 'All right. That's enough. Ian, give us a minute, please.'

'Alan, I really think—'

'I said, "Give us a minute." Not "Would you like to give us a minute?" '

Ian returned the laptop and file to his case and walked out, taking care to slam the door as he did so.

25

'I HAD TO let him have his head,' Sir Alan said. 'You can be sure he'll give all that to our friends in the Security Service, and I wanted to see how you'd react.'

He poured Kate a glass of water. She drank it gratefully.

'You look like you need something stronger,' he said.

'If you were a proper boss, you'd have a flask in your pocket.'

He smiled and reached into his jacket. But it wasn't for any kind of alcoholic sustenance. With a magician's flourish, he took out what looked, at first, like playing cards, and placed them face down on the table. Kate could see that they were SIS staff security passes. Six in all.

'The Russians knew that you were going to be on Andros very shortly after the decision to go was taken. Regardless of whether or not the foreign secretary is a Russian asset, we cannot avoid the fact that we have a traitor inside our organization. So, who is Viper?'

He looked at the cards.

'Six people had enough information to allow the Russians to act as they did.'

He turned over the first card. 'Sir Alan Brabazon, better known as C.'

Then the second. 'Ian Granger, director of Europe and Russia.'

And the third. 'Danny Simmonds, Operations.'

'Danny didn't know what we were intending to do there.'

'But he knew the location. He knew you were tracking the *Empress*. He would have assumed it was connected to what you had learnt in Istanbul.'

'True.'

He was behaving more like a croupier now, in a high-stakes poker game. 'Kate Henderson, Russia Desk. Julie Price, Russia Desk.' He glanced up at her again. 'And, finally, Ravindra Singh, Russia Desk.'

He removed Rav's card from the circle he had created. 'And then there were five. Why did they kill him?'

'He called me from Zürich. He said he had something on the transactions to the foreign secretary's offshore company. Proof of the Russian connection.'

'Was anyone else aware of it?'

'No.'

'Was *that* why he was killed?'

'Until we come up with a better explanation. And I don't include a gay-sex game gone wrong. I can't find his laptop, phone or briefcase.'

C stared at the cards before him, absorbed, as if trying to force them to give up their secrets. He reached forward. 'Julie is a recent graduate recruit from the most thoroughly vetted generation in our organization's history. So, while she *could* be an agent, it seems unlikely.'

'Unless there's more to her affair with Ian than meets the eye.'

'Hmm. An attempt to cover her back?' C toyed with Julie's card, sliding it in and out of the circle, and ended up leaving it in.

'Operations is a big unit,' Kate said. 'They don't assign themselves. How could the Russians have *known* Danny would be in a position to help? The description we overheard on the *Empress* doesn't fit him.'

'Correct.' C moved Danny's card to the side of the table. 'So that leaves four: Julie Price, Sir Alan Brabazon, Kate Henderson and Ian Granger. The fact that Julie chose to have an affair with Ian seems out of character and surprising. The way in which you claim to have been given twenty-four-carat information as a Valentine's gift is not credible. And Ian's desperation to heap suspicion upon you is in itself suspicious.'

He pointed at the picture of himself. 'But how much better than all of that it would be if the Russians had the officer who holds the ring as their man.'

'If you mean to unnerve me at this point, I'd like you to know you're doing a great job.'

He sat back. 'I've liberated you from the clutches of our friend there.' He gestured to the door Ian had just left through. 'But purely temporarily. I want you on that plane to Greece. I'd like to use the time we have left to work every angle within reach. I'll keep the security detail with your family – around the clock, if need be – and you'll have a close-protection team with you abroad.'

'I don't need—'

'After what happened to Ravindra, it's not something I'm willing to compromise on.'

'Are they protecting me or watching me?'

He gazed at her steadily. It was impossible to read what was going on behind those eyes. 'Don't push your luck, Kate.'

She stared at the newly painted cold grey wall behind his head. 'All right,' she said. 'We'll go ahead as planned. But we'll come up with a different story for Ian. That way, if we see the Russians respond, you can at least narrow it to a choice between him and me.'

'But it must be *your* story, Kate. And you must tell *only* him. Otherwise, *I*'d be able to point the finger of suspicion.'

'That doesn't lift my spirits much further.'

'You have to keep in mind the possibility that the person you seek might be me.'

'What I keep in mind is – if that's true, then I'm in the deepest trouble. To misquote that Blair-era civil servant whose name I forget, you're fucked, I'm fucked, we're all fucked. So I'm not sure it's worth thinking about.'

Kate emerged onto the Victoria Embankment and stood in the lightly drifting rain for a few moments. She looked skywards and let it fall upon her face. Then she caught a cab to her car, drove home and parked opposite the entrance to the house. She could see one of their minders lurking in the shadow of a tree a little further down the street. The light in her bedroom was off.

Inside, she spent a few minutes being briefed by the head of the security detail. Her close-protection team would arrive in the morning. The rest of them would divide themselves between Stuart and the children. Kate was free to crawl upstairs to bed.

Fiona and Gus had dragged a mattress into their parents' bedroom and were asleep head to toe, their faces ghoulish in the halogen glow of the street lamp. Jed lay between the mattress and the wall, but Kate was beyond even remarking on this strange development in their domestic arrangements.

She elected to undress in the bathroom, brushed her teeth, then crept into bed. She kept her distance from Stuart, so as not to wake him, but he snuggled up to her, and wrapped his arms around her waist.

'Are they asleep?' she whispered.

'Can't you hear them snoring?'

Kate listened to Gus's ragged wheezing. It reminded her of the nights they'd had him in their room when he was a baby.

'Remember when we used to go on holiday and all sleep in the same room?' Stuart whispered.

'Our most romantic phase.' She pressed herself back into him, so that his breath was on her neck.

'Where were you tonight?'

'We lost someone.'

'Christ.' He raised himself on an elbow and gently turned her over so that she was facing him. 'Who?'

She wiped away a tear, and realized she could barely speak. 'Rav.'

'Oh, my God, Kate.' The bedsprings squeaked as he rolled onto his knees. 'How? Where?'

'I found him . . . hanging in his flat.'

'Jesus!'

'Careful,' she breathed. 'You'll wake them.'

Unable to hold back the tears any longer, she swung away from him and curled into a ball.

He gathered her up in his arms. 'I'm *so* sorry, my love. I know how much he meant to you. Was it . . . suicide?'

'No.'

'What happened?'

'I don't really want to talk about it.'

'Of course. Just . . . rest.'

'Someone murdered him.'

'Why would anyone kill Rav?'

'He called me from Switzerland. He had evidence of James Ryan's Moscow link.'

She felt him shake his head. 'Jesus. Is that why the protection team is still here?'

'No. They're here to watch me. I think the men who came round to scare Fiona and Gus were a set-up.'

'A set-up?'

She extracted herself gently but firmly from his grasp and sat up in bed. He knelt opposite her. 'I told you we have a mole, someone at the top of the Service. I think he or she might be trying to make it look like it's me.'

'What? How?'

She turned away from him, wondering how much she should say. But she had to tell someone. 'Sergei has been feeding me information. It was he who first tipped me off that some of the most senior figures in the Russian Intelligence Service were meeting on a super-yacht in Istanbul.'

'How did he know that?'

She turned to face him. 'He's never come onto our radar before. That's not unusual. Sometimes they keep agents in deep cover inside the diplomatic service for a long time without using or activating them. But then he started to get in contact – just with small titbits at first, but it gradually became more serious.'

'Shouldn't you have refused to accept anything from him?'

'Maybe, but the letters came in the post. It would have been hard not to read them.' Stuart was obviously bridling, so she turned towards the window. 'It turns out that he's in the GRU, which is fighting a bitter turf war with the main foreign intelligence service. And not only that, he appears to be at a high level within it, too, close in some way to its chief.'

'Why is that a problem?'

'Because Sir Alan and Ian think I knew that and failed to disclose it.'

'And why would you have done that?'

'Ian is trying to suggest that the only reason I could have kept it a secret is that I'm working for them.'

'That's absurd.'

'Yes, but right now it makes about as much sense as any other theory and Ian can be bloody clever when he sets his mind to it.'

'So is Ian the mole?'

'He might be. But he's also weak and paranoid, so it could just be that he's panicking and trying to make sure the finger of blame doesn't point at him, regardless of whether he's guilty or not.'

'You have to stop this, Kate. It's madness. You have to get out.'

'I can't stop.'

'You *have* to. What about Fiona and Gus and . . .'

She raised a hand to his cheek. 'I can't. Not now. If I don't finish this, who will?'

Stuart got up. He skirted the still sleeping children,

tweaked the curtain and looked down into the street. 'It is *not* our fight.'

'Then whose is it?'

'How can you be *sure* you have a mole? How do you know they're not playing you?'

'Because it's my job to know.'

'How do you hunt him?'

'The same way we always hunt moles. We channel them towards the noose, then pull it tight.' Kate lay down. 'I'm sorry, I need to sleep. I know this is very hard for you, but it's what I signed up for. It's my responsibility, my . . . duty. And I don't have any choice but to go on.'

Kate turned away from him again. Stuart got back into bed and she pressed her back against him to make it clear this was not rejection. She took his hand and wrapped his arm around her waist.

'Is it a bit weak to admit that I'm frightened?' he said.

'No. I am too. But we'll come through it.'

'Could they come after the kids?'

'I . . . don't think so.'

'But they might come for you?'

'I can look after myself.'

'Like Rav could, you mean?'

Kate didn't answer. She could hear his breathing and sense his alertness. 'I have to go away in the morning, my love.'

She could feel his body tense. 'Where to?'

'I can't say. We're in lock-down. I'm sorry, but do you mind holding the fort?'

'For how long?'

'The honest truth is, I don't know. A few days. A week, maybe.'

'Of course, Kate.'

He only ever used her name when he was irritated or upset. She waited for the inevitable withdrawal and he duly rolled away. 'You knew it would be like this. I told you.'

'Perhaps you did. But I don't mind admitting I'm not as tough as you are.'

'We're all tougher than we think.'

He didn't answer.

'I may be gone before you wake up.'

'Okay. Good luck.'

'Thank you.'

He went silent again. But she could tell he was still wide awake.

'I love you,' he said.

'I love you, too.'

'Brilliant,' Fiona said, from the mattress on the floor. 'Can we all go to sleep now?'

26

THE EASYJET FLIGHT direct to Mykonos touched down in a howling wind. The descent had been bumpy as the plane twisted in over the windmills and the whitewashed houses of Chora, and the fishing boats in the bay.

The wind tugged at Kate's hair as she came down the steps to a few spits of rain on her cheeks.

Julie met her and they didn't exchange a word until they were in the taxi. Tears rolled down Julie's cheeks and Kate pulled her head to her chest. For a moment, they embraced.

Julie straightened. 'I didn't sleep a wink last night,' she said. 'I just couldn't believe it. What have they found?'

'The inquest will say he accidentally hanged himself while taking part in a sex game. The Russians very carefully and deliberately made it look like Gareth Williams.'

'The guy they found zipped up in a bag?'

'Yes, sorry, before your time. He was a really bright guy working on how the Russian Mafia and oligarch class

299

were laundering their money. We should have learnt our lesson.'

'Why Rav?'

'A similar reason. He had proof about the foreign secretary. He rang me to say so. That call must have signed his death warrant.'

'Have *we* found the proof?'

'C has our people in Zürich trying to locate the woman he met there, but I imagine she will have disappeared as well.'

'Was she for real, or a set-up?'

'I guess we'll never know.'

'Where is the close-protection team?'

'I stood them down at the airport this morning. It caused quite a stand-off, but I want us to handle our own security.'

With its brilliant white houses and churches, dark blue shutters, domes and narrow patchwork of alleys, Chora was every tourist's fantasy. Lost in thought, Julie didn't seem to notice any of it. Kate decided to save it for later, and closed her eyes. She'd been up and out of the house painfully early, had dozed fitfully on the flight and her neck ached.

She'd called Yusuf in Istanbul and asked him to take up residence in Athens airport security. She could have asked the local station chief, but didn't know anyone there well and, more than anything now, she needed someone in place whom she could trust. She'd then called Ian to tell him she'd received a tip-off from her source that Mikhail was aiming for Santorini – so their entrapment operation would be focused there.

'More misinformation, no doubt,' he'd said.

To which she'd replied, 'Perhaps. But what they then choose to disseminate will tell us something pretty revealing.'

In any event, the trap was set. There was no one more

qualified to spot a Russian wet team than Yusuf and his family. If the Russian team hit Athens and went on to Mykonos, Ian was not the man she was looking for. If they boarded a vessel bound for Santorini, her noose would tighten. She didn't doubt that the Russians would want to be where she was.

Even as the last whispers of summer faded into winter on the island – such a climate reminded her that autumn was a quaint and peculiarly English notion – the streets remained busy. Jeeps and scooters and quad bikes wove and swerved and tooted their way through hordes of pedestrians.

Julie had rented their base through Airbnb. The apartment had a roof terrace with spectacular views of the town and the hills beyond it, which boasted no shortage of Chora's trademark windmills. Danny had set himself up on the roof, beneath a canvas awning, and the surveillance teams were all in place.

She could see the *Empress*, anchored offshore. As always, Igor's super-yacht was hard to miss. And Danny's screens were already fired up with the live feeds – eight in all – from cameras attached to the surveillance teams. Kate put her hand on his shoulder. 'Hello, my friend.'

He responded with a wistful smile.

'Coping?'

'Depressed about poor old Rav, like everyone. But we're going to nail these fuckers, right?'

'Yes, we are. Got anything?'

'Not a dicky-bird. We think he must still be on board, but have no evidence of it as yet.'

'What are your plans?'

'Everyone's out now, but we'll work a shift system overnight.'

Kate unpacked in the room she had been assigned, went

to the bathroom and washed the grime from her face. By the time she returned to the roof, the red sun was sinking behind the windmills scattered across the neighbouring hillside, no doubt launching a thousand Instagram boasts as it went. Kate sat next to Julie, took off her shoes and pressed her feet against a warm stone pillar.

The roof terrace was sheltered by a glass wall, but the wind worried away at the canvas awning above them, and the clatter of its metal fasteners reminded her of a yacht's lanyards beating against its mast on a stormy night. Julie lit a Marlboro, took a few puffs and passed it across.

'Stuart will bloody kill me if he finds out,' Kate said, after inhaling more deeply than she'd meant to.

'Something tells me that's going to be the least of our worries.' Julie took back the cigarette and dragged on it long and hard, then watched the smoke curl upwards until it was whipped away by the breeze. 'So,' she said eventually, 'what happened?'

'Do you really want to know?'

'Of course.'

'I found him hanging naked in his living room. Not a mark on him that I could see.'

They waited for a while, keeping track of the feeds. A light or two sparkled across the water from the *Empress*, but there was no sign of anyone arriving or leaving.

Kate took Julie out to a local supermarket. The alleys around their apartment were filled with tourist shops, selling locally crafted jewellery, accessories, T-shirts, dresses and beachwear. A small and well-stocked supermarket supplied them with lettuce and tomatoes, arborio rice, stock cubes, onions, chillies and mushrooms, which they cooked together in companionable silence.

'He's never going to disappear, though, and neither is Lena,' Julie said at length, as she diced and fried the onion. 'Jason hasn't, and he died a long time ago.'

'Do you want them to?'

'Yes!' Julie grappled with Kate's question for a moment or two longer. 'No. Of course not. I just want them to be here.' She stared into the pan. 'Are you ever frightened, Kate?'

'Pretty much always, these days.'

'Of what exactly? The idea we might be next, or the implications of whatever the truth turns out to be?'

'Both. And more.'

'As I lay awake last night, I thought about how much worse it must be for you. You have children, a husband, so much more to lose.'

Kate stopped chopping the mushrooms and gave her a hug. 'I'm very lucky,' she said. 'And I'd rather die than have any harm come to them. But you have your whole life ahead of you, with the strength and talent to make it wonderful.'

'Some days I think that. Others I don't.' Julie gave the onions a stir. 'If I was a mother . . . I really don't know that I could do what you're doing. Would I be here, now, if Jason was still alive? I'm not sure. But you aren't stepping back or wilting under the pressure, are you? You're a formidable opponent, and they must know that. I don't know that I could be.'

'You're the most resolute young woman I've ever met.'

'That's only because I have nothing to lose.'

'You're twenty-seven. You have *everything* to lose.'

'Twenty-eight, actually. And I still can't afford my own place. I don't have any of my own time. I'm fucking a guy I don't give a shit about, and who doesn't give a shit about me . . .'

'Why?'

She shrugged. 'I've asked myself the same question. Then I realized I already have the answer. It's because I don't give a shit about him. And he doesn't give a shit about me.' She gave Kate a rueful smile. 'Weren't you in Russia when you were my age?'

'Younger, the first time. And that certainly had its moments. At the end of my tour they threw me into Counter-terror. That was where I met Rav. We shared rather a lot. Many, many nights in Lahore and Peshawar and Kabul – and a whole lot of other places – when we talked like this.

'I'd just had Fiona and Gus. They were tucked up safely in their cots while I was out there wondering whether I'd see another dawn. It didn't seem to make much sense, to be honest. I thought about quitting a hundred – no, a thousand – times. But Rav saw me through, which is one of the reasons I'm not going to throw in the towel now.'

'How did he see you through?'

Kate thought about the many answers she could give. 'Plain old-fashioned decency is high on the list. And, in the end, the simple fact that he believed somebody has to do this. It *must* be done. So, if we hang up our boots and go home, another poor soul will have to step up in our place.'

'That's the speech all front-line commanders have doled out since warfare was first invented.'

'Perhaps because it's true.'

'I've spent a lot of time in this job trying to push death to the back of my mind,' Julie said. 'For ages, I didn't care – or didn't think I did. Rav used to know my true feelings better than I knew them myself. He'd say it was all cool, because we could make sensible decisions that would minimize the risk. There was no reason to suppose this life was any more

dangerous than crossing a busy street or being an account-
ant and cycling home every day in a world full of articulated
lorries.'

'I always envied him that quiet conviction. When I was in
my teens, I thought we'd all live for ever. I didn't have a
brother who became a random target on a big red London
bus. The first time I was forced to confront the fact that
death didn't just happen to other people was when my dad
died. But it didn't make me fear it. It made me fear not making the most of life.'

'Having children changes everything, doesn't it?'

'The biggest wake-up call ever. And a tightrope act without a safety net. When they were born, I felt the greatest
need to help make the world a better place. But for every
minute of every surveillance op, I was tortured by the
thought that I should be standing outside their bedroom
door to make sure they were still breathing. And the real-
ization that I did fear death after all. Their death. I'm
paralysed by fear of their death. And Stuart's, obviously.'

'I guess we can only do our best. I think that was what
Rav was trying to tell me.'

Kate added the mushrooms to the onions, as Julie continued to stir. 'That's where my mother's been so helpful.
She made me feel that my best is a long way from good
enough.'

'Do you believe in God?' Julie asked.

'No. But I'm old enough to recognize that we simply have
no idea what lies beyond the boundaries of our knowledge
and to take some comfort from that ignorance.'

'I don't know what that means.'

'In my youth I looked for answers with a terrible urgency.
I craved certainty. Then I started telling myself that, in the

end, we have to accept there's a vast amount we just don't know.'

Julie's face creased into a grin, and then she began to giggle.

'Here I am, musing upon the infinite mysteries of the universe, and you're pissing yourself with laughter,' Kate said. 'What's that about?'

'It's about you talking bollocks. You still crave certainty. You still believe you can show your mum she's wrong.'

Kate poured in the rice. 'You're really going to mess up this risotto,' she said, 'if you don't keep a proper eye on it.'

'Mrs H, you're truly an inspiration to us all.' Julie turned down the flame, then draped both arms around Kate's neck and kissed her cheek. 'And while we're on the subject of truth, I know you know about Ian,' she said.

Kate pursed her lips.

'Do you think a lot worse of me?'

'Safe to say he wouldn't be my choice. And from the way you've always talked about him, I didn't think he'd be yours either.'

'I shouldn't have said those things. It was a childish attempt to convince you – and perhaps even me – that it wasn't happening.'

'You've been lonely. I know that.'

'It really is just sex. I don't have time to date, and he seems to want it badly. Even if that doesn't necessarily mean he wants *me*. It's an arrangement.' Her eyes sparkled. 'And I do find him weirdly attractive.'

'From everything else you've said tonight, I'm not sure I entirely believe that.'

They took a bowl of risotto and salad up to Danny and ate

their home-cooked feast on the floor below, enjoying the candlelight, and the silence.

'This risotto is actually quite good,' Kate said, when she had almost finished.

After their gin and vodka experience on Andros, they'd agreed to limit themselves to a glass of wine each, and Julie took a last gulp of hers. 'He's a different man away from work, you know. He's almost schizophrenic. In the office, he can't contain his ambition. When he comes in, he thinks the world is against him. But he's—'

'Married.'

'Yes . . . There is that. But it's complicated.'

'It usually is.' Kate touched her wrist. 'If he's two different men, how do you know which is the real one? And how do you know there aren't more than two of him?'

'I didn't think you'd understand.'

'I'm not judging you, Julie.'

'But you are judging him.'

'Not yet.'

'I suppose you wonder if I'm Viper.'

'Why would I?'

'You might think fucking him is out of character and that it could be an attempt to cover my back.'

'Your . . . affair surprised me. But it shouldn't have.'

'Why?'

'Because, despite your fantastic strengths, you're bruised. And lonely. You've learnt to bury what you really feel beneath a coat of armour.'

'That's what spies do, isn't it?'

'You might have convinced yourself that this is a comfortable transaction. Just sex. But I'm not sure it's going to end like that. You don't think you've let him in. But I can't help seeing it differently.'

'Thanks, Mum.'

'Seriously. You've made yourself vulnerable in ways I don't think you want to admit. And I hope he doesn't treat you too badly. But he will hurt you.'

'And you won't trust me now?'

'I know you, Julie. You're my friend. You're not Viper – you could never be Viper.'

'How can you be so sure?'

'Because I've been in this business a long time. So let's make a simple pact: we won't talk about Ian, and you won't discuss our work with him. When he does hurt you, you have my shoulder to cry on. And in the meantime, we carry on as we always have.'

'Okay.' Julie smiled. 'It's a deal.'

'Apart from anything else, I now need you more than ever.'

They immediately disobeyed their own wine rule and took the rest of the bottle up to the roof, but Julie didn't say another word. There was an intensity to her that felt like a mirror to Kate's younger self, but there was a distance sometimes, too, as if the issues she was wrestling with were not the ones she'd articulated.

Kate handed Danny another bowl of risotto, which he attacked with a relish that reminded her inescapably of Gus.

'What's this?' She pointed at the TV debate unfolding on one of his screens.

'ITV. Our two candidates.' He turned up the volume.

James Ryan had clearly hit his stride. 'I think what they did to Imogen was *absolutely* disgusting. Needless to say, I myself have led a life of blameless virtue . . .' He waited for the ripple of laughter from the audience. Or perhaps he was looking around for a mirror so that he could admire himself.

'If we could keep this within the realm of the vaguely credible, Foreign Secretary . . .' the presenter said.

'My point, exactly! As I've often said, there but for the grace of God, and the rest of it. The fact is, none of us are expecting to be hailed as Vestal Virgins, but the Russians have done a genuinely disgusting – I mean *revolting* – thing. When did they record this tape? Why did they record it? Why have they released it?

'Well, I think we all know the answer to that. They wanted to throw this election, as they have so many others around the world, into complete chaos. And I have to say that, so far, assisted by some unduly obliging, so-called media pundits, they've succeeded. We cannot allow this to continue. We simply cannot go on like this. That is my contention. We must remove this cancer from the heart of our national politics, and the easiest way to do that is to ignore it.'

The presenter turned to Imogen, on the other side of the podium. 'What do you think? The foreign secretary is trying to help you here, is he not?'

'No, he isn't. Ignorance is most emphatically *not* bliss. As ever, my not totally honourable friend's apparent generosity of spirit helps me a little but helps him a lot. And that's very much the way he likes it.'

'Come on, Imogen,' James Ryan blustered. 'For God's sake—'

'No,' she said, tight-lipped. 'I will not "come on". I'm accused of being an adulterer. I hate that charge more than almost anything else that could be thrown at me. I've hurt my family deeply. I cannot begin to put into words how much I regret that. But no one is accusing me of betraying my country. No one seems to doubt that the Russian Foreign Intelligence Service had me under observation and cruelly breached my privacy. I don't know why they did, but I'm pretty sure I know why they chose to release it at this particular moment.'

'Honestly, Imogen,' Ryan said, 'for Pete's sake, can't you see? They were hoping we'd be standing here having just such an argument. This is what they want.'

'No, James. They're hoping you'll win. And if you're happy to benefit from this piece of arrant chicanery, you're a lesser man than even I perceive you to be.'

'Go on, Imogen,' Julie whispered. 'You tell him.'

If Imogen had intended to tease out his mean streak, she was doing a grand job. His head dropped a little. He turned to the presenter. 'I'm afraid that my opponent here, to whom I've been trying to extend the hand of friendship tonight, as you have seen, is now using this business – quite bafflingly – against me. We all know this is how our enemies operate. We understand that igniting this kind of argument at the heart of our democratic process is exactly what they hoped to achieve. I can only regret that the Education secretary has now chosen to do their work for them.'

'The charge,' Imogen said, 'is that you are an agent of a foreign power. It is one that we know MI6 is currently investigating. And I certainly hope they conclude their work before this leadership election is over. We cannot afford to doubt the fundamental loyalty of our prime minister. I know politics has become unpredictable of late, and a dirty word, quite understandably, to many, but if we allow these people to triumph, we may as well all pack up and move to Moscow.'

'Utterly preposterous,' Ryan blustered. 'Like I said, she's doing their work for them! It's tragic. And disgraceful.'

'Any movement in the real world, Danny?' Kate asked.

Danny minimized the ITV feed and brought up the static picture of the *Empress*. The yacht was in almost total darkness. 'Are we sure he's still there?'

'Unless he's shape-shifted and become James Ryan.'

Danny insisted he was happy to stay up all night, but Kate said she was tired. She would turn in and wake at four to relieve him. She went downstairs and WhatsApped Stuart: *Watched some of it. Good on her.*

Double or quits. And he doesn't fight fair, so why should we?

Kate lay back on her bed: *All okay at home?*

Yup. All good. Fi and Gus with me now. We'll go home as soon as we wrap this up.

Please tell me they haven't seen the video.

Everyone has seen the video, he replied.

Kate must have fallen asleep almost immediately, because the next thing she heard was the sound of the alarm drilling itself into her head. The wind had got up again too, rattling the windows and whistling across the rooftops.

She straightened her clothes, ran a brush through her hair and went up to the roof. The clank of the awning fixtures was intrusive and threatening. By the light of the moon, she could see the white horses whipping across the water.

'Morning,' she said to Danny.

He smiled. 'If you say so, boss, but it probably still qualifies as night, don't you think?'

'Go and get your head down.'

Danny remained reluctant, but she insisted they needed to pace themselves. Julie had left her cigarettes out, so Kate took one and smoked it. By the time the first fingers of light felt their way over the horizon, the pack was almost empty.

Danny reappeared.

'Not what I'd call an epic sleep,' she said.

'I tried.' He looked at the detritus in the ashtray. 'I see devoting yourself to a long and healthy life is going well.'

They sat in easy silence for a while.

'Tell me something,' Kate said. 'If you were working for the Russians—'

'Purely hypothetically speaking, I imagine.'

'Purely hypothetically speaking, yes. Picture this: a desk officer has identified someone who is willing to work for you, in a first-world country with a highly competent internal and external intelligence service – in other words, the kind you'd need to treat with more than a little ... respect. How would you advise the agent and desk officer to communicate securely?'

'Assuming they could be listened to and overlooked at any time, you mean?'

'Yes,' Kate said. 'Assuming the imminent possibility of close surveillance.'

'Some kind of app buried within an app, probably buried within another app.'

'In English?'

'Oh, I don't know. I'd probably use WhatsApp. Everyone has it – there's no reason not to. It's end-to-end encrypted, so I'd hide something in there – a folder that would be bloody hard to find unless you really knew what you were looking for.'

Kate thought about this. 'Okay. But *we* have to hand in our phones, laptops and so on for random vetting. And it's no different elsewhere in Whitehall. So . . . let me ask you a slightly different question. If I had something of the kind you suggest on my iPhone, would our people find it when I handed it in?'

'Probably.'

'Why? You said you could hide it well.'

'I could. But they're good at finding stuff. The best.'

'So, how would that be a sensible way to communicate?'

Danny sucked his teeth. 'There's no totally foolproof way. Not in this day and age. There are just clever dodges and tricks that might work for a while. All I'm saying is, if you were asking me to set this up, that's the bit of the jungle I'd explore.'

'But then I'd repeat to you what you've just said to me – I need to be able to communicate quickly and easily, but I also need it to be a hundred per cent safe.'

'Impossible.'

'Think about it.'

Danny took the last of Julie's cigarettes. He never smoked. Almost never. 'Maybe a second device,' he said. 'Something like that.'

'What do you mean?'

'The point of maximum threat is when you're asked to hand in your device. So the problem is less in the everyday. I'd focus on how to beat the call-in.'

'Go on.' Kate had a terrible feeling she knew what he was going to say.

'Two identical devices, synced up and running all of the same programs. You could pick up one and then another – they'd look and feel exactly the same and have the same information on them, except one is clean, the other has the app buried in the app, or whatever you're using to exchange information.'

Kate stared at the *Empress*, out there in the darkness.

'You don't look very happy about it,' Danny said. 'But I think that's quite a clever idea.'

'It is, Danny. Thank you. Go to the top of the class.'

'You want me to talk to anyone about it?'

'No. Thank you.'

Julie came up to join them. 'It's the wind,' Julie replied. 'It's so loud.'

'Welcome to Insomniacs Anonymous,' Danny said. 'You may now begin our twelve-step programme. Just one entry requirement: bring more cigarettes.'

'There's a carton in my bag,' Julie said. 'You fucking get them.'

Kate kindly volunteered, and went to make coffee. She did that a lot, for the rest of the day. It seemed that no matter how hard they glared at the floating palace in the cove, they couldn't will it, or anyone on it, to swing into action.

Time crawled by.

Kate and Julie shopped for food again, and allowed themselves to be distracted by one or two clothes shops. Julie bought a striped beach dress. 'I only got it because you liked it,' she said, as they wandered back to the apartment.

Kate put an arm around her shoulders. 'Yes, darling, I know. And I do. Though it's a bit on the revealing side, and I'm worried that the boys might like it a little *too* much . . .'

They made prawn linguine together.

'Danny wants to cook tomorrow night,' Julie said. 'I hope the office bean counters recognize how many euros we're saving them.'

'On past experience, I'd say their gratitude is likely to be underwhelming.' Kate started putting together a salad. The ingredients weren't the freshest she'd ever worked with. 'Have you spoken to your dad since you got here?'

'I talk to him every day.'

'What about?'

'Everything.' She grinned. 'Er, no. Not everything. My fears, my hopes. I spend quite a lot of time wishing aloud that I was less emotional, and he unsettles me by saying that I'm very like my mother.'

'From your description of her, you're nothing like your mother.'

'Hmm. Maybe I am, maybe I'm not. The older I get, the more I realize that you basically *are* your parents. Or become them, anyway. I mean, you have all the same characteristics, though it takes you time to spot which bit comes from where. Most importantly you inherit their value system, wholesale.

'Your teenage years are just a long period of radical delusion. Once you get beyond them, you start to see the reality and choose which of those values you wish to reject or replace. The rest rolls on from one generation to the next.'

'I'll tell my kids that. They'll be over the moon.'

'They're lucky. You know they are. And I bet they do, too.'

'They might say different.'

'Not if *I* asked them.'

They plated up the pasta and loaded a tray.

'Do you think you should have another go with your mother?' Kate asked. 'On the grounds that it's a relationship one should probably never give up on.'

'Do you still try?'

'Yes and no. I do, but usually end up wishing I hadn't.'

A Greek flag flapped above the balcony of the neighbouring

hotel. Given what a mess the country was in, Kate rather admired the determination of the locals to remain proud of it.

'There's something terrible about the fact that the one seal of approval I still seek is the one that will never be granted,' she said. 'I've spent my whole life trying not to *be* her, but I still want her to celebrate me as *me*. Even if it's only once. So when I go round there I don't know whether it's an act of kindness – of the type my father admired and exemplified – or just another exercise in self-harm that I should have grown out of long ago.'

'What does Stuart say?'

'He's trying to ban me from going. If he thought he could get away with it, he'd put arsenic in her tea. He's quite practical like that.'

'I love your husband.'

'You're welcome to him.'

'Ha!' Julie grabbed the tray and headed upstairs. 'You don't mean that. You're lucky, and if you don't know it, you're a fool.'

'Actually,' Kate said, as they stepped on to the roof, 'I do know it.' Then, mostly to herself, 'But I am a fool.'

They ate while staring at the *Empress* on Danny's central screen. There were two lights on now, and zero movement.

'We should make a TV series of this,' Julie said. 'Kind of like *Gogglebox*, but marginally less compelling. The real work of SIS: watching paint dry.'

At around eleven, Kate went to bed. She was halfway through getting changed when Yusuf sent a WhatsApp message: *Still no sign of anyone.*

Kate thanked him. She thought for a moment, then sent a

WhatsApp to C: *No sign of anyone rerouting to Santorini. So either too smart, or not Viper.*

His response was immediate: *It must be you, then. Or me.*

Must have left my sense of humour somewhere else, she replied.

You should never leave home without it.

There was a rap on the door. 'Something's happening,' Julie said.

27

KATE FOLLOWED HER onto the roof. The *Empress* was ablaze with light. Half a dozen crew milled around on deck.

'Moving on?' Kate asked. 'Or coming ashore?'

Moments later, Mikhail climbed down into the launch and headed towards the shore. The closest surveillance officer picked him up on the quay and his camera treated them to the full benefit of Mikhail's white skinny jeans, patent-leather shoes and brightly coloured shirt, open almost to the navel.

'Are those flamingos, or just pink splodges?' Julie said. 'Whatever, that's what I call dressing for a night out. I think we're in business.'

The first camera remained static as he walked into a beach bar called Neptune. Danny switched to the second surveillance officer's feed as he followed Mikhail inside. The place was heaving, the music loud and the lights on low. It didn't take long to spot that the men were mostly talking to the men and the women to the women. 'Bingo,' Julie said.

The surveillance officer was clearly going to have difficulty keeping his camera on target in there without drawing attention to himself, so the Russian swam in and out of focus. He cut a lonely figure at the bar, not yet in conversation with anyone, but clearly hoping to be.

'Let's go,' Kate said.

'Where to?'

'We're not going to catch him sitting here.'

Julie struggled to keep up with her as she threaded her way through the busy streets. 'What's the plan?'

'I don't have one,' Kate said. 'We're going to have to make it up as we go along.'

'What are we doing in a gay bar?'

'What do we usually do? We're a couple, looking to swing.' She turned towards Julie. 'You put your arms around my neck last night. In about ten minutes, you're going to have to kiss me on the lips.'

The Neptune was even noisier and more claustrophobic in reality than it had seemed through the surveillance lens. Kate made her way to the bar. 'I must be the oldest woman in here by about a decade,' she said.

'Don't worry, Mum,' Julie yelled. 'I don't think you'll be alone for long.'

'Very funny,' Kate said. 'What do you want to drink?'

'Oh, shit, I don't know. Mojito? But don't make the mistake of thinking it's just one and I'm yours.'

Kate ordered two and they huddled up close to the bar, since there wasn't much choice to do otherwise. Out of the corner of her eye, Kate could see that Mikhail still hadn't hooked up with anyone.

She and Julie exchanged small-talk and pretended to sip their drinks. A trio beside them moved away and created some space. It was quickly filled by a tall and very pretty blonde girl with a dragon tattoo that was creeping out of her crop top and trying to give her a love bite. 'Hi,' she said. 'You spoken for?'

Kate didn't know quite how to react.

'No,' Julie said firmly, and smiled.

The girl offered her hand. 'I'm Stacey, and, as you can probably tell, I'm from the Land of the Free.'

They shook.

'Whereabouts?' Julie asked.

'Michigan originally, LA more recently. But I mostly talk about Beverly Hills because no one ever wants to hear about Michigan and I don't blame them. I don't either. Where are you from?'

'London.'

'Are you a couple?'

Kate concentrated very hard indeed on sipping her cocktail.

'Yes,' Julie said. 'She's old enough to be my mother, but we try to gloss over that.'

'And you like to play sometimes?'

Even Julie looked a little nonplussed.

'Sometimes,' Kate said. 'Depends who with.'

Stacey moved closer. 'I'm good with three, but happy to go with more if you'd like.' She shook out her hair.

Kate could see now that her irises were fully dilated, and not just because of the intimate lighting. The girl was as high as a kite.

Stacey leant in and somehow managed to nibble Kate's ear. 'So how did you guys hook up?' she breathed.

'Oldest story in the world,' Kate said, taking half a step back. 'We worked together and . . .' she ran her fingertips down Julie's bare arm '. . . things kind of went from there.'

'Where's work?'

'A very boring department of our government. The passport division. So if you ever need to get into the UK, you know who to call.'

'I *love* London. I had a blast there. Do you ever go to Daphne's?'

'We don't go out much in the city. You know how it is.' Mikhail was talking to a toned twenty-something guy who looked like he'd come to a fancy-dress party as Michelangelo's *David*. If Michelangelo's *David* ever bothered to get dressed. 'What brings you to Mykonos?'

'Oh, just living the dream, I guess. I was in TV production in LA, but they were a bunch of sleazeballs, so I had to get outta there. I saved my nickels and dimes and decided to keep travelling until they ran out. So you might need to buy me a drink . . .'

Kate waved at the waiter. As she ordered another mojito, she noticed that Mikhail and his new best friend were getting along very nicely. So nicely that he was caressing the guy's shirt pocket. It was time for them to move. She handed Stacey her cocktail when it arrived. 'Sorry,' Kate said, taking Julie's hand. 'Nature calls. If you know what I mean.'

'Jeez,' Stacey gasped. 'Was it something I said?'

'It's not you,' Kate said. 'It's us.'

Julie followed Kate as she slalomed through the throng. They reached the decking that led onto the beach. The DJ was now playing George Michael. 'It's not you, it's us,' Julie said. 'Nice one. And you know how I love it when nature calls, but can you let go of my hand now?'

Kate released her. 'Time for an argument. Keep it going through the bar. Your hands are younger than mine, so I'll bump and you search.'

'What am I looking for?'

'Room key card. I'm betting it's in the guy's shirt pocket. Mikhail isn't about to fuck him on his dad's super-yacht, is he?'

'You never know with these Russians. What are we arguing about?'

'My decision to dodge a threesome.'

'You're bloody enjoying this, aren't you?'

'Hello, Kettle, Pot calling . . .'

Kate leant forward to kiss her on the lips, and got a slap on the cheek in return. Aghast, she put her hand to her face, then turned and strode away. She didn't get far. Julie grabbed her arm and spun her around. 'She might not have been your type,' she screeched, 'but she is mine.'

'Grow up, Julie, for fuck's sake.'

'You're just a jealous bitch. You're *always* spoiling my fun.'

If there hadn't been so much at stake, they'd have struggled to get through it without dissolving into laughter, but Julie made a convincingly vicious young lover and the argument had all the conviction of a real one as Kate thumped into Mikhail and his statuesque young friend.

'Hey,' Mikhail said. 'C'mon . . .'

Kate feigned surprise. 'C'mon what?' she snapped.

Julie gave her a drunken shove, then fell back and breathed mojito fumes over Mikhail's companion's chest.

She must have been successful, because she then stormed off. Kate followed her. They kept walking until they were out on the beach. 'Result,' Julie whispered. Her cheeks were flushed with excitement. She held up two cards in the darkness – a room key and a driving licence.

'You're a clever girl. If I was gay, I'd definitely want to sleep with you.'

'In your dreams, Grandma.'

Kate turned and gazed out to sea. 'Are you hearing all

this, Danny? We've got the key. He's staying at the Chora Beach Club. His name is Yorgos Mistolis.'

'You bet I'm hearing it,' Danny said. 'I love it when you girls talk dirty.'

A surveillance team was in place by the time they got to the beach club. Danny had located Yorgos Mistolis via its billing system. Room 1101 was right on the beach, simple to locate and equally simple to break into. They had it wired in less than five minutes, then hightailed it back to the roof of their apartment. The feed was high definition.

'Let the circus begin,' Julie said.

'That might be in rather poor taste,' Kate replied.

'After your performance this evening, I'm not sure you're in a position to cast the first stone.'

Kate and Danny both helped themselves to Julie's cigarettes. 'Just to be clear,' Kate said, 'I don't actually want to watch this. I'm just going to wait up until we're sure we've got them.'

'I find gay porn quite a turn-on,' Julie said.

'Men only or women too?' Danny asked.

'Both.'

'What are you doing after the show?'

They didn't have long to wait. And there wasn't much in the way of foreplay. The two men were barely in through the door before they were going at each other.

'I'm leaving before the interval,' Kate said. In fact, she stayed long enough only to note that they both looked as if they'd spent a lifetime in the gym.

'Good call,' Danny said. 'I think this'll go on for a while. And the dialogue is shit.'

'Call me when it's over.'

*

Kate tried to sleep but her mind wouldn't let go of the conversation she needed to have in a few hours' time. Was he really scared of his father? Was it credible that Igor did not know of his activities? And was it possible that, like so much of what had happened since Istanbul – in fact, since that first conversation with Sergei – all this could be interpreted as another attempt to set her up?

She must have dozed off because sunlight was creeping through the shutters as Julie gently shook her awake. 'You're on, boss,' she said. 'He's getting dressed.'

Mikhail was riding a scooter back into town, weaving to and fro across Danny's screen, his shirt half open.

'Looks happy,' Danny said.

'So would I be, if I'd just had that much sex,' Julie said.

Kate handed Danny her phone. 'Can you load up last night's stuff?'

'You'll be pleased to know I've put together some edited highlights.'

'How lovely. How long did it go on?'

'About three hours.'

'Jesus Christ.'

Kate watched Mikhail pull up in front of a café. Danny switched to the next camera. The operative wearing it followed Mikhail inside and took a seat far enough away from him to avoid invading his personal space.

'Perfect,' Julie said.

'I've learnt to worry about perfect,' Kate said.

'But we've been thick on the ground, and haven't seen a hint of anyone else.'

'I know, but we didn't on Andros either, until Rav and I were mugged by the wet team. And Lena still paid the price.' Kate stood. 'Come on, we haven't got the luxury of introspection.'

Julie delivered Kate to the café on the back of her scooter. Its layout was almost identical to that of the bar they had been in last night, with a spacious deck leading to the beach, but Kate was spared the pulsating bodies and the pounding beat. It was empty except for their surveillance guy studying the menu in one corner and Mikhail in another. Kate smiled at the waiter, steeled herself, then took a seat opposite her target.

'Good morning,' she said.

He looked up at her impassively. 'Oh, it's you again . . . let me guess. Your name is Jane or Susan and you're from the British Secret Intelligence Service.'

'How did you work it out?'

'Call me a fucking genius.'

'I could be an old friend of Katya's from Downe House or—'

'I know who my friends are. And you didn't go to Downe House.'

'Would you mind if I ordered coffee?'

'I don't mind if you shove a lacrosse stick up your arse, Jane. Or Alice. As long as you very quickly fuck off.'

Kate waved at the waiter. 'A cappuccino, please.'

She looked at Mikhail.

'I've ordered,' he said. 'Though I shan't be staying long.'

'You shouldn't rush. After what I've just seen, I'd say you need to replenish your strength.'

Mikhail stared at her. 'So, let me guess again. Some of your rather sad and voyeuristic operatives installed cameras in my new friend's bedroom. You've just enjoyed several hours watching two well-endowed and not unattractive men have vigorous sex. And you were so turned on by it, that you've come to ask me for my autograph.'

'That is not correct in every particular.'

'You're thinking that your duty as a woman is to tell my wife.'

'I've certainly admired your wife from a distance.'

Mikhail shook his head. 'It's so late, it's early. And as you clearly don't need me to tell you, I didn't get much sleep. So I'm even less interested than usual in playing your stupid games.'

'I wouldn't call this a game.'

'So where do we go from here? You're going to send the footage to my father. You think I care?'

'No, Mikhail. We're not going to do that. And since you are neither naive nor stupid, I'm not going to pretend our hand is stronger than it is. But what we want isn't very substantial either.'

She paused long enough for her cappuccino to be delivered, then brought out her phone and played him thirty seconds of Danny's edited highlights.

'If we sent this footage to your father, I think it would be painful. But since I suspect he isn't in awe of your machismo anyway, it's not going to change the course of your life, or his, all that much. So we wouldn't do that. What we *would* do is send it to his opponents or, at least, one of their choicer websites. That would humiliate, embarrass and possibly damage him. I think you *would* pay a heavy price for that.'

'Or he could find out I've been talking to you, in which case he'd kill me.'

'Now I hope you're exaggerating. He's bad, but he's not mad, your father, as you must know better than anyone.'

'So what do you want?'

'We have a problem. As you must be aware, we recorded your father and some of his former SVR colleagues in the

326

boardroom of the *Empress*. So we know you have at least one agent at the heart of our political establishment, and a well-placed informant, codename Viper. I need to know who they are.'

Mikhail smiled. 'This is amusing. And you think they would tell *me* who these people are?' He stared at her. 'You know I work on the Polish Desk, right? I mean, if you really want to trade one of your second-rate operatives in Warsaw so I can maintain the illusion that I'm the Kremlin's answer to James Bond for a little longer, we might be in business. But . . .' He raised both palms. 'Seriously, *this* is why you came?'

'You're saying you weren't party to any of those conversations?'

'I have *no* idea what you're talking about. Or, at least, I didn't until I read about the foreign secretary in *The Times*.'

Kate leant forward, elbows on the table. 'Perhaps your father didn't share this with you. And I doubt he educated you at Eton so you could spend your life in Russian intelligence, so I guess this phase is designed to familiarize you with your system. But you were aboard the *Empress* when Lena was killed, and I'm afraid I refuse to believe you didn't know about that.'

Mikhail's eyelids flickered. He wasn't the ruthless bastard his father was.

'So how did you find out Lena was working for us?'

He gazed over her shoulder, out to sea.

'Let me make this clear. Given how much time you've spent in the UK, I think you know I can be relied upon to be as good as my word. We're interested in one trade. Give me something that might allow me to track down your agents and I'll let you go. Withhold what you know, and I'll make sure that not only is your father gravely embarrassed by this footage, but you're on every sanctions list circulated by every country any old Etonian is ever going to want to spend any time in. And, believe me, however tough you think you are, I can see very clearly you're not cut out to spend the rest of your life in a Moscow apartment block.'

'I have nothing to trade,' Mikhail said. 'Honestly.'

'How did you know Lena was working for us?'

'A message from Moscow, saying someone on board was passing information to the British and we needed to eliminate him or her.'

'Who's *we*?'

'My father and me.'

'When did you receive this information?'

'I can't remember.'

'How did you receive it?'

'We use WhatsApp, like everyone else.'

'May I see it?'

He almost handed over his phone, then thought better of it. 'This is all you're going to get. It's all I have. So do I have a deal?'

'Yes.' She held out her hand. 'Now give it to me before I change my mind.'

Mikhail scrolled through his phone and pushed it across to her. 'That message only.'

Kate took a shot of the screen and stood up. 'Good luck, Mikhail. I hope, for your sake, that we don't meet again.'

'I can assure you we won't.'

Kate slipped her phone back into her pocket. She had less than she'd hoped for, but more than he thought he'd given.

28

KATE TOOK JULIE and Danny back to London with her. The surveillance teams would de-rig and return in their own time. She got back to the office in the late afternoon and went directly to the basement, a long, dimly lit room with a dirty grey carpet, a low ceiling over walls with faded paint peeling in the corners and a bank of more than two dozen screens covering every aspect of and approach to the building, both inside and out. The hidden cameras were located as far away as Vauxhall Bridge Road and the Embankment to the north of the river, and those on the roof gave a full 360-degree view of the surrounding area.

Internal Security was run by a man called Jim, who had spiky dark hair and large round glasses. The internal CCTV footage was stored digitally, and it took Jim a while to locate the feed that covered the Russia Desk's lifts. Kate and Julie stood either side of him as he fast-forwarded through the afternoon she had pinpointed with a little help from Mikhail.

'There,' Kate said. She checked the time. 'Five eighteen.'

'Jesus,' Julie whispered.

'Play on,' Kate instructed.

Jim hit the space bar again and they watched as Kate turned left to her office and Ian right to his. Their eyes followed Ian until he exited the frame.

'Freeze there,' she said.

They peered closer at the shot of Ian taking his phone from his pocket.

They thanked Jim and didn't speak again until they were in their own office with the door closed.

'It doesn't prove anything,' Julie said.

'The timing fits.'

'Yes. There is some circumstantial evidence. Your meeting with C is over by a quarter past five, yet Mikhail has his warning half an hour later. But it doesn't narrow things down conclusively and the fact that Ian is in a hurry to whip out his phone doesn't prove anything at all. In theory, it could still be you, or C himself.'

'Or you.'

'I thought you'd ruled me out.'

'Technically, we're all in the frame. But neither of us can claim that you're truly objective.'

Julie looked through the internal window, towards Ian's office. 'What should we do?'

Kate picked up her bag and slung it over her shoulder. 'I'll think of something. If either Ian or C asks, say I wasn't feeling well and had to go home. We'll speak in the morning.'

'Novichok poisoning?'

Kate smiled. 'A mild tummy bug should suffice.'

'Are you sure you're going to be all right?'

'I'll be fine.'

'You think I'll tell him?'

'Perhaps.'

'And that's why you made sure I saw the footage.'

'If it's Ian, no one can save him. Not even you. And you shouldn't want to. If we lose battles like this, our country doesn't belong to us any more. And it never will again.'

Kate strode home. The strap of her bag dug into her shoulder enough to give her a sore back by the time she arrived at her front door. The sole remaining member of the security detail told her the family had gone for a walk in the park.

He withdrew discreetly to the living room and left Kate in peace in the kitchen. She made herself a cup of tea and checked the mail. There was no mistaking the handwriting on the third envelope down, and her heart thumped a little harder as she opened it.

I have the proof you need, Sergei had written. *Come to the dacha. Come alone.*

The envelope had been posted from Kotka in Finland, just over the border from Russia and only a short drive from Sergei's family dacha.

Kate burnt his note and the envelope in the sink, sluiced the ash down the plughole, then sat at the kitchen table in silence.

Eventually she retrieved her coat from the hall and went out. She half expected to bump into Stuart and the children as she skirted the park, but she reached her mother's building without seeing them. She looked up, hoping the light would be off on the eleventh floor and she might be able to turn away with her conscience clear. But she was disappointed.

Lucy sat alone, gazing out over the London skyline. 'Hi, Mum,' Kate said.

There was no answer, so she repeated her greeting, but Lucy didn't stir. 'It's Kate,' she said. 'Your daughter.'

'Perhaps I did make mistakes,' Lucy said.

Kate sat next to her by the window. 'We all make mistakes.'

'Your father said you wanted him to leave me. I thought that was very cruel.'

'I just wanted him to be happy.'

'He was happy with me.' There was a long silence. 'But perhaps I did make mistakes.' Lucy turned to her. 'Where have you been?'

'At work.'

'You're always working. That was one of your father's mistakes.'

Kate had steeled herself not to rise to the bait. 'Would you like a cup of tea?'

'No, thank you, dear. I have more tea in here than a Calcutta street trader. I don't know that it's doing me much good.'

'Can I get you anything else?'

'No. Why are you here? I only saw you at the weekend.'

'I came to say goodbye.'

'For ever?'

'I don't think so. Just for a little while.'

'Well, I know how important you are. "She's practically running the government," our friends used to say. You must be *so* proud.' Lucy turned back to the window. 'Ambitious Kate. Clever Kate. All those As in all those exams. Still, you've got what you wanted.'

Kate knew her mother well enough to be certain she should leave it there, but she couldn't resist ignoring her own advice. 'And what did I want?'

'To prove you weren't me. And now you can parade your virtue and your happy family for the world to see.'

'It never ceases to amaze me how such a benign-looking

woman can have such an acid tongue,' Kate said. 'But I might be gone for a while and who knows what will happen in the meantime? So, if you want our last words together to be harsh ones, then carry on as you are.'

Lucy made her wait so long for an answer that Kate wondered whether she had toppled back into the dementia pit. Eventually, without turning her head, she said, 'I don't. Have a good trip.'

Kate stayed there as the minutes ticked by and then, very quietly, got up and left, a new layer of loneliness wrapping itself around her heart.

At home, Stuart and the children's welcome was as immediate and warm as her previous encounter had been grudging and cold. They were relieved to have her back. She went through the motions of engaging with everything they said, but she was not in the moment. She didn't know why she'd said goodbye to her mother. She couldn't bear to do it to her children. She was going away again, early in the morning, she said. It would be the last work trip for a while and she hoped she would be away only for a day or two.

Fiona asked if anything was wrong, but the evening haze continued all the way up to the moment she joined Stuart in bed. The concern in his eyes was raw. 'Are you all right, my love?' he asked. 'You don't seem yourself.'

'Don't I?'

'No. Even the children noticed. What's happened?'

'I went to see my mother. It was worse than usual.'

'Yes. She called when you were on your way home. She said you'd come to say goodbye.'

Kate lay down, facing away from her husband. 'I don't want to see her any more.'

Stuart gently coaxed her towards him. 'Your mother is a gold-plated, diamond-encrusted bitch, but that's not the reason, is it? What's happened?'

'I can't talk about it, my love. The conclusion of something.'

'Of what?'

'Everything I've been working on for as long as I can remember.'

Kate turned away from him again, so Stuart swung out of bed, circled around it and sat beside her. 'Please tell me.'

'I have to go to Russia tomorrow.'

'I thought all members of staff were banned from travelling to Russia.'

'We are. I'll have to go in under cover.'

'That's an insane risk.'

'It may be, but I don't have a choice. Someone has agreed to give me evidence—'

'Sergei?'

She couldn't bring herself to lie to him. 'Someone has made contact to say he has evidence to prove who's been betraying us. That's all I can say, so please don't question me any more or attempt to dissuade me. I wouldn't go unless I absolutely had to. I'll be all right as soon as I'm back. It'll be over. One way or the other.'

He touched her cheek. 'You know I'm here for you, don't you? Right behind you. Always have been, always will be. But are you sure it's right to go? There must be another way.'

'Yes. It is right. So, please, if you'd like me to go and sleep in the spare room, that's fine. I have to be up really early . . .'

Stuart withdrew. He switched off the light, but in the darkness she could tell that sleep eluded him, too. It was a long time before he succumbed to it.

When she was sure he was finally asleep, Kate got up. She emptied the bag she'd taken to Mykonos, filled it with cold-weather gear, then went down to the kitchen. She opened her laptop and sent a message to Ian and Sir Alan, separately but identically: *My source says he has proof of who has betrayed us. Am on my way to Russia to collect. More to follow.*

She WhatsApped Julie and Danny, asking them to meet her at Heathrow, then crept back upstairs. Gus did not stir as she kissed him, but Fiona was awake as soon as her mother's lips brushed her forehead. 'What are you doing?'

'Just kissing you before I go.'

'You never do that.'

'I always do that.'

'Not in the middle of the night.'

Kate sat on the bed beside her daughter.

'What are you doing, Mum?'

'I have an impossible few days ahead, my darling. But I have to go, and I don't think I can do it without your support.'

'What do you mean?'

'I think you know what I mean. Those men outside our house? They're there for a very good reason. And I have to settle the matter now. I don't think it's going to be easy.'

'Will you be all right?'

'Yes, I believe so. Otherwise, I don't think I could say goodbye to you and your brother. But I don't know precisely how it's going to end.'

'What about Dad? Surely you couldn't say goodbye to him either . . .'

'Exactly.'

'Is everything okay?'

'In this room? Yes. In the country? No.'

'But *you*'ll be okay? You're not going to take any . . . risks?'

'There's just something I need to do, and then it will all be over.' She smiled at her daughter. 'How is my new friend?'

'He likes you.'

'I apologized for misjudging him.'

'I know.'

'I should have apologized to you, too. I should have trusted your judgement.'

'You don't have to apologize to me. I deserve all the shit I get.'

'Well . . . some shit, perhaps. But not all of it.'

Fiona wrapped her arms around her mother's neck. Her tears were damp on Kate's cheeks. 'I love you, Mum,' she said.

It was the warmest hug she'd had for years and it made the walk out into the chill night the bleakest she had endured.

Kate called an Uber. She wanted her movements to be traced. And as she got into it, she looked back to see that her bedroom light had been switched on.

Kate spent half an hour with Danny in Carluccio's at Heathrow as he passed her the equipment and explained how she could rig it. Then they all boarded the flight to Helsinki.

29

THEY HIRED A car at Helsinki airport and didn't stop until they reached Kotka, where Sergei's letter had been posted. Kate had first come here with him on a day trip from the dacha to the Finnish capital. It had changed considerably for the better – and worse – since then. A major port in the Gulf of Finland, it had once thrived on its paper mills and other light industrial output, but globalization had taken its toll and the evidence was clearly visible in the ill-kept apartment blocks in the outer districts, gloomy now as the grey afternoon crept towards dusk. But the harbour had been spruced up and the coffee shop they stopped at, overlooking a tall ship by the quay, was a temple to Scandinavian minimalism.

They didn't talk much. They had agreed to part there. Kate would go on alone. 'Are you ready?' she asked, after they had sat in silence sipping coffee.

They nodded.

She hugged them both. 'I wish I was coming with you,' Julie said.

'No, you don't.'

'I'll happily come.'

'I need you here.'

Julie gazed at her. 'It's reckless to go alone, Kate.'

'It's reckless to go at all. Taking you would be even more so.'

Kate got into the car to forestall any further discussion and drove away without looking back. She only glanced in her rear-view mirror as she swung right at the end of the quay and saw that Julie and Danny were both still standing on the pavement, watching her.

It began to rain, the dull drizzle in flat grey, almost winter light, which made life in England feel like a ray of sunshine. And as she drove on with the pine forests to her left and the Gulf of Finland stretching away to the horizon on her right, she was so absorbed in a cascade of endlessly repeating thoughts and theories that it felt like only minutes later that she began the approach to the Vaalimaa border crossing. European and Finnish flags tugged violently in the breeze as she joined the queue.

Kate tapped her fingers on the wheel in the way Rav used to.

The rain strengthened. She inched forwards, listening to the steady beat of the windscreen wipers. The control booths were a blaze of light in the gathering gloom.

She reached the front of the queue and presented her passport, which said she was Ebba Johansson from Stockholm. Every MI6 officer at grade three or above had at least five, under assumed names, to allow them free movement. If pushed, Kate could speak fluent enough Swedish to convince anyone other than a native. But that didn't stop her chest tightening and her breath quickening as she drove across the tarmac to the Russian side.

There was a short queue there, too. She breathed deeply, and tried to prevent her heart thumping its way out of her ribcage.

As she wound down her window again, the Russian guard, a great bear of a man with a thick black beard and ruddy cheeks, grunted and stretched out a hand.

'*Dobry den,*' she said, as she gave him her passport.

He opened it without a reply, and entered her details into his computer. Kate kept her gaze away from the armed guards sheltering from the rain.

Time crawled by. She closed her eyes. If they had broken her alias and arrested her now, it would change everything.

The guard stamped her visa page violently and handed it back, still without a word. She drove on, relief flooding through her.

The rain strengthened again, billowing across her path, so that the journey onward was painfully slow. But as she turned off the main road to Vyborg and headed towards Sokolinskoye, a shaft of bright evening sunshine suddenly danced across a windscreen soon speckled with grit from the road surface.

As she bumped along the pot-holed track that finally wound through the pine forest to Sergei's parents' dacha, Kate felt suddenly, exuberantly, at home. She hadn't realized how much she had missed this place, which had remained unchanged since the Tsarist era. The track emerged beside the water, which glowed a rich orange in the sunset.

She could see a few brightly coloured dachas scattered through the woods, until the light faded and the sea merged with the sky. And at last she was on the gentle slope down towards the beach. A final turn to the right, and there it was in the sweep of her headlamps, its once neat green wooden cladding, shutters, balcony and white-framed windows faded by neglect.

Kate got out of the car. The night was eerily still. She knocked once, but no lights flickered on, so she opened the door and slipped inside. The interior was damp and chilly. A moonbeam fell across the crowded bookshelves on the far wall.

'Sergei?'

There was no answer. She slid open the box of matches that lay beside the candle on the table and lit it. The dacha had never had electricity and nothing had changed.

She glanced about her. All along one wall there were pictures of Sergei in various ice-hockey teams, beside those of the St Petersburg squad; his father had looked after their stadium. The gramophone still had pride of place on a wooden bench, with the family's vinyl records stacked neatly on the windowsill.

The room was dominated by an enormous stone fireplace, which faced a worn leather sofa and two tattered chairs. Someone had laid a fire and left a box of matches there too. Kate lit it and drew the rudimentary curtains to shut out the night.

The fire here burnt better than any she'd encountered before. She lit more candles and it wasn't long before the interior of the cabin was as cosy as she remembered it. She put on *Passion for the Russian Revolution 1917* performed by the St Petersburg Philharmonic and conducted by Yuri Temirkanov, whom Sergei had taken Kate to see on many occasions during that long winter in his city.

She went upstairs, candle in hand. There were two rooms,

both with small double beds covered in furs. One was where Kate had normally slept, the other where she had longed all night to join him.

She had taken the precaution of stealing some cigarettes from Julie, and back downstairs, she sat and smoked one by the fire. But the growing warmth of the ancient building, and of her nostalgia, still failed to put her mind completely at rest. Perhaps, she thought, that was his intention.

After a few hours of listening to the crackle of the flames and the rustling of the trees, Kate felt hungry enough to venture into the tiny back kitchen. It was damp, like the rest of the cabin, and looked as if it had recently been cleaned. There was no fridge, but the cool-box contained some borscht in a bowl covered with clingfilm and a bottle of red wine from the Crimea with a corkscrew taped to the side. There was little doubt it had been left for her. There were no curtains at the window, nothing to shelter her there from the looming menace of the forest.

Kate ate gratefully and drank some wine by the fire. And still the night delivered nothing but the occasional plaintive cry of the wind. Once or twice she moved to the front window and pulled back the curtain, but all she could see was the moonlight on the water.

Eventually Kate screwed up her courage and stepped out into the darkness. Though she was certain she hadn't left it open, her car door was banging against a naked trunk. She circled in front of the vehicle and pushed it shut.

She snapped around.

'Sergei?' she yelled, but his name was immediately smothered by the forest.

The shadows were making a fool of her. She walked away from the house along the sand. In the days she'd come here with him, she'd loved the cabin's splendid isolation, but her surroundings were now closing in on her.

She started to see shapes and faces in the darkness. She turned back. The door to the dacha was open and yet she was certain she had closed that too. This time she locked it behind her.

'Sergei?' she called again, but there was no answer.

She picked up the wine bottle as a crude weapon and crept back into the kitchen. Once she was convinced it was empty, she swapped the bottle for a knife and climbed the stairs. There was no one in the bedrooms either.

She took the furs from the beds and carried them down to the fire, curling up in front of it, trying to console herself with the memory of having done so, often, with him. She had cast the die. Now she could do no more than wait.

Not for the first time, Kate found that intense fatigue could overcome even acute fear, and she awoke as the first hints of morning slipped in beneath the simple cotton drapes. She stood. The fire had burnt out. The air in the dacha was damp and cold again. She drew the curtains, to be greeted by autumn sunlight shimmering on a flat, calm sea. The wind had blown through, taking her fears with it.

She stepped out of the dacha and walked past the car onto the beach. There, in the sand, she saw her footsteps from the night before.

And then another set, beside her own, which very clearly belonged to a man.

Kate looked about her. In this still, quiet place, there was no sign of life. She adjusted her clothes and walked on, her eyes fixed upon the path at the end of the beach, which led up a small incline to a clump of trees.

The sand was damp, her footfall heavy, but she could still hear her own breathing. She stopped again and looked back towards the dacha, then checked her pocket to be sure she still had her car keys.

She continued towards the trees, and there he was.

She found she could no longer move as he walked slowly towards her.

'Hello, my love,' Stuart said.

Her reply caught in her throat. But the strangest part of it was the feeling of relief that swept over her. She had come here to confront a fear that had been eating her alive. The truth was some kind of release.

'It had to be you,' she said. 'Ever since the appearance of that magically crack-free iPad. And the way you looked at Imogen. I've been such a fool.'

'The sins of the flesh can make fools of us all.'

'To betray me is one thing, but to betray your country, as you've been so clearly doing, is of a different order of magnitude, don't you think?' She slowly shook her head. 'Did the condom wrapper I found in the rubbish belong to you, after all?'

'No. My . . . liaison with Imogen . . . was very brief, and a long time ago.'

'I guess you owe it to me to explain how you could have been so stupid.'

'They start in such a small way, Kate. You know how they work. I guess it's what you do, too. And you convince yourself it won't really matter. What was I? Just a civil servant in the Department of Education. Who the fuck cared if, once in a while, I lunched at a good restaurant and shared the Whitehall gossip? They must have heard it from a million different places. But then they have you. And they start turning the screw.'

'I hope at least you're going to tell me that Imogen Conrad was the fuck of your life. That the betrayal and misery you've unleashed was, on some level, worth it.'

He took a step closer. 'You're so inflexible, Kate, so unyielding, so . . . certain. I—'

'Stay where you are and just tell me *why*.'

'Because I'm human. Because I made a mistake. Because I knew you would never accept or forgive it. Because I didn't want to hurt you. And because the price I was being asked to pay by the Russian Embassy seemed—'

'You mean the SVR.'

'Yes, yes . . . of course. I didn't understand at first who I was dealing with, or maybe didn't want to. But what they were asking for . . . it seemed a much smaller price to pay than the alternative, which would have been to destroy our love and wreck our family.'

'How long have you been fucking her?'

He shook his head. 'I said, it was only ever once – well, a few times, on foreign trips a long time ago. But they had a recording.' He looked as if he was about to cry. 'And I couldn't bring myself to break your heart.'

'*My* heart.'

'All right, my own. The children's. But what was the alternative? To confess and destroy our family? I just—'

'To confess and let me make my choice.'

'But I knew what choice you'd make. You would never have forgiven me, Kate. You know that. And what the Russians were asking for didn't seem so . . . serious, so terrible by comparison. I'm sorry, I know I should never have done it. I know you'll despise me, but—'

'Don't whine at me, Stuart. I don't want to hear that you're the victim in all of this.'

344

He closed in on her again, but she raised her hand silently and stepped back. She felt, suddenly, as if the ground was opening beneath her feet.

'I'm *so* sorry, Kate. I've been a fool. Worse than a fool. Much, much worse. I know the pain it will cause you. But it doesn't have to be the end of everything we've built.'

He couldn't keep the desperation from his voice now. And it only made it worse. She couldn't believe that the man she saw and heard was the one she had loved for so long, reduced to a pathetic, whining traitor and adulterer by the brief promise of Imogen Conrad's loins.

'There is a way out of this, Kate. It doesn't have to destroy everything, our family, Fiona and Gus's health and happiness—'

'A way out?' She couldn't keep the contempt from her voice.

'Please, Kate. Will you at least listen?'

'Where's Sergei?'

'They said he would come to no harm.'

'Where is he?'

'St Petersburg.'

'The SVR detained him?'

'Yes . . . yes.'

'And they faked the last letter, inviting me here to the dacha?'

'No, I think the letter was real. They've had him under surveillance.'

'So this is their fight back against the GRU and its influence on the president?'

'I don't know. I asked them not to hurt him.'

'But only if you can get me to agree to what you're about to propose?'

'Neither of us has a choice, Kate.'

'Don't we? How convenient.'

'If you agree, life can go on. I know it will be difficult and there will of course be . . . adjustments. And I'll have to win your forgiveness. I don't doubt how tough that will be. But I forgave you your time with Sergei here—'

'You had nothing to forgive. I was *never* unfaithful to you.'

He stared at her. 'If you agree to let me be, we'll both go home to the life we love. If you don't, our children will be orphans.'

'I presume you asked Rose to step in and look after them? Or did you get on a plane and leave them to fend for themselves?'

'Of course I didn't. I dropped them at her house in London after you'd left.'

'What did you tell them?'

'That I had to do something to help you.'

'And as Viper, it's been your job,' she said, 'and I guess will now be mine – if I fall in with your plan – to support the foreign secretary once he walks into Number Ten.'

He didn't answer her.

'I assume he *is* the Russian spy we're really looking for?'

Stuart just stared at her, the colour rising in his cheeks. It was a question she knew he would have been instructed not to answer.

Kate breathed in deeply. She thought of Lena's naked body on the slab in Athens. 'You bastard,' she whispered. 'You weak, pathetic bastard. Lena is dead. Rav is dead. And now you have the gall to stand here and ask *me* to betray my country as the price of *your* sins.'

'Kate . . .' He took another step closer.

'Stay where you are.'

346

'Come on, Kate. This is our life. The whole world is a cess-pit. They want very little of us. Just to help, once in a while. To give their interests a hearing. Is that *so* bad?'

Kate stepped back. She wiped a tear from the corner of her eye and tried to clear her mind. 'I'm wired. And your masters must have known I would be, which is why you were instructed not to answer my question on the foreign secretary. Even now they're too smart to give me the proof I need.' She looked out across the water. 'Danny is over there, the other side of the Gulf, recording it all.' She turned back to him. 'So what now, Stuart? My husband, my love? Are you going to shoot me – and orphan our children, as you said? Are you really going to do that, with the world still listening? No,' she said. 'Of course not. Even you're not that much of a bastard. You came to say goodbye. And as for your people listening and mine recording over the water, we're at check, and checkmate will elude us both. For now, at least.'

She turned and walked away.

'Kate!'

She climbed into the car, turned the ignition and drove away. She saw a lonely figure stranded on the sand in her rear-view mirror, but she didn't turn back.

She remained staunchly upright all the way into the forest. Then she stopped, bent over the steering-wheel and cried until her stomach hurt.

She took a T-shirt from the bag she had never unpacked and wiped her eyes, then pulled the car back into the centre of the track and began the long journey home.

Epilogue

AS SCHOOL PLAYS go, it had been tolerable. Kate and Fiona chatted politely to some of the parents over warm white wine afterwards. Despite the presence of many of her own friends, Fiona had not strayed much from Kate's side all evening as they waited for Gus to emerge.

By and large, both children had responded to the events of the last few weeks as well as Kate could have hoped. She had told them the truth – what other choice did she realistically have? – and had tried her level best to make Stuart sound like any middle-aged man having a rush of blood to the head, a spin that she thought neither of them bought, but which had perhaps allowed them to lock away the darker elements of his behaviour in a place where they could deal with it another day.

Or, at least, she hoped so.

Kate had consulted a child psychologist about it, and a bereavement counsellor. They'd done their best, but neither of them could claim any experience of a man who betrays his family *and* his country.

That said, they'd already progressed quite substantially on the practical arrangements. Kate had stressed that Stuart's decisions did not change his love for them (how she'd hated having to give that speech) and she knew, despite her inner rage, that she had to do something about it. So, at some point in the future, she would facilitate the children flying to see Stuart at a neutral, pre-agreed location far from his new life in Moscow.

In the meantime, she'd had to tell them both that their father would never be able to set foot in the United Kingdom for as long as he lived, which they had found extremely hard to take.

'So he'll never be able to come to another rugby match?' Gus had asked.

Fiona had enquired, later, if he'd be able one day to walk her down the aisle.

'Only if you get married somewhere outside this country,' Kate had said. The bereavement counsellor had advised her never to lie to the children, difficult as that would undoubtedly be.

It was in the nature of her work, perhaps, that small-talk about school runs and the inadequacies of various teachers or individual school policies frequently seemed like tales from a different planet, but today Kate found it especially difficult to concentrate. She sipped the wine and nodded a lot. Gus came running in to say he'd like to go home with Pete Markell and she said that would be fine.

She noticed Fiona's gaze continually flicking back to her and took it as a sign she wanted to leave. She picked up her coat and came to retrieve her daughter. As they walked down the endless hallway, Fiona slipped her hand into her mother's.

They continued in companionable silence until they reached the entrance lobby. There, above the coat pegs, was a wide-screen television, sometimes tuned to a school policy notice but otherwise defaulting to Sky News. As they passed, they saw the new prime minister, James Ryan, sweeping into Downing Street.

Kate and Fiona stopped to listen. For a man with the undoubted gift of the gab, it was a pretty uninspiring speech. 'I intend,' he said, 'to govern for all the people of this country, which is going to require some bold and visionary thinking.' It was a version of governing for the many not the few that they all trotted out. For all she knew, they might even have meant it.

Another woman had come to stand alongside them. Maggie, or perhaps Marjorie – Kate's memory failed her – a fussy mother of one of the many academic geniuses in Fiona's class, a woman whose horizons had never stretched far beyond Fulham. 'Didn't the press say he was a Russian spy?' she said. 'Honestly, what nonsense they do come up with!'

'What nonsense indeed,' Kate said.

As the woman bustled off, Kate glanced at her daughter and they smiled at each other, then walked out into the rain, hand in hand.

Acknowledgements

My wife Claudia has been a partner in the writing of all my novels and screenplays ever since we started work together on *Shadow Dancer* twenty-five years ago, so my primary and heartfelt thanks go to her. And we would not have got anywhere without Mark Lucas as our agent, who is simply a genius. But don't tell him that. We'd also like to offer heartfelt thanks to Bill Scott-Kerr, a brilliant editor, publisher and friend.